VIRTUE

Serena Mackesy

ARROW

Published by Arrow Books in 2000

1 3 5 7 9 10 8 6 4 2

Copyright © Serena Mackesy 2000

Serena Mackesy has asserted her right under the Copyright, Designs
and Patents Act, 1988 to be identified as the author of this work

Published in the United Kingdom in 2000 by
Arrow Books Limited
20 Vauxhall Bridge Road, London SW1V 2SA

Random House Australia (Pty) Limited
20 Alfred Street, Milsons Point, Sydney,
New South Wales 2061, Australia

Random House New Zealand Limited
18 Poland Road, Glenfield
Auckland 10, New Zealand

Random House (Pty) Limited
Endulini, 5a Jubilee Road, Parktown 2193, South Africa

Random House Group Limited Reg. No. 954009
www.randomhouse.co.uk

A CIP catalogue record for this book
is available from the British Library

Papers used by Random House
are natural, recyclable products made from wood grown in
sustainable forests. The manufacturing processes conform to
the environmental regulations of the country of origin

ISBN 0 09 941475 9

Phototypeset by Intype London Limited
Printed and bound in Great Britain by
Cox & Wyman Ltd, Reading

For Asif

Acknowledgements

My agent, Jane Conway-Gordon, whose magnificence knows no bounds. Kate Elton at Century for her dedication, sound judgement and endlessly tactful delivery, and Anna Dalton-Knott for her painstaking care and vital comprehension of bad jokes. Asif for general Asifness and practically everything else as well. Titus Andronicpuss for constant disruptions, and his auntie Tracy for saving his life, Mum, Dad, Will and Cathy for being the backbone of my existence, and my friends, who have shown me how damn sweet life can get.

Prologue

Unforgettable

Were someone to conduct DNA sampling on the remains of Marshland Mary, the jute-wrapped peat burial preserved like a squashed Klimt painting in a glass case at Ditchworth museum, they would find that her descendants have scarcely moved five miles from where she lived and died. There have been Burges at Belhaven since well before the land got its current name. By the time the furriner Moresbys were given everything they could see from Marksman's Hillock – which in East Anglia is a lot of land – in exchange for a certain facility with a bodkin and a vial of adder juice in the post-Hastings mopping-up operation, the Burge family had been scratching a living from the soil thereabouts for well over a thousand years. Not that they have ever discussed the matter, or indeed given it much thought. People only tend to keep family records if they feel that there has been some distinction to show off, and, while each generation has known the skills of fencing and digging and raising a fine batch of hunting fodder and tipping their caps with just the right combination of humility and dignity, the chief achievement of the Burge family lies in its singular economy with words. Throughout the ages, when the wedding trestles have been brought out, the Burges have sat in corners eating pickled sweetmeats and silently holding out their mugs for refills. And it is, after all,

1

these peculiarly taciturn qualities that have kept the Burges in the employ of successive generations of Moresbys when their more loquacious neighbours have had to up sticks and head for less heated parts of the country. For if there is one quality a great family values in its retainers – above, even, the ability to do huge amounts of work without complaining – it is discretion. And discretion the Burges have in spades.

And they're good at getting up in the morning. If you don't tend to waste precious resources sitting up after dark discussing the current political situation, deconstructing your relationships and comparing tattoos, mornings present little by way of problems.

Before dawn on a Monday in late March, a day when the least possible number of visitors is expected at Belhaven Great House to disturb – or, worse, witness – the planned operations, lights are on in two of the tied cottages of Belhaven village. Behind light cotton curtains, heavy hands reach for army-surplus trousers, large wool-covered feet emerge from beneath the bedclothes and plunge into trouser legs, sweatshirts go over sleep-vests and woollen hats over mussed hair. Down in kitchens, slices of Wonderloaf forsake their packaging, PG Tips swills in teapots and the sound of that long, post-sleep evacuation rings out through bathroom windows. Burges don't waste time; they will never do one thing when they can do two.

Derek Burge is the first to emerge in his wellingtons, for the gamekeeper's cottage is a hundred yards further down the Belhaven road, which doubles as a drive to the Great House. Derek is the younger of the Burge brothers; dark, hairy of arm and relentlessly reliable, he walks, boots shushing on the tarmac as though raising the feet is a waste of effort, down the road, glancing neither left nor right. There's little, after all, for him to see in a village whose every inch he has known since childhood.

Derek Burge reaches the head gardener's cottage, crunches over the frost-pocked gravel round to the back door, where he drops into total stillness. His breath flumes from his nostrils and from time to time he shifts from one foot to the other to encourage his circulation, but otherwise there is no sign that anything is happening behind his eyes at all. Behind the door, the odd muffled clunk and scraping suggests that his older brother, George, is pulling on his own wellingtons and preparing to emerge. George's wife, Margaret, insists on grilling his Wonderloaf for him on the grounds that he needs a proper breakfast inside him, and he is consequently always a few minutes behind schedule, as he has never got used to the change of routine in the seventeen years of their union. So Derek waits, hands deep in pockets, while Margaret finds his brother's beanie, and, in the fullness of time, the door opens.

The two nod in greeting, and set off. Not a word passes between them as they negotiate the length of the Great House drive, and George precedes his brother through the gate in the wall that separates the family chapel from the rabbit-mown lawns of the house. Neither asks after the other's well-being, or what he watched on the television the night before, what he might be planning to watch tonight. Neither remarks on the majesty of the ancient oaks studding the parkland that spreads across the landscape around them to the nearest horizon, on the progress of the spring, which is beginning to dot the rough-hewn grass with daffodils, or the beauty of the mackerel sky breaking into ecstasy above them. And, though their minds must both be on the task ahead, not a word, not even a joke to alleviate the inevitable tension, passes a pair of lips. Silently, the two men cross the grass to the back of the chapel, where the door to the crypt already lies open.

The Duke of Belhaven emerges: tweed jacket, flat cap, cavalry twill trousers, brown suede brogues, spots of colour patterning the apples of his cheeks. 'Morning,' he says, as though this is just another day. The Burges nod. 'Good morning, Your Grace,' they say, only, with their remarkable taciturnity, the entire phrase comes out as a single word: 'Grease'.

Gerald Belhaven rubs his hands together in his leather gloves, stamps a couple of times to acknowledge the cold and his appreciation of it, and says, 'Well, might as well get on with it, I suppose.'

The Burges follow him down the stone steps into the basement of the church where an iron-barred gate is hidden behind a slab of oak. Despite the fact that this place is only officially visited when there's been a death in the family, the steps leading down are worn; the fourteenth-century builders of the chapel failed to notice that it lies directly in the line of a small stream that only springs to life during the height of winter, and by the time the error was noticed, the building was half-finished. A drain was quickly installed at the bottom of the stairs to prevent the scions of Belhaven from floating away, but the steps themselves have done service as a decorative waterfall for centuries now, and thriving lichen has made the going entertaining.

Nonetheless, the medieval architect did his job, and the interior of the crypt beyond the drain is dry enough that coffins, as long as they are lead-lined and left as undisturbed as possible, can on the whole protect their contents until those contents have become inoffensive.

The Duke and his servants make their way past the drain-pool, weave their way among ancient bones in search of their quarry. Here, the glorious Moresby family lies at peace, rotting gently among their peers and relations. On the left, Guy de Mauxbois, trusted camp follower and, as it turned out, accomplished assassin, who established the family line in this windswept enclave, slumbers in an elaborate stone sarcophagus − or at least what could be found of his bones, dug up by his descendants when this crypt was established, does. The skull, strangely, was never reunited with the body. On stone shelves that line the walls are memorial tablets to George, last Baron Moresby and first Viscount Ditchworth, who received the title from Henry VII two weeks before he finally succumbed to wounds sustained in battle the year before, and Harry, fourth Viscount Ditchworth, lost at sea off Virginia while establishing a tobacco plantation for Queen and country. Above and below the fourth Viscount, his first wife, Arabel, who tragically died from a surfeit of almonds in her thirty-seventh year to heaven is commemor- ated; her widower was so grief-stricken that, on the advice of his friends, he took another wife, seventeen-year-old Catherine, three weeks later. Tragically, she, too, failed to outlive her spouse, being found at the bottom of the great staircase fifteen years later, having tripped on a carelessly discarded ermine tippet. The Viscount was drowned before he was able to marry again.

The Burges follow His Grace past Red Malcolm, famed for his beard and his battleaxe, past Benedicta Belhaven, whose husband, despite a singularly obvious lack of achieve- ment, received a dukedom from Charles II in recognition of his contribution to the well-being of the monarch; past Henrys and Geralds and Dianas and Sarahs; past children lost in hunting accidents and dowagers dead of gout; past adul- terers and soldiers and philanthropists and scholars (well, one scholar: Charles, sixth Duke of Belhaven, whose *History of the British Aristocracy* lies as good as new on the shelves of the Bodleian to this day); past gluttons and ascetics; past bashful debutantes and stern matriarchs. Torchlight bounces off the vaulted ceiling, breath hangs in the air like steam from a carny attraction, and not a word is spoken. At the back of the basement, Gerald Belhaven slips between the coffins of Thomas Belhaven, whose command of the tragic Nineteenth Light was one of the more discussed events on the Crimea, and Henrietta, responsible for the considerable collection of Chinoiserie that lines the canton room on the first floor of the Great House. He plays his torch over the simple wooden casket that rests against the wall, checks the nameplate as though he had not himself overseen its being placed there. Nods.

'Here we are,' he says, and the Burges start forward to take stock of the task in hand.

It's not a particularly big coffin, for its occupant was famous for the frailty of her build. Simple but dignified, it is carved from the wood of a 600-year-old oak that had been felled the winter before her death, in one of the series of storms that are still talked about in the area and very nearly resulted in the disappearance of Ditchworth Old Town beneath the North Sea. The plaque, too, is simple but dignified, a plate of shiny brass, only slightly discoloured by the intervening years, on which only a name and two dates are to be discerned. 'Godiva Fawcett', it reads, '1950–1985'. There is nothing else, for nothing else is necessary to add: that simple name, those tragically short-lived dates, is enough to bring tears to most eyes.

Godiva has been dead fifteen years now, though those who mourned her then mourn her still. That glorious face is still now, the hands that danced crossed across her breast, those eyes, green like emeralds, green as Tara, green as the bottom of a Hollywood swimming pool, dropped closed in modesty, those lips, that braved the disapproval of society in support of the needy, pressed together in quietude. Godiva, so lovely, so missed, is to be moved today to her final resting place in the mausoleum built fifteen years ago for her followers to visit, though it was tacitly agreed that to leave the body within while public emotion was at its height was asking for trouble. As it is, the statue that graces the front of the building has had to be replaced three times after well-wishers armed with chisels took a few too many souvenirs. But the worst of the furore has died down now and the shrine gets only a hundred or so visitors each day, swelling to maybe a thousand on special anniversaries, and Gerald Belhaven feels that the time has come to risk moving his stepmother to where she is meant to be.

The three men stand for a moment, contemplating the casket. And then, at a nod from the Duke, the brothers step forward and grip the casket. Bend at the knees, as working men have always done without the aid of ergonomists to tell them how, lift. Apart from a small grunt that issues from Derek, who is at the front end and taking the weight of the head and shoulders, neither says a thing about their burden, which is surprisingly heavy. It would hardly be appropriate, and anyway, Burges know better than to voice comments on anything to do with The Family.

Gerald Belhaven stands back, arms crossed over the little paunch that has started showing under his checked lawn shirts since he turned forty. The Duchess calls it his 'food baby', and likes to make a show of patting it in public. Emotion is one of those things that the Belhavens were trained out of some time in the eighteenth century, and this playfulness is part of the reason that the current Duke is widely believed to have one of the most stable marriages in the aristocracy. Gerald's mother was his father's second Duchess, Godiva his third and last.

The gap between Thomas' and Henrietta's tombs is narrower than anyone had remembered, and the Burges have to tip the last Duchess on her side to get her through. Shoulders sloping, Derek Burge's face turns suddenly puce, and a small hiss of air escapes from between his teeth. 'Are you all right?' asks the Duke, mildly concerned, for no one has ever heard a sound of pain from a Burge. Derek nods and mutters, 'Ar', between gritted teeth, and they're through to where the plain sailing begins. 'Want to put it down?' enquires the Duke. Burge minor shakes his head, and the brothers plough forward.

Across the floor they plod, these three conspirators, landing heavy footfalls on the heads of Moresbys loved and Moresbys lost, Moresbys great and Moresbys fallen, Moresbys in heaven and Moresbys in hell. They reach the stairs. Though winter is over and the waterfall has dried up, the lichen is thick and new on the stone and slippery underfoot. Slowly, the Burges edge their way upward, Derek in front and George following in the rear to take the worst of the load. Derek, the strain of his weak shoulder showing on his face, gets halfway up before his brother reaches the bottom. And then disaster walks in.

Three steps up, George gets his right wellington halfway on the step, puts his whole weight down upon it. It grips, and he moves confidently forward, lifting the other foot to go one step higher. And as he does so, the balancing foot shoots backward with the speed of a fairground ride. One moment he is upright, the next he has tumbled face-down upon his load, and it has come crashing to the ground.

'Careful!' cries the Duke, as though such advice will somehow save the day. For two seconds, two long, teetering seconds, the whole shebang rests in the powerful hands of Derek Burge. His eyes pop, tendons stand out in his neck, the corners of his mouth pull down to reveal the dentures beneath. Fingers vainly strain to dig into unyielding wood, arms try to clamp themselves round their load, knees buckle to allow a gentle landing for this end of the box, but in the end it's all too much to bear. With a roar of despair, he concedes defeat, the fingers unclamp and the coffin crashes to the steps. Clatters, bump–bump–bump, all the way down into the crypt, carrying the slipshod George before it, and comes to rest with a sickening crack, half-on and half-off the staircase. George is pinned into the drain and the Duke, dropping his torch in his horror, plunges them all into total darkness.

Silence for a moment, broken only by the tick-tick-tick of settling wood, then George groans and begins to extricate himself from beneath the load. Derek stands halfway up the stairs, hand clamped to his torn shoulder muscle, and peers into the gloom. 'Is everyone all right?' cries the peer and, scrabbling about, finds the torch to illuminate the scene once again.

George is out from underneath, literally if not metaphorically, and sits against the last resting place of Richard, eighth Baron Moresby, rubbing the back of his head where it has caught an almighty crack when he went down. Derek starts down the steps, stops when the torchlight falls upon the scene below him. His mouth, whose gulps for air have made him look like a landed monkfish, drops open, the skin hanging slackly around his jaw suddenly revealing the fact that Moresbys have not, over the millennium, been entirely averse to a spot of *droit de seigneur*. He looks, at this moment, almost exactly like his employer, who is frozen, gape-mouthed and fish-eyed, on the far side of the accident.

'Oh, your Grace,' says Derek Burge. 'Her Grace, Your Grace. Her Grace.'

The coffin, after fifteen years in these damp surroundings, has split open on impact, and its contents are on display. But they are not as you would expect. Instead of the sludge of decay, the air is scented with attar of roses: a perfume that everyone who knew and loved her associated with the Duchess throughout her prominence. And there she lies, framed in her plushy satin bed: Godiva Fawcett, later Godiva Moresby, fourteenth Duchess of Belhaven, mourned the land over. Godiva, whose ice-white skin and perfect features hid a heart that beat for the poor, for the lost, for all those who suffered. Godiva, whose death sparked worldwide lamentation, pilgrimage, promises of improvement, expressions of love. Godiva, whose life was carpeted in thorns and whose death was carpeted in flowers.

Head pillowed by the softest of silk, she lies with her eyes open and bright as her last moments on earth. Roses touch those lifeless cheeks, still full and rounded over the narrow, tilting jawline. Her white-blonde hair curls and shines as though newly washed. And that rosebud mouth still smiles, still pouting, unchanged in its fullness and promise by the fact that the soul has fled. There she lies, Godiva the Good, flawless hands crossed over a bosom so full and so perfectly rounded that it is hard to believe that it will not, even now, heave and shudder as she draws a breath.

'My God,' says Gerald Belhaven. 'My God.'

George has raised his head to see, and sits back against the eighth Baron, face shining with astonishment. And he opens his mouth, and utters the longest speech that has ever been known to pass those heedful lips.

'It's a fucking miracle, that's what it is,' he says. 'A fucking miracle.'

Chapter One
GeogSoc

Once we're in the taxi and he's tickling my earlobe with the edge of his finger, the nagging feeling of discomfort gets worse. At some point, this guy's going to want me to call him by his name, and I can't for the life of me remember what it is. Brad? Troy? Jake? Something monosyllabic, I remember that, and one of those close-to-made-up names they have on Australian soap operas. Roo? Cal? Butch? Or maybe I'm inventing this, because he said he was once in an Australian soap opera, which isn't that surprising, because if you divide the population of Australia by the number of soap operas they turn out, everyone in the country is likely to pop up washing cars and saying 'G'day' over any given fifteen-year period.

Jam? Bug? Park? Sim? I know I should know, but you know how your memory develops holes, usually just when you're about to make a really important point, or when you're trying to say 'thank you' in Turkish, or when the plod want to know where you were on the night of the 17th, and, though I have a clear picture, when I close my eyes, of Lindsey shouting 'Anna, this is . . .' over the top of several heads and a flower arrangement, after that it all goes blank.

Biff? Barf? Lung? The thing is, I know that this is a problem. Because however much men like to think of themselves as roaming wolves, however much they joke about not knowing what, or who, they were up to last night, the fact is that they get as upset as women do by the idea that someone doesn't actually know their name. They turn all droopy and sit on the edge of the bed with a sheet draped over their groins needing to be comforted. And it's worse when they've made it perfectly plain that they've mastered your name within seconds.

Lid? Mig? Grog? Goddamn, I've got to take memory lessons. He's one of those people who make sure they get your name fixed in their head in the first minute by repeating it over and over. 'Hi, Anna,' he said. 'How ya doing, Anna? Who do you know here, then, Anna? Can I get you a drink, Anna?' And of course, I was so fascinated by watching those white, even pearlies, the I-may-wear-factor-20-lotion-but-I'm-out-in-the-sun-all-day skin tone, the natty bleached-by-the-sea mop-top, and feeling myself overwhelmed by Thursday-night lust that I forgot to reciprocate. So now here I am barrelling down Kensington Gore, catching sight of the cab driver watching us in his rear-view mirror and thinking: Christ, Waters. Not even bothering to learn someone's name is seriously slaggy. I mean, it's a simple matter of etiquette, isn't it? The rules of promiscuity: carry condoms, never go anywhere where you don't know the address, be immaculately polite.

And he's rather nice, actually, this strange Aussie – Gruff? Brig? Dim? Nice enough to deserve better than to have someone reduce him to the status of nameless boy-toy. I mean, I'm not *that* hard. Not so hard that I don't know how I'd feel if someone turned round and called me Jane.

To my surprise, he hasn't gone straight for the tits, but seems to be taking a lot of pleasure in running his hand over my stomach, caressing my hips. In the orange glow of the street lights, I can see that his eyelashes are long enough to brush the tops of his cheeks. Maybe he's a habitual specs wearer, has taken them off in the hope of being more attractive. Only specs wearers have eyelashes like that. I used to have eyelashes about an inch long before I got the contacts, not that anyone ever got the opportunity to appreciate them.

The cab lurches – probably on purpose – as it rounds the corner at Knightsbridge, and Jib? Dick? Bob? falls briefly onto me with his full body weight, which is fine by me. Hand on my thigh for purchase, he says, 'Oops', flashes a complicit grin and leaves it there. I love men – well, most of them, anyway. I love their puppy-dog naughtiness, the way that, even when they must be 99 per cent sure why they're in a cab being speeded across London by a woman they've only just picked up at a party, they still have to play these little hunt-and-chase games, convince themselves that they've somehow persuaded you against your better conscience. As we sit at the Sloane Street lights, Door? Bunk? Rod? runs a thumb over my thigh against the direction of the hairs – the weather turned warm enough, thank God, to ditch tights a month ago, and I've already gone a nice balcony gold right up to the knicker line – and I can't resist a little shiver. It's partly for real and partly for effect. If I can't remember the guy's name, I might as well make him feel that the oversight comes from an excess of passion.

It works. Fag? Hung? Lard? grins, wraps his arms round me and crushes me to his chest like an over-affectionate grizzly bear. 'Shit, you're great,' he says. 'I never thought my luck would be in tonight. My word.'

I think I'm probably the only person who would have expected their luck to be in at a talk to the Royal Geographical Society, but I like a challenge and it's all too easy in bars and clubs and parties. But I seriously thought, when

I saw the Atlas of Geographers gathered around the half-dozen bottles of Chilean Cab Sauv, domed heads hovering over beards as they fiddled with the toggles on their anoraks and got into almighty rages with each other, that I was going to luck out tonight. I mean, you could sleep with just anybody, but that's not the point, is it? That's where the line between bad and sad is drawn: bad girls sleep with anyone who looks like he might be good for a laugh; sad girls sleep with just anyone.

So thank God for Pad? Blip? Rug? It would have been a wasted night, otherwise. I get the cab to drop us off on the embankment, help him haul his backpack onto the pavement and lead him down the road to the gate. 'Christ,' he says. 'Where are you taking me? You're not some sort of psycho-killer, are you?'

I turn and look over my shoulder at him as I punch the keys on the gate-pad. 'Could be. Why? Are you scared?'

Hilarious. For a second he shows all the signs of controlled panic: wide eyes rolling round, trying to look through the back of his head for an avenue of escape, chest pumping as he gets that creeping feeling that he might just have to run for it; hand gripping and loosening on the strap of the rucksack as he wonders if he's going to have to ditch all his worldly belongings in the rush to get away.

So I burst out laughing, point at him and say, 'Come on, bozo. Have you seen the size of me? All you need to do to stop me is hold me at arm's length.'

He's not sure whether he's embarrassed or amused. Decides that being amused is probably the best way of getting his naughties tonight, smiles sheepishly. The gate beeps and clunks open.

'Come into my parlour,' I say, gesture him through.

He steps into the yard, stares around and goes, 'Coo', or

one of those other words people use when they come into our yard for the first time. 'Come on,' I say, but he is saying, 'What the hell *is* this place, anyway?' which is what people tend to say when they've finished saying 'Coo'. Well, it's pretty amazing, in the middle of all this prime real estate, to find yourself in the middle of a couple of acres where nothing moves, no one's parked a BMW and there's not a scrap of chromed handrail to be seen. Okay, so the railway lines might put some people off, but you'd at least expect some far-thinking council to have built an estate here.

I take hold of the strap of his rucksack, start to pull him in the direction of the tower. I'm used to the yard now, don't have to run with my eyes clamped on the path in front of me to get through it, but it still spooks me a bit. All those empty spaces; you can never guarantee what's going to be in them. 'They're old boat sheds,' I inform him.

'Boat sheds? This far back from the river?'

'It's not that far, really; less than a hundred yards. There's a lock going down to the river, only no one ever notices it because the main road goes over the top.'

'Christ,' says Matey. 'And you live here? How d'you get to live somewhere like this?'

'My flatmate. Her family had it back when it actually was a boatyard. They're those sort of people who never get round to selling anything.'

'Strewth.'

I suppress a giggle. Hearing an Australian say 'Strewth' is like hearing a Scotsman say 'Och aye'. You simply don't believe that they really say it until you're actually standing next to it.

Round the D-shed, under the rowan, over the lock bridge and we're at the porch. Zak? Pack? Shack? stands with his back to me as I fiddle with the keys and mumbles about the industrial wasteland around him. 'Actually,' he says, 'this is pretty cool when you get used to it, isn't it? I mean, like, nobody has this much space in a city. And it's just you and your flatmate?'

'Mmm. Yes. Harriet.'

'You could have,' he says speculatively, 'like, a real commune here. Well, obviously not a commune, this isn't the sixties, but one of those places where all your mates could land when they've been travelling. Those sheds would be amazing for parties. Like, a big house area in one, and maybe seventies or trance or something in another, and a big chill-out area in the third, maybe some cushions under that tree we came under, candles, body piercing . . .'

And then just as I'm thinking: hang on a minute, sonny. You've not got your feet under the table yet. Christ, you've not even got them inside the front door, he breathes, warm and damp, on my hairline just behind my ear, and I remember what I've got him there for.

We go backwards into the hall, locked together like velcro Care Bears, and he drops the backpack just inside the door. Manoeuvres me towards the stairs, which doesn't take much manoeuvring as I'm waltzing back with him. I get my foot on the first step, and finally our faces are almost level. We haven't bothered with the lights; nobody bothers with lights when they're drunk and horny. He hitches his arms around my waist and simply lifts me from step to step, our crotches grinding hard with each swing, and I'm really looking forward to this. I haven't got laid in two weeks. If I don't get this guy horizontal – or as near as damn it – soon, I feel like I'm actually going to burst out of my pants. And from the feel of him, I think he might do the same thing.

His foot lands on something which splits, crunches and scatters over the stairs.

'Shit,' he mutters. 'What's that?'

'Christ. Bloody Harriet.'

'What is it?'

'I don't know. She's always leaving things on the stairs. I knocked over an entire bag of plaster of Paris the other day and then she dropped a bottle of wine on it. She would have let it set, as well.'

'Sounded like split peas to me,' he grunts.

'What the fuck would she want with split peas?'

'I dunno. Cook with them?'

'Harriet doesn't cook. She's posh.'

He feels for a foothold among the scattered whatevers, hikes me up another step. 'Christ, it's lucky you're so little. How many steps are there here?'

I push him off, start running up them. 'A hundred and eighteen.'

'What?'

I get up to the first-floor landing, outside the bathroom. Call down as he thunders up behind me, 'A hundred and eighteen!'

He catches me up between that landing and the one outside my room, grabs me behind the knees and flips me handily to the stairs. Panting a bit, I notice, but not so much. Some people are so winded by the time they've got up here they're no good to anyone for ten minutes. But not Lug. He's all over me like bath oil, has his hands under my skirt, gripping my buttocks, and is making it very clear that he's up for a bit of a party. And my insides are doing that familiar cha-cha-cha and I'm already starting to sweat a bit.

'Jeez, you're gorgeous,' he says, which of course means, 'I'm so horny my geography teacher would look gorgeous', but hell, I don't care, it's not like I've never said anything like that myself when I thought I was going to get a good

17

going-over, then he gets his hands inside my pants and starts to pull them off. Lovely, lovely, lovely. He's got button flies and they're practically popping. There's no way we're making it any further up these stairs.

I manage to unplug my mouth from the fine game of tonsil tennis we've got going, and say, 'Have you got any condoms?'

'Shit, no,' he says. 'Down in my backpack. Christ.'

''S okay.' I've still got my bag with me, so I look for my purse, find a johnny in behind the business cards and pull it out. I know they're always telling you that men think that women who carry condoms are slags, but I'm a happy slapper and I don't care what anyone thinks. I like scoring, I like getting my legs round a nice warm man and seeing what we can do for each other. Call me a slag, it's fine: I'm having a good time.

'Oh, thank Christ.' He snatches it from my fingers, rips the wrapper open with his teeth, kneels up to put it on. A lock of bleached hair flops into his eyes and I look at him and think: yeah, sweet guy, spends a lot of time doing point-less physical things; this will be fun. He meets my eyes and his face melts into one of those soppy, puppy-dog smiles that breaks your heart. 'Are you ready for this?'

Am I ready? I've been up for it for hours, you fool; just come here and do your thing.

Downstairs, there's a crash. Then Harriet's voice floats up, 'Oh, pants. Who bloody broke my bag of popcorn? Anna! Are you up there? Did you break my bloody popcorn and just leave it on the stairs? I nearly broke my bloody neck, you stupid cow. Where the fuck are you?'

My lovely boy is sheepishly trying to stuff himself back into his trousers, jaw hanging in panic. I sit up, pull on my knickers, haul my top back down over my tits. 'Yeah, I'm up here,' I call down.

'Well, what are you doing leaving popcorn all over the stairs?'

'I didn't know it was popcorn. I didn't turn the light on. Anyway, it's you that left the stuff on the stairs in the first place.'

Her footsteps clomp in our direction. Muscleboy sighs with relief as the last button pops somehow back into its hole and Harriet comes round the corner: navy-blue pleated hockey skirt halfway up the thighs, white blouse liberally stained with gravy and red wine, striped tie at half-mast, high-heeled T-bar sandals, blonde hair tied up in a pair of plaits coming from the top of the head like Pippi Longstocking, filthy old riding mac thrown over the top. Harriet has worn that riding mac every day of the ten years I've known her, and it's never been cleaned. Which at least means that she can travel on the tube unmolested.

'Oh,' she says to the slightly pink bambino beside me. I didn't ask him, but he looks in this light as though he might be in his gap year. 'Don't get up.'

He doesn't, so she continues, 'Let's not bother with introductions, eh? I daresay I'll forget the minute you tell me, anyway. Is that your backpack I fell over when I came in?'

'Yeah,' he replies.

'Ah. Backpacker, are you?'

'Traveller, actually.' He tries a tentative smile.

'Ah, yes. Tourists without baths.'

I close my eyes and pray: please, please don't let him start explaining the difference between a tourist and a traveller.

God answers my prayer. He just grins and says mildly, 'Yeah, I reckon. But we have email addresses these days as

19

well so we can keep in touch with all the other travellers and never mix with the natives.'

Harriet seems satisfied with this, continues up the stairs, hops over his knees. 'I've had a shitty night. Totally shitty. Like, shit city with the fan turned on. You won't mind if I don't stay and make small talk, will you?'

She looks seriously grim. Harriet puts so much effort into work that she's often totally drained when she gets home. Sometimes she's so tired that I don't just find myself running her a bath from pity, I have to come back and haul her out of it, or she'd just sleep there until she died of hypothermia.

'No worries,' says Thunk.

We sit together on the steps listening to her plod up to the living room, her voice, sweet and loving as she greets Henry, who must have been waiting just inside the door for hours. 'Hello, my darling. Hello, my fine gentleman,' she coos, and the door clunks to as he yowls in response.

Lug-Mug-Fug says, 'Is she always that charming?'

'No.' I have my hand on his knee, but somehow the atmosphere has slipped. Something of Harriet's contempt still hangs in the air, and there's nothing like contempt to kill the sexual urge. 'I think she liked you, actually.'

'Aouh yeah?'

I love the way Australians can fit three vowels – sometimes even four – if you've ever heard a Melbournite refuse a drink, you'll know what I mean – into a word where every other nationality would make do with one. I nod non-committally.

'Guess she must've liked school, if she's still dressing like that?'

Irritably, I shake my head. 'Don't be stupid.' I can't be bothered to explain.

He puts his hands out in defence. 'Okay, okay. Sorry. No need to drop the dummy.'

I shrug. Think, well, might as well get something going again, stand up and say, 'Might as well go to my room and try again?'

He struggles to his feet. 'Sure,' he says, 'but I could do with a drink, maybe? You got anything up there?' Puts his hand out and runs it over my breast, and I realise that the mood is still there, shallow buried, ready to come out and play again with a tad of encouragement.

Smoothing my skirt over my thighs, I turn upward. 'There's bound to be some wine up in the kitchen. My room's the next one up.'

He takes this as an invitation to go in and get settled. Gives me a don't-be-too-long kiss, says, 'Strewth' when he turns the light on, and I leave him to it.

Stump on further up the stairs. I'm sure there is a bottle of plonk somewhere, probably a bottle of house wine from the restaurant which sometimes just falls into one or other of our bags. From above, I can hear the boom of the television and the clatter of dishes. Henry is sitting at the head of the stairs, the king demanding his dues before anyone can pass. 'Good evening, Your Majesty,' I chuck him behind the ear and he rewards me with two smacking kisses, one down one side of the nose, one down the other. 'H'raaow,' he purrs.

'How are you this evening?'

'A'morrwai,' he replies, 'm'you?'

'Fine, thanks.'

'Good,' says Henry, stands up to usher me into the royal receiving rooms. Walks regally ahead of me with his tail proud in the air, plumps his bottom down on the rug to the side of the door and begins to play the cello. I rub him on the back of the neck and proceed into the living room.

Harriet is eating a sandwich and pulling off her tie while watching the ads on Channel 5. 'What's on?' I cross over to the fridge – the living room, which takes up the whole top floor of the tower, triples up as a kitchen and, over by the windows on the opposite side, a studio where Harriet splashes glue, paint and bits of whatever she's found in a skip onto the carpet, and smears the walls with blobs from her oily rags. The whole place has a permanent light scent of turpentine, coupled, occasionally, with the unwashed-hooker smell of Copydex. Sometimes you see a faint look of fear cross people's faces as they are about to light a cigarette; more often, you see fear on their faces when they think they might be asked what they think of Harriet's work.

'Foft porm,' Harriet splutters round a mouthful of cheese and onion. 'Veeve Frenf meople memp on a micnic and vem all veir mloves fell off.'

'Mmm.' I look in the sink cupboard, where the wine rack lives. God knows why we have a wine rack. I bought it in a rush of optimism when the Belhaven estate said we could have the tower and it's never had more than three bottles in it since. I think I had this fantasy that we'd get cases delivered by a discount warehouse, maybe have dinner parties or dos with cheese straws and things involving anchovies. I find a bottle of Prefect's Perks, the second-from-bottom house wine from which Roy makes far the biggest mark-up on the grounds that the kind of people who order the second-from-cheapest in order not to look mean deserve everything they get. 'You know you've got a right to be fed at work, don't you?'

Harriet swallows the last of her sandwich, breathes fetidly

over me. 'It's all tapioca and spotted dick on the menu tonight. And fish cakes with mashed swede.'

'Ah.'

I fish in the drawer for the corkscrew, settle for a knife. 'How was your evening?'

'Shitty. Totally shitty. Though I managed to give someone a caning he'll never forget. Who's the man-child?'

'Dunno. I found him at the Royal Geographical Society.'

'Does he have a name?'

I look at her, shrug. Then I have to laugh, because I'd been hoping I'd get away with it, and you never get away with anything with Harriet.

Harriet makes a disgusted face. 'I'm so glad,' she says, 'to see your sense of responsibility growing with age.'

'Yeah, but Harriet, have you seen the size of his feet? I couldn't resist.'

Harriet's eyes roll upwards until the pupils disappear beneath her eyelids. She wags her head from side to side and goes, 'Gaah! Filthy manky old slag.'

I wave the bottle at her. 'Glass of wine?'

'What will I catch?'

Henry turns a somersault on the rug, stretches his legs out in front of him, lets go the gentlest, most subtle of farts and looks painfully smug. Harriet picks up an old coffee mug with green paint stains around the middle and says, 'All right, then.'

I cross the room, give her a share. She grunts, drinks, says, 'Disgusting' and turns up the sound on the telly as the ads come to an end and the music for the news headlines begins.

'See you later.' I walk back towards the door with my bottle, rub Henry's tummy as I go and am rewarded by a slash of teeth and a couple of rabbit-kicks. Then, behind me, 'Fuck!'

I turn. Harriet has many different levels of 'fuck', and this one sounds alarmingly like a force nine. It's been a while since the word cracked over the air like splitting timber. 'What's up?'

'Motherfucking bitch,' snarls Harriet. 'Bloody sodding hellfire. Who the fuck does she think she is? What the—'

I bound back into the room, heart pumping. On the screen, though I can't hear anything over Harriet's cusswords, flash pictures of Godiva, a lingering helicopter shot of the park at Belhaven and a set of archive pictures of the hysteria at the funeral. 'What is it?' I raise my voice over her cussing. 'What's happened? Harriet, shut up, I can't hear!'

Harriet turns round, face like a radish and the sort of snarl I haven't seen for six, seven years ripping her upper lip back from her teeth, throws her mug of wine at the wall. 'Damn her. Damn her bloody eyes. Goddamn it and fuck it all to hell.'

'Harriet!' I've jumped over Henry and made it back to her side, but the picture has changed now to shots of the little black pepperpots that pass for women in Afghanistan. 'What is it?'

'Damn her,' shouts Harriet. 'The bitch has been dead for fifteen years, and she still can't keep out of the limelight!'

Chapter Two

Under Siege

His name, it turns out after all that speculation, is – wait for it – Nigel. Obviously, he stays the night, sleeping like a baby until after ten o'clock in my bed while the chickfest goes on upstairs, and I take the opportunity, while Harriet is in the lav at around five o'clock, to sneak a look, with a sinking stomach, at the passport in the front pocket of his rucksack. Nigel. And there was me thinking he was a child of the outback, his name formed in the red dust of Alice. Actually, he's just finished his teacher training in Canberra and is fitting in a few months' life experience before he commits himself to the geographical enlightenment of the youth of East Perth. That's what he was doing at the RGS: trying to make contacts he could get to come and give talks if ever they were on the south-western edge of the world.

He tells us this as he slurps coffee with alarmingly lavatorial sounds and fries up a couple of kilograms of bacon he's found in his backpack. He's a wonderfully normal object in the midst of our controlled hysteria. He acts like there's nothing unusual about the situation, though I guess he must have heard *something* when he came up looking for me after I'd been gone forty minutes last night. He's normal enough that we can afford not to be that attentive, having been up all night with Harriet pacing the floor and me removing breakable objects from her path, but we nod and uh-huh at the right places, and Harriet says something damning every five minutes, so I don't think he notices anything much.

Eventually, around eleven o'clock, with the sun streaming onto the balcony and Henry throwing him don't-you-have-any-manners? looks from the top of the dresser where he likes to settle among the odd pieces of Sèvres that we brought up from Belhaven and have never actually had the occasion to use, Harriet lights a cigarette, picks up her glue pot and says, 'Listen, Nigel, I'd love to stay and chat all day, but Anna and I both have work to get on with.'

'Aouh yeah?' responds Nigel. 'Whadda yer working on?'

'I,' says Harriet grandly, 'am making an eco-mosaic.'

'Right.' Nigel peers at the accumulation of feathers, bits of old sardine tin, wine-bottle labels, chunks of pavement, skeletal leaves and dessicated rabbit turds that she's built up on her corner table (the rabbit turds having been drying on a sheet of reflective aluminium out on the other side of balcony from where we sit) and smiles. 'So that's what the popcorn was for, yeah? Going to use it to fill in the bits in-between, like—'

'A gravel pathway,' Harriet finishes. 'Well, yes, I suppose you could express it in simple terms like that. But it's actually a metaphor for—'

'I get it.' Nigel nods thoughtfully. 'A metaphor for the waste and decay in modern society. Sort of, we think we've tamed nature with our cities and our infrastructures, but actually it's rotting all around us, right?'

'Right,' says Harriet, looking pissed off.

He grins. 'Trustafarian, are you?'

Harriet's voice goes dangerously quiet. 'What makes you think that?'

'Well,' – he scratches the back of his neck, narrows his

eyes as he looks about him – 'sort of stands to reason. You live in a huge industrial space in the centre of a prime real-estate area, you dabble with minimum wage jobs to be out there with the people, you haven't seen a hairbrush this side of graduation, you stay up all night obsessing about your mother and you make pictures out of animal droppings. You've either got a rich dad or you're care in the community.'

I stay stumm. I hardly know the guy, for God's sake, and I'm not going to get in to the subject of the employment prospects of the daughters of saints with just any old geography teacher. I think he's expecting her to get riled and show her teeth; Nigel, it turns out, is a serious wind-up merchant despite the love beads and the multicoloured cotton plait round his wrist. He leans his bum against the cooker, folds his arms loosely and smiles at her. Looks faintly disappointed when she suddenly smiles back.

'Yes. Maybe both, even. D'you want another cup of coffee before you fuck off?'

Nigel grins, reaches over and presses the tit on the kettle. 'Sure. Don't mind if I do.'

Which is when the phone rings. Harriet looks at it. I look at it. Neither of us makes a move towards it. Nigel snorts.

'Christ,' he says. 'You two really are the ticket, aren't you?'

Harriet gestures him to be quiet as, after two rings, the answerphone clicks in. I check my watch: eleven thirty-five; just enough time for a coffee, a briefing and a couple of phone calls while the features editor is in morning conference. Our number's not that hard to come by; the phone will be ringing off the hook all day now with Glendas wanting to know the inside track on Harriet's emotional state.

Harriet's voice. 'This is a machine. If you leave a message, it will not steal your soul. If you're lucky.'

27

The hum of a dead line. Always works with journalists. The machine resets and the phone starts ringing again. Nigel looks from me to Harriet and back again, shrugs, and goes back to filling the coffee pot.

'This is a machine,' says Harriet again. 'If you leave a message, it will not steal your soul. If you're lucky.'

After a couple of seconds' thought, a voice says, 'Hello. This is a message for Lady Harriet Moresby. This is Leeza Hayman calling from the *Daily Sparkle*. I'm writing a piece about your mother for tomorrow's paper and I need to speak . . .'

Harriet slides the volume control over to zero, claps the glue pot down on the kitchen table and picks up the coffee pot. 'I remember Leeza "Godiva would be turning in her grave" Hayman. A hypocritical alcoholic who drank three bottles of wine on expenses and wrote them down to me.' Nigel raises an eyebrow, puts four spoons of sugar in his mug and stirs.

I quietly move the glue pot onto a newspaper, say, 'Ignore them. You know that's what you have to do.'

'Oh, well, that's all very well for you to say—' she starts, remembers that it actually is all very well for me and shuts up.

'Why do I know that name, Moresby?' asks Nigel, pouring me a cup.

The phone rings again, almost immediately clicks off.

'Because it was my mother's married name,' snaps Harriet.

'And what was her original name?'

'Pigg.' Harriet says the word with the contempt of a good Imam. 'But you wouldn't have heard of that. She had a few names before she settled on Fawcett. And then she married my father and turned Moresby for a few years.'

I can see the grey cells heating up as he makes the connections. Clunk. Fawcett. Clunk. Moresby. Clunk. Important enough to be getting phone calls from journalists. Clunk. Harriet. Clunk. Around twenty-eight years old, hair so blonde it's almost white, slender, cute little button nose, emerald eyes, dark brows, cupid's bow lips; she may be covered in paint, nails bitten to the quick, hair tied back with a bulldog clip and cunningly disguised as a tramp, but the resemblance is unmistakeable. A huge neon exclamation mark lights up above his head.

'Christ!' he cries. 'You're Godiva Fawcett's daughter!'

'No shit, Sherlock,' she says.

'You really do swear a lot, don't you?'

'Too fucking right. I went to a convent school. Well, several, actually, in a row. It's a classical part of the education. Any other questions?'

'Well, yeah, only about a million. But—'

'Yeah, yeah. I know. First you want to say how much you loved her and though you never knew her you felt that she touched your heart and made you a better person. Spare me.'

Nigel bursts into a gale of raucous laughter. 'Touched my heart? I wasn't but six when she died and it was on the other side of the world, for God's sake. I was more touched by Skippy the Bush Kangaroo. Oh, sorry.' He suddenly remembers that this is someone's dead mother he's talking about, looks guilty like a schoolboy caught behind the bike sheds, then puzzled by the look on Harriet's face.

'No, no,' she says, 'it's fine.'

An awkward silence. Nigel slurps his coffee, then says, 'If you don't mind me asking, why are you ignoring the answerphone? Has something happened?'

We glance at each other.

'Yes.' I decide it's my turn to do the talking. 'You could say that.'

'What?'

Harriet hauls Henry down from his eyrie, tucks him rebelliously under her chin and starts planting kisses on the top of his head as I talk. He wriggles for a bit, says 'Naao' a couple of times then gives up, straddles his front feet either side of her neck and submits grumpily to her caresses. Henry is wonderfully, moggily yellow with eyes the same colour as Moresby mother and daughter. The contrast with her hair is like gold set among diamonds; they glitter together as though they had been made that way.

'You know,' I say, 'that Godiva was buried in a special mausoleum at the family house in East Anglia after she died?'

Nigel nods. 'Bellevue? Something like that?'

'—haven. Well, it didn't actually happen entirely like that. The fact was that Gerald – that's Harriet's half-brother, who inherited after their father died, he's about fifteen years older than us and sort of stood guardian for Harriet most of the time, even while Godiva was still alive, she was always so busy doing good works, you see, and fighting the estate for a share of the will – anyway, he decided that it probably wasn't such a good idea to actually bury her on the spot because of the way the crowds were going on in the first few years.'

Nigel nods again. I'm going to have to do something about his name. 'I heard about that,' he said. 'I heard it got pretty ugly now and again.'

'That's putting it mildly. There were a couple of times when someone got in there with a crowbar, and another time when some eighteen-carat nutter turned up with dynamite to blow the whole shebang sky-high. Well, you can imagine . . .'

There's a moment there where I can see a tasteless joke hovering on his lips, but he suppresses it.

'Anyway,' I continue, raising my voice while Harriet drops Henry onto the top and shows a sudden and noisy interest in washing up. 'He decided a week or so ago that it was probably safe to move her out of the family crypt and into her real one. He's never liked having her buried with the rest of the family. There's bad blood there, still, after all these years, and if it hadn't been for the press coverage, he'd never have let her be buried at Belhaven at all. So he couldn't wait to get her up and out of the church. But there was some sort of accident. I'm not sure what, but her coffin was broken open—'

'The whole bloody place is run like some sodding Laurel and Hardy movie,' interjects Harriet, slams a handful of cutlery undried into the drawer.

'And it turns out,' I continue, 'that her body's pretty much perfectly preserved.'

Nigel thinks about this for a moment. 'Christ,' he says. 'And—'

I nod. The phone rings once again, cuts off.

'Some bird called Margaret Burge called the *Mail*. She's married to one of the guys who – Hey, Harriet, I thought the Burges were meant to be, like, dumb?'

She waggles her head. 'Margaret's not a Burge, is she? Seems she's been a frustrated blabbermouth for the last two decades. She was Godiva's number one fan. Along with everyone else in the world.'

'And that's roughly it. So now it's business as usual: Godiva back in the limelight, us having to keep the answerphone on and stay indoors as much as possible for the next week and read quotes that someone at the *Sun* made up and everyone else repeats the next day because they couldn't get one either. Look. There's half a dozen of them out there already.'

'Mmm.' Nigel opens the balcony door, steps out to have a gander. Milling about down by the gates (we disconnected the buzzer at six this morning) is a knot of people: two twelve-year-olds in power suits, two middle-aged men in the sort of anorak that the owners believe to be endowed with magical self-cleaning properties and a chap with short hair in what looks like a pinstriped suit. On the far side of the road, a couple of mid-market saloons sit by the river, sheltering working teams whose photography allowance runs to a car. One of them presses on the buzzer as we watch, as though they believe that we are as likely to pick up after a hundred rings as after one.

'I see what you mean. Still. They don't look too threatening. I'd have thought the two of you could take them on.'

The phone goes again, clicks over to answerphone, clicks over to fax. Chirrups and starts to buzz. 'Christ,' says Harriet, 'can't they get the message?'

I glance at the cover sheet as it emerges. ''S okay. It's from my mother.'

'Tell you what,' says Nigel, 'I could throw them off the scent a bit on my way out, if you like.'

'Oh, leaving now, are you? *Thanks,*' says Harriet.

'Well, you did want me out of here ten minutes ago, didn't you?'

'I can change my mind if I want to.'

'I've got to catch a plane at two thirty. Much as I'd love to stay here and shoot the breeze with you two lovely ladies – ' Harriet pulls a face at the mention of ladies. She doesn't much like being reminded that she is one for real ' – I'm supposed to be in Dublin tonight.'

'Oh, well then. Off you go,' she says like a schoolmarm dismissing an eight-year-old from detention.

'I'll see you later.' He heads for his rucksack, brushes past me and says, 'And I really hope I see *you*.'

Actually, I hope he means it. He may be called Nigel, but his forearms are covered with shiny golden hairs and I can just feel them brushing the small of my back. Damn. I can't afford to get worked up about someone who's just leaving.

As he passes the fax machine, he rips off the paper, scans it and begins to hand it over. 'She says she knows you're screening and to call her—' he begins, then stops. Looks back at the cover sheet and over at me.

'Christ. You mean I almost got my hands on some Nobel totty?'

I sort of wriggle and gesture uncomfortably. If there's one thing that can be guaranteed to turn a guy off, it's the thought of my mother.

He looks me over, and he seems to be pouting. 'You don't look like her.'

'No. I, um, don't.'

Nigel lays down the fax paper, rubs his arms, where all the hairs are suddenly standing up on end. 'What the hell have I walked into?'

He regards the two of us with a combination of fascination and horror. Shakes his head and says to Harriet, 'And to think I was feeling sorry for *you* a second ago. Bloody hell.'

And then he addresses me. 'What the hell's it like having someone like Grace Waters for a mother?'

Chapter Three

Happy Families

I'll tell you what it's like having Grace Waters for a mother. Imagine, for a moment, that you're back at school. Imagine that you wake up one day, and you're seven years old, and confined within the walls of a school where you were placed at birth. Only, it's not your common-or-garden school with start times and end times, with break times and lunchtimes: it's a 24-hour-a-day, seven days a week, 365 days a year hothouse where no failure is brooked, no slacking permitted. And imagine that this school is not just a school, but a country in its own right, a country established on a windswept island in the Atlantic that has, by mutual consent of all governments worldwide, been declared both independent and a site of special cultural interest to be defended at all costs.

And imagine this: however hard you try, however diligently you apply yourself to meeting the exacting standards of this school, however late you stay up frowning over your homework, however you strive to show enthusiasm for your subjects, however enthusiastically you pant up and down the hockey field, you still remain the class lummox, still the unpopular one, still the one that everyone takes last, and unwillingly, onto their teams, still the one whose report cards read, monotonously, Could Do Better. You suspect, because you have stumbled, on the beach, across a short-wave radio that occasionally crackles into life to tell a joke or describe an activity you've never encountered, that some dreadful error is afoot and that you've been mistaken for some other, higher being. But you know that the expression of such thoughts is forbidden and punishable by detention, or being sent into coventry by classmates and teachers alike.

And imagine this: this country has been thriving for a whole generation before you were born. The laws have been tested and no one in the previous generation has found them to be bad laws. The original legislator is, in fact, venerated close to godhead; statues of him are scattered about the place and his collected quotations are brought out to support every decision, quell any signs of rebellion. And as you know nothing else, you have to believe what you are told: that your silent world of work and diligence and trying always to please the legislators is the only possible way to live, that all other options are inferior ones, that you, and your fellow citizens, have achieved the pinnacle of what human life has to offer. What would you do? What would you think?

I'm talking metaphorically, of course. My real life was far duller than that. But just as crushing.

When I met Harriet, I had been dying, bit by bit, for seventeen years. Harriet Moresby saved my life. And I don't just mean the time she did it literally.

I'll tell you what it's like to have Grace Waters for a mother: it's like growing up in purgatory with none of the entertainment value. Yes, I know. The great Grace Waters. Feminist heroine, saviour of humanity, Nobel laureate, role model to millions, leader of civilisation. The Grace Waters whose medical work transformed your life, whose musical works enrich it, whose feats are more than merely legendary.

You probably read those colour supplement interviews

where celebrities are asked to choose their fantasy dinner party guests. Have you noticed that my mother is always among them? All the usual suspects: Marilyn Monroe, William Shakespeare, Diana Vreeland, Mick Jagger, Godiva Fawcett, Henry Kissinger, the Dalai Lama, Steven Spielberg, the Prince of Wales, Groucho Marx, Jackie Kennedy-Onassis, Elvis Presley, their current partner, Rupert Murdoch, their interior designer, Gianni Versace, Socrates, Dorothy Parker, Charles Darwin, Richard Dawkins, Oscar Wilde, my mother. They always crease me up, those articles: silly people attempting to add gravitas to their personality by listing people they've heard of.

I mean, you don't think they really mean it, do you? You wouldn't really want my mother at your dinner table, would you? Sitting there in her high-necked Laura Ashley flower prints (as she always says, there is no reason why a woman cannot display intellect and also look feminine), her hair with its white streak in the centre parting swept up into two batwings on either side of her head, looking for all the world like a paint-free, bespectacled, floral Cruella de Vil and curdling the cream in your vichyssoise.

Let me tell you about my mother, the great Grace Waters. My mother has been famous practically all her life. She first became famous when she won a scholarship to Cambridge at the age of twelve to read physics and philosophy, and the papers divided themselves into separate camps, often within the same publication, filling the comment pages with con-gratulations for effort rewarded and hysterical defences of the sanctity of childhood. Ask your mother about her. She will tell you about the clips of Grace's serious little face above her serious little crushed-strawberry tweed coat, the sight of her lost among giants, tiny little body wrapped in a gown that had had to be custom-made in order not to trip her up.

The chances are that she will also mention Grace's father. He was always there by her side, Peter Waters, the child staring silently into the camera lens as he spoke of his pride, his dedication and the sacrifices he had had to make to get her to this point so young.

But that's not all. Unlike many child prodigies, my mother came true to her promise. At fourteen, she graduated and embarked on her doctorate. At sixteen-and-a-half she completed her first thesis, and began teaching people years older than herself. And it's not as if she has one of those narrow, focused minds that can see only one subject. She may have gained her original distinction for counting particles in stellar nebulae, but her second doctorate was awarded for her discursive way with the meaning of life. The Nobel Prize in medicine she won for two things: the cancer immunisation discovery that showed millions the possibility of a life free from fear, and the world's first foolproof, pope-proof, side-effect-free contraceptive, which she developed to cope with the consequent population boom. Boy, how you loved her for that, and rightly so. Thirty thousand bunny rabbits might disagree, but the end always justifies the means.

And then there's the rounded character; my mother is Renaissance Woman and no one can forget it. An entire evening was dedicated to her musical works, knocked out as relaxation after a hard day's thinking – you can fit a lot into your day if you only sleep four hours a night – at the Proms last year. The premiere of her Fantasia for xylophone, harp and tabla received the usual ten-minute standing ovation, Grace nodding modestly in her stalls seat.

Nobel prizes are like swimming badges in our house; win one, you win them all.

There are things, though, that my mother won't be winning any prizes for. She won't be winning any popularity contests, for a start. To quote the woman herself, in one of her rare interviews, in *New Scientist*: 'The desire to be liked is one of the most destructive urges where original thought is concerned. Popularity is, in its very essence, the antonym of excellence.' She won't be winning many prizes for her sense of humour, either: one of the phrases that still echoes from my childhood, applied to other people as well as to me, is: 'Oh, I see. You're trying to be funny.'

Grace Waters won't be walking away with gongs for hospitality, warmth, empathy or even elementary psychology in the near future. She won't be tearfully accepting accolades from the Best-Dressed Boffin Society, the Good Neighbour Trust or the Friends of the Stiletto. The National Humility Co-operative won't be beating a path to her door, nor will the Society for Cordial Relations. And she certainly won't be polishing any cups or shields from the Tea and Sympathy Brigade. Actually, this saviour of human life is one of the heroines of the capital punishment movement. She once referred to recidivist offenders as 'a cancer in our society which, like all cancers, must be excised to save the body'.

Let me tell you about my mother. She may be brilliant, she may have helped the world, she may be the person you all admire the most, but she is also the coldest person I have ever met. Cold, rational and full of contempt for anyone who fails to live up to her standards.

My mother spent two decades trying to replicate her father's own success. For two decades, her pet project was to create me in her own image. And to my shame, she almost succeeded.

Chapter Four

Tea and Sympathy

Harriet always gets into these states when her mother comes back into the public eye. I know she talks like a bitch about her mother, dismisses her with a snarl, but it's not really as simple as that. I mean, yeah, in some ways it is. Godiva was, all told, pretty dodgy on the mothering front: absent where mine was all too present, mercurial in her affections, throwing her arms around her daughter in the presence of cameras and forgetting to come back for access visits for months on end when they weren't there, but you know, despite everything, Harriet loved her. Godiva had a way with her, a way of opening her eyes wide and confessing her weakness that could bring any child back into the fold. It's the other people who claim that they felt the same that set Harriet off: the strangers who elbowed their way into the limelight, wept crocodile tears, claimed kinship and friend-ship and stole Harriet's tragedy for their own. Harriet's hatred of hypocrisy comes from that time, and she never really had anyone around to teach her how to hide it.

And off he goes, my unused lover, slouching through the early summer sunshine down the path and over the lock, backpack hanging casually from one shoulder. We take turns to watch through the periscope I won in a raffle five years ago – we hardly want to go out onto the balcony and wave

– as he presses the exit button and steps through the gate and is surrounded, in two seconds, by a dozen gannets with their notebooks and cameras and boxy tape recorders.

Nigel recoils, pantomimes surprise, then he throws his long arms wide in an exaggerated shrug. Flings his head back in laughter, shakes it vigorously.

'He's talking to them,' says Harriet in tones of horror. 'The bugger's *talking* to them!'

I pat her arm. 'He did say that was what he was going to do,' I remind her.

'Yes,' she replies, 'but there's no need to get so pally.'

My mate. She won't be reasoned with.

Then her pursed lips soften, her jaw drops ever so slightly. 'Well, I'll be buggered,' she says.

I grab the periscope. Nigel is loping off up the embankment, and, to my amazement, the gents and ladies of the press are scattering, some following him, some getting back into their cars, some hailing taxis, some heading in the direction of the tube. Well, I'll be blowed.

'You have to marry that man,' says Harriet, 'and have his kids.'

Which makes me smile. Because I'm still living out my adolescence and have no intention of marrying anyone until I've tested a lot more of the available options. But you never know: maybe he'll come back and at least give me some chance to practise.

My mobile rings. I check the display before I pick up. You never know, after all. But it's Mel. Phew. 'Hi, honey.'

'Where are you?' she asks.

'At home.'

'Oh. Did you know your phone's switched off? I've tried about five times and it always goes to answerphone.'

'Sorry,' I say. 'We've switched the volume down.'

'I'm not surprised.' Mel is neither fazed nor curious. That's the great thing about old friends. Mel met me when I was still in my chrysalis phase, helped us move into the tower, went through the tenth anniversary commemoration celebrations with us; she hardly needs telling about what's going on.

'That's why I was ringing,' she continues. 'Are you two okay?'

'Oh, I'm fine,' I say. 'Lovely's in a bit of a state.'

Harriet snatches the phone from my hand. 'I am *not* in a state,' she announces. Oh yeah, I think, that's why I've been sitting on the sofa hugging you half the night and watching you smoke your head off the rest of it.

Harriet listens while Mel talks. 'No,' she replies, 'I'm just furious.'

Another silence. 'Well, of course it's a shock . . .' she says a bit less certainly. That's one of Mel's talents. Being one of those people with a regular job, paid holidays, time to read, she's done so much self-actualisation she never has compunction about asking the direct question that needs to be asked. 'No, well, what do you think?' asks Harriet. Then, 'Yeah. They were camped outside the gates first thing this morning, but they've gone now. For the moment, anyway.' She listens again. 'Well, I'd love to, darling, but we've got to work tonight.' Another pause. 'No. Roy will totally lose it if we both don't turn up at five hours' notice.'

Harriet laughs. First actual laugh all morning. 'You have no idea how much I'd like to do that,' she says. 'And I'll tell you what. When I do, I'll shove the ping-pong bat right up there after it. But not when we're both totally skint and we're getting better tips than we ever have in our lives.'

She looks at her watch. 'Sure. Are you sure? Why aren't you at work? Well, okay, then. That would be nice.'

Laughs again. 'Totally shitfaced. But I can't really afford to, not if we're on duty tonight. Tea any good?'

While this is going on, I'm keeping an ear on the conversation and an eye on my mother's fax. Boy, my mother doesn't bother to waste words. Under the address, the string of letters after her name and the five phone numbers, in her scrupulous handwriting, each t crossed firmly with a tiny bar that never strays into another letter, all curlicues and flourishes cut down for waste of time, Grace has written:

As you do not see fit to answer your emails, and as I am unable to access you by telephone, I am sending you this to inform you that you are expected at the Blackburn Lecture, on Sunday week at 18.45 prompt, Arlosh Hall, University College. Please confirm this with me at your earliest convenience.

Blimey. Nigel softened *that* one up a bit.

I'd forgotten, actually, that The Dragon was back in the country next weekend. Thank God, at least she doesn't seem to want to have one of our dinners. Lindsey calls them Trials by Food, and she's not far wrong.

Harriet hangs up. 'Mel's coming over, and Dom,' she announces. Dom and Mel live together. As a couple. As one of those couply couples who not only look alike – masses of chestnut curls, wide, honest eyes – but seem to know, most of the time, what the other is thinking.

I love them, but my heart sinks. Oh, God. Does this woman never sleep? We've been up for well over twenty-four hours and I feel that every bit of me is flaking off. I twist a smile onto my face.

Suddenly, Harriet looks concerned.

'Oh, God, sorry, Annie. I thought it would be okay if it was those two. I'm sorry. I didn't think. I'll call her back . . .'

I shake my head. 'Don't be silly. I'm just tired.'

She cons my face. 'You look awful.'

'Thanks.' I boot the computer up.

'What are you up to?' she asks.

I hand her the fax. 'I thought I'd better answer this before she comes round in person.'

Harriet reads it properly for the first time. Perches on the edge of the table, frowning. 'Does she *have* any other tone than commanding, your mother?'

'Not to me, no. I've sometimes seen her talking to people as though they were almost her equal, but that's only other Nobel winners and profs and things. And I think most people are quite grateful never to have to see her social face again once they've seen it the first time.'

'No!' Harriet lifts her eyes from the paper. 'All these years I've known you and you never told me she had a social face! I've never seen it!'

Harriet has met my mother three times in the ten years we've been friends. On the first meeting, my mother treated her to the bug-under-microscope thing. Since then, it's been strictly Immigration Officer. Grace isn't stupid, after all; she knew almost immediately – probably before I did – that her grip had weakened when Harriet came on the scene. I don't think, though, that she knows just how much.

I demonstrate. Open my eyes as wide as they can go, draw my upper lip up towards my nose so that my front teeth are exposed, tilt my head slightly to one side and, in a tone both bored and patronising, I say, '*Really?*'.

'Jesus Christ!' Harriet actually starts back for a second and lets out a little shriek.

I've practised my mother's social face in the mirror, so I know that I look like the bastard progeny of a mechanical midnight coupling between Margaret Thatcher and Nosferatu, but even I am unprepared for the strength of her reaction. Then she bursts into a laugh. 'Your mother,' she declares, 'is the scariest woman in the world. Holy cow, I thought you were going to eat me.'

I return the smile, turn back to the screen and click 'compose message' with the mouse. Begin to type my mother's address until the address book clicks in and completes it for me. There are eight messages from Grace in the inbox, all sent in the past twelve hours, with a noticeable gap between 1 a.m. and 5 a.m. her time. She's not changed her sleeping habits, then. It was only after I had the fifth twelve-hour lie-in of my life, at the age of eighteen, that I discovered that my perpetual tiredness was actually related to chronic sleep deprivation. Before then, I had never woken without an alarm or a shaking in my life.

'So how often does she do that, then?' asks Harriet.

I type 'Sunday week' in the subject box. 'Not often. But we'll probably be seeing a bit of it after the lecture. There's a reception.'

'Ooh,' says Harriet. 'Ooh. Can I come? Let me come! *Please* let me come. Please! You didn't tell me there was going to be a party.'

'No.'

I type:

Sorry. Didn't log on for twelve hours. Thank you for the invitation for Sunday week at University College. I will be there at 18.45 prompt.

There's no point in holding back on the irony when writing to Grace, as it all goes straight over her head anyway.

'Oh, *pleeease*,' says Harriet again. 'You know how I love

eating cheese on sticks with a load of academics. Go on. I promise I'll be good.'

'No, Harriet,' I repeat firmly.

'Sometimes,' she says, 'I think you're ashamed of me.'

She knows this isn't true. But we have to go through this ritual every time there's a Waters evening. I'm not ashamed of Harriet. I'm prouder of Harriet than anything else in my life apart from Henry, who we both burst with pride about whenever he speaks his mind, but I can't afford to have my cover blown. If Grace is ever going to find out the truth about me, I need to have done something with my life first. Wait for Sunday week and you'll see what I mean.

'Yes,' I reply. 'I am ashamed of you.'

'Fair enough,' says Harriet, and I click on send.

The buzzer goes. We thought it was probably safe to reconnect it now that the press had left but, just in case, I make my voice gruff and answer in the guttural accents of Mitteleurop. 'Vat do you vant?'

'Hi, Annie,' says Dom. 'It's me.'

I buzz him in. Henry plops down off the sofa where he's shown all the signs of being stuffed for the past hour, and goes down the stairs to greet him. That's another reason we're so proud of Henry. Whenever the door goes, he always assumes that the visitor is there for *him*. What a dude.

They arrive together five minutes later, Henry hanging over Dom's shoulder like a big fur stole, Dom perspiring lightly from the climb wearing a knock-off designer suit as befits his position on the lower rungs of his chosen career. 'I brought some white wine,' he declares. Dom enjoys a sweeping generalisation as much as the next man, 'because girls like white wine. Mel's not here yet?'

'No.' Harriet, unprompted, crosses the room and actually gives him a hug. Dom is one of a very few men that Harriet

45

actually has strong affection for. Him and Shahin, and a gay guy called Stuart who used to be a trolly dolly on British Airways until he went off to Barcelona to set up a beach bar with a boyfriend he met in a hotel in Thailand. Harriet used to spend hours at a time watching tapes of *Baywatch* with Stuie. We both miss him. Harriet is comfortable with Dom because she met him as Mel's main squeeze and he's never shown a flicker of interest in her other than as a boy with tits. Which, come to think of it, is why she likes Shahin and Stuie too. You know, you get like that when you look like Harriet.

Harriet relieves Dom of his plastic bag, and sets to with the corkscrew. 'Harriet,' I warn, 'work.'

She just pulls a face and pours the plonk. And somehow I find myself accepting a glass.

'So,' begins Dom, 'Mel says you've been besieged.' He sits down, and Henry readjusts himself to fit the new posture.

'Eugh,' says Harriet. 'Do you know who had the nerve to call? That Leeza Hayman thing. She was clogging up our answerphone at eleven thirty this morning.'

'Agh, God,' says Dom.

'I'm surprised,' continues Harriet, 'that she was able to do anything at eleven thirty in the morning, the amount she drinks.'

'I think,' says Dom, 'that Leeza Hayman probably stopped having hangovers some time in 1978.'

'Oozy bitch,' says Harriet. 'Doing the old best-friends routine. I'll give her best friends.' Harriet hates Leeza Hayman. Hates her with poison, with bile, with a vengeance.

Dom, who's been working in PR for a while now, says, 'You know, it mightn't be such a bad idea to bury the hatchet with la Hayman, Haz. Or, at least, let her think she's not got to you. You know what it's like with the press. They'll always have the last word if it kills them.'

'Balderdash,' Harriet replies. 'Poppycock and hogwash. It won't be the last word that kills that bitch if I ever get my hands on her.'

Dom gives her that reproving-but-indulgent look that always drives her on to greater extremes.

'I will be mortal enemies with that woman until the day I die,' says Harriet, with magnificent exaggeration. 'She needs to know that not everything she does is going to be forgotten. She needs to know that wherever she goes, however she disguises herself, however long she lives, I will be there, hunting her down and waiting for the kill.

'And besides,' she finishes, 'I like having enemies. It's good practice, and it stops me killing my friends.'

Dom, her friend, laughs and reaches out to snake his arm round the back of her neck. 'You,' he says, 'are all mouth and no trousers.'

Harriet flashes wicked green eyes at him, says, 'Just you try me, sonny.'

'You're okay, then,' says Mel from behind us. Mel is our keyholder, poor lamb, which is a more onerous job than you would think as we're both pretty good at leaving things on the bus. But at least she doesn't have to wait to be let in like everyone else.

Harriet is breezy now. You get new people in the room and, even when they're people she knows as well as these two, Harriet always has to turn breezy. 'Laughing,' she replies. 'Wine in the fridge. Wash yourself a glass.'

Mel looks at me. 'You okay?'

I nod because, essentially, I am, though three sips of wine have turned me into a sleep monster. I check my watch. Four hours till we have to be at work.

'You look like shit,' says Dom.

I do wish people would stop saying that.

'She hasn't had any sleep,' says Harriet. 'And I interrupted her in the middle of her favourite hobby.'

'Oh, no!' cries Mel. 'You mean that little Aussie cutie went to waste?'

Less of the little, I think. But blinking, I nod again.

'Lindsey said she'd never seen anybody work that fast,' says Mel. 'She said it was a record even for you. She said one minute you were talking to some bloke with a beard about sustainable teak production and the next you'd legged it out of the door with some boy with love beads.'

'Well, she introduced us,' I protest. 'And anyway, I gave it at least half an hour.' Okay, so that was a bit fast, but you tend to know, don't you, in the first five minutes?

'Are you ever going to settle down?' asks Dom from the lofty height of a seven-year involvement. Mel and Dom met, in the Proper Manner, at an interview weekend for a traineeship in the City (which neither of them won), and have been a Couple, no vacillation, no humming and hawing, since precisely ten days later.

Harriet and I catch each other's eye. And then we start to laugh. We laugh till tears begin to squeeze from our eyes, until Henry raises his head from Dom's shoulder and treats us to a sleepy glare. And then Mel starts to laugh too, and finally, after a minute's 'No, but seriously's', Dom's shoulders start to shake and he joins in. 'Sorry.' He giggles. 'Sorry. Silly me. That's about as likely as Harriet taking up housework.'

Harriet pats him, pulls herself off the sofa and finds another bottle of wine in the fridge. Opens it, tops the others up, comes in my direction, but I wave her away. She looks concerned. 'Are you okay?'

'Yeah. But I think I'm going to keel over, hon. Honestly. I don't think I'm going to make it through tonight.'

Mel sits forward. 'She's kept you up all night again, hasn't she?'

'It's fine.'

'Well, Anna, why don't you go and have a rest?'

'I'm fine.'

'No,' Mel says. 'You're not fine. You've gone green. Go to bed.'

The pull of my lovely deep bed is getting stronger as she speaks. Suddenly, the thought of being anywhere other than wrapped in my chenille bedspread, buried among my velvet cushions, cosseted by my azure walls, is enough to bring on a tantrum. I find myself agreeing. Stumble to my feet, saying, 'You won't let Lovely get too pissed, will you?'

'No,' says Mel.

'And someone will wake me at five?'

'Yes,' says Dom.

'Okay,' I say. 'I think I have to if I'm going to make it through tonight. I'll see you later.'

Chapter Five

1949: Piggs on the Beach

'Look at me! Look at me! Look at me!'

Geraldine Pigg, seven years old, balances on the break-water as the wind whips her hair across her face and into her mouth. Geraldine's white-blonde colouring is set off by a pink tutu, navy sandshoes and, perched on the top of her head, a sequinned cardboard tiara. She raises her hands, touches the tips of her fingers together above her head and repeats the cry, 'Look! Look at me!'

Fifty yards away, the rest of the Pigg family, wrapped firmly in overcoats against the gunmetal sky, sets out the day's festive luncheon. Irene Pigg, hair protected by a clear plastic pac-a-mac headscarf printed with gaily waving umbrellas, finds hard-boiled eggs, salt, pepper, bread and, from the bottom of the picnic basket, a nice tin of Fray Bentos.

'Ooh.' Her sister-in-law, Ivy, desists, for a moment, from the demanding task of adding condensed milk to four cups of tea poured from a large Thermos flask that Stanley Pigg has carted like the Crown jewels across the shingle. 'Corned beef! We *are* in for a treat!'

Irene starts to hack at the tin with the rust-stained can opener she has kept in her handbag ever since the time when she found herself spending twelve hours in a bomb shelter with only a keyless tin of sardines for sustenance. 'Well,' she replies, 'I always say, there's no point in being married to a butcher if you can't occasionally benefit from the stock.'

Geraldine, high upon her perch, realises that her audience is not with her. 'LOOOOK!' she howls into the wind, lifts one foot from the top of the old railway sleepers and holds it out to the side at hip level.

Stanley Pigg leans forward in his deckchair. He has tucked an old scarf round his neck to keep out errant breezes, so that his face is only visible between moustache and the tweed cap that matches his scarf. 'I'll have that cup of tea now, if it's not too much trouble,' he says with the untroubled authority of one who can lay his hands on corned beef whenever the need should arise.

Ivy passes Stanley his own special Bakelite mug, the red one he has had since his own childhood, stained a rich brown on the inside with the residue of a thousand consoling cuppas. Behind him, his daughter waves and wobbles, her eyes never straying from her potential audience.

'Do you think,' asks Ivy, 'that we ought just to look at your Geraldine and get it over with?'

'Leave her,' replies Irene, never looking up from the loaf as she slices and butters, using the basket lid as a board. 'It'll only encourage her.'

Ivy thinks for a while, cracks open the shell on an egg and begins to unpeel it. 'So why,' she eventually says, 'if you don't want her attracting attention, did you let her come to the seaside in her ballet costume?'

Irene sighs. 'You have no idea' – the corned beef is sliced up thin and laid across the bread. She produces a pair of tomatoes from a paper bag, pares them as TV chefs will do fifty years later with garlic and razor blades, and lays them over the beef – 'how hard it is to get Geraldine out of her ballet costume. It's as though she had been welded into it.

51

It was either let her wear it, or die fighting. We'd never have got here otherwise.'

In the background, Geraldine, finding that the parallel-leg thing just isn't doing it, leans forward and points her toe out behind her. She is, it has to be said, remarkably sure on her feet for one so young in such a high wind. Even the gust that blows violently up the crotch of her tutu is insufficient to produce a diversion. 'Look!' she shrieks, but the grown-ups sit obdurately with their backs to her.

Geraldine puts the foot back onto solid sleeper, thumps her fists into her sides. Geraldine doesn't like her parents much. They're not the people, with their sensible clothes, their sensible picnics, their careful budgeting, that she would have chosen had she been given the choice. But since the weather has driven all the less hardy holidaymakers off the beach and in behind the steam-covered windows of the Cozee Nook teahouse, they're the only audience she has. She reaches up, tucks her hair behind her ears and pouts.

'Sometimes I wonder,' says Ivy, 'if she's really your daughter at all.'

'Steady on,' says Stanley, who's the wag of the family, 'what are you implying about my good lady wife?'

Ivy laughs and elbows him in the knee, which is the only part she can reach from her perch on the tartan rug. 'Now, don't go on, Stanley. You know what I mean. Some sort of mix-up in the hospital or something. I mean, she hardly takes after any of us, does she? When was the last time there was a blonde in the family? And as for the showing off, well – I don't know where it comes from, I really don't.'

'Well, it must come from your side,' says Irene. 'The last time anyone got up in public in my family was when our George was made jury foreman in that burglary trial in 1937.

And then all he had to do was say 'Guilty'. I don't know. Rich Tea with that, Ivy?'

'Mmm! Can't beat a Rich Tea with a cuppa, I always say. Stanley? Rich Tea?'

Stanley Pigg shifts in his seat, shakes his head. 'Can't stand 'em,' he says. 'Dry and dull as ditchwater.'

'Dull! A Rich Tea biscuit? Are you mad?'

'Mad,' mutters Ivy.

'Completely barmy.' Irene takes back the biscuit tin, presses down firmly on the lid.

'I might have another one of those in a minute.' Ivy sounds ever-so-slightly plaintive.

'Ooh, sorry, love.' Irene re-produces them and each helps herself. The three sink back on their seats and fall into mutual contemplation of the glories of nature: the crashing waves, the suck on the shingle, the flock of seagulls attracted by the teeming life in the warm outflow of the gasworks.

'This is the life,' says Stanley. 'You can't beat a good day out at the seaside.' He tucks his scarf further in around his chin and basks in the silence of agreement. A shriek from behind and the shush of body hitting pebbles. Then a wail, quiet with shock at first, then building with outrage as the wailer realises that no one is looking.

'Oh, dear,' says Irene, 'I have to look now, I suppose.'

'Leave her. She's only trying to attract attention.'

The wails rise higher and wilder on the breeze. Evidently, the injured party is not in immediate peril. 'Aaaah! Aaaah! AAARRRGH!'

'Oh, well,' Irene puts her hand down on the ground, 'I suppose . . .'

What she sees brings her immediately to her feet and bustling over to where her daughter hunches at the foot of the breakwater. Geraldine caught her thigh as she fell and has torn a hole four inches long in the skin, from which blood runs freely, soaking tutu, sandshoes, white socks. Her face and hair are covered in a sticky brown residue where she landed head-first in a patch of sea-tar-covered seaweed.

'Ooh, ooh WAAAH!' she howls. 'Aah! Waah!'

Irene kneels beside her stricken daughter. 'What have you been doing? Look at the state of you! What on earth . . . ?'

'Aargh!' yells Geraldine, then says, through a gout of snot, 'I was trying to get my foot up by my ear to show you, and I fell off.'

'Well, really, Geraldine.' Her mother produces an off-white handkerchief from her coat pocket, spits copiously on it and starts to rub at her daughter's wounds. 'I don't know what possessed you. Now look at you. Haven't I told you that you'd get into trouble with your showing off?'

Geraldine flinches at the touch of the handkerchief. It does hurt, for her mother's impatient ministrations aren't the gentlest, but there is element of the Maria Martens in the way she flings herself backward, hand over face, as she suffers her fate.

'That'll scar now, you silly thing.' Irene puts her face up close to the cut, sees that, though ugly, it probably isn't life-threatening. 'And your tutu's ruined. I hope you've learned your lesson, my girl.'

Geraldine sniffs, and a fat tear runs down her cheek. She has already mastered the art of storing up tears so that they roll individually, like glycerine drops, from her eyes, rather than massing in salty puddles round her nose. 'Well, it's all your fault,' she announces.

'And how do you come to that conclusion, young lady?'

Geraldine sits up straight, says imperiously, 'Well, if you'd only looked at me when I wanted you to, it would never have happened.'

Chapter Six

Chelsea Ladies' College

Roy is standing with his hand on his hip when we come in, and, from the twisted, Mr Punch grimace on his face, I get the feeling that the hand I can't see is probably scratching his arse. 'Girls,' he says, and goes back to staring at the greenery in the window, which has turned once again to brownery.

We go, 'Roy,' and drop our bags and coats in the under-stairs cupboard behind the bar. Even though we haven't seen a journalist since Nigel persuaded them all to scatter this morning, we couldn't really risk leaving the tower in full uniform tonight. Harriet goes to the loo to put her hair in bunches and do her make-up: bright, childlike colours smeared over the eyelids (peacock blue), cheeks (round splodges of embarrassment pink) and lips (slut-red; we may be pretending to be schoolgirls but the punters like their schoolgirls tarty) and to change into stockings with her miniskirt. I don't need to make so much effort. Where God blessed Harriet with one of those knowing, adult faces that convinced the nuns that she was up to no good when she was about six, he blessed me with the sort of face that gets carded by bouncers well into its thirties. School uniform looks perfectly normal on me, under a cover-all coat; I just look like I'm dressing my age.

I pick up a pile of clean napkins from the counter, make a start on laying them out on tables.

'I don't understand' — Roy fondles the curled leaves of a weeping *ficus*, which crackle between his fingers — 'what's happened. Is it the light in the window, do you think?'

I shrug, place a napkin in the middle of a place setting made up of adult-sized red-plastic-handled training cutlery and those heavy Arcoroc beakers that bounce when you throw them. You need beakers that bounce in here; and you need sharp reflexes to dodge them. 'No good asking me, Roy. I'm crap with plants.'

'Oh, well,' says Roy glumly, 'maybe that's it. I used to have a green finger until you two came along. This whole window used to be like a jungle. I had everything here. Banana plants, weeping figs, aloes, rubber plants, agaves, avocado, spider plants, yucca, swiss cheese, ferns, cacti: everything all in one window. You couldn't see in, you couldn't see out. It looked lovely. And now look at it. Either you've cursed them all, or you've got some virus.'

'Bollocks,' says Harriet, emerging from the loo with her woolly stockings rolled down over rubber bands to hold them at just-over-knee-height. 'People don't carry plant viruses. You're imagining things again. Just keep feeding them that fertiliser I gave you and you'll see what happens.' She takes a wad of napkins from me and starts folding them, yawning widely, gets halfway down the table, then looks up, says, 'So what treats have you got in store for us tonight, then, Roy?'

Roy has a look at the reservations book. 'Two stag parties, a birthday party and three corporates. Biggest table fourteen, smallest seven. Birthday starts at seven, corporates seven thirty, eight, eight thirty, stags are staggered at nine thirty and ten. Specials are Welsh rarebit, bacon roly-poly, tapioca and jam but second two corporates are on the set menu as they've got Japanese with them.'

'Oh shit.' Harriet slaps her napkins down on the table, throws herself into a chair. 'You didn't tell me there were going to be Japanese tonight.'

'Of course I didn't. I knew you'd find some excuse not to come in if I did.'

'Too bloody right,' says Harriet, lights a cigarette. Jiggling her foot in her five-inch tranny-shop stiletto, black kohl pencil smeared beneath her eyes, she looks exactly like a petulant twelve-year-old who's tarted up her uniform in preparation for the trip on the school bus. Which, of course, is exactly what the job requires. Roy couldn't believe his luck when the two us walked in here in search of a job. At the time, we couldn't believe what Shahin had told us about the tips. We do now, though. But I don't think either of us realised how hard we'd have to work for them.

'Presumably they'll be wanting the Sapporo, then,' I interrupt. I can't face a fight today. I think we need to keep on Roy's good side at the moment. I know we're his best waitresses, but he's not the most kindly of employers, and I have a feeling that there might be some unscheduled absences coming up in our part of the rota. Fortunately, even Roy recognises that this job is a tough call, so he has six waitresses, and none of us works more than three nights a week. You won't believe it, but the tips really are good enough to survive on that.

'There you go, there's the spirit.' Roy points at me as I dig out the keys to the cellar. 'That's the sort of attitude we need, milady: not your shan't do this, shan't do that. Why can't you be more like your friend here? She doesn't mind what . . .'

His voice fades as I go past the fusebox down the basement

stairs, into a jumble of exchangeable table tops, broken chairs, blackboards, tablecloths, the washing machine and tumble dryer, metal drums of rice, baked beans, semolina, tapioca, flour, raisins, the desk and computer, the toolbox, cardboard boxes full of receipts mouldering in wait of the bookkeeper and enough bottled beer to refloat the *Titanic*. From the corner, a couple of hundred spiders watch silently as I edge my way past the maypoles left over from Roy's 4th of June (a free flower-edged boater with every jug of Pimms!) and the giant mortar boards from the graduation promotion (degree certificate with every bottle of champagne!). I reach gingerly down behind the walk-in freezer and nab the vodka bottle. Take a large gulp from the top, sneeze, gag, take another one. Harriet has her mother's theatrical background to fall back on when we're out there performing; I need a bit of help from time to time. I'd burst out laughing, otherwise. Or crying. If I've got two lots of corporates and a stag party, I need to be half cut. I mean, don't get me wrong. Most of the time I enjoy my job; it's just that even I can see that it's a weird way to make a living, and it can get to you sometimes.

Behind the Tsing Tao, I locate the case of Sapporo. Bring an armful up the stairs; if Roy wants the whole case carrying, he can bloody well do it himself.

Just as I reach the top of the stairs, there's a shriek from the kitchen and the swing door bursts open in a pall of smoke. Shahin must have put the bangers on to cook, then. I can hear him cussing out of the back door. The whole neighbourhood can hear him cussing out of the back door. 'Crazy motherfuckin' hangdog sonofabitch forget you!' he cries. Shahin's colloquial English has the old-fashioned elegance of a language gleaned from American shows watched on a secreted satellite dish in downtown Tehran. He's one of the weirdest shags I've ever had: all 'Ooh, baby

baby give eet to me,' and 'You like that, baby?' Not scary, you understand, just a bizarre combination of Starsky and Hutch and Dick Dastardly. Very clean, though: fingernails scrubbed to porcelain, and he's never held it against me that I didn't go back for more. Didn't just not hold it against me: turned out to be a total sweetie, actually. Set me and Harriet up with Roy when things went pear-shaped at the Bean-Bag Bar. Shahin loves it here. Thinks it's hilarious. 'Best job I ever freakin' had,' he says. 'But I don't understand this spotted deek. Are all this airheads crazy, or what?'

'And I see you girls are back in trouble again,' Roy's voice drones on. He's obviously not drawn breath since I went downstairs. Maybe I should have stayed down there.

'Not in trouble. It's nothing we've done,' Harriet says wearily, finishing with the ashtrays and rolling her eyes in my direction. It's pretty clear that this isn't going to be a good night. I'm exhausted already. I love her, but a night up with Harriet is the equivalent of an Airtours flight to the Caribbean. Well, not as boring, perhaps, and posher, and usually the plumbing holds out for the entire night, but apart from that, it's close-on the same. That familiar not-quite-there feeling hovers over my cotton wool-wrapped brain and each limb feels like it's got an exercise weight strapped to it. Jet lag. Why did I have to get a friend who gives me jet lag?

'Yeah, but your mum's back in the limelight again.' Roy isn't giving up. I really wish Shahin had never let on about our backgrounds.

'Don't start,' says Harriet.

But he does anyway. 'What beats me,' he starts, 'is how someone with your background, all your advantages, has ended up where you have.'

'I said,' says Harriet, 'don't start, Roy.'

The phone rings. Harriet plunges onto it. 'Good evening,

Chelsea Ladies' College?' She listens. 'Yes, of course. You're the nine-thirty party, yes? Name of Michael? Sure. Has he been a very naughty boy? How naughty? Well, obviously I can give him a good whacking, but for very naughty boys there's the blancmange option as well. Only ten pounds. Of course. What time would you like it? Well, I'd suggest we do it pretty soon after you arrive. It'll break the ice.'

Roy hurries out to the back to tell Shahin that he needs to put a blancmange on.

'No,' says Harriet. 'I'm afraid we'd have trouble with our licence if the serving staff stripped. It's to do with the fact that we're all dressed as schoolgirls. But I'll tell you what we can do. We have an arrangement with an agency. We can get a schoolmistress to come in and do that for you if you like . . .'

I look at my watch. Forty-five minutes before curtain up.

Chapter Seven

Education, Education, Education

There's always a bit of a lull on the food front around ten o'clock; we like to let them polish off their sausages and mash before we put on the show, and try to hold back the puds until afterward. It cuts down on food fights. Shahin, in the kitchen overseeing a vat of sultana-studded semolina, peruses the pictures of Godiva's purple-rinse fans gathered at the gates of Belhaven in the *Sparkle* and says, 'Jesus H. Christ. You grow up in this house?'

Harriet, polishing the dishwasher stains off the Arcoroc, nods nonchalantly. 'Holy sheet,' says Shahin. 'What's it like living somewhere like that? You been there?' he adds to me.

'Yes.' I used to go down and stay there during the vacations after my grades dropped at university and Grace started sending the heavies round to give me talkings-to.

'So what's it like?' he asks again. Like most of the Persians I've met, he's fascinated by the details of other people's wealth.

'Not that great. Mostly ghosts and dodging sightseers, and interminable stand-up drinks with the local hunt. And spending thousands of pounds on microfibre longjohns.'

Shahin stirs the semolina, has a taste. I can feel him wishing for rosewater. 'Longjohns? What is longjohns?'

'Those long thin trousers you wear under your trousers.'

'Oh. So was cold, then?'

'Yes.' I finish separating eggs for the next batch of the two gallons of custard the restaurant gets through each evening, and glance guiltily at Harriet. Slagging Belhaven off is her birthright, after all, not mine. 'And damp. It's below sea level, you know. The kind of cold that gets right through your skin into your bones.'

She gives me a smile of consent under her eyelashes. 'Godiva wouldn't go there at all in the winter,' says Harriet. 'And I spent my entire childhood dodging from radiator to Aga. The minute you aren't actually *sitting* on a radiator, clothes start to rot on your body and your fingers start to drop off.'

Shahin looks up from the *bain-marie*. 'Sitting on radiators? Isn't that meant to be bad for you?'

Harriet clucks. 'Of course it is. Why do you think they call them stately piles?'

Shahin pours a gallon canister of milk into a cannibal-sized saucepan, turns on the heat beneath it. 'So, tell me. If you grown up somewhere like that, why you need to be working here?'

'Oh, darling,' she replies, 'it doesn't work like that. People like me never have any money. It's all tied up in land, which you're not allowed to sell because you're supposed to be a guardian for the next generation or some bollocks like that.'

He chucks five vanilla pods into the warming milk. Shahin can never quite get his head around the less-is-more philosophy. 'No,' he declares. 'I doane bliv you. English peoples always saying "I got no money, I got no money," but is not true. Is cultural thing, like when taxi driver in Egypt say "as you like" so he can see how much money you got and double it. You must have money.'

Shahin has a directness that's difficult to resist. Harriet

never can. 'Of course I've got money, doughbag,' she replies. 'It's just that it's tied up in a trust and I don't get my hands on any of it until I'm thirty, and that's only if the trustees approve. It's quite a common thing, that. No one in Britain thinks their children are capable of handling money before they're thirty.'

He's ripping the top of a huge bag of sugar open with a knife better suited to chopping up recalcitrant children. 'Is no way you can get before?'

'No,' she replies. Then, 'Well, I could get married.'

Then we all laugh.

'Maybe,' says Shahin, 'you need to like men a bit before you get married.'

'I don't not like men,' she protests, 'it's just that I've never met a man who wasn't an arsehole.'

Shahin turns and throws her one of his specialist 'my eyes are velvet cushions, rest on them' soppy looks, says, 'You are saying you doan like your Shahi'?'

'Well, I'm not bloody marrying *you*,' she replies, and he gives her a flash of gold-capped horse-teeth, laughs.

'Crazy chicky,' he says, which is about the highest compliment in his vocabulary, after sonoffabeetch.

Roy puts his head round the swing door, clears his nose. 'Oi! Any chance of someone doing some work around here?'

We turn. 'What?'

'Table eight are ready for their spanking,' he barks, disappears.

Harriet unpeels herself from the oven doors where she still naturally comes to rest despite ten years away from Belhaven, picks up her cane and her table-tennis bat and stalks towards the 'Out' door on her dominatrix's heels. 'You ready?'

I nod, collect the blancmanges on their paper plates from

the counter and fall into line ahead of her. I always go first; coming up to Harriet's shoulder, I would never be noticed at all if I went last. We wiggle to work ourselves up to maximum velocity in our Wonderbras, check each other for inappropriate hairs, say our grace. 'Spanking builds character,' I tell her.

The response comes, 'It never did me any harm.'

I turn as Roy drops the volume on the sound system and hits the dimmer switch, I kick the door open, and, clomping forward on my big black Caterpillar boots, shout, 'Right! Is there a Roger Herriot in the house?'

Harriet raises herself up and inhales until the buttons on her blouse groan under the stress.

'Have you been a very naughty boy?' she asks.

'Yes.' Roger, her victim, bent over the table, confesses.

'How naughty?'

'Very naughty.'

'What have you been doing, you evil boy? Have you been sneaking off and watching Matron undress with your little binoculars again?'

'Yes.'

'Yes what?'

'Yes, madam!' He cries, and his friends snigger with joy: Urk, Urk, he called the waitress madam, Urk.

'And what else have you been doing? I suppose you've been naughty in the showers again, haven't you?'

'Yes, madam!'

'You have?'

This is my cue to step forward. I come round to stand at her side, prime myself with a blancmange in each hand. I always have to avoid Harriet's eye at all costs at this point in the proceedings, because if there was one moment of communication between us, we would probably both lose it, collapse in hysterical laughter and have to stagger off to the kitchen to recover. It happened once, and Roy docked our wages. But it's amazing: even after three months of doing it, I still find the prospect of flanning someone irresistibly funny.

'You're a dirty, dirty little boy!' storms Harriet. 'And you know what we do to dirty little boys around here, don't you?'

His friends start thumping the table: the drumbeat of the British bully preparing for the kill. Harriet puts a fist on a hip, drops her head to one side so her pigtails bob. 'Pants!' cry the mob, and other tables drop their conversations to watch. 'Pants! Pants! Pants! Pants! Pants!'

'Stand up,' orders Harriet. Her victim uncurls to face her, flushed with drink, excitement and being the centre of attention. He gives her a sheepish grin and she pouts bossily. 'No good smiling here,' she says, 'you can't charm your way out of your punishment. Now, drop your trousers.'

The boys burst into a rapturous cheer. Roger starts to fiddle with his buttons. 'Hurry up! Hurry up!' I order.

'Please, miss.' He tries to look boyish and appealing, but I can practically smell the dribble coming out of the side of his mouth. 'I can't do it by myself.'

Wanker. There's always one. Every night, someone who fails to distinguish between a novelty waitress and a flycatcher.

'Sorry, sonny,' I snarl. There are times when you have to turn on the thumbscrews, put them in their place without putting them off the fun. It's the fact that we mastered this art so quickly and he was able to save himself bouncer money that keeps Roy employing us despite everything. 'If you're after a classy bird, try Stringfellows. We expect our pupils to have mastered their trousers by the time they come to this establishment. Now, drop 'em!'

'Now!' repeats Harriet, points her cane at his crotch.

Obediently, he lets his trousers fall open. He is wearing white boxer shorts underneath, cute widdle piccies of dancing pigs popping out from behind his striped shirt tails.

That's enough for me. I step forward, grab the flap of his trousers and neatly drop a blancmange inside, grind it in, safely keeping hands away from flesh, with the paper plate. As the refrigerated jelly hits his skin, his back arches back involuntarily in shock, as it always does. And I leap into the air and land the second blancmange full in his howling face.

A great bay of male approval. Not approval of what I've done, of course, but rather joy at the sight of another man humiliated. The noise always makes me want to duck and hide, but I stand my ground and wait while Harriet steps forward once again to take the spotlight.

'Time,' she says quietly once the cheering has died to a gurgling mutter, 'to take your caning.'

'Oh, God,' says Roger, wiping blancmange from his face. 'Not more.'

'Any more of that, and it'll be twelve of the best,' she snaps. Sometimes I wonder how much acting goes into Harriet's role. I know this for a fact: Harriet, having grown up in a family where men were little more than tools for women's advancement, has only a small supply of respect for them. Plus, of course, she was educated by nuns. 'Now, get over that desk and take your whacking.'

I lead him by the tie to the podium in the middle of the room, bend him over the inky desk upon it and quietly slip the scissors from the pencil slot. Once Harriet's done, my turn comes.

This is her divine moment, the moment she always makes

the most of. Stalking up and down the podium, she slaps the cane into the palm of her hand as the room rustles to the sound of readjusted trousers. Harriet bends over, showing both stocking tops and knickers, and a small groan rises from the assembly. 'Are you ready?' she asks.

The question is ostensibly aimed at Roger, but a dozen voices mutter, almost involuntarily, 'Oh, yes.' Men. Can't live with them, but threaten to paddle their arses and they'll be yours for ever.

'Well, *get* ready.' Harriet brandishes the cane under his nose, bends it until you think it must snap, then gets behind him. Places it on his buttocks, and the hairs on his legs stand on end. 'Count with me,' she tells the audience. Pulls her arm back to its fullest arc.

'One!' they shout. And Harriet, with the deftness of one who has had years of practice, suddenly produces the ping-pong bat in her left hand and brings it down upon Roger's backside. For this is the secret of public violence: maximum drama, maximum pain, but woe betide the restaurant that leaves a welt in the age of litigation. The crack rings out over the audience, Roger yelps and Harriet pulls her arm back for another shot.

'Two!' Whack.

'Three!' Whack.

'Four!' Whack.

'Five!' Whack.

'Six!' Whack.

I step forward. 'Whaddawe say?' I cry.

'And one for luck!' they scream in return, and Harriet brings the paddle down for one last lick.

Harriet is panting as she helps Roger to his feet, plants a thick lipsticky kiss on his left cheek while I do the same on the right, deftly cutting the end off his tie at the same time. We always keep little souvenirs of our victims; Harriet includes them in collages and I turn them into funky little play-toys for Henry. 'Well done,' we say.

'Thank you,' he mumbles through the tears pouring down his cheeks.

Harriet shakes her head. 'You truly are a sad individual.'

'And you are a goddess,' he replies.

Chapter Eight

The Front Room

What people don't realise is that after-hours drinking joints are not actually there to service the coke-addled networking ambitions of thrusting media Turks, but are, in reality, there to provide places where the people who have been servicing them can go for some post-work R&R. All the restaurant and bar staff in central London are members of each other's clubs, and all the door staff at all of them know the other people on the restaurant circuit. The coke-addled media Turks are there to subsidise the leisure of the leisure providers. You know those people you see waltzing past the queues, the ones who don't even have to hand over their names to have the velvet ropes snapped open for them? They're not big faces in the record industry; they've probably just got off work at a bar in Mayfair. People dedicate their whole lives to finding out the secret of being on the guest list, and never discover that it's this: if you want access to all of London's leisure facilities, get a job as staff.

Once the last customer has been dispatched, singing and gurgling and walking gingerly round the weals on his buttocks, we drag Shahin via Victoria station and the papers for a drink at the Front Room. The Front Room is a Manchester theme bar, complete with tasselled lampshades, swirly carpet, flying ducks and ceramic sauce bottles, on each of the tables that line the walls. I think the decor was meant to be an Ironic Statement. The joy of it is that, instead, everyone who goes there treats it with a Coronation Street cosiness that would probably seriously depress its designers.

Harriet and I kiss Alexi, the bouncer, and he unclips his velvet rope to usher us inside. Then everyone kisses Jasmine, who used to work with Harriet at Ollie's Bar, and Harriet requests a huge vodka and tonic. I have a double espresso because I think I'm going to die any minute now. I'm not sure what I'm doing still up, to be honest, except that I'm too wired to go to bed. Shahin orders tea. Not very late-night London, I know, but there you go. Bet you don't always start banging them home when you get in from work either. We find a worn brown velvet sofa whose headrest is protected by white lace antimacassars encased in plastic and slump down to read.

Godiva has made the front pages of everything but the *Financial Times*. Even the *Guardian* has a downpage piece under the headline 'Feminist icon re-emerges as saint? 'It's a miracle!' screams the *Sun*. 'Blessing of Belhaven', says the *Mail* with characteristic alliteration. The *Independent* has a half-page photograph of the scrum of photographers outside the gates of the Great House and the headline 'Fawcett exhumation renews hysteria'. I like the *Sport* best. Its headline merely reads: '36–24–34: Godiva's body found unchanged'.

Jasmine brings the drinks. I sugar my coffee heavily and read the '20 things you never knew about Godiva Fawcett' column in the *Headline*. No 12 is 'It is estimated that Godiva's patronage raised over £30m for charity – £180m at today's rates. The biggest single fundraising effort was when she lent her image to the One World Fair and Ball at London's Alexandra Palace in 1981. Guests and visitors donated over £1m between them, though administration costs reduced the take to just under £70,000.' At No 19 – well, you have to scrape the barrel if you're looking for things people don't know about someone as famous as Godiva – is 'Godiva wore a size 3 shoe, the same as Grace Kelly, Boadicea and Geri Halliwell.'

Harriet reads impassively. There's no sign of emotion on her face; she's been too well trained to let it slip through. I know, though, that there's stuff going on behind that porcelain mask; I've known her too long to be fooled. I sip my coffee and feel an almost instantaneous jolt. Not from caffeine, though: Jasmine has added about half a pint of brandy to the mug, which is one of those things that bar people do as little gifts for other bar people. Damn. And I was going to get a good night's sober sleep tonight.

Shahin puts down his copy of the *Daily Extra* and gives his verdict. 'Crazy fuckin' English peoples,' he says. 'Always death, death, death. This lady, she been dead for how long now?'

'Fifteen years,' says Harriet.

Shahin takes a loud slurp from his cabbage-leaf teacup. Pulls a face. 'And another thing. How come you got to put milk in your tea? Always. Horrible.' He emphasises the 'h' roundly from the back of his throat, a sound that suddenly turns this simple adjective into a blissful onomatopoeia. I'll never pronounce it the old way again.

'Don't think of it as tea, Shahin, think of it as penance.'

He pouts, waggles his head, rests his cup and saucer down on his doily. Jasmine has brought us a cakestand full of sweet treats, apologising for the lack of lardy cake due to a bit of a rush when the staff of lastminute.com had a corporate bonding session. Shahin picks up a Fondant Fancy, sniffs it, puts it back.

'Oh, that's nice,' says Harriet. 'Remind me to eat your toad-in-the-hole next time I'm in.'

He grins that sly Persian grin, that 'I cheat at backgammon and you'll never find out how' smirk. 'I remember when your mother die,' he says.

'Died, Shahin,' says Harriet. 'She died.'

He frowns, waggles his head a bit more. 'Yeah, I know. We find out about it even in Iran. I was maybe eight years old.'

'Jesus,' Harriet interjects. 'I've heard of showbiz ages, but I don't think I knew there were kitchen ones. You're saying you're twenty-three?'

'Yes.' He breaks open an Eccles cake, sniffs, and puts a shred in his mouth. Pulls a face like a disgusted camel and spits it into his hand, and from his hand transfers it to the ashtray. 'Gaad. This you call food?'

'It's a special kind of rural cuisine, Shahin.' I pat his shoulder. 'More decorative than edible. I don't think you're actually supposed to eat it.'

He licks the back of his hand and does another couple of faces. Yes, I think, I really did sleep with this man. I think it was something to do with his eyes being like glittering pools of oil in the desert or something. That, or vodka and the small box of honey-soaked cakelets he brought me from the Reza Patisserie one afternoon. Like I said, he's a total sweetie.

'Crazy. Crazy people. Who makes food that is not for eating? Anyway, day she die was on Iranian TV. Whore from England dies using Moslem children for puppets for TV. Pictures – not many pictures. They say she dress like prostitute all the time, sleep with many man, was perfect example of how Western morality spit in the face of God, that her death is example of God's wenchance. Then I switch over to CNN, that my dad had though could be put in jail, and is all these people weeping on screen, tearing hair and beating their face and saying she was angel, she was most beautiful woman who ever live, she was kind, she was great moral leader, I love her. It was just like when motherfuckin' bastard Khomenei die . . .' Shahin never says the Imam's name without the preceding two words. He feels that the entire Iranian revolution was carried out as part of a dastardly plot to personally rob him of the opportunity to eat at McDonald's and wear sunglasses as a teenager.

Harriet stubs her cigarette out on his old teabag. 'Get to the point, Shahin.'

'So.' He looks again at the Eccles cake, shakes a Marlboro from the pack in his breast pocket and starts waving it about. 'The point is this. Which was she, this mother of yours? She was angel, she was whore? You never talk about her. In all the time I known you, you never mention.'

Harriet thinks for a bit. Says, 'I suppose she was something a bit in between, really. Only she was good at the presentation. She did stuff that was – well, I don't know – pretty awful, really, but somehow she managed to emerge smelling of roses every time. She had that sort of charisma. I mean, I loved her. She was a pretty crap mother most of the time, but she could charm the arse off you. You know. She'd turn up three days late for your week's visitation rights, and she'd be all presents and apologies and compliments, and you just couldn't stay angry for more than ten minutes. And she had that effect on everyone. I think people just didn't want to believe that someone that lovely could have really done all the things they heard about her. So they just didn't. They just blocked it out.'

'And that's how you get to be saint, these days?' Shahin lights his cigarette, pours out another cup of tea, adds milk.

'Well, yeah. Sainthood's all in the perception, isn't it? And the point was, it's not whether my mum was good or bad either way, is it? It's the fact that she was famous enough for it to count.'

'What do you mean?'

'Look.' Harriet flips her stocking-clad feet, the stilettos long since consigned to a plastic bag, onto the top of the fold-out space-saver lounge-dining table. 'You're not virtuous these days unless you're famous. It's fame that makes people virtuous. All those nurses and carers and Médecins Sans Frontières, all the Christians and Moslems and charity workers and mine-clearance experts and people who find people's wallets in the street and hand them in intact, and the good coppers and the kindly priests and the soup-kitchen volunteers and the people who make a habit of giving money to beggars: they're just doing what they ought to. Look at Mother Theresa: she was a straightforward nun, doing her nun thing, albeit pretty effectively, until the celebs started beating a path to her door. She saved thousands of lives on the streets of Calcutta, but she was admired because of her connection to the rich and famous. If you're famous, and you put your arm round one mangy-looking poor person, you're a saint. That's what my mother did. And in a way it's what Anna's mother did too. Think about it. Nowadays, Anna's mother is a Nobel cult figure with a following of millions and as much research money as she could ever want. Before she got picked up by the newspapers, she was just the local weird kid who preferred reading about quantum theory to smoking on the village bench. But once everybody got to know who she was, she turned into an example to us all.'

Harriet pauses. Recrosses her ankles. 'Which is why,' she continues, looking at me now, 'you and I will be lowly sinners all our lives.'

'I know,' I say. 'But don't you prefer it that way?'

'Oh, yes,' says Harriet. 'Christ, yes.'

Chapter Nine

LEEZA HAYMAN
She Says What She Means, and She Means Business

Sometimes I'm ashamed to live in this country. And sometimes I'm proud. But what I'm proudest of this week is that I write for a paper that reflects the real views of real people. Since Friday, we have heard nothing from the twelve-year-olds who write for the 'highbrow' – for highbrow read boring – papers but complaints about the so-called 'hysteria' that real people have reacted with when it emerged that Godiva Fawcett's body has been found to be uncorrupted after 15 years in her grave.

According to certain so-called experts, this shows that people – for 'people' read you and me – have their priorities all mixed up. I suppose, according to them, we should all be putting our priorities into handing out money and flats to any asylum seeker who jumps off a lorry in Dover, and investing money that could be spent on shortening NHS queues in drop-in centres for one-legged lesbian Bengali single mothers.

Godiva, they say, was a figure-head, a showbiz personality who got too big for her boots. We should forget about her and start getting our priorities right. No doubt they mean things like setting up Aids awareness programmes for three-year-olds, or funding alternative theatre groups to 'educate' teenagers in homosexual practices in schools. That's what the loony liberals who are so scornful of Godiva want to do with your hard-earned tax money, you'd better believe it.

Well, not me, mate. You may be too young to remember the things that Godiva Fawcett did for this country, but I do and so do millions of ordinary people whose lives she touched in the last century. And I've got a few facts for you:

FACT: Godiva Fawcett was a self-made success story, and one of the most accomplished actresses that Great Britain exported. But of course, she didn't make black and white subtitled films about starving pearl divers in one of the fashionable spots in the Third World, so no doubt the socks and sandals brigade will never have heard of mere popular hits like 'Beach Bunny Massacre' or 'The Power Game'.

FACT: As a single mother myself, I admire Godiva's courage in continuing to show public affection to her daughter despite the suffering her father had put her through. Furthermore, she was, despite all the unhappiness in her own life, the most hospitable and encouraging person you could ever hope to meet. I will always remember when, as a tyro reporter, I was sent to interview her over lunch at her favourite restaurant, Le Gavroche. She was honest and forthcoming about herself, and full of good advice. 'Leeza,' she said to me, 'it doesn't matter what other people say, if you're true to yourself and your own opinions, you can never go wrong.' I have followed her advice, and have always found it comforting when I have doubts or depressions of my own.

FACT: Godiva raised over £3bn for charity. The do-gooders like to think that they have the monopoly on giving, but the truth is that it was Godiva's efforts that really raised people's awareness.

FACT: While governments claim they will perform miracles, Godiva genuinely did. Stories abound of people who received psychic comfort from this wonderful lady, children who laughed for the first time when exposed to her love, of remissions in cancer cases after visits. The government may harp on about how they're going to bring about a revolution in our health, but 20 years ago Godiva was going out and *doing* it.

FACT: She proved to all of us how a girl from even the most under-privileged of backgrounds can make something of herself in this world. Godiva always avoided talking about the great sadness in her childhood that led her to change her name and cut off all contact with the past, but we all know that she was the victim of terrible demons that she never entirely came to terms with.

FACT: We all loved her. The vegetables-have-souls brigade may claim now that it isn't so, but there wasn't a single person in this country – apart from snobs and ivory-tower academics – who didn't feel personally touched by her, because she was very much one of us. She put her arms out and embraced us all, and we loved her for it.

What I am saying here is this. Godiva was the closest thing to a saint that this world has known for well over a century. She loved without discrimination, she gave and forgave without any thought for her own interests, she brought about miracles in a cynical world and she died a martyr for her own causes.

I've done my homework, and guess what? This recent discovery at Belhaven qualifies this wonderful woman for sainthood. And that's what I think she should be. If you think so too, write to your MP. Not that they'll pay any attention, if past history has anything to say about it. This government will never let the people's choice be a saint. She didn't come from Islington after all, did she?

© Daily Sparkle 2000

Chapter Ten

Too Much Coffee

Stupid. I've been sleepwalking for the past eight hours, and what do I do? Drink three giant mugs of Jasmine's special coffee and find myself, when Harriet finally allows us to go home, wide-awake and jittery with caffeine, head buzzing slightly in that too-tipsy-to-go-to-sleep, not-pissed-enough-to-pass-out in-between state. A nice cup of Horlicks, that's what I should have had: a nice cup of Horlicks and some vitamin B. But no. At three in the morning, with Harriet, who practically fell asleep on the stairs and had to be dragged up the last two flights, spreadeagled in her bed snoring, I am jittering around the living room like a great big jittering thing, drinking gallons of water and stuffing all the high-carbohydrate foods in the house into my jittering gob.

This is not good. I'm not good at being alone and wakeful late at night. I'm not one of those people who can settle to watch bad pop videos on the telly, or read a book or embroider or something. I've never shaken off my early training; if I'm alone late at night, I start to obsess. About everything. Like: what the hell am I doing with my life? And: if something happens to split us up, how would we work out custody of Henry? And: what happens if Godiva really does become a saint? Are we going to have to start going to church? And: why, after all these years, is it that my mother can still turn me into a quivering jelly from the other side of the Atlantic?

I know there will be an email waiting from her. Might as well get it over and done with. Take another glass of water over to the computer and go online.

She answered within five minutes of me sending mine. Of course, people in America remain permanently online because they don't run up backbreaking phone bills if they do. But all the same: it would be so nice if just once in her life Grace had gone 'Oh, look, an email. I'll make a cup of tea and then I'll answer it,' or 'Oh, sod it, I'll wait till the red bill comes.' It would make it so much easier to relate to her as a human being.

Thank you for having the courtesy to reply. Please be prompt, and please study the guest list. There will be important people there, and I expect basic courtesy.

No sign off, as usual.

The quivering jelly replies, 'Of course. I will look forward to seeing you. Anna'. Underneath her message, in the inbox, a strange address: Zapp2001@backpack.net. It takes me a minute to work out who it's from.

Hi there, wildgirl, and salutations from County Cork. It's great here, though there seems to be an Internet cafe in every town, so instead of the craic you've just got all these people staring at screens and talking to their cousins in America. Just wanted to know if my attempts at getting rid of your visitors the other day did any good. Also to say that getting waylaid at the GeogSoc was probably the most exciting thing that happened to me in London! You're quite a girl.
yr knight in shining armour, Nigel

Love-beads! I click on reply and start to type.

You! How are you! Thanks: your ruse worked brilliantly. What did you say to them? There's not been a sign since. How long are you there for? Coming back through London at all?
Love, wildgirl

Oh, goody. I still haven't forgotten the way he looked on the stairs. I do hope he'll come back through and make a night of it. Something nice to think about. Maybe I'll be able to get to sleep, if I turn in right now.

So I do. I really try. It's half past three and even Henry's ready to come to bed. He's been looking reproachfully at me for ages now. Trots after me as I go downstairs and climb into bed.

And I manage to think about fun things for precisely two minutes. And then I start to worry again. Why the hell did my bloody mother have to come back now? I don't have time. I don't have time. It takes concentration to psych myself up, and there's Harriet in a state and the press sniffing around looking for her, and I have to get my hair done and find some clothes and the fridge hasn't been cleaned for months and I don't even know where University College is and I don't even have a proper job and do you think she knows?

Fuck it. Sit up in bed, switch on the light. Everything is as usual: a scatter of clothes, silk scarves tied round the foot of the bed, curtains blocking out the daylight that will come creeping in in a couple of hours. I've got a nauseating sense of impending doom. You can't just retrain yourself. I've had a sense of impending doom for as long as I can remember: a certainty that retribution is going to come screaming down on me one day, whatever I do. Damn it, I *like* my life. Why do I have to feel guilty all the time?

Is this how she feels? Is this how Grace feels? Is this perpetual gnawing fear of discovery a by-product of our upbringing, or is it the fact that I've thrown away all her expectations, that I am what she would call a failure, that every time someone finds out who I am, they look at me in confusion? I can see it written all over their faces: what the hell went wrong? How on earth did someone like her produce someone like you? Whatever happened to all that promise? Surely you should be head of department some-where, at least?

Late-night heebie-jeebies: I hate them. I wanted to do something with my life, I really did, but *you* try carrying a name like mine around with you and see what people offer you. All I want is to be normal. I want to have a good life, a real life: a life that doesn't involve the isolation of wild success, a life that doesn't involve the endless self-castigation of failure. But you know, you present a CV, and people can't help but put two and two together: my name, where I grew up, my seventeen O levels and my five A levels, the degree over and done with before I was twenty, and it has the weirdest effect. Everyone is scared to death. You would have thought that they would look at me and see the mess I am, but they don't. The arty people think: oh, God, how on earth are we going to cope with someone who evidently hasn't had a day's emotion in her life, who's going to be logical and clinical and never let her discipline down enough to allow inspiration to come in? And the scientists? The money people and the people who deal in calculation, logic, all the things the artists project on to me, that isn't there? Obvious, isn't it? None of them want me around. They're all convinced that if they let their guard down for one minute, make a single slip-up, it will get back to Grace and they will feel publicly humiliated. They all think I'm a spy.

Usually, what I would do when I get into this state is wake up Harriet. And I would go on about it, and Harriet would say look, calm down, you're great, you're doing brilliantly, when our money comes through we'll open the gallery and you can sell my paintings and everyone will love you and want to suck up to you because you can sell theirs as well. We're fine, we're great, we're having a good time. We're still young and we're still going out; look at the people who love you, look at the friends you've made, look at the progress you've made. That's what we both do for each other when the screaming fear gets to us in the middle of the night.

But that isn't an option tonight. All I'm doing is obsess about normal stuff. Harriet's the one in trouble; Harriet's the one who needs help and love right now. And Harriet needs sleep.

Again I search my head. Does Grace wake in the night and feel like this? Is this why she never sleeps? Is what she's done the same thing to me as that Peter Waters did to her?

Chapter Eleven

The Golden Child

I, like Harriet, have a trust fund of my own, a pot that will eventually buy me my freedom. And the irony is that the money comes from the man who put me in chains in the first place. My grandfather, Peter Waters, wrote one of the biggest bestsellers of his era, and, as someone who liked to think he was cleverer than the authorities, he left the proceeds not to my mother, the cash cow, subject of the book, but to me, when he died.

The grand irony of my grandfather's literary success is this: he never realised that of the 8 million people who bought *Sowing the Seed: How I Brought My Daughter up a Genius*, 7,980,000 of them bought it as comedy. Presumably the other 20,000 actually followed his advice on the upbringing of their children. Certainly, I have a collection of roughly that many letters thanking him for his ruminations. Sometimes it makes me nervous: all those people, fifteen-odd years older than me, who went through the same life. What are they like now? And what if the 20,000 letter-writers are only the tip of the iceberg? What if, say, a million people followed his advice? That's only one in eight, after all, of the people who bought the book. And if, say, they had an average of 1.5 children (the Waters method is so intensive it rather precludes the possibility of large families), and only one in a hundred of those children proved susceptible in the long term, that still means that, spread across the developed countries of the world, there are some 15,000 second-generation Graces. Single-minded, voraciously knowledgeable, evangelistical, unforgiving. I have been known to wake screaming from a nightmare where they have all got together and are tracking me down. Imagine: pursued by 15,000 zombies in cardigans.

But, like I say, that wasn't why most people bought the book. Carolyn, my grandfather's secretary-cum-housekeeper, remembers vividly the book's role on the dinner-party circuit in the sixties; the most popular game of the time, aside from finding uses for car keys and Mars bars, involved guests competing to find the most extreme example of banality employed to support insanity. Ever popular was 'Under no circumstances permit the child to run aimlessly about here and there, hither and yon. A running child is not a concentrating child.' 'Attention to detail is the core of all achievement. No picture can truly be in perspective if the details are wrong' was another frequent winner.

She also says that Peter used to tear round bookshops demanding to see the manager when he found his tome under comedy, and fired off letters to editors complaining bitterly when the error was perpetuated in print.

He was, of course, a great writer of letters. A writer, and filer, and triplicator. I still have, in the trunk where his fan mail resides, a box file of correspondence, spanning fifty years, with the various editors of the *Times* crossword ('Recidivist? There is no example of this back-formation in my dictionary . . .'). I have a folder of complaints to local councils about wastage ('Why do your officers deem it necessary to append postal enclosures with paper clips? I calculate that at a rate of 400 letters per day, the council is wasting

£500 per year on paper clips alone . . .'). I have an envelope of replies from the Queen ('Her Majesty has asked me to thank you for your interest and assure you that we take all correspondence seriously . . .'). And another ('while we take your point about the use of the split infinitive, we feel that the grammatical abuse in the phrase "To boldly go where no man has gone before" has become synonymous with the programme . . .') from the duty officers at the BBC. I'm not sure why I keep them. Maybe one day I'll throw them away.

So what sort of person was he, this super-parent whose obsession was such that he did little, at least on the surface, for himself after the birth of Grace? I remember him more as a beard. As a superbeard. He had one of those carpet beards that covered everything from neck to eyes – or at least to the point at which his square, steel-rimmed spectacles started – and by the time I can remember, the beard was a couple of inches thick. He was a tall man, and thin and tweedy, and being told by him to speak in full sentences was rather like being ordered about by an over-solemn bottlebrush.

If I'd been a psychologist looking for a Ph.D., I think I might have chosen Peter as a subject. But he wasn't stupid, and must have known that people would be queuing up to spot his pathological traits, so little remains in terms of history surrounding him. What we do know is this: until the birth of his daughter, Peter Waters was a minor civil servant whose role in Whitehall was unknown in the outside world but made him deeply unpopular within. He lived at first alone then, in his forties, with his much younger wife, Sylvia, in a modern three-bed semi in Amersham, and was employed to root out waste and petty theft across the Home Office. He wasn't exactly the man with the keys to the stationery cupboard, but he was the man with the requisition forms.

In the years BC (Before Child), Peter spent his days stalking the corridors of power, clutching sheafs of pink and yellow paper. No one ordered a bulldog clip, a pad of carbon paper, a box of pencils, a rubber band without triplicate copies of the requisition landing on Peter's desk. And Peter, who had worked out optimum-usage graphs for every piece of equipment known to office life, would consult his charts (a sort of embroidery pattern of tiny coloured X's on squared paper) and see that everyone's orders were, as it were, in order. And if he felt that some filing clerk was going through too many paper tab labels, or that typewriter-ribbon usage in surveys didn't accord with their production, he would leave his windowless cubbyhole and creep on silent soles to the offending office to demand an explanation.

'He was the most feared man in the ministry,' says an anonymous former colleague in a profile in the *Mail* the week of his death in 1980. 'We all dreaded his approach, because a visit from Peter Waters meant hours discussing how exactly one went about using the amount of paper one did. But you have to hand it to him, it worked. Stationery wastage was at an all-time low while he worked there, and had almost doubled within a year of his leaving.' This may sound like a petty sort of achievement, but Peter Waters saved the ministry some £15,000 a year when he was working, and this was in the 1930s.

And then came the years AD, or After Daughter. 'To be honest,' says the same anonymous source, 'the birth came as a bit of a surprise to all of us, as no one had thought – not that we discussed that sort of thing much at the time – of Peter and Sylvia as a couple who made much of their marital status. He was older than her – at least fifteen years – and we'd always assumed she had married him for security rather than passion. He seemed such a dried-up chap, sort of dessicated, and she was a mousy little thing. There were a few unkind jokes going around. It's always the quiet ones, that sort of thing. But I don't think that anyone doubted Grace's paternity for very long; it became very obvious that Peter was absolutely besotted with her. Which was great for us. Suddenly, we were able to have two pencils from the stores at a time . . .'

When Grace was three months old, Sylvia Waters made herself scarce from the family home, leaving only a note and a collection of embroidered napkins behind. No one knows what the note said. Peter destroyed it the day he found it, and the following day handed in his notice at the Home Office. 'I have a duty,' said his letter of resignation, 'to ensure that my daughter, who now finds herself, through no fault of her own, handicapped in comparison with her peers, has the best start in life I can give her.'

I still don't know if this letter was disingenuous or not. It's chicken and egg, isn't it? Had Sylvia stayed, would Peter have developed such an intense passion for his daughter? Or did she leave because, the incubation period over, her family had no further use for her services?

Whatever, the one-parent unit turned out to be surprisingly well equipped to cope without the attentions of a mother. At forty-four, Peter had over twenty years of index-linked civil-service pension built up, and was able to take retirement on compassionate grounds. Well, possibly a combination of compassion and relief, the pensions department being as vulnerable to cross-examination on the subject of India rubbers as any other. And as he had never been known to spend a penny on frivolities, the Amersham house, bought fifteen years earlier on a mortgage, was as close to paid off as scarcely mattered.

'I had a choice,' he writes in *Sowing the Seed*, 'between

my own satisfaction and the future of my daughter. Many parents, too caught up in the here-and-now, choose their own, short-lived gratification. I do not think that I will lay myself open to criticism when I claim that I had a higher calling. Better a childhood dedicated to work and thought, than a lifetime filled with the inevitable mediocrity of play!'

Grace was born in 1938, when the Luftwaffe was still a gleam in Hitler's eye and property prices in the London hinterland still relatively high. Presciently, and within six months of fatherhood, Peter had sold Amersham and taken his pension to rural Shropshire, where land was cheap and farm cottages were being sold off to make way for combine harvesters.

Peter applied successfully for the right to home-school his daughter – the local council, overwhelmed by the influx of half-starved evacuees, asked fewer questions than they might have done at another time in history – and he and Grace spent the war, through rationing and gas masks and Haw-Haw and put that light out! and scrap drives and Winnie and *For Whom We Serve* and the Queen looking the East End in the face, and *Hitler Has Only Got One Ball* and 'We shall fight them on the beaches,' locked in their cottage, scrimping for light money, sending off for cases of books from country-house sales, raiding the libraries, wasting no time. Day by day Grace grew, in stature and mind, never mixing, never exposed to the paucity of expectation the world applied to others her age, never taking her eyes, or her mind, from the deadly serious task at hand. While Hitler's star waxed, and waned, and eventually went out altogether, Peter Waters ploughed ahead with his own plans for world domination.

Chapter Twelve

Good King Hal

'Get off, Henry.'

'Naoo,' says Henry, digs his claws into my T-shirt and buries his face in my neck. Absurdly spoiled by two bossy mummies since we hauled him out from the giant-sized polyfilla drum that someone had shut his blood-covered kitten self into and thrown over our wall, Henry believes that I am actually a cushion rather than a sentient being with a life beyond his well-being, and insists on climbing onto my bosom the moment I settle anywhere. It's my own fault. If I'd occasionally pushed him off when he was young he might take no for an answer.

'Muum,' he sings into my ear and busses me, continental-style, on either cheek with his snotty wet nose. Yawns into my face and I turn away. Harriet's been feeding him pilchards again.

I'm almost awake, now. You can't stay asleep while being rubbed with cat snot for all that long. I give up, accord him his dues. 'Good morning, Your Majesty,' I say, glance at the clock and correct myself. 'Good afternoon, Your Majesty.' It's after three o'clock. Having worn myself out fretting, I've been asleep for almost seven hours. I pinch the acupressure points on Henry's ears and he responds with a purr like a train going through a tunnel. 'Thank God for you, my darling,' I thank him. 'Thank you.' Henry has a great talent for dispelling nightmares. He never gives you a chance to carry on obsessing where you left off. Not when you could be obsessing about him instead.

I've been sweating in my sleep. There's no specific clear memory, but since I finally lapsed into unconsciousness some time after dawn, it's been a morning of vague nightmares: dark, looming shapes, fog-shrouded rocks, uncontrolled flight. And now my mouth is all furred up and my armpits smell like half-ripe brie. Which is funny, because I had a chunk of half-ripe brie for supper between spankings last night. The sort of customers we get only like their brie half-ripe.

Bath. I sit up, deposit Majesty on the bed and peel off my T-shirt. Very definitely not good. The brie has ripened beneath the cotton, has a salty undertone. Bath, coffee, fag, another doze on the sofa and then it's time for work again. Who said night workers had empty lives?

Henry follows me down to the bathroom. Stares longingly up at me as I pee, pretends to be terrified as I flush, bolting from the room and sticking his head round the door jamb a couple of seconds later to see if I've noticed. You've no idea how much I love this cat. Sorry.

I put half a bottle of baby bath under the running tap and climb into the tub. Henry jumps up onto the shelf beside it, sits there staring down at the bubbles, occasionally reaching out with a tentative paw to pat at them. Henry loves bubbles. He has fallen into the bath three times, but he's never learned. And nor have I. You'd have thought that I would have clicked that having a wet cat in the bath with you was a recipe for lifetime scarring, but I never have. He runs away when I turn on the shower nozzle to wash my hair.

Better. Still weary to the bones, but clean is a help.

Harriet's painting, a pair of surgical plastic gloves protecting her hands so the punters don't get too frightened when she passes them their bread-and-butter pudding. Her face is screwed up with concentration, a blob of grey-blue decorating the side of her mouth where she's stuck a brush between her teeth. She has been working for the past week on an unusually cheerful and straightforward piece: two blue and white vases, one containing pristine white lilies swanning gracefully over glossy spear-shaped leaves, the other crammed higgledy-piggledy with a handful of crushed and dying red roses. The two pots lie on a highly polished mahogany table top, either side of an indistinctly handwritten letter and a wedding ring. It may be melodramatic, but it's rather lovely, and what's more, you can actually see that Harriet has mastered the skill of transferring an image from the real world onto canvas. You don't get to see this very often. It was a while before I established that she could do it at all. She spent the whole of her first year at the Ruskin fooling about with expanded polystyrene and bits of battery-heated wire. Mostly, as far as I could see, making a variety of models of her own initials and exposing them to different lighting effects.

'Hi,' I say.

'Hi,' she replies. 'I was just wondering if I ought to come and get you up. Bad night?'

'Yup.'

'Me, too.'

'Sorry.'

'Hardly your fault.' She dips her paintbrush in a smear of black on her palate, starts to brush in dark edges around the rose petals. Frowns again.

'It's lovely,' I comment.

'Hmm,' she says. 'It's not finished yet.'

'Doh. Yes, I know that. I was just saying.'

Harriet smiles.

'Do you want coffee?'

She nods. 'That would be nice. What kept you awake?'

'Coffee. Tiredness. Thinking about stuff.'

Harriet shakes her head reprovingly at me. 'Stuff. Really, Anna. You should know better than to think about *stuff*. Always a bad idea.'

'Didn't you sleep, then? I thought I heard you snoring.'

'Oh, yes,' says Harriet. 'I slept all right. It was the not being able to wake up bit that was the problem.'

Ah. I put the kettle on.

'Anybody call?' I ask, and she shakes her head.

Then I remember. 'Hey! Guess who emailed me last night?'

'The Pope,' she says. 'The President of the United States. Keanu Reeves. Mahatma Ghandi. The man who runs the dog traps at Walthamstow race track. My old maths teacher. Norman Wisdom. Roy's old auntie in Pinner. Nope. I give up. Who did email you last night?'

'Ha ha. Nigel.'

'Who's Nigel?' asks Harriet. Then, 'Oh.' A little pause. 'And what did *Nigel* have to say?' She pronounces the name with exaggerated enthusiasm, a prep-school heavy-handedness I've never been able to master.

'Nothing much. He's in Ireland.'

'Yeah,' says Harriet, 'I think we know that. And?'

'And nothing much.'

'What? No protestations of everlasting devotion? No money orders? No tickets booked for you to join him?'

'You are so sharp,' I say, 'you'll bleed to death.'

'So when's he coming back?'

'Dunno. Why?'

'So I can buy some bloody earplugs, that's why,' she says. 'Or leave the country before the tidal wave.' She smiles and goes back to her painting for a moment, then looks up again. 'So did you answer him?' she asks.

I grin. 'What do you think?'

Harriet sighs. 'Go on, then. Go and see if he's written back.'

Of course, I forgot to turn it all off last night. Can't even remember if I hung up. It's certainly offline now, but there'll probably be one of those mysterious five-hour calls on the phone bill again.

I sit in the desk chair, log on and the computer makes a jungle monkey shriek to say that new mail's arrived. Not Nigel. G.Waters@thoughtlab.ac. 'So grateful you can fit me in to your busy schedule,' Grace writes. I don't even bother to respond. No point. Henry plods into the room, jumps up onto my lap, gets onto his back legs and drapes his front half over my shoulder. Purrs, rubs his ear against mine. Wraps his front paws round my neck. 'Mmm. Waarm.'

What can you do? I pick him up, turn him upside down, shower his noble, battered face with kisses, rub his shredded ear and put him on the floor. 'Whyyy?' he cries. 'Whyyy?'

'No,' I say. 'I have to occasionally do things that don't involve your comfort.'

'Awww,' he says piteously. 'Haaard.'

'Can you leave that on?' Harriet interrupts our chat. 'I might as well see if I've got anything while we're there.'

'Sure.'

Henry, bored with looking plaintive, pounces from three feet away and sinks his fangs into my ankle. We think he thinks this is funny. Once he'd got over the horror of being an abused baby he turned into a cat of consummate violence, who would pick a fight with anyone from Rottweilers to toddlers. Which is how he got his name. Harriet's hands and arms were so covered in bite and scratch marks that he inevitably ended up being called Henry Tudor. Maybe you have to say it in a London accent.

I kick him off and he retires to the sofa and starts to lick his tummy. After a couple of seconds, I log out and go over to join him. He looks up, startled, pretends not to have the foggiest idea who I am.

'You done?' Harriet picks up a turpsy rag and starts to dab it over her canvas.

'Yeah. What are you doing?'

Harriet has finished her painting. Except that she hasn't. Because now that she's made this simple if lovely thing, she's methodically going over it with the rag on which she has wiped her paint and glue brushes for the past three years without a wash.

'Harriet! That was lovely!'

Harriet says nothing, but suddenly runs her arm, swoosh, across the whole canvas, splodging vases, wood, flowers and paper into each other. Where once there were shades of light and dark, minute gradations in stem and petal, there's now, well, a lot of dark brownish, lumpy blobs obscuring something that looks like it might have been quite nice. '*The Artist*,' she announces, '*Views Love Through the Eyes of The Philosopher*.'

Ah. She's been to the Saatchi gallery again. 'Great,' I say. 'Perhaps you could diddle around with the title a bit.'

She lays down her rag, comes over to the computer and logs into her hotmail. The keyboard gathers another few smears. Well, it's her computer. 'By the way,' I say, 'are you ever going to do anything about that popcorn?'

'What?' she says vaguely. Then, 'Oh, yes. I promise I'll clear it up.'

'And throw it away?'

'No. No, I want to do something with it. Definitely. It will make the most wonderful mosaic tiles. Honestly.'

'Yes, well at the moment it's just making brilliant ball bearings for people to tread on on the stairs. And Henry's doing the weirdest things in his poo-box. You know how much he loves sweetcorn.'

'Okay. Sorry. I'll empty it.'

There's little point in pursuing the matter. She'll clear it up when the muse strikes, and at least she's not a bloke, strewing underpants everywhere and complaining because no one's cleared them up. I stretch, get up and go onto the balcony to look at the view while she reads her mail. I love this view. Way below, that mysterious rush-hour traffic you get at weekends even though everyone's supposed to be at leisure edges along the embankment, parping and booping out the London chorus. A train comes out of Victoria and rattles its way south, heads poking from the windows in the vain quest for air. There's a dredger on the Thames just emerging from under the bridge, the matte black of its livery standing out like Darth Vader against the glittering flow tide. High, puffy, cotton-ball clouds float over the power station, drifting on towards the Eiffelesque radio mast at Crystal Palace.

I look out and think: yeah, I love this city. It may be full of sharks, but there's nowhere else I'd rather be.

'Bugger,' says Harriet.

I come back in. 'What gives?'

She pulls a face, nods at the screen. 'Nutmail.'

'Oh.' I look over her shoulder. Someone called A.Friend-@stinky.com has been writing to Harriet. Or at least they're writing to Bitch From Hell hoping that she will both return and rot there.

Whore. I hope you catch the plague you so richly deserve. Who do you think you are, that you believe you're above the morals of ordinary, decent people? You were given everything and I was given nothing, but at least I don't cavort naked for my personal gratification. Get some self-respect, or get off the planet.

'Ah. Fan club's back, then.'

'Yeah.' She goes into admin, cuts the standard text and pastes it into a reply.

Dear A.Friend, I thought you ought to know that someone showing obvious signs of instability is using your email address to send abusive messages on the Internet. If you are at all worried, I would suggest you contact your service provider immediately.

Yours sincerely, Harriet Moresby.

92877763@number.com writes:

It used to be that the sins of the fathers were visited on the children. In your situation, the rule seems to be reversed. Remember where you came from, and the debt you owe!

'Hmm,' says Harriet. 'Could be spam, I suppose.' Replies anyway. Last week we had three faxes from the Bible Decoding Society inviting us to join them for an evening's cipher-breaking at the Cumberland Hotel. Eventually, Harriet faxed them back with a note saying, 'The Bible wasn't written in code, it was written in Hebrew,' and the faxes stopped. What was a bit worrying, though, is that they must have bought their fax list from the people who send us weekly offers of cut-price pornography. God and Mammon walk hand in hand in this world.

'Well, at least somebody remembers who I am,' she says.

'If I didn't have the Godiva club, I might as well close down the account, for all the good it does me.'

She's laughing as she opens a missive from Asfiggis@anon.com, and it takes a few moments to kill the giggle, though the message itself takes no more than a second to read.

'Oh, shit,' she says.

Asfiggis has one thing to say, and it's the sort of thing you don't want to read. **I know where you live,** he says.

Chapter Thirteen

The Poisoner

I was sixteen when my stomach ulcer and I went up to university. Sixteen and absolutely ignorant of all the things 'normal' people take for granted, like friendship, or late-night singing sessions, or microwaves, trainers and oven chips, or *EastEnders*, or the difference between a flare and an A-line, or *Catcher in the Rye*, or vodka and orange, or full-day lie-ins, or the vital importance of the offside rule, or why everybody loves Jimmy Stewart, or backpacking, or horoscopes, or washing 'n' going, or how to balance on heels, or how to make a water bomb from a condom, or agadoo-doo-doo, or crisp sandwiches, or riding bikes without hands, or copping a feel, or lesbianism, or parents who dance embarrassingly at parties, or crying yourself to sleep over someone who's dumped you, or sibling rivalry, or chocolate in bed, or *Smash Hits*, or Purple Ronnie, or detention, or food fights, or afternoons in the movies, or homework excuses, or Valentines, or lipsalve, or fuck-me shoes, or Narnia books, or pot noodle, or charter flights, or Saturday jobs, or any of the myriad subjects with which our generation breaks the ice and finds things in common with each other.

Instead, I knew about maths and physics and chemistry and biology and geology and art history and musical theory and magical realism and philosophy and economics and geography and algebra and trigonometry and the *Lives of the Masters* and Shakespeare's symbolism and political history and ancient history and astrology and law and engineering and the poetry of Ezra Pound. I knew about tutors and summer schools and tests and S-levels and evening classes and extended essays. I knew about prizes and plaudits and wouldn't you all like to be like Anna while my contemporaries stared at me with those blank stares that said no more effectively than any words could do. 'No,' said their unmoving faces, 'we don't want to be like Anna. We don't want to be picked last for the teams, overlooked for the plays, left off the party lists. We don't want to be the one who sits in the single seat behind the coach driver, gets her essays read out in class, gets moved up a year, has special dispensation to spend breaktimes in the library. We want to be young, free, popular. Why should we want to be transformed into the dumpy one just because it's what teachers like?'

Dumpiness isn't a physical thing, it's an emotional one. Do you think that someone like my mother would have let me be unfit for even a minute? I had no concept of the point of team sports, but daily calisthenics and tri-weekly aerobic workouts made sure that under the plain navy jumper and the shapeless polyester skirt was a body well-suited to survival, pumped with enough blood to maximise the brain but not so much as to tip it over into Beckhamhood. But all the same, I was the dumpy one: dumpy of appearance, dumpy of personality. The one who paused slightly when someone tried to engage her in conversation and replied, 'I don't listen to pop music.' The one who looked on at experimental make-up sessions with the bemusement of a biologist encountering a new and slightly revolting aspect of arachnid group behaviour. Come on, you had one of me in your class: the silent one whose hand went up dutifully whenever the teacher asked a question; the one with the smooth-brushed ponytail and the on-the-knee skirt; the one you used to go home and tell your mum about how awful she was.

Well, just be glad you weren't her. Just be glad you didn't lie awake after your ten o'clock optimum-sleep bedtime, watching the lights move across the ceiling, hearing the neighbouring kids at play and wondering what was wrong with you. Be grateful that you could yell at your mother, tell her she hated you, didn't understand you, was ruining your life, and be able to expect her to yell back until you were both in tears.

Just be glad you weren't brought up by the book, and be particularly glad that your grandfather didn't write it. It always entertains me when I hear a certain type of pushy parent talk of hothousing as though it will inevitably produce some rare and beautiful blossom: do they not know that cacti grow in hothouses? And that the largest orchid in the world gives off the stench of rotting cadavers?

And because of my unspeakable training, I nearly missed Harriet altogether as she wafted past on a cloud of saddle soap and *eau de Givenchy*. I was so well trained in disapproval and standing back that had it not been for Harriet's temper I'd have been another statistic by now. Harriet, raised in privilege by people whose basic idea of education was learning how to get out of a sports car properly, represented everything that I'd been taught to despise: the old world of contacts and consanguinity, a world where familiarity with the uses of a running martingale was far more important than familiarity with the works of Goethe.

And besides, she was up to something pretty outrageous when I first spoke to her. It was around our fourth or fifth day in halls, and I was up at my usual six o'clock, heading down the corridor in a terry bathrobe for a good stimulating lukewarm bath in preparation for another long day at the library. I was worn out, not from a routine that I'd known since I could remember, but from lying awake at night listening to the shrieks and giggles of my contemporaries as they discovered the joys of student life till two, three and four in the morning. I was so tired, I was even beginning to contemplate trying coffee. Shampoo clutched to bosom, I toddled down the silent parquet, turned the corner and very nearly went A over T as I tripped over the crouching form of Harriet Moresby.

I recognised her, of course; she lived next door, after all. I'd even, once or twice, muttered a half-hearted greeting to her as I slipped past her ever-open door on the way to a lecture. I'd watched in astonishment as a stream of absurdly unpractical objects were carried into her room on the first day by a pair of glumly silent countrymen whose wellingtons shrieked agonisingly on the parquet of the corridor: oil portraits, ball dresses, heavy tapestry curtains three times the length of our windows, Turkey rugs, champagne bowls, what looked like a huge sword, or at the very least its handle and scabbard, saris, cherubs that held aloft candle sconces, a stuffed trout in a glass case, sixteen pairs of scuffed stilettos, an ice bucket shaped like a top hat, three cocktail shakers, an urn full of ostrich feathers. I know that someone like me should have found all this impossibly glamorous, but the truth is that I just found it confusing. I mean, what on earth does one do with an urn full of ostrich feathers?

Swathed in strapless gold satin, high-piled hair beginning to come down at the edges, riding mac dropped carelessly on the floor beside her, Harriet squatted, bag open, by a giant Benares ware planter that held a rather manky-looking umbrella tree. As I appeared, and swerved violently to avoid somersaulting over her shoulder, she looked up guiltily, dropped a small brown bottle down to her side and said, 'Oh, it's you. You're up late.'

Up late. What on earth was I supposed to make of that? A lot of the time, through my youth, I'd felt that I was trying to make contact with aliens from another planet when I tried to engage someone else in conversation. It was only just beginning to occur to me that it might be *me* that had landed from Saturn. 'I've just got up. What are you doing?'

'Just got up?' She made a valiant attempt at changing the subject. 'What are you, a rower? You can't be. You're far too small. Oh, of course, you must be a cox. How brilliant. I wish I could work up enthusiasm for team sports. I'm sure I'd have got a better UCCA report—'

'I don't row,' I replied. 'I need to get up at this time to be ready to go to the library for nine.'

And then Harriet burst out laughing, which was the last reaction I had expected.

'LIBRARY?' She howled. 'NINE?'

'What's so funny about that?'

'You're a student, for God's sake. You're not supposed to go to the *library*. What are you reading that you have to be in the library for?'

She was trying, as she spoke, to slip the brown bottle into her bag without my noticing. 'Physics and philosophy,' I said, stretching my neck to catch sight of the label.

'Christ!' she cried. 'Kant for Cunts! You're kidding! I never thought I'd meet anyone reading that.'

Believe it or not, I'd never in my life heard anyone employ the C-word in conversation, though of course my full and rounded education had apprised me of what it meant. So I tried my mother's line on cussing, which had always seemed to work before.

'Swearing,' I announced imperiously, 'is the last resort of the inarticulate.' I wasn't sure what to do with this glittering creature who seemed unable to take anything seriously.

She responded with another peal of laughter. 'Yeah, right. Which is why I was president of my fucking debating society.'

The bottle, which had dribbled a bit while she was pouring, slipped from her fingers and landed at my feet. The label, face up at last, revealed it to be a small flask of Roundup.

Our eyes met. 'What are you doing? You're poisoning that plant?'

'Well, yes, of course I am,' she replied airily, as though it was the most normal thing in the world.

I hadn't expected her to reply with such honesty. For a moment, I was lost for words. Then, 'That's college property,' I said.

Still down on her haunches, Harriet attempted to engage my look with a naughty, complicit one of her own. Suddenly I was horribly aware of my stodgy dressing gown, my hairy legs, my tortoiseshell hair clips.

'It is,' I insisted.

'Well, it may be, but it's also an abomination,' she replied.

'What do you mean?'

'Look at it.' Harriet pinched a leaf with spiteful intensity. 'You can't have something like this in a house. It doesn't flower. It doesn't do *anything*. It just sits there being ugly and every now and again the kind of person who likes polishing houseplants comes along and polishes it. I mean, have you ever stood there in Homebase and watched the kind of people who buy houseplant polishing equipment?'

I thought for a moment, thought about the houseplant in

my room and the fact that I'd only the previous morning spent ten minutes buffing up its leaves with a spray gun and a soft cloth. I coloured slightly. Even I could see that there was something a bit – well – not right about polishing houseplants.

'People who polish houseplants,' announced Harriet, 'are the kind of people who say "Shoes *off* the carpet" when you go round their houses. They have little notebooks in which they write down every last penny they spend. They buy greatest hits compilations because they're better value. They get in panics if they eat more than three eggs in a week. They never go to bed when there's a dirty cup in the house. And they say "Pardon" when they mean "What".'

She sat back, obviously expecting some sort of reaction from me. And I, fairly certain that what I was meant to do was disapprove, but unable to find the words, simply gawped at her from behind my specs.

'Never mind,' she said, and I knew that I had in some way failed a test that had been set me. 'The point is, they shouldn't be encouraged.'

'It's still college property,' I said obdurately. 'You shouldn't be destroying other people's property like that.'

'Chill, Anna.' She got to her feet and I realised that she had a good nine inches on me. I also realised that, although she knew my name, I had not managed to master that of a single one of the people on my landing.

'No one's going to miss an umbrella plant,' announced Harriet. 'Trust me. No one's ever missed an umbrella plant. Good Lord, it was probably *left* here by a student who saw the light in the seventies. And the poor old scouts have been cursing having to maintain the sodding thing all these years, going, "Why won't it just *die*, Beryl?" and never getting their wish. I'm doing everyone a favour.'

Once again, I gawped. I was in way over my depth, and I knew it.

'You can't claim it's a thing of beauty, can you?' she asked quite kindly.

'It's still a living thing.'

'No,' she said firmly. 'It's a living thing when it's in the jungle. In a corridor, it's a stick with some green stuff stuck on that takes up space without contributing to form. It's an abomination, Anna, and it should not be allowed to live.'

Suddenly, I noticed a glint in her eye that I wasn't really sure what to do with. She was either laughing at me or she was seriously unhinged. Maybe both.

'You're not going to stop me, Anna,' continued Harriet. 'I'm going to kill them all. Umbrella and yucca and avocado grown from the stone and spider plants and weeping figs and century plants and cacti. Especially cacti. They're all dead. All of them. This is my mission in life, my ambition, my vocation. I will not rest until every pot-grown cactus in the world has been exterminated. Do you understand? Exterminated.'

And suddenly, the glint was gone as quickly as it had come.

Harriet picked up the riding mac, which was still a light shade of fawn in those days, hung it from her shoulders and smiled sunnily at me. 'I must get to bed,' she said. 'It's been a long night. Have a nice day and don't work too hard, will you?'

Like I say, I almost missed her.

Chapter Fourteen

Sunday Week

Once again, the gates of Belhaven are as familiar to the reading public as the gates of Buck House, and small buses full of American tourists have taken to decanting on the verge outside to pronounce on Godiva's beauty, her goodness, their sense of kinship with her, how much they miss her. Mrs Violet Bock of Stanton, Missouri, recalls the time when she was brought out of a diabetic coma by being shown a photograph of Godiva. 'She was an angel,' she says. 'It was a miracle. I had been three days in the hospital hooked up to insulin drips, and within a few hours of my daughter putting her photo at my bedside, I woke up.' 'I have always wanted to come here and thank her,' concurs her daughter Wanda. 'My only regret is that I got here too late to do it in person.'

Gerald performs with his usual charisma, saying, 'I'm frightfully sorry, but I really don't have a comment to make for the time being,' through the window of the Range Rover before locking himself into his flat in the Albany and taking the phone off the hook. Poor George Burge has been forced to move in with his brother for the duration, and speculation is rife that the Burge marriage is probably doomed.

But while the fans have something else to focus on, at least they're not focusing on Harriet. There have been no more scary emails, but all week Harriet has sat in front of the telly watching the news with bitter astonishment as new strangers appear to testify. And even though she says that if they're testifying on screen they've got less time to testify to her on the Web, I know that it's affecting her beneath that defiant surface.

I watch her shake her head in disbelief as more middle-aged matrons swear that their bad luck changed for ever when they put a photograph of her mother in their lounge, how a hug from Godiva brought about a remission in their dead sister's cancer, how they found their lost wedding ring after asking for help from the dead Duchess, and I know that things are not good for her. I even wonder, for a moment, whether to relent and bring her to my mother's reception, because I don't like leaving her alone when she's miserable. But then I think: yeah, but what's more miserable than an evening alone with the telly? An audience with Grace Waters, that's what.

I'm always glad if I have a few days' notice that I'm going to be seeing Grace, because, even with all the practice I've had, it takes me a while to get ready. Pathetic, I know, but if you lead a double life to keep the peace, there's stuff you need to do to get back into the swing of what you've been doing in the life you don't live. So on Monday I have a haircut, toning down my usual black to more of a filing-clerk brown, and get into practice at wearing my specs, which are so thick that they tend to make me a bit queasy for a couple of days after I first put them on. On Tuesday I go to Debenhams and buy a shirtwaister in navy with a pattern of ivy leaves in white upon it (because I feel that Grace would notice if I turned up in the same clothes over and over). On Wednesday I spend the afternoon in front of the mirror practising the meek and birdlike look – the sideways glances, the pecking head movements, the apologetic, self-deprecating responses – that satisfies my mother that my respect is intact. I follow this rehearsal up with an hour's work every day to be sure. All my spare time on Thursday, Friday and Saturday is given over to reading back copies of the *Librarian*, to which I subscribe, and getting myself up to speed on indexing advances and man-management techniques for those who would rather spend their time communing with books.

I work in the library at King's College, you see. Grace is a bit disappointed that I work in a library, not, say, on the cutting edge of biotechnology, but she's just about learned to live with it, and it's a considerable improvement on the alternative.

Actually, Mel is the one who works in the library at King's College, but her colleagues feel enough pity for me that they've fallen in with the fantasy and are all ready at the drop of a dictionary to say that I'm on holiday/sick leave/at lunch if Grace were ever to call. Not that she ever has; Grace is the kind of person who would always rather not communicate face-to-face if she can help it. We meet maybe three times a year, and otherwise all our contact save dire emergencies is done by fax or email. In fact, I didn't see my mother's signature for a full eight years until she started appending a Paintbrush version dropped down from her Series 5 into her desktop; now all her communications are polished off with a neat 'Grace Waters' at the bottom.

But here we are, it's Sunday Week and I'm standing on the edge of one of those rooms you find in every academic establishment whose designers have deliberately robbed it of all features and whose governing body have named it after the least memorable person ever to have worked there. This one is called the Martin Crawley Function Suite and its sixties architect obviously believed that windows were, on the whole, an unnecessary distraction. It does, in fact, have two of the things, running from floor to low-slung, acoustic-tiled ceiling, but neither is more than a foot wide, and both are tucked away behind wide concrete supporting pillars in order that the room needs to be lit at all times by the unshaded strip lights set among the tiles. Someone else has then decided to disguise the lack of glass by hanging plain grey curtains the length of the wall, a grey echoed by the wear-well carpet on which we are standing. The podium-stage at the far end of the room is built in oak-stained pine and sucks any light that might be foolishly generated by the pale faces about me into itself and re-emits it in grey to match the room.

I'm taking a breather. Mother's lecture was, as usual, way over my head – a switch clicks in my head when I hear the words 'molecular biology' and I turn into one of those people whose jaw is perpetually tense with not being seen to yawn publicly. Even the inclusion of slides doesn't help, and the strain of smiling gamely is beginning to tell. Ditto the strain on my eyes. I ache to pull off the hated glasses – my eyes are so poor that looking through them is like watching the world from inside a goldfish bowl – throw them at the nearest domed forehead and rub hard at the bridge of my nose. I've had two and a half glasses of white wine vinegar and the desire for nicotine has never been stronger.

Grace, half a head taller than most of the men who sur-round her – despite her position as feminist icon, she likes to be surrounded by men – stares at me over the crowd. And for a moment the social face drops. Turns into a mask of displeasure. You're not mixing, says the look. It is your duty to mix. Then the upper lip raises itself and she tilts her head again to indicate that she is listening. And I find myself wondering spiteful thoughts about whether Peter taught her to do that, or whether it's what she learned from her readings of Proust.

I hoist my daughter-of-the-genius yoke back onto my shoulders, smile dimly at a man whose swollen dome of a forehead suggests that he is probably either a professor or an encephalitic. He knows, of course, who I am: they all know who I am at these functions, though I doubt that a single one of them would recognise me in the street.

'Hello,' he says. And, I think, reaches the end of his conversational skills.

I beam hopefully at him. He beams back. Then after a bit we get embarrassed, make 'hmm' 'haa' noises and start beaming at the room. Oh boy, academic drinks parties. They're probably not so bad if you're an academic yourself, because at least then you have professional sniping to fall back on.

Two men in cardigans – one yellow, one blue – are indulging in a spot of professional sniping beside me at the moment. Yellow cardi says, '. . . hasn't published since 1994. God knows how the poor thing got tenure.'

'Well,' red cardi replies, 'there was that article in the *New Scientist*.' And then they both laugh. 'What did you make of tonight's little speechie?' asks red cardi.

'Well, between you and me,' says yellow cardi, then suddenly notices that I'm standing there and changes tack. 'Brilliant as ever,' he says. 'She never fails to surprise, does she? Why, aren't you Anna?'

I make a jerky pigeon-peck of assent, smile my I'm-harmless smile, reply, 'Yes.'

He sticks a hand out. 'You haven't changed a bit,' he says, which all my mother's admirers say to me whenever we meet. If only they knew. 'I haven't seen you since you were twelve.'

Okay. That narrows it down to a couple of hundred bald men in cardis, then.

'Hello,' I reply, shaking the hand. 'Have I really not changed since I was twelve?'

'Not a bit,' he says. 'This is Barnabas Mitchell. Works for Wellcome. Barnabas, Anna Waters. Daughter of our esteemed hostess.'

'Ah!' says Barnabas Mitchell. 'How do you do?'

'Very well, thank you.'

'Good show tonight, I thought. Always a pleasure to hear your mother's thoughts. Most – um – thought-provoking . . .' He trails off.

'Good,' I reply. 'And what do you do for Wellcome?'

'Research,' he says.

'What sort of research?'

'Pest control.'

'Yes?'

He nods. Doesn't elaborate. Sometimes being around scientists is like being at a convention of spies: everyone is so possessive of their intellectual copyright, so scared of industrial espionage, that they practically tap the sides of their noses and say 'Walls have ears' if you try to ask them anything in detail.

'I'm not actually interested!' I want to scream. 'I don't give a toss about your new insecticide recipe! I don't want to know about your human genomes or your hairy aphid contraceptive programme! I'm a waitress! I like pop music and staying up late and action movies and going on package holidays and getting chatted up in dark corners and dancing and lying around all day reading OK! magazine!' Instead, I say, 'I hear they're good to work for.'

'Oh, yes,' he says, then continues with something so up its own bottom that I want to smack him. 'Their remuneration package is quite satisfactory,' he says.

Aaargh. Get me out of here.

A waiter is suddenly hovering at my elbow. 'Excuse me, miss,' he says, and from the expression on his face I can see that he feels a deep, raw pity for me. 'Your mother wants you.'

'Ah. Okay—' I correct myself. 'Certainly. Thank you.'

'You're welcome.'

I take the opportunity to return my half-drunk vinegar to his little electroplated tray and squeeze between knots of people to where my mother stands clutching her glass of plain mineral water. Arrive and stand politely, obediently, awaiting acknowledgement. You don't interrupt Grace Waters. It would be like hugging the Queen. I swore I wouldn't do this, but I just have to check my watch. Immediately wish I hadn't. It confirms to me that what has felt like three hours has actually only been twenty-five minutes.

Even as Grace's conversations go, this one seems to have reached the apogee of stiltedness. For The Woman Who Expects to Be Listened To seems to have hooked up with The Man Who Listens to Nothing. Grace isn't a great one for small talk herself, but the man who stands beside her is one of those who assume automatically that anything anyone says to him while he's standing up must be small talk and must, therefore, instinctively be tuned out. So Grace says, 'It seems as though the Harvard chair will go to Jenkins, then,' and he, gazing over her shoulder, sighs and says, 'Evidently,' before blinking into space a couple of times. And when, after a silence that suggests that she is hunting for something more to say and he is thinking absolutely nothing at all except that he would like to be somewhere else, she observes that she had been expecting the dean of studies to put in an appearance this evening, it seems like the effort of replying 'Really?' might actually kill him.

Look: I have conflicts about my mother. And in situations like this, I feel sorry for her as much as I feel the fear. I mean, look at her. This isn't like going to a parental cocktail party and trying to behave well in front of their friends. Grace doesn't *have* friends. She has colleagues, and admirers, and sponsors, but she doesn't have friends. She doesn't have people she kicks around with making up stupid puns, she doesn't have drinking buddies with whom she can shrug off her woes by having a big night out, she doesn't have anyone to ring up and sob on when the going gets rough. People don't seek her advice about their love lives or their frustrations, or come to her with that emptiness lurking inside us all that occasionally just needs to be filled with stupidity: if Grace's phone rings, it's someone who wants her input on committee structures, or cell structures. And that's why I keep my end up for her. I know it's weird, but I know that how I perform matters intensely to her. I'm not here to give her back-up, to save her from dullards or gather stuff to gossip about later: I'm here as another part of her success story. You know how all parents want to show their children off in their best light? With Grace it's much more than that. Grace wants her daughter to show Grace off in *her* best light.

So after another pause where each of them twiddles their glass and holds an arm folded across their body, she turns to me and says, 'This is my daughter, Anna.'

'Richard Jones,' he says, sticks a hand out behind his back to shake mine.

'How do you do,' I ask, and receive no reply.

'Richard,' my mother announces, 'is looking for a head librarian.'

112

Oh, bugger. She will keep trying to push my career ahead. 'Oh, yes?' I ask politely. He nods. My mother names a university in the north of England and I quail. It's a good university: with a famous library full of papers donated by famous people, one that no one in their right mind would turn down. Unless, of course, they weren't a librarian at all.

'Anna,' she says, never one to beat about the bush, 'is a senior librarian at King's College.'

'Oh yes?' he asks, as though she's just told him I work in a hardware shop.

'Anna,' says my mother, 'needs to move up to head librarian.'

'Oh, yes?' Richard Jones seems to have something stuck in his back teeth. Either that, or this conversation is making him dyspeptic.

He suddenly asks me a question. Academics, I've found, generally don't regard librarians as being part of their own, more as people who man the specialist hardware shops they patronise. 'Like being a librarian, do you?' he asks. I blink a couple of times, say, 'Yes. Very much.'

'Why,' he asks, 'would anyone want to be a librarian?'

Well, I don't bloody know, do I? Mel seems pretty content, and she gets to go home at five most days, which is pretty rare in itself these days. 'It's a privilege,' I reply, 'to spend one's days surrounded by the works of great minds. And a privilege to help people further their own knowledge.'

God, I can talk bollocks when I want to.

'Know Siegfried Marriott?' he fires.

Hah. Trick question. Mel told me about this guy, who retired last year after a small scandal concerning marker pens. 'I haven't seen him since he left,' I say. 'But they hope to restore the Donne to close to original condition.'

Richard Jones nods at the air. 'Send me your CV,' he says.

'I will,' I lie, 'thank you. I'm most grateful.'

'I haven't given you the job yet,' he says.

And you never will. Grace turns to me. 'Who have you spoken to this evening?'

'Um, I—' A load of blokes in cardis who haven't seen me since I was twelve. 'Several people.'

'Names?' she barks. Mother is wearing a fetching ensemble printed with forget-me-nots, frilled at neck and cuffs for extra coverage.

God, what does she do that turns me into an amnesiac? I can't remember a single person I've spoken to, a single conversation I've had. Well, I can, but they've all consisted of brief and stilted attempts at getting me to tell them what my mother is up to while keeping what they themselves are up to quiet. I take my specs off and start to polish them on the cuff of my shirtwaister to give myself a moment to think. 'Dr Lewis said he enjoyed your lecture very much,' I venture. Lewis has to be common enough a name to get away with.

Grace snorts. 'Dr Lewis? Jack Lewis?'

'Yes,' I try.

'He's not here.'

'I thought – I thought—'

'I do wish you would make an effort to get things right,' says Grace. 'If you mean that fool Roger Lewis, I'm hardly going to be pleased to hear his opinions.' She stops, narrows her eyes and stares at the side of my nose. 'What's that?'

Oh, bugger. I play dumb. 'What?'

'Don't say "what",' she says automatically as though I'm still five years old. 'On your nose. Have you had it pierced?'

'Mother!' I protest. I'd thought the hole was pretty inconspicuous.

'You have! You've had it pierced!'

'Don't be silly, Mother.' Think fast, girl. 'It's a blackhead,'

I explain. 'I know it's huge, but I didn't think it was *that* huge.'

She is unconvinced. 'Really,' I start again. 'I've used everything on it and nothing works. Ghastly, isn't it?'

'Please don't use florid terms like ghastly,' she says.

'Sorry,' I say humbly. Change the subject as fast as I can. 'Can I get you another drink, Mother?'

She looks down at her half-drunk water. 'I have plenty, thank you.'

Aaaargh. Oh, God. 'It must be warm by now. Why don't I get you a fresh one?'

She looks suspicious. Grace finds all solicitous behaviour suspect. Then she pushes her glass into my hand and turns away.

I trot off and find a waiter. Pop behind a pillar and down a glass of vinegar in one. It doesn't do to get drunk at things like this, but you need back-up. Then, thanking my lucky stars that my mother is only in the country three or four times a year, I bring her a new glass of water, a couple of chips of ice still visible on the surface.

Grace is talking to a different bald bloke with specs. This one has, poor woman, a twittery wife in tow, a cuddly-looking, countrified woman who should, by all the laws of nature, be wearing a hat with fruit on it.

As I put Grace's glass into her hand, I see that the poor love is making a terrible fool of herself. Doesn't know how to dig herself out of the hole she's stepped into. Because, trying to be nice, she's gone and told Grace how much she admires her. 'I've always wanted to meet you,' she twitters. 'I'm *such* an admirer.' You practically hear the hiss as her husband sucks air through his teeth.

Grace looks down: cons the motherly hips, the turquoise-knit two-piece, the black patent shoes, the puffy ankles, the giant just-in-case handbag, the trusting smile, and I think, God, Mother, please don't. Just this once, try being nice. She doesn't really admire you, she's only saying it to be pleasant. There's no need to—

'Thank you,' says Grace. And for a second I think: maybe she's psychic, maybe she's picked up my silent plea, maybe this innocent matron will come away—

'And which aspect of my work is it that you most admire?' asks Grace.

Balding man and I let out tiny groans, groans so small that I wouldn't notice his if my ear weren't so sharply attuned to the sound.

Cosy wife looks taken aback, her mouth a little 'O' of shock for a moment. And then, poor fool, anxiety drives her forward. 'Well, everything, really,' she states. 'It's all your work I admire.'

'*All* my work?' asks Grace. 'How nice. And which aspects in particular?'

Cosy wife goes pink. Can't think of anything to say.

'Are you a physicist?' asks Grace.

Cosy wife, pinker than before, shakes her head.

'A biologist, perhaps?'

'No.'

'Ah,' says Grace. 'You're a musician.'

'I play the piano . . .'

'You play the piano.'

'Not very well. Just as a hobby.'

'Ah, good. Well, it's very *nice*,' says Grace, 'to have the admiration of a fellow hobbyist. I merely write music as a hobby as well. And what do you do?'

All this time, her eyes are boring into the bowed skull of her victim. That'll teach you to smalltalk me, she is saying.

That'll teach you to approach me as an equal. So unnecessary. So my mother.

'I think,' stutters the vanquished one, 'I'll powder my nose.' She looks in her handbag, finds a folded hankie, stuffs it up her sleeve and flees to the loo.

Mother turns to the husband. 'I believe I remember you,' she says. 'What do you do?'

Chapter Fifteen

Gentlemen of the Press

Might have guessed the lull wouldn't last. On Wednesday – Wednesday is usually a quietish night, so when we had a rash of bookings, one or other of us should have smelled a rat – the restaurant is full of tabloid journalists. Well, it wouldn't be Thursday, because that's when the PR freebies happen, and nothing keeps a hack away from her freebies.

We can tell they're tabloid journalists because the men are wearing the sort of suits you usually only see on Egyptian policemen, the women are all in need of a meal (and a deep conditioning treatment), and they're all sitting around muttering things like '. . . waiter pushes the door open and there she is giving him a blow job. Checked into rehab in Arizona the next day' and '. . . doing cocaine on the table in full view of everyone when she was seven months gone. No, straight up, I've seen the photos'. And besides, they would hardly be broadsheet journalists; broadsheets never waste budgets on things like this when they know they can write about what the tabs have been saying the next day.

And another way we know that they're tabloid journalists is that Leeza Hayman is one of them. Leeza let-me-tell-you-something-Mr-Blair Hayman, scourge of the immigrant, terror of politicians, voluble single mother who seems to be out at Showbiz Parties and Trendy Nightspots so much that one occasionally wonders if she would actually recognise the child in question were they to bump into each other on, say, Piccadilly Circus.

We catch one glimpse of them through the kitchen door and retreat behind Shahin. 'What the hell happened?' asks Harriet. 'What the fuck are they doing here? How did they find out?'

I shake my head. I've no idea.

'You like maybe I go and hit them with my ladle?' asks Shahin. He always has the best ideas. For a moment, I'm tempted: the idea of Leeza Hayman being pursued around the restaurant by a howling Iranian cook is almost too good to pass up on. But Shahin only says these things for effect. I go out and beckon to Roy, who is standing behind the bar rubbing his hands together. He catches my eye, jerks his head around and comes through.

'What?'

'Out there, Roy. Tabloid journalists.'

'Really?'

Roy is so surprised, looks so innocent, that I know immediately who the culprit is. And so does Harriet. She starts swearing. 'Roy, you really are the biggest shit I know. You're a treacherous scumbag and I fucking hate you. What do you want? You want me to go out there? What the hell did you think you were doing? You've thrown me to the wolves, Roy, you bastard.'

'Harriet! Harriet!' Roy tries the soothing-voice-of-reason act. 'What makes you think they're here for you? It could just be a coincidence.'

'Oh, yeah, right, and my *arse* is a coincidence,' she snaps. 'You total gobshite pig-bastard. You've got another think coming if you think I'm going out there.' She starts pulling on her coat, heading for the back door into the alleyway.

Roy comes round the counter to block her passage. 'Don't be silly, girl. Come on. You can't just walk out!'

'Just fucking try me!' she snarls.

'Harriet!' Roy jabs a finger at her face. 'If you go and leave me understaffed when we're full, you're not coming back. Do you understand?'

'Well, you should have bloody thought about that before you rang every paper in the country,' she says. 'Get out of my way.'

'I mean it,' he warns.

'Tough titty,' she shouts. Steps round him and stalks into the night.

Oh, great. Just when I think things can't get any worse, I find myself facing the mob alone. For a moment, I'm tempted to go with her. Very tempted. I can't believe he's done this to us. But I look up and see his face, and I think: Christ. We've not been paid for a fortnight. We'll both end up with nothing to live on if I walk too. So instead, I say, 'You're a bastard, Roy,' and vacillate by the door.

'I don't know what you're on about,' says Roy.

'Oh, yes you do,' I reply.

''S up to you,' he says. 'Believe me, believe her. Just remember, you're never going to earn like you earn here anywhere else.'

So I think: what do I do? I can't afford to drop out of this job, not with all that money owing. And something naive and optimistic and stupid in me makes me think that maybe I can throw them off the scent. Leeza will recognise me, knows I live with Harriet; maybe I can make out that there's been some sort of mistake, that it's only me who works here. And I'm not a story in myself: or not at the moment, anyway, while Godiva's so hot.

I shake my head.

'There are people in there want drinks,' says Roy. 'Either you get out there and serve them, or you get out. It's your choice.'

'Fuck you, Roy,' I reply, and stalk out into the arena.

Leeza is her usual voluble self. Patting her striped-blonde bob, and fingering her glass of dry white, she's saying, 'I'm going to have to sack that nanny. Now she's come over all employment laws with me. Says if I want her to babysit I've got to pay her overtime, if you please. And now it's National Insurance this and minimum wage that. I said, "Well, I'd like to see you get National Insurance in Kosovo, madam," but it's like talking to a brick wall.'

She's sitting next to a man, of course. He sups his lager, says, 'Well, you don't want to give her too much time off. She'll only be off begging at Marble Arch.'

'Probably takes my kid with her as an accessory,' Leeza snarls. And all the time she's saying it, she's watching for Harriet.

I think, well, might as well get it over with. Go over and say, 'Hi, Leeza. What a surprise.'

Leeza hams up the least convincing show of astonishment I think I've ever seen. Well, apart from Godiva's when she won Woman of the Year in 1979. I may be sour on Grace, but I'll say this for her: she doesn't bother pretending she didn't expect to win things. Actually, I'd love to see the camera on her face the day she *doesn't* win a prize: now, *that* would be worth seeing.

'Why—' She bats her eyelashes. Leeza's eyes are robin's-egg blue, enhanced by blue eyeliner and copious amounts of glossy white highlighter on the lower lids. Batting her eyelashes must have got her a long way before she turned forty. 'It's . . .'

I don't bother to say anything. She knows who I am. I

know that she knows who I am and she knows that I know that she knows who I am. So it's hardly worth the waste of breath.

'. . . Angie, isn't it?'

A good try. I smile. 'Everything all right for you, Leezy?'

She bares her teeth. It's like being threatened by a Sindy doll. 'Fine.'

'Here on a story, are you?'

Another bat of the lashes. 'Noooo. Gosh. No, I'm out with a few friends and we thought we'd come and see this place we've heard so much about.'

'Oh. That's interesting. Only, we've got the *News of the World* in tonight, and the *Mirror*. What a coincidence.'

'Nooo!' she says again, though she must recognise most of the people sitting round her. Then she rallies. 'And how's your flatmate – what's her name?'

'Harriet.'

'That's right. I heard she was travelling in Australia.'

No you didn't, I think. At least, not most recently. Nigel's red herring has worn off at last, more's the pity.

'Nope,' I reply. 'I don't know what gave you that idea.'

'So tell me.' Leeza leans forward. 'Any extras on the menu?'

Her companion is drinking it all in. Hacks often work in pairs on this sort of job: witnesses. He has the sort of hair that looks like a wig: that Elton-style boyish pudding basin that never really looks convincing on anyone older than thirteen.

'What sort of extras?' I know we're totally in the clear. Roy may be a sod, but he's not a fool.

'We heard,' says Leeza, 'that you could book escorts through this place. Get your dinner with all the trimmings, as it were.'

I sigh. 'What do you want, Leeza? You're going to have a lot of trouble making something like that stick, you know.'

'Well, I don't know,' she says. 'You could always sue. But mud sticks, as I'm sure you know.'

'What do you want?' I repeat.

'Just an interview with Harriet.'

'You know I can't give you that. I don't have the first idea where she is.'

'You do, Angie.'

'Anna. It's Anna. And I don't.'

'Well,' says Leeza in a tone that's half wheedle, half bully. 'I suppose we'll have to go ahead with the feature we've got. The Sunday will love it. You could give us a quote, of course, put your side—'

'No.'

She starts on the old patter, but I've heard it too many times to be taken in. 'Look, Anna. We're going to run the piece anyway, so you might as well talk to someone. It'll look much worse if you don't put your side of things; perhaps you could put us right on a few things. Give us your point of view.'

I shake my head. Roy is doing the same to the guys from the *News of the World*. Now that his bait is gone, I guess he's realised that he needs to do some damage limitation. Doesn't want his precious restaurant turning up in a real-life exposé all of its very own.

Leeza turns nasty. 'I can fucking destroy you,' she says. 'I can put your name all over the papers and have the police watching this place like hawks. All you have to do is tell us where she is. We don't want to do anything nasty. We just want to talk to her. We know she's been working here. You don't think she'll want to give some sort of defence for herself?'

'Not to you she won't, no. She wouldn't have anything to say to you at all, even if she did work here.'

'You're a fucking fool, Anna. I'm giving you one more chance, and then . . .'

I'm cursing inside. I want to reach out and slap her, but know that this is my route to the front page. 'No, Leeza,' I repeat. 'I have absolutely nothing to say to you. I don't know where Harriet is, and if I did I wouldn't tell you. There's nothing for you to see here, and no story. Perhaps you'd just like to leave now? Your bill's on us with our compliments, of course.'

'Oh, no.' Leeza sits back and folds her arms. 'We've booked a table and we're staying. And we'll be back tomorrow night, and the night after that and the night after that until you tell us . . .'

The kitchen door bursts open with a force that suggests that it's been kicked from the inside. Harriet, still in her gymslip, with ping-pong bat, tennis racquet, whip and cane in hand, stalks through, shrugging off Shahin, who seems to be holding onto her arm and begging her. A silence so complete we could be wearing headphones falls among the diners, punctuated only by the pop and whizz of cameras. Hand on hip, she marches to the podium, heels clicking sharply on the floor. Steps up, drops the lash of the whip down over her shoulder, looks slowly around to afford every photographer in the place the opportunity to take her best angle.

'Right!' she barks, and the customary rustle of adjusted trousers fills the air. 'You've all been very naughty and you're going to have to take your punishment. So we'll start with the naughtiest.' Her glittering eye roves about the room until she spots our adversary sitting by my elbow. 'Is there a Leeza Hayman in the house tonight?'

Chapter Sixteen

LEEZA HAYMAN
When a spade's a spade, she's not afraid

My gran, who was the wisest person I ever knew, had a saying that went like this. 'Leeza,' she'd say while she whipped up a batch of her famous Victoria sponges (unlike some people, I didn't have the luxury of a stay-at-home mum, and I spent a lot of time round my gran's helping her cook for the entire family when they came home from their shifts at the factory), 'if it walks like a duck, and talks like a duck, then it is a duck.' Well, if ever I had proof that this was true, I saw it with my own eyes on Wednesday night.

Imagine my feelings on Wednesday when I went out for a quiet dinner with a couple of colleagues. At a so-called restaurant in one of London's ritziest neighbourhoods, we came across a scene of debauchery that would make your hair stand on end. In a room that was done up to look like some sick version of the classrooms your kids and my kid go to every day, two young women pranced about in gymslips and stockings, spanking the diners.

Okay, you say, these things happen in the world. People have to make a living, and beggars can't be choosers.

Well, let me tell you something. These girls weren't beggars. Far from it. These were young women who had been brought up with all the advantages handed to them on a plate. Unlike some of us, they had the best schooling, the best parenting, the best start in life that anyone could want. And who were these lucky young women? Why, Harriet Moresby, daughter of Godiva Fawcett, and Anna Waters, daughter of the famous Grace Waters. Yes.

As regular readers of this column know, I am a huge fan of Godiva Fawcett, and have been pushing, against all the might of the government, big business and the powers that be, to have her made a saint, or sanctified, to use the nobs' word for it. Not that they'll let it happen, of course: she was too difficult for them, with her love of the weak and the needy,

125

and her stint as a UN Goodwill Ambassador showed once and for all that if there was one person who worked outside the establishment and was capable of embarrassing it, it was Godiva.

And if there's another woman I think should be in line for the honour, it's got to be Grace Waters. I've always said, if I had the perfect dinner party, the two female guests I would really want to be there would be Godiva and Grace. If ever two women deserved sanctification, it would be them. And if it wasn't for the government's pathetic excuses – that Godiva wasn't a Catholic, that Grace is still alive, that it's not down to him anyway – it would have happened already. They're saints in my heart, anyway.

So what must these women be feeling now? I know how I'd feel. I've tried all my life to do something good, I've never been a stranger to hard work, and honesty, and decency, and nor are these two girls' mothers. And this is how they repay them. When they realised that they had been caught out, how do you think they reacted? Shame? Embarrassment? Apologies for spitting in the face of everything that is moral? No. They just carried on as if it were a normal night in their den of iniquity. I'll tell you, I hugged my son very tightly when I got home that night, even though I had to wake him up to do it.

Of course, I wasn't born with a silver spoon in my mouth, so maybe I'm just ignorant, and no doubt the stuffy papers will be falling over themselves to come up with liberal excuses for this behaviour, but here's what the real people will think. What is the world coming to? What chance is there for our children if people with all the chances can go so bad?

Well, let me tell you something. Sometimes there's nothing you can do. I met Godiva several times before her tragic death, in fact, I would go so far as to say that she counted me as a friend. She was charming, witty, caring, kind and always happy to help me out. I have never met Grace Waters, but reports say that she is the same way inclined. I interviewed Godiva's daughter on the tenth anniversary of her mother's death, and a more proper little madam you've never met. Defensive, drunk, foulmouthed and disrespectful. Waters, who by all accounts has been hand-in-glove with her for nearly ten years, seems to have developed much the same characteristics.

There's only one conclusion any right-minded person can draw. That these marvellous women made the mistake of loving their kids too much. You can do that, you know. Harriet Moresby and Anna Waters are classic examples of overloved, overindulged children. Spoiled rotten, in other words. Remember this if you don't want your own children to turn out to be junkies, or thieves, or greedy little slovens. Because if it looks like a slut, and it talks like a slut, what do you reckon it is?

© Daily Sparkle, 2000

Chapter Seventeen

The Bus Stop

Lindsey is reading Leeza Hayman out loud, and tears of laughter are pouring down her face. 'Because if it looks like a slut, and it talks like a slut, what do you reckon it is?' she cries, pointing at me and dabbing at her face.

Lindsey, Harriet and I all worked together in Chee's cocktail and burger bar in Covent Garden when we first came to London. It was Lindsey, in fact, who first introduced me to the joys of tabloid newspapers. Before I started borrowing her copies of the *Sun* in meal breaks, I'd only really ever read the *Grauniad*.

She needs to shout to be heard over the crowd, even though the five of us are squashed cosily together in a four-person booth, and we only got that by dint of fast elbow work and deadpanning. We're still having to pretend to be unaware of the people we beat to our table, who are standing over us in the baleful hope that they will somehow be next in line when we leave. I don't know why. If ever a group of people looked like they were dug in for the night, it would be us.

The Bus Stop is heaving, even for a Friday night. We perch on the red plastic vandalproof benches that line the booths, clutching the three magic markers we've managed to secure in case anyone wants to do a graffito. Tables consist merely of narrow planks on which to rest one's drink; there are no ashtrays, cushions or bins and the concrete flagstone floor is littered with fag butts, bits of paper and spilled drinks by the end of the night, waiting to be washed down with hoses in the morning. The only decorative flourish is a digital screen on the end wall, which alternately flashes the word 'Loading' and a jumble of asterisks. When you first come in, the door people give you tickets with the time on. Once you've bought your first round, you then have to wait an hour before you are allowed to approach the bar again. Still, at least you're then allowed to buy three drinks at once. 'A woman making her way in the world,' I shout, 'and anyway, it's hardly Leeza's place to throw stones. Everyone knows she wrote her first hundred columns on her knees.'

'And the next hundred on all fours,' growls Harriet.

Dom says, 'Have you heard from your brother at all?' and Harriet shakes her head. 'I don't suppose I'd hear from him if there was a death in the family, let alone a resurrection. Gerald is so wet, they've got him plumbed into the sprinkler system at Belhaven. Saves a fortune in rates. It would never occur to him to call me and let me know there was a crisis.'

'So how about you?' Linds turns to me. 'Your old girl been in touch?'

I shake my head. 'Fortunately, she went off to Geneva straight after the party thing. If I've got any luck, she'll have missed the papers.'

'And if she hasn't?'

I shudder. 'I'm having dinner with her on Thursday. I guess I'll find out then.'

'Jeez,' says Lindsey, 'seeing your mother twice in less than two weeks? That must be a record, mustn't it?'

I give her a look.

But at least she's sympathetic. 'Poor old you. Call me if you get scared, won't you?'

'Thanks.'

'I'm in Edinburgh on Thursday, and Friday. But you can call me on my mobile.'

'Thanks. You're a star.'

Meanwhile, Mel continues to cross-examine Harriet. 'So what are they going to do with the body?'

Harriet shakes her head. 'How would I know? She's only my mother. Gerald will probably leave it up to the Burges, and the Burges will try to sneak her back into the crypt, only one of them will manage to drop the coffin out of an attic window and crown a tourist underneath or something.'

'What do you want done?' Mel, who likes to think of herself as 'good' with people – and to do her credit, often is – asks. I think that Mel has a bit of a fixation about death and bodies; she certainly never avoids a chance to ask detailed questions.

'Well – ' Harriet polishes off her first sidecar and slides the next along the table until it comes to a rest in front of her, ' – obviously she can't go in her mausoleum now that they've gone and got the fan base all worked up. They'll be trying to break in and cop a feel again. I don't know. The Fawcett Memorial Trust were on the phone yesterday, suggesting that we hold another memorial service.'

'Say,' Lindsey sparks up at this, 'what a great idea! Then we could all go! I haven't had an excuse to buy a really extravagant outfit for ages.'

'Yeah, right,' says Harriet. 'Another round of churchgoing is all I need.'

'Yes, but your mother's never been a saint before,' says Mel.

'It would be brill.' Dom lights a cigarette from the butt of his old one and drops the butt on the floor. 'Just think. You could round up all the children she visited and fly them in, and maybe you could get Elton John to sing a song. *Dirty Little Girl*, perhaps, or *I'm Still Standing*.'

'Yeah, and Geri Halliwell could take some time off from her hectic round of UN engagements and mime to a valedictory address,' says Lindsey.

'Yes, and Ann Widdecombe could pull a face for the opposition, and we could all dress up as film roles she played.'

'Oh, yeah,' says Mel. 'Bags I *Beach Bunny Massacre*. I loved *Beach Bunny Massacre*, especially the bit where Godiva runs all the way up the shoreline in a bikini—'

'And her tits don't move,' the three of them finish.

No one seems to have noticed that Harriet has dropped out of the conversation.

'Who do you think they'll get to conduct the service, do you think?' asks Dom.

'Oh, no one less than Papa himself, of course,' says Dom. 'After all, if she's going to be a saint . . .'

'Saint, hah!' Lindsey leans forward, shakes her hair about, embarks on another round of Godiva-bashing. 'I mean, if I ever heard a joke, that's got to be it. I mean, if you two qualify as sluts, then I can hardly see Godiva getting through the Virtue test. The woman had more pricks than your average rose grower.' Mel and Dom and Lindsey, having known the two of us for years, are not subscribers to the 'criticism is sour grapes' society of Godiva admirers. Of course, it was the fact that they never were that let them through Harriet's barriers in the first place but I try to kick Linds under the table anyway, because I can see that Harriet is going through one of her don't-knock-my-mother moods.

'Well, there *was* Mary Magdalene . . .' Dom says doubtfully.

'Yeah, but Mary Magdalene had at least repented. All Godiva ever did was blame other people. And anyway, what would we call her? Our Lady of the Make-up Counter?'

'Saint Godiva of Silicone Valley, patron saint of nude scenes,' says Mel.

'Godiva Polygamous / pray for me / let me get my / alimony,' chants Dom. 'Perhaps she should get a special dispensation for excellence in motherhood.'

And this one is enough for Harriet. She tips over her last sidecar, gets to her feet, and finally everyone takes a moment to look at her.

'Please stop talking about my mother like that,' she says. She says it calmly, but her face is white. 'I know what you all think of her. I know what most of the world thinks of her apart from the nutters who want to believe she had some sort of direct line to God. Christ, I know what *I* think of her. But she was still my mother. She was still my mum and she still used to tuck me up in bed when she was home, and she still bought me birthday presents and told me about periods and rang me to say goodnight. I know she was crap. I know everything about her faults. I was the one who had to live with them. And no one's ever let me forget them. Why do you think I don't tell people who she was? For God's sake, for every person that tells me she should be a saint, there's someone else who tells me she should have been burned at the stake. I don't want to hear any more. You may think she was a saint, you may think she was a witch, but some people actually knew her as a human being. She may have been a silly bitch, but she was still my mum, and I still loved her. Please don't forget that. She may be a joke to you, but she was still my mum.'

We call it a night relatively early. The after-pub crowds

haven't even hit the streets by the time we start our silent walk home, just the occasional couple locked into each other's arms, tired travellers trundling suitcases from airport train to Pimlico flophouse, fourteen-year-olds with nowhere to go since they closed down the youth clubs. Harriet is monosyllabic through most of the journey, and I don't push her. If you push Harriet, you get nowhere. She always has to work through her rage before the truth comes out.

And eventually, halfway down Buckingham Palace Road, she speaks. 'I'm sorry,' she says. 'I sort of put a downer on the atmosphere tonight.'

Which is true, but not in the way she feels. Harriet has that brittle upper-class dislike of emotional behaviour, feels that it should be kept away from the social arena, and is always annoyed with herself if she lets the side down. But the others, overcome by guilt, fell over themselves to change the subject and make up to her, which of course meant that everyone immediately stopped behaving naturally.

Normally, Godiva doesn't even come up in conversation that often, and normally, a couple of jokes are fine. Because despite her outburst tonight, Harriet manages, on the whole, to tread the fine line between her mother's iconic status and the reality of her life with remarkable equilibrium. It's just that life isn't very normal at the moment.

'It doesn't matter,' I reply, 'I don't think anyone's going to hold it against you.'

'Yes,' she says, 'but they're going to think I'm completely mad. I mean, what was I doing? Mummy wasn't like that at all. Where on earth did all that bollocks come from?'

'Sometimes she was like that,' I remind her reasonably. 'She was really sweet to you some of the time.'

'When it suited her,' adds Harriet gloomily.

I don't know, but I've sort of got the impression over the

years that this is true, to a greater or lesser extent, of quite a lot of parents. That image of self-sacrificing selfless devotion as the median of motherhood is, as far as I've seen, as much of a myth as Godiva's sainthood. It's one of those myths that keeps society going, but the only people who have ever lived up to it to the letter have probably produced some seriously fucked-up children. I mean, it's bad enough carrying Grace's expectations around on my shoulders, but imagine the burden of guilt if someone had sacrificed *everything* for your well-being.

Then Harriet says, in a small voice, 'Why can't they just leave it alone? Why can't they just—' She pulls up by an empty coach stop and puts her hands over her face. 'I don't understand,' she moans through her fingers. 'I don't understand what I'm meant to do. What am I meant to do?'

I put a hand on her shoulder. 'I don't know, sweetheart.'

'I—' says Harriet, and then she goes quiet. Even after all these years, she still hates people to see her cry. She finds it difficult to deal even with me seeing her, despite the countless times I've sobbed and railed in her presence and she's loved me none the less. So we have a tacit pact, which is that she lets me see, and I pretend not to have noticed. I move the arm from her shoulder and put it round her waist, rock her against my side until the long, slow breaths she's been taking die down. Then, standing on tiptoe, I smooth a stray lock of hair from her forehead and plant a kiss where it has been.

'Harriet, there is nothing you can be doing.'

'I can't win either way,' says Harriet. 'Someone's going to be offended whatever I do. I'm not going to lie. Why should I?'

'You don't have to. Harriet, the people who matter know. It doesn't matter about the rest.'

'But it does,' says Harriet, hands still over her face. 'It does when they think they can tell me about it. Every single bloody day I get a dozen emails, or letters forwarded by the estate, or someone says something to me in the street. I've changed my email address three times and they just find it out again. I can't stand it. I never asked to be a public person. No one ever asked me. Why can't they leave me alone?'

And once more, her breathing gets long and heavy and she falls silent. God, Harriet, I wish you were better at this sort of stuff. You're so damn good at doing it for other people, but you just won't let go yourself.

I put my other arm round her. She stiffens, then relaxes and allows a tiny sob to get out round the palms of her hands.

'Oh, darling,' I say. 'I wish I could make it all go away, but it won't. You've just got to tough it out and remember how much we all love you.'

A louder sob, a judder in the shoulders.

I make the sounds I've heard people make to small children in the street. 'There,' I say soothingly, hug her closer. 'There.' And I say, 'It's okay, sweetie, I'm here. Don't worry. I'm here.'

And she does what she always does. After five minutes, she straightens up, wipes her hands upward over her face to clean the tears away and says, 'God, what bollocks. Sorry.'

''S okay.'

'Total loss of dignity there. Sorry.' She starts to walk homeward, hands sunk in the pockets of the riding mac, heels scraping on the pavement.

'I'll be holding it against you,' I reply.

She throws me a watery grin and we walk on in silence until she thinks of something to talk about. And eventually she does. 'Tell you what. I've got to think of something to do to that bastard Roy.'

'What were you thinking of?'

'Well, I'm not sure,' she says. 'I've already poisoned his bloody plants. I was wondering if we could maybe do something to his wardrobe.'

Roy is temporarily living in the flat above the restaurant while builders fit an all-gold bathroom in his newly built loft apartment. 'It's a possibility,' I say. 'But we'd have to be careful. We really can't afford to lose our jobs right now, even if he is a bastard. What were you thinking about?'

Harriet laughs. 'You know what I think?'

'No, darling, I don't. That's why I'm asking.'

'Do you remember the time Henry left that vole on that fun-fur you left on the stairs?'

Hard to forget. He did it in a warm snap in the winter. It was two weeks before I felt a need to pick the coat up again, and by then the only possible course of action was to throw up a couple of times and then stuff it in a bin liner. You would never believe that something so small could give off so large a smell.

'Well, he left a large mouse on the doormat about a week ago. I've been saving it in a plastic bag by the boiler.'

I laugh. 'You are an evil genius, Dr Moriarty.'

She laughs back. 'There is no evil, Mr Holmes,' she replies, 'only genius. And Iranian chefs with spare keys.'

'When're you going to do it?'

'Ooh.' Harriet is amazingly good at swinging her mood back when she wants to. 'I thought as soon as would probably be best.'

We swing into the home strait, discussing the details of our revenge: how I can keep him talking while she sneaks upstairs, best ways to hide the thing in a wardrobe so it won't be discovered until the damage is done. Direct action is Harriet's forte. She long ago gave up bothering to reason with people; gets quite Old Testament when she thinks that someone will never see the error of their ways.

Under the street light outside our gate, a figure that's been squatting up against the wall uncurls, stretches and stands, hands on hips, watching our approach.

'Oh, bugger,' hisses Harriet. 'Who the hell is that?'

'I don't know. Journalist?'

'At this hour? Christ. It must be a fan. Oh, God. Do you think he *really* knew where I lived?'

'I don't know. Oh, God. What should we do?'

'Well, there's nothing we *can* do. We're not going to get into the house without going past him.'

He waves. Oh, bloody hell. What do we do? Wave back?

Then he starts to walk towards us, back to the light so we can't even see if his face is friendly or otherwise. We slow our pace to a crawl, tensely waiting to see what his next move is going to be.

Then a broad Australian tenor booms out across the night air. 'Chroist!' it calls. 'I thought youse goys were *niver* gaingda come home!' and, with a yell of delight, I throw myself on top of him.

Chapter Eighteen

Love You to Death

That's the difference between Harriet and me. I, cosseted, hothoused, watched over, guarded and given more attention than any child has the right to expect, have never been able to love my mother, dearly though I have wished that I did. Harriet, neglected, deprived, exploited, shoved from pillar to post and often treated more as accessory than dependent, loves her mother dearly, desperately, however much she wishes she didn't. Fifteen years on, Harriet mourns Godiva with the immediacy of yesterday, hungers for her with the ferocity of wolves.

Harriet has never forgiven Godiva for dying as she did, rails against her and spits on her memory with an orphan's fury, and in the night, when she thinks no one can hear, the sound of her sobs drifts down the tower stairs and fills me with pain. Me, I've pretty much forgiven my mother for living as she has lived; pity her as the victim of my grandfather's zealotry. The tears I used to cry for lovelessness dried the day I decided to live, and though sometimes other people's stories of shared intimacies at kitchen worktops fill me with a false nostalgia for an experience I never had, at least I never have to live with those shrieks of frustration, the howls of mother–daughter provocation, the rage of closeness.

But imagine Harriet's childhood. Only child of a third

marriage that had imploded by the time she was six, boarding at seven, half the holidays in a great cavern of a place avoiding a half-brother who resented her and a father who had never really got over the fool he'd made of himself over her mother, the other half in hotel rooms and rented flats waiting for the moment when the photo-op would begin. If you're our age, you probably remember Harriet from the background of many of Godiva's public exploits: Harriet in a baseball cap, Harriet shyly and solemnly attempting to converse with a Namibian starvation victim, Harriet in a miniaturised version of her mother's scarlet ball dress at some charity occasion, Harriet receiving a cuddle from the loving mother. Because that's part of the deal for a child of the Famous: the offspring of the prominent aren't just there to be a drain on finances and pass on their genes, they are there to emphasise their fecundity, highlight their affections, illustrate their humanity. Well, obviously, I wasn't; I was there to illustrate my family's superiority, but as such I at least had the good fortune to be kept away from the scrutiny of the camera.

And here's another thing: when Harriet lost her mother, her tragedy was never her own. She became a thing to be pawed, confessed to, someone to share the pain of people who never knew her mother. Wherever she went, women would approach with pictures, mementos, stories, as though sharing them with her would somehow confer Godiva's benediction upon them, make their grief real and justifiable. She was discussed on television, hounded from school to school, given advice on problem pages, hugged in the street by strangers. And none of these strangers, these people who wanted a piece of her, ever started a sentence with any word other than 'I'. 'I was so devastated at the loss of your mother.' 'I don't know if I can go on now she's not here.' 'I got so much inspiration from her.' And as she got older, it was 'I just have to touch you; you look so much like her,' and later 'I can't believe someone so dainty could have a child as big as you,' or 'I just had to tell you about the time when . . .'

It wasn't hers, but it was. Godiva left no one else behind to mourn her. Husbands, family, friends: all the others had been shed, one by one, bit by bit, as she scaled the heights of virtue and the memories of intimates became increasingly inconvenient. So there was only Harriet, among the croco-dile weepers at the empty graveside; only Harriet and a million bereaved admirers.

As a matter of fact, Godiva being so famous and her public so hungry, the footage she saw on the news was the first intimation she had that her mother was dead. The film was in the can and beamed into newsrooms across the world several hours before protocols could be put into place and a responsible adult sent out to tell the daughter formally. Godiva died at four thirty in the afternoon Middle Eastern time, and the story made the six o'clock news bulletin in Britain, just between tea and prep at Harriet's third boarding school. This was a school that had some pretensions to producing children with a broader spectrum of knowledge of the world than who was related to whom and how much their fathers owned, and the six o'clock news was mandatory for everyone before prep.

Harriet can still recite every detail of the moment: how she was sitting cross-legged on the floor in the third row among her contemporaries, how she had just mastered the fifth stage of cat's cradle and was showing it to Marcia Tennent who was sitting next to her. Her voice goes dead as she tells you the details; it's as though she is telling them under hypnosis, as though her voice is no longer conscious, but coming from somewhere deep inside her, a place that in her waking moments is as obscured from her as it is from the rest of us.

It was a sunny day and she wanted to be out playing at being a horse in the woods behind the school. She had a huge ink stain on her fingers from where her biro had collapsed during history. Farial Prakash–Taylor, sitting in front of her, had a pair of gauzy, iridescent butterflies attached to her hair slides and she wanted to reach out and see if they would change colour when she touched them. She had a hole in her sock, hard on the calf where she had caught it on the corner of the lockers in the changing rooms; it was beginning to ladder and she knew she'd get some sort of black mark for it. The carpet in the television room was a rather attractive Morris willow pattern, faded almost to oblivion.

'The music came on, and then I don't remember much,' she says. 'There was someone screaming, and I realised it was me.'

I also remember the day Godiva died. Even in my ivory cocoon, it wasn't possible to miss it. And besides, it was the topic of the day for our evening debating session. The evening debate was a crucial part of my education: Peter had instituted it with my mother when she was five years old, and she'd been doing it with me, on the evenings when she was at home, of course – the demands of a career like Grace's didn't allow her, thank the Lord, to give me quite the same amount of quality time as she got from Peter – since I was around seven. By the time I was four, everyone had acknowledged that I wasn't quite on the same fast track as my mother had been, so everything came a little later in my upbringing than it had in hers.

The evening debate took place after supper, which was

always strictly at eight o'clock for optimum digestion. My day was timetabled down to the last ten minutes. When I was eleven, around the time that Godiva died, it went thus: Six thirty a.m. get up. Six forty a.m. ten minutes' stretching exercises. Six forty-five to five past seven a.m. breakfast (high-bran cereal, fruit, vitamin pills). Five past seven to seven fifteen a.m. dress. Seven fifteen to seven forty-five a.m. piano practice *or* t'ai chi, alternating days. Seven forty-five to eight thirty a.m. prescribed reading (I was, by this stage, on Goethe, Rousseau and – selected – Chaucer: I had, of course, done the entire works of Shakespeare by the age of nine). Eight thirty a.m. travel to school. Eight forty-five to twelve thirty p.m. normal lessons. Twelve thirty to two p.m. lunch (packed, of course: high-energy salad with three types of sprouted beans, lean meat or cheese, wholemeal bread, live yoghurt – how I hated that sour-milk taste, unsweetened even by honey! – fruit, vitamin and mineral supplements, echinacea, royal jelly); special dispensation to miss break and replace it with coaching in: algebra; linguistics; physics; chemistry; piano (a different lesson each weekday). Two to four p.m. normal lessons (obviously, with my special coaching, I attended certain lessons with classes even further above my age group, something which caused endless time-tabling grief for my school. Nobody, however, ever complained; I was, after all, a prestige pupil). Four to four fifteen p.m. travel home. Four fifteen to four thirty p.m. free time (to include snack of wholemeal bread, salad, fruit). Four thirty p.m. coaching as above. Five thirty to six p.m. homework. Six to six thirty p.m. watch the news. Choose subject for evening debate. Six thirty to seven p.m. home-work. Seven p.m. supper: lean meat, steamed vegetables, carbohydrates. Seven thirty p.m. finish homework and/or hand over to Mother for evaluation while preparing for evening debate. Eight to eight thirty p.m. evening debate. Eight thirty to nine thirty p.m. prescribed reading: fiction, poetry, selected drama. In my twelfth year, I read the works of Jane Austen and Anthony Trollope in their entirety. I've never been able to read them again. Nine thirty p.m. bath, tidy bedroom, prepare uniform for following day, finish off any homework left over. Ten p.m. bed.

That was weekdays, of course. Weekends weren't anything like as much fun.

It was inevitable that I should pick the death of Godiva Fawcett as our debate subject that night. It was the lead story on the news and, aside from anything else, I was deeply moved by what I had seen. And Grace's reaction to my choice was equally predictable. The Anglo-Irish Agreement was in full swing at the time, after all, and we had only spent three debating periods on the subject so far.

'Why,' she asked when I announced my chosen topic, 'do you believe that this is a subject worthy of discussion?'

Even for Grace, this was a pretty blunt way of opening a debate. The purpose, after all, was that I should learn to conduct discourse fluently and in full sentences on any given topic. 'I – I thought it was very upsetting,' I replied. 'The only moment of death I have seen before on film was the footage of the Kennedy assassination, and I found it both distressing and moving.'

'Both distressing *and* moving?' asked my mother. 'Can you give me an example of something that is distressing *without* being moving?'

Had I been older, I think I would probably have been able to reply that the sight of Margaret Thatcher's wholesale dismissal of the miners' distress of the year before was distressing without being moving, but at eleven I wasn't endowed with the courage to disagree. 'I'm sorry,' I mumbled. I got marks out of twenty for my evening debate; it was evident that I was down to nineteen-and-a-half after a single sentence.

She waited. I continued. 'I feel that the manner of her death will have a considerable impact on our society. According to the news reports, people are already conducting a vigil outside her house in London.'

'And besides a group of silly people indulging in hysteria,' said Grace, 'what impact will this have?'

'Godiva Fawcett,' I said, 'was a popular figure with many people across the world. She was a prominent spokesperson for many charitable causes, and the organisations involved will have difficulty in replacing her with as charismatic or as energetic a figurehead.'

Believe me, this really was how I talked back then. Compressing words, non-sentences – anything more than the mildest deviation from grammatical laws was rarely tolerated under the Waters roof.

Grace folded her arms, stared grimly at me across the table.

'And what is the function of a charitable figurehead?'

I thought. 'To bring the public's attention to an issue. To promote an emotional involvement that might not otherwise exist.'

'And why does the public *need* to have an emotional involvement with issues that affect strangers? What purpose does this serve?'

'Well, obviously—' I started, then winced. That'll be another point off the total. 'Sorry. I believe that the purpose is to emphasise the importance of charitable giving. I believe that it has been established that those who feel they have an understanding of an issue are more likely to donate funds to its solution.'

'Feel they have an understanding, or have an understanding?'

'Feel – have – either . . .' Whoops. Not a full sentence. Seventeen and a half.

'And how do you feel that this benefitted Godiva Fawcett?'

'Gosh. I don't. I was under the impression that charity figureheads take on their roles in an attempt to give something back to the world.'

This didn't please her at all. 'Give something back? What, precisely are they *giving back*? Are they donating funds? Are they donating skills? Does a single individual benefit directly from their actions?'

By now I was close to tears. I knew what I had seen on the television, and it had upset me as much as it upset everyone else who saw it. Grace excepted, of course.

'Yes!' I snapped, losing two points for direct contradiction. 'Didn't you *see* it? She saved *five* children! Didn't you see?'

'What I saw,' said Grace, 'was a silly and egotistical woman taking an unnecessary and ill-advised risk and losing her life as a consequence.'

Sort of true. But what are acts of courage other than unnecessary and ill-advised risks? If a man charges a machine-gun post, would he do it if he stopped to weigh up the risks first? Do we refuse injured firemen their disability allowances? I found myself, not for the first time in my life, speechless. Lost a point. Fourteen and a half.

'And what I also saw,' continued Grace, 'was a fading actress, who had been exploiting other people's misfortunes to bolster her own popularity for years, take advantage of a situation to ensure that she would maintain her popularity in perpetuity.'

'Mother!' I cried. Lost half a point for raising my voice. 'You can't say that!' Fourteen.

'Direct contradiction,' she said. Thirteen and a half.

'But—' Thirteen. You don't start a sentence on a conjunction. 'I know what I saw. I saw an act of extreme courage and self-sacrifice. I saw someone who didn't care about the consequences to her own life as long as other people were in danger. I saw something I will never forget, and I don't think anyone else will either.'

Sadly, no one ever deducted points from Grace's score. 'Oh, very reasoned,' she said. 'Such an impressive argument. Have you listened to nothing I have taught you? Or are you simply obtuse?'

I stopped mid-flow, apologised. 'Sorry, Mother.'

'And the reason for your apology?'

'I allowed emotion to dictate my reasoning.'

'Exactly. And why is this particularly appropriate to the debate in hand?'

Good Lord, I'm only eleven. 'I'm not sure.'

'Because,' she explained, 'Godiva Fawcett represented the emotion-over-reason brigade. All of her public work consisted of direct appeals to the emotions. She never asked her audience to think, merely to feel and act accordingly.'

'But—' I began. Stopped. Too late. Twelve. 'If the outcome is desirable, should the means of bringing it about matter?'

'What,' she replied, 'makes you believe that the outcome was desirable?'

'She raised huge sums of money. People made charitable donations as a direct result of her appeals. Of course the outcome was desirable.'

Definitive statement based on generalisation. Eleven out of twenty.

'Were I less controlled,' said Grace, 'I would be angry

about this idea that the world is made better by charitable donations.'

'*What?*' Ten and a half.

'The world is made better by action,' said my mother.

'Surely—'

She interrupted. I lost half a point.

'It is not people like Godiva Fawcett who change the world,' she said. 'It is not people who give themselves a glow of self-satisfaction because they've given something away. It is the thinkers. It is people such as myself who set themselves goals and work to attain them. Those of us who work exhaustively and without asking for thanks or affirmations. These emotional gestures are meaningless. They are a waste of time. They are an insult to those of us who are *really* changing the world.'

Suddenly I noticed that there were little spots of colour on the point of each of her cheekbones, and I realised something I had never seen before. The great Grace Waters, icon of reason, is driven by emotion after all, and it's one of the basest emotions imaginable. My God, I thought, you're jealous. Despite all her prizes, and accolades and affirmations, the votes of thanks, the standing ovations, she was eaten up with jealousy of a dead woman.

Of course, I didn't say anything. By then I had learned which thoughts to share and which to hug to myself, which would keep things simple and which would bring cold and unreasonable punishments down upon my head.

'You're right,' I admitted. 'You win.'

And by conceding, which I always did, I brought my points down below the halfway mark, so I would be assigned another essay to write on the subject at the weekend. It would have happened one way or another, whatever I did; might as well get it over with.

But you see, even I owe something to Godiva Fawcett, even though time and acquaintance have taught me that the manner of her death was little reflection of the manner of her life. She meant many things to many people. To some she was a role model, a figure of admiration, someone to emulate. To some she was a miracle worker, the figure who came to them in a dream and cured them of their sciatica. To some she was a joke, a B-lister who came to surprise us all. To Harriet she was the mother who, though she was scarcely there, left a gaping void by her departure. Some see her as a saint, some as a sinner, some as an expert manipulator and queen of spin.

And me? The day Godiva died was the day that the small seed of doubt within me that my famous mother might not be infallible after all finally felt the blissful touch of rain.

Chapter Nineteen

Princess Incognita

A recently uncovered A++ essay from 1952, found among a bundle of others in the basement storerooms of Warrington Primary School (formerly Warrington Church of England First School) and currently on display as part of the lottery-funded 'Warrington Education: Past Successes, Future Principles' exhibition at Warrington Central Library. The exhibition has been a remarkable success, attracting some thirty visitors over a six-week period.

My Family by Geraldine Pigg aged 12

Once upon a time, I was born. My father was a king and my mother was a queen, and I was called the Princess Incognito. But my mother had a fairy godmother and they forgot to ask her to the chrissaning. Fairies get very cross when they are not asked to things they should be asked to, so my mother's fairy godmother turned up all in black and stood over my cradle. And she said, 'You have forgotten to ask me and now I have to have my revenge. The Princess Incognito will die within ten days.' But my father's fairy god-mother was able to undo some of the curse but not all of it and she said, 'The Princess Incognito will not die but you will never see her again as she will have to go and live with another family and they will change her name and however long you search you will never find her.'

So then she took me and put me with the family I live with now and they are called Mr and Mrs Pigg. My 'father' is called Stanley and my 'mother' is called Irene and her name was Mimms before she got married and before they had me they could not have children before so they are very pleased to have me and they called me Geraldine. They own a butcher's shop on Corporation Road and we live above the shop and they had enough meat to eat even during the war when no one had meat except when they had rashers and then it was mostly offle and mince most of the time. Sometimes we go to the seaside and on Saturday afternoons we go to the park after the shop is closed except when it is raining and we go to the cinema.

I like films with Cary Grant in mostly and also ones where the princess is saved by the dashing cavalier as it reminds me of what my real life was like before I came here even though I should have been too little to remember. My mother likes knitting and my father smells of pork chops even when he has had his bath. But I do not think that they know that I know that I am not their real daughter or that I remember that I used to live in a palace and have silk sheets and baths every night in rose petals.

Mother wants me to pass the higher certificate so that I get a good job as a secretary or even a teacher. All the girls in my class have no imagination and want to be shop-keepers and secretaries and some of them nurses. They call me Her Ladyship just because I have higher ambitions, and want to make something of myself and speak properly and that. They play praticle jokes on me and try to get my clothes dirty by tripping me up and throwing things, but I don't care because it is beneath me to care. And anyway, I know that one day I shall be rich and famous and I can sweep past them in my golden carriage as I pass them on the street. In fact, I will go back to the life I used to live before I came to Warrington, and then they will all be sorry.

Chapter Twenty

Anna Gets Dressed

'So I reckon you're in for a bit of a spanking on Thursday, then,' says Nigel, back from Ireland and two days ensconced in the tower. Well, in my bedroom. We made an effort to go upstairs once, but it didn't last. He's lying on my bed like a well-warmed cougar, arms behind his head, hair roaring across the red velvet cushion he's using for a pillow.

'You never know,' I reply, 'I might have got away with it. I've not heard a peep.'

Nige snorts with derision. 'I think a woman as intelligent as your mother will have worked it out by now.'

'Ah, but you forget. Women like my mother don't read the tabloids.'

Early evening sun streams through the window and plays lovely little games with the golden hairs on his thighs. I reach out and run my finger over them, brushing them ever so lightly so that they bend like a cornfield in a breeze, and he grabs my wrist and pulls it away.

'Excuse me,' he says, 'but we hardly know each other, do we?' Then he gives my left breast a caress and plants a friendly kiss firmly on my lips.

Which turns into a longer kiss. And a hand on my arse pulling me hipbone to hipbone.

Oh, bugger. I would so like to stay. I push him off.

'Honey, it's half past five. I have to be in the restaurant for six.'

'Go on,' says Nigel, like a man deprived, 'just a bit longer.'

I'll tell you what: this boy was worth having back. He fucks like he's rocket-fuelled. Give him the occasional bacon sandwich to keep his strength up, and he'll keep a smile on your face all day.

'Oh, honey, I can't be late tonight. Roy's pissed off enough as it is. Can't you stay a bit longer?'

'Wish I could,' he mumbles, 'but my ticket's not refundable. Just a quickie, huh, Anna? You know you want to.'

Of course I want to, but I can't. Push him away with a firm but gentle hand on the chest, sit up.

He turns onto his back, pulling another cushion over to cover the bulge under the sheet. 'Ah, well. Worth a try. Can I come back and try again when I get back from Barcelona?'

Reluctantly, I've got my feet on the floor already. 'I'll probably have to hunt you down and kill you if you don't.'

'Cool.'

I'm pretty sure there are a couple of clean blouses still in my drawer. There should be twenty-odd coming from the laundry tomorrow. This isn't the sort of job where you can recycle your uniform with a couple of squirts of Febreeze and a bottle of Chanel; it's the sort of job that would make a washing-powder ad. Anna Waters talks about Raz Automatic, 'Jam stains, custard stains, gravy stains: I get them all in my work, and they're the worst stains to get out. I was in despair until I found Raz . . .'

He watches me rummage, says, 'So your guts will be garters, then.'

'Probably. That's why I live each day as though it were my last.'

In the wardrobe hang four identical gymslips, striped ties pre-knotted round the neck of each hanger.

'Anna?'

I put a hanger on the bed, take a clothes brush to my straw boater. I'm the best turned-out schoolgirl in London, though I say it myself. I look over at him, say, 'Yes?'

'Why don't you just tell her you're a grown-up now and she'll have to lump it?'

I slump on the edge of the bed. 'No way.'

'Why not?'

'I'm a coward, I guess.'

He digests this.

'You've got to stop some time, Anna.'

I try a bright smile. 'Not now, though, eh?' Stand up and go in search of a push-up bra and some frilly white knickers.

He pushes himself up in bed, pulls up his knees, wraps his arms round them. 'It's difficult, you know, for someone like me to understand someone like you. No one ever gave me a hard time when I was a kid. I don't suppose it's the same with you, is it?'

I sit down again, with my back to him, shake my head. 'Look, Nige, don't get too heavy, huh? I'm having a good time now, and that's what matters.'

He's quiet for a bit, then, 'Still, I bet you did well at school, huh?'

'Shut up, Nigel.'

'Tell me. Teacher's pet, were you?'

'Shut up!'

'What's the problem? Must have been great, passing exams with flying colours, everyone wishing they were you . . .'

I turn round, glare at him. 'It wasn't like that at all. It was shit, if you want to know. It was absolutely shit. There wasn't a single day when . . .'

He starts back in mock fear. 'All right! Keep your hair on! I was only saying!'

'Well, don't say! You don't have the first idea what it was like being me! Being younger than everyone else in your year by two years so that no one wanted to be friends with you. Having everyone call you a suck-up because you always knew the answer to everything, and all the teachers thinking you were a smart-arse and being too scared of your mother to say so. It wasn't fun at all!'

'Okay,' he says.

'Well, you started it! Do you know what it was like being the unfashionable one, the one who never knew who Simon le Bon was, or Madonna, or what the difference was between a gym shoe and a trainer? I bet *you* were never the one who everybody groaned about when they were made to be your partner in a crocodile. I bet *you* got to go out and play with your mates after school. I wouldn't have been allowed to even if I'd *had* any mates. All I had was bloody reading lists and maths tutors, and . . . and . . . and weekly reports from every one of my teachers, and a nightly hour where my mother and I discussed a nominated topic of conversation. Christ, I'd never even *spoken* to a boy when I went to university. No wonder I'm still living out my adolescence now. Why on *earth* should I tell her anything?'

'Woah,' he says. 'Sorry. Raw topic. Should've thought.'

As quickly as I got angry, it's over. I collect a pair of hold-up stockings from the bedside table, begin rolling them down to toe level to put them on.

Nigel puts a hand on my arm. 'Look,' he says, 'are we still mates?'

I look down at him. You can't be angry with someone as straightforward as the golden boy. At least, I can't. 'Don't be stupid. Of course.'

'Gissa kiss, then.'

I lean back, give him a kiss, let myself sink into his arms and accept a cuddle. He's got nice arms, Nigel. I love men's arms. I love most things about men. I still feel sad that I didn't get to find out how much until I was nineteen.

He takes a stocking from my hand, looks at it.

'How do these things stay up, anyway?'

I show him the sticky rubber bands inside the embroidered bit. 'Perspiration.' Nigel gets a naughty look.

'Nice.'

'Stop it.'

'Will you let me dress you?'

Now, this one's new on me. 'You couldn't wait to get my clothes *off* a short while ago.'

Silence.

'All right, then.'

He leaps eagerly out of bed, bears down on me, stocking in hand. Points at the armchair and says, 'Sit!'

I giggle, sit down, cross my legs at the knee and kick.

'Stop that. Come on. Be serious.'

'Serious?'

'Point your toe.'

I point my toe. He drops to one knee, slips the stocking over my foot, runs his hand over my ankle, smoothing the black nylon on its way, up my calf, over my knee, spreads the top over my thigh and, licking his finger, runs it round the inside of the rubber bands.

'You've done this before.'

Nigel looks up, grins, snaps the stocking down on my thigh.

'Ow!'

'No complaining. This is a professional service. If you

154

want to register a complaint, do it to the management in writing. Other foot.'

I point my other foot, and he repeats the process, only this time, he plants a little kiss on the inside of my knee before he covers it. 'There. You'll have to carry that around with you all night now.'

'Thank you, sir.'

'We aim to please.'

This is, like, the single sexiest thing a man has ever done for me. He picks up the knickers from the bed, arranges them on the floor so the leg holes are unobstructed, tells me to step into them. Then he crouches down and slides them up my legs, over my buttocks, quickly slips his fingers inside the elastic to settle them into a smooth fit.

'You *have* done this before!'

Now he's got the bra in his hand. 'If madame would care to lean forward,' he says, 'we can proceed.'

I obey. His hands gently cup my breasts, and a small, involuntary shiver runs down my spine. Then he's pulling up my straps and expertly hooking me up at the back, doing a quick check to see that the side panels aren't rucked up.

'Now I *know* you've done this before.'

But he's holding out the blouse, unbuttoned. I slip my arms into the sleeves, let him shrug it onto my shoulders and come round to face me while he slowly, carefully, slips each tiny mother-of-pearl button into place. 'A fine piece of tailoring, if madame will allow me to be so bold,' he says.

'Thank you,' I reply, but somehow I seem to be a bit breathless when I say it. He returns to the bed, hooks the tie over his arm, comes back with his thumbs hooked through the straps of the gymslip. Pulls apart the pleats of the skirt and holds it above my head. 'And now for the crowning touch,' he says, waits while I lift my hands over

155

my head and drops it down so it falls in one movement over my body. Slips the tie under the collar of the blouse, wiggles the knot up until it's tight. By now, I've got a silly, unstoppable grin on my face and I'm just staring up at his mouth through my eyelashes.

He leads me across to the full-length mirror, positions me in front of it, standing naked behind me, hands on my shoulders. 'So,' he says smugly, 'does madame approve?'

I turn to face him. 'Nigel?'

'What?'

'Maybe just a quick one, eh?'

Chapter Twenty-One

A Dinner Date

Roy is too scared of even the thought of my mother to refuse me the night off, so I brush my hair down, don a new charity-shop shirtwaister in pale blue with a tiny red pinstripe, polish up my glasses and thank God the Aussie boy isn't around any more to see me. I think, maybe, if he saw me like this he would have kissed me goodbye, perfunctorily and on the cheek, for good. And then I set out across town for my fatal dinner date.

She's picked the carvery of a bland concrete hotel near Marble Arch. We're not eating there because she likes the food – I was brought up on the same strictly balanced low-protein diet that Peter raised her on, meat being a substance that fired inconvenient and distracting passions – but because she prefers the combination of anonymity and obsequiousness afforded by these diamond-carpeted monuments to mediocrity; no fashion victim she. And besides, she's staying upstairs. My mother likes Holiday Inns, Mövenpicks, Copthornes and Thistles. She likes mass-purchase local prints, curtains on sticks and paper-wrapped water glasses. They ground her; they make her feel at home.

As usual, nervousness makes me early. No one would ever have believed me at school, but I always experienced pangs of fellow feeling with the naughty girls I'd pass lined up outside the headmistress's office. Although Grace limited her travelling during my childhood, I never got used to the pang of unfamiliarity and faint dread with which I anticipated her return from work at six thirty each day. Went-the-day-well enquiries always had a faint flavour of interrogation about them in our house: you vill anzer ze kvestion. Rezisdance is fudile.

I announce myself to the maître d'. I never recognise anyone working in these places. I don't know where they come from, or where they go to. No one I know has ever worked in one, or known anyone who worked in one. It's as though they've been dug up from some service-ethic mine outside Birmingham and will, in the fullness of time, be shipped off second-hand to hotels in Sheffield. He scarcely affords me a glance, merely says, 'Yes, madam, she's already waiting,' and leads the way to the table. Madam. No one ever calls me madam in the real world. They've been calling me it around my mother since I was fourteen.

It's a bit of a shock to find her waiting at the table already. Grace usually makes a point of arriving five to ten minutes late wherever she goes; not late enough to be rude, but leaving things long enough to quietly emphasise that she's worth waiting for. But here she is, looking like the big old spider that she is, eyes multiplied and blinking behind her bifocals.

I approach, give her the statutory peck on the cheek and take my seat. A Mediterranean-looking youth of about fifteen immediately shoots forward and shakes my white linen napkin into my lap. 'Can I get you anything, madam?' he asks.

Yes, please. I'll have a bucket of gin and a straw and a handful of barbiturates. And maybe if you had a bottle of poppers handy, that would be nice. I could do with a laugh, and my headache's not going to get any worse. 'I'll just have some fizzy water,' I say.

My mother is silent. This isn't all that unusual, as she doesn't believe in small talk and despises those who do. 'How was your flight?' I ask. 'How's Boston? How're the lectures going? What was it like going on *Newsnight*? Is Paxman as terrifying as he seems or is he just an interrupting boor? That's a lovely brooch, where did you get that? What happened about the latest round of grant applications?'

I realise that I am prattling, and also that I am doing so to cover the fact that not one word has issued from her mouth. She is looking particularly severe tonight; she has scraped her hair back into a bun so tight that I think the skin at the front of her face must split from the pressure, and she has, for some reason, swapped her usual face-softening neck frills for a prison-warder-style grey tweed suit with a lilac blouse underneath. She watches me burble, her fingers running up and down the stem of her water glass.

The waiter returns with leather-look plastic-covered menus in maroon and, rather optimistically, a wine list in royal blue. My mother waves them away without looking at him, for she is continuing to stare at me in much the same way that police inspectors study suspected child molesters on ITV cop dramas. I finally run out of things to blather about and say, humbly, 'What's wrong, Mother?'

A silence. A small patch of red begins to form on the skin just above her collar. Oh, bugger. I'm in for it now.

'How's the library?' she asks eventually.

There's no way out of this; whatever reply she gets will be the wrong one. So I say, 'Well, I didn't want to tell you until I'd sorted out another job, but they had a round of budget cuts and had to lose some staff. So I'm not working there any more.'

It's a terrible thing, this lying, but the awful thing is that, once you've got into the habit of lying to someone, it's practically the most difficult habit to break. I lie to Grace pretty well as much as I talk to her. I think: okay, this time you're going to have to get it over with, face her and tell her the truth, and once you've done it the first time, it can never be as bad again, and then when I gather my breath and open my mouth, the most absurd catalogue of falsehoods pours out and it feels as though there's nothing I can do about it. I lie to Mother reflexively, idiotically and without control; I know I'm being stupid, that it's much harder to remember one's catalogue of lies than just live with the consequences of truth, but it's as though I'm under someone else's control. God, I might as well have been brought up a Catholic.

'So,' I finish, 'it's a bit of bad luck, but I'm sure it will be fine in the long run.'

'Oh, really?' Mother sips her water, places the glass carefully back on the table in the exact spot where its base had left a circular mark before.

'Well, you know,' I mutter.

'I don't,' she says. 'Why don't you tell me about it?'

'Well—' Oh, God, what do I do? Why didn't you give me one of those thick, twittery mothers like Mel's got, who would reply to the announcement that you'd been on a day trip to the moon with a gasp of admiration and a whooshing, '*Really?*' Or a cuddly mum like Lindsey's who thinks that everything that makes her children happy is okay unless they're actually crack-whoring or robbing sub-post-offices with sawn-off shotguns. Or Dom's mother, who's seen so much in her years in A&E that nothing comes as a surprise to her. Or Shahin's mother, who thinks that the sun is actually generated by his flatulence and sends him regular care parcels full of pistachios and postcards of Isfahan even though he writes her about two letters a year in return.

'I, um, well—' I begin, then revert to my childhood tactic of staring down at the table in total silence.

'And presumably you're working here,' she says, placing Sunday's *News of the Screws*, the one with the front-page photo of Harriet and me standing in front of the desk, both leaning on a slim, bendy whitewood cane, on the white tablecloth, 'because you're desperately hard up and will do anything to pay the rent?'

Well, um, yes, sort of, but that's not going to do me any good. Face burning, I continue with my in-depth study of the pattern on the tablecloth. Not a word issues from her lips. By saying nothing, she's giving me all the slack I need to hang myself, I'm aware of that. Whatever way I jump, I'll end up dangling in the breeze.

'No,' I mumble after a wait that draws itself out beyond the minute.

'No what?'

'No,' I say, 'I'm not doing it because of that.'

There's another silence and I risk a snatched glance at her. The blotch has spread to her cheeks and her lips are white from pursing. I've never seen her so angry. She feigns astonishment. 'Well, this must be a world first. The truth coming from the mouth of Anna Waters. And what do I owe the honour of being the first person to experience *that* to?'

She's so angry she has actually allowed herself to indulge in a dangling participle. I'm going to cry if this goes on much longer. I'm aware that the waiter is hovering just behind my left shoulder, and that, having sized up the situation, he quietly makes himself scarce.

'So what do you have to say?'

161

I shake my head. Misery has sucked the words right out of my head.

'You're not even going to apologise?' hisses Grace, and to my astonishment, I find myself shaking my head again. What's happened? Even yesterday I would probably have meekly said I was sorry and taken my punishment. But I'm not. I'm not sorry. More than that: it's what I've chosen to do, and even if I'm not using my education, I'm still doing something I'm really good at, and I'm proud of that.

I look up, face that steely glare and lock eyes with her. 'No, I'm not. I'm not going to apologise. I know it's not what you had planned for me, but this is what I've chosen to do. I'm sorry you don't like it, but I won't apologise for my life.'

A double blink, and the lips bleach a little more. I raise my chin and stare her out. You may be my mother, I think, and hope she's picking up my thoughts, but you're not my proprietor. This is what I am, and you're going to have to get used to it in the end.

She blinks again, takes another, measured sip from her glass and puts it back in its allotted position. Then she speaks.

'You disgust me,' she says. 'You are a disgusting individual. I gave you everything. You had the best nutrition, the best education, the best stimulation. I surrounded you with people who would set you good examples, I gave you everything you could ever need to take a place in the world with respect, make a decent life for yourself. And now look at you. You've sunk to your own level, you're down there where you belong.'

Numb with misery, I refuse to respond. Let her. She can't say anything she's not said before, can't do anything she's not done before. I'm past this all now, Mother: there is nothing you can do to me.

Then she says something I wasn't expecting. 'I should never have got you,' she says. 'I should never have tried this experiment.'

Oh, Christ. This is one step too far. I leap onto the moral high ground. 'Parenthood is not an experiment, Mother.'

And she gives me a small, twisted smile of triumph, the sort of smile that makes your heart lurch in your body. Sips once again from her glass, specs glittering, then smiles again.

'Oh,' she says, 'but in our case, it was.'

Chapter Twenty-Two

Stocious

I do what anybody with any sense would do under the circumstances. I go out and get stocious. Catch a cab, raging, to Brewer Street, drop into the loos at Jennifer's, put on some smudgy, red and black face paint, change into the black Lycra shift I keep balled up in my bag for emergencies, stuff the detestable shirtwaister into the bin with the paper towels, replace my nose ring, sink a couple of Manhattans in one and, bawling into my mobile, set off into the Soho night. Because, fuck it, I'm young, I'm bright, I'm in London and I just don't give a damn.

Nobody is answering their phone. Harriet, Dom, Mel, Shahin and everyone has their phone switched off. Stand outside a knocking shop that advertises 'Geniune School-girls!', and shout messages begging them to call me onto their answering services. And then, because I'm not drunk enough yet, I stop off at the offy and buy a half-bottle of vodka to swig in the street like a wino, and go shopping to rid myself of the last remnants of my hateful news.

The shoe shop in Old Compton Street is still open and I blow eighty quid on a pair of blue sequinned slippers that I know are going to disintegrate the minute I hit a patch of spilled beer, and drop my sensible black T-bars into a passing wastebin. From a guy with a felt-lined metal suitcase, I buy rings: lots of rings; huge, chunky, primary-coloured plastic things with seahorses and glitter and neon flowers preserved for ever in their depths, and he throws in a pair of big, bobbly earrings made from Christmas tree baubles which bang against my cheeks as I walk and will no doubt have turned my piercings green by morning. Thursday night: Soho is wild with overexcited queens and tarts and strippers and beggars and Muscle Marys and office workers and media players and restaurant people and minicab touts and students drinking absinthe and grubby old blokes in raincoats and ladies coming out of the side doors of the musicals tying up their headscarves to save their hairdos from imaginary rain and coffee addicts jittering on the pavement of Frith Street and sturdy beggars and bridge-and-tunnellers and fourteen-year-olds from Hampstead in designer boob tubes and heavy-eyed kids from Staffordshire staring hungrily at the video arcades and Greek fellas licking their fingers and counting mysterious wads of cash held together with rubber bands and City boys looking to get their braces twanged and fashion PRs trying to stay upright on shoes that were made for window displays and huge men with ponytails and dark suits crossing their arms outside low-lit doorways.

I buy a double espresso from Bar Italia, drink it standing up on the pavement with a thousand other people, set off to wander the area, hopelessly looking through bar windows to see if I can see one of my friends. Oh, God, where *are* you? I know you're around here somewhere: the whole world goes to Soho on a Thursday night unless they're working. My feet hurt, my head hurts, and there's a ball of red-hot metal working its way through my guts up my throat. I try to put it out with a swig of vodka, get a look from a yuppie couple on their way to a yuppie fucking restaurant with white tablecloths and five sorts of bread. Well, fuck you too. Can't you see through your privilege to spot that I'm in pain?

Try Harriet again. Still on answerphone. Get through the message and shout, 'Where *are* you? For God's sake, where *are* you? Call me. For God's sake call me, I need you!' and hang up.

Seconds later, my phone rings. It's Mel. I can scarcely hear her over the background bedlam. 'Where are you?' she bellows.

'Oh, God. In the middle of Greek Street.'

'Oh, right. Why? What are you up to?' she asks.

'I'm getting drunk,' I reply. 'I really need to get drunk. Have you seen Harriet?'

'No,' she says. 'I spoke to her earlier. She said she might come out but she wasn't sure.'

'She's got her phone switched off now. I don't know where to find her.' I really need to talk to Harriet. My friends are kind, sweet people, but Harriet is the only one who actually knows.

'Don't worry,' says Mel, 'I'll text her. Are you okay?'

'No,' I say. 'No, I'm not. I'm stone cold sober and I've just had one of the worst nights of my life.'

'What happened?'

'I don't want to talk about it,' I say, though of course I do.

A slight pause as Mel takes this in. Then, 'Okay. We'll come down. We'll meet you in the Steam Room. Give us an hour.'

I hang up, cut down Bateman Street and hang a right down Frith. Outside the Pitcher and Piano, a group of schoolboys is laughing and pointing at one of their number, who is throwing up noisily and generously. Not, naturally, in the gutter, or against the wall, but in the very centre of the pavement. I think that this must be some masculine rite-of-passage ritual I've not been let in on; you're not a man, my son, until at least three thousand people have had to take flying leaps to avoid your vomit. I hang a right back into Old Compton, walk west to Wardour, wiggle through into Brewer Street.

Pause on the corner of Great Windmill Street and send another text message to Harriet. 'Where are you? Am distraught. Call me. Going to Steam Room. Find me. Please.'

Not the best place to pause. When I look up from the phone display, the bloke with only six fingers is grinning toothlessly at me from less than two feet away, saying, 'Big Issue.'

'How did you know?' I ask. He looks blank.

'Never mind.' I dig in my bag, find a couple of coins, drop them into his hand.

'Thanks, love,' he says. 'Much obliged.'

I put my hand out for my magazine. The grin comes again. 'You don't mind,' he asks sweetly, 'if I keep the *Big Issue*, do you?'

You can't refuse a good scam. Not if it's offered with chutzpah. ''Course.' We grin at each other. He smells of old vodka and loose boxes. At least I know there are people in a worse state than me.

'Have a good night, love,' he says. I thank him for his wishes, jump over a spilled bin bag, skirt a puddle, cross the road to avoid a group of Leeds fans besieging a kebab shop, slip off my coat and push open the door at the top of the stairs to the Steam Room.

A blast of jungle, a wave of heat so ferocious you think that something must be seriously wrong. By the time I'm halfway down the stairs I'm coated in sweat and the neat alcohol I've already consumed has just got a couple of pints neater. Lovely. Save money. Dehydrate yourself and cut out the middle man. At the bottom of the stairs, a corridor leads to a door behind whose glass all you can see is a cloud of damp heat and the occasional glimpse of a body part. I drop the coat in with a girl who sits by a permanently working fan, a pint glass of iced water by her elbow, and go inside.

If there is a hell, the Steam Room must be the closest approximation on earth. I think people only go there because it's such bliss to come out again. In a typical forty by forty Soho basement, sixty-odd twentysomethings bathed in ninety-degree heat pumped out by two giant fan heaters, slip and slide in the pool of perspiration on the floor, flimsy clothes clinging to pain-wracked bodies. I fight my way to the bar, order a triple vodka and soda, rummage around for cash in my bra. I am actually losing weight as I stand here, I can feel it.

A tap on my shoulder, and Mel is there. 'Hi, kiddo,' she yells into my ear. 'I'd forgotten how vile this place was. You got a drink?'

I nod, wave my vodka and souse my thirst. Dom gives me a big kiss on the cheek while she hangs over the bar and orders. 'Heard you were in a state!' he shouts. 'What's been going on? Where's Harriet?'

'Dunno,' I reply. 'I'm fine, really. Just had dinner with the old girl.'

He grimaces.

I think for a moment, and start, 'Actually, something really—' but he's helping Mel with her purchases and not looking in my direction. By the time he's turned back, I've changed my mind.

We go and sit on the sauna-style wood-slat benches that line the walls and Dom shouts, 'Remind me why we come here again?'

'I think,' I tell him, 'it's because no one can ever think of the name of a bar when they're talking on a mobile phone. The only places they can think of are places they *don't* want to go to.'

'Ah, right,' he says.

I take a large slurp of my drink. A very large trainer lands on my lovely new shoe and, soaked as it is with other people's sweat, it splits open like a swatted mushroom. 'Fuck,' I mutter. Suddenly things get a bit blacker. Suddenly, I really don't want to be out. I should never have believed my first urge. I want to be at home with the duvet over my head and Henry curled up with me.

Dom has fallen to jiggling in time with the music pounding from the eight four-foot speakers ranged around the room. He's a restless presence, slapping his thigh with his open palm, nodding and tapping his foot to produce a constant, irritating chafe against my leg. I gaze around and see that everyone in here is doing the same; the benches are stacked with bobbing heads, jaws slackened, eyes vacant, having fun. I think I'm getting too old for the cutting edge of leisure. I find myself longing for somewhere where I can simply get my elbows on a table, my bag between my feet and hear what more than one person is saying at a time. I want nice light lounge music to soothe my harassed mind with a BPM that doesn't raise my heartbeat above its already elevated rate. Everyone is having a good time but me. I wasn't meant to have a good time. What on earth made me think I was?

I burst into tears. Not showily or loudly, but my nose fills with snot, my lower lip trembles and my cheeks are soaked. I didn't cry in front of Grace – you never really cry when you get the shock; it's only afterwards – and now the misery surges up and takes over my whole world. My shoulders are shaking. I bow my head and let the tears drop onto my thigh. Oh, God, I wish I were dead. Why didn't you just kill me at birth? Why didn't you give her a dog, a monkey, a dolphin, a computer to play her games with? What the hell did I do to deserve a life like this? Where the hell is Harriet?

Nobody notices. Dom jiggles on and Mel is conducting a conversation in sign language with a boy who I vaguely recognise by his haircut. I hunt through the zip pocket of my handbag and find a wad of old loo roll, which I squash into a ball in my hand and surreptitiously use to wipe either side of my nose and catch the drips coming from its end. But they just keep coming. I try to take a deep breath to clear my head, but halfway through it turns into a sob.

Even Mel hears it. Turns to look, and her face drops. 'What is, it, Annie?'

I open my mouth to tell her, but another sob comes out instead and cuts off my words. I shake my head, clutch my snotrag tighter and start to bawl.

Mel glances over my shoulder at Dom, puts her arm round me. 'Come on,' she says. 'Come with me.' Pulls me to my feet, puts her other arm round the front of me so I'm buried in her T-shirt and pushes a path for the two of us through the crowd to the ladies' toilet. By now I can barely walk, certainly can't see in a straight line; all I can do is give myself up to Mel's guiding arms. She drags me past the queue, pushes the door open and props me up against the sinks, where I tip forward and shudder while she holds me up by the shoulder with one hand.

'What is it, Annie? What's happened?' Mel is terrified, I can hear it in her voice. 'Talk to me. What happened?'

And all I can manage to articulate in return is, 'She hates me. She h-h-*haaates* me.'

'Who?' Mel reaches round me, wets a couple of paper towels and presses them against my face as though cleaning away the mess will make me stop. 'Who hates you? Oh, Annie, what's happened? Please tell me. I don't understand. Who hates you?'

But I can't say anything more, just let the sobs rip their way up my throat, tumble out of my hanging mouth. I'm a mass of slobbery, slippery misery, mascara all the way down to my smile marks, red eyes, salt in my hair. Mel gives up, just puts her arms round me and lets me slobber on her bosom, another drunk chick crying in a nightclub lavatory.

Then a sound of running feet from the corridor outside and a bang as the door is pushed open. And Harriet's voice, going, 'Where is she? Annie? Where are you? Annie?' and Mel lets go with one arm to beckon her over. Then she's there, holding me up, cheek pressed against my own, and she's going, 'Annie? Oh, Annie darling, what happened? It's okay now, sweetheart, I'm here. What happened, Annie? Oh, darling, what did she do?'

Chapter Twenty-Three

1990: The End of the Line

I stand on the chair and take a final look around. Scuffed cream walls, heavy thirties carved mahogany wardrobe containing a selection of knee-length skirts, cardigans, coats, blouses, washed and pressed and hung carefully on hangers to prevent creasing, three pairs of dowdy brogues. Divan bed, single pillow, candlewick bedspread, regulation wavy pattern, pale pink. Sixties 'Look, no handles!' chest of drawers, veneered in wood-effect melamine, containing socks, white knickers, bras in white and natural, sleepwear, jumpers, cardigans. Orange, black and purple half-length curtains whose pattern declares that they originated in the seventies, just like me. The desk, wood-look melamine to match the drawers, is under the window to make use of the sill as extra shelf space; like the rest of the room, it is scrupulously tidy, books lined up with their edges flush both with each other and the edge of the desk, computer cleaned each day with anti-static wipes, drawers containing drawer dividers containing pens, pencils, rulers, set squares, compasses, protractors, A4 printer paper, lined notepads. Carpet in wearwell red. Imitation tweed armchair. Kettle. Tea, Nescafé, milk. Three chocolate-coloured earthenware mugs, three teaspoons, three plates, three knives, three forks, three dessertspoons. By the desk, an umbrella plant, four feet high, bought by my mother as a gift to add a personal touch to my college accommodation.

I look, and I think: the five months you've lived here, you've left no mark of yourself on this room at all. All they'll have to do is take the books back to the library and straighten the bedspread, and no one will ever know that you were here in the first place.

And then I kick the chair out from underneath me, and drop into space.

The moment I begin to drop, a voice inside me goes: *Stupid, stupid, stupid*, and I realise that I don't want to die. Then the rope reaches its end, and I realise that I *really* don't want to die like this. *Stupid, stupid, stupid*: seventeen years of intensive education, and I can't even tie an effective hangman's knot. Instead of the quick snap of the neck and oblivion, I've tied a slow and vicious garotte.

I'm making noises; scrunching, gurgling noises from the throat where I try to force my windpipe open and only spittle emerges. Try to force a hand in under the rope, can't do it, scratch skin until blood flows. Sound of breakers crashing on a distant beach, red pain as larynx bends and tries to snap. White lights. I feel my tongue swell and force its way between slack lips, eyes begin to force way out between stretched lids. *Stupid, stupid, stupid*. I'm going to die and I don't want it to be this way.

My legs dangle and flail and drum against the wall, the chair, on its side, is just one inch beyond the reach of my stretching arch. Suck at air, get phlegm, can't choke, nowhere for it to go. Got to do something. Stupid. Air hisses out like a cat throwing up, but nothing goes in.

Reach up above my head and grab the rope. Haul. Shoulders, upper arms, wrists, scream in pain; this is not an angle arms are supposed to lift body weights at. But, God, the rope loosens slightly, or stops tightening, and by wriggling I am able to inhale, tiny gulp by tiny gulp. I can't see above my head, don't know how far I am from the hook from which I'm dangling. Try to pull myself up towards it, but the rope is behind my head and it's like doing body lifts backwards.

This isn't going to work; I'm getting enough air to slow down the onset of unconsciousness, but it won't stop it. I dangle like a kosher chicken, slowly kick the life from my limbs. So now I'm going to die by crucifixion. People died on the cross of strangulation; pain and blood loss and strained and broken limbs would push them into coma, and, slumping forward, they would cut off their own windpipes. I can't keep holding myself up like this. Thirty seconds more, maybe, until a muscle gives or something pops in my brain and I drop back into endspace.

White light intensifies, but black encroaches around the outside of the picture. And through the roar of the breakers, a new sound: thump-thump-thump-thump-thump-thump-thump-thump. Not rhythmic like the whoosh of my blood, but angry and off-beat and – coming from outside my head. Someone is banging at the door. I kick hard against the wall, try to shout, but no sound comes. Don't go away. Please, don't go away.

'Open the fucking door!' she shouts. 'I know you're in there! I can hear you! Open it!' and she thumps again.

I drum against the wall. My arms have reached the end of their strength. Strain. Beg myself for more power, but nothing's going to work. Against all my will, my hands drop open and I fall once again to the end of the line.

Three thumps, louder than the last, and the door bursts open. Harriet Moresby crashes through, face purple and constricted with anger. She's shouting, 'Don't you ever,

ever—' and then she gapes. Eyes almost as big as my own bullfrog bulgers, blonde hair fixed on the top of her head with a biro.

'Oh, shit,' she says.

Then she turns round and leaves the room.

She left me. She left me. I don't believe it. *Of course she left you. You think you deserve to have her stay?*

And then she's back, and she has something in her hand. Something long and black, like a pole. I can't see anything, really, now; white light and darkness are turning red. I know what this is. The veins in my eyes are popping. I'm dying.

The krish of metal on metal, then she leaps upward in front of me, brings her hand across above my head. Hits the rope, makes me jump and jiggle, closes the last little gap in my windpipe. I start to struggle, fight, beat at her with my hands.

'Stop it!' Harriet stuns me with a single, sharp but deadly, punch to the face, leaps once more and slashes, and I tumble to the ground.

She drops on me in an instant, slapping away my scrabbling hands, getting her fingers under the knot, pulling. It won't come. 'Don't move,' she snarls. Takes the Belhaven sword, one of the many *objets de la guerre* I saw coming through her door at the beginning of the first term and with which she's cut me down, pushes the tip into the centre of the knot and strains.

The sword, sharp as the day it was used on the eighth Countess, lurches forward, slices the skin of my shoulder and embeds itself in the floor, and the knot, cut at the bottom, unravels. Nothing happens. I'm still choking. Harriet pulls me upright, bangs on my back with such violence I think my heart will jump from my chest. And with a ghastly squeal, my windpipe comes open and I breathe. Collapse

175

and lie there, heaving and shrieking, while my deliverer kicks the door closed and starts to pummel me about the face and shoulders with her fists, to shout in my face.

'Don't you ever, ever do that again!' she screams, slaps my cheek, hauls me up by the collar of my shirt and shakes me. 'If you ever try something like that again, I'll fucking kill you myself!' Slap. 'You stupid, stupid, stupid bitch! What the fuck do you think you were playing at?'

And then she does something I don't expect: she hauls me into her arms and bursts into tears.

'Are you all right? Are you all right, Anna? God, I'm sorry. I'm sorry. I'm such a fucking bitch. I didn't mean it. Tell me you're all right!'

My throat hurts so much that I can scarcely make a noise, but I grunt and nod into her neck. Which hurts as well. My entire upper body is on fire.

'What were you *doing*? What were you doing? You can't – you can't—' and then she simply sobs, and I sob too.

I doubt that I will ever get to the point of wanting to be dead again. It hardly seems possible to me that I am the same person now, the girl on the floor, crying for the first time in someone else's arms. Too long alone, too long a prospect of being alone, too tired, too weak: you take a child and you raise her apart from that which is gentle and that which is kind, and you tell her every day that life cannot get better than this, and one day, she will know that if life will never get better, then she wants no life at all.

Ten years ago, give or take a few months, the day my life almost ended, the day it began.

Harriet, on the carpet, pulls back, wipes her face with her sleeve, wipes mine, says, 'I'm sorry I hit you. Did I hurt you?'

I shake my head.

'Is it because of what I said earlier? I'm sorry. I didn't mean it.'

Ah but you did, I think, but as it wasn't that, or was only partly that, I shake my head again. Many words are spoken in anger. Suicide is a dirty revenge.

'Why?'

I don't know. How do you explain?

'I can't,' I rasp. 'I can't do it any longer.'

And instead of asking me what I mean, or telling me I must, she just puts her arms back round me and rocks. Harriet Moresby, superbitch, embraces the world's dullest woman and saves her life.

'Stupid thing is,' she says, 'now I'm responsible for you. One minute I'm telling you I wished you'd fuck off and die, and the next minute I've got to keep you alive.'

I don't know what she's going on about.

She tuts, tucks my hair behind my ear and continues, 'The Chinese say that if you save someone's life, you're responsible for everything that happens to them after that because they wouldn't have a life if it weren't for you.'

I snuffle, wipe my nose. 'The Arabs say that if someone saves your life you have to dedicate your own to them in return.'

'Christ,' says Harriet. 'If I ever get caught in a house fire, remind me to do it in Jordan.'

Chapter Twenty-Four

Theory of Relativity

Extract from a lecture given by Grace Waters to the University of Michigan to mark the award of her second Nobel Prize, 3 April 1973.

. . . Throughout my life I have been aware of the lively and, frankly, often rather silly discussion of the circumstances of my upbringing. I have been variously described as an automaton, a role model for my generation, a stunted shadow of a teenager, a shining genius, a victim, a saint and even a monster. As you can no doubt see, what I am is a fully-formed human being. No machinery under this skin, I can assure you! (Pause for laughter.)

However, those who felt they had a right to dissect my early life were to some extent correct in doing so, though no one person has really managed to touch upon the full truth. But being the one who knows best about it, I can tell you that I have emerged with an understanding of the human potential for achievement and a vision of how this potential may be tapped. Intelligence, as we understand it, is not a simple question of who your father and mother happen to be. To believe so is to capitulate to the same erroneous beliefs to which those religious groups who believe in pre-destination cling. To believe so is to condemn vast swathes of humanity to a future as second-class citizens. To believe so is to dispense altogether with the concept of free will.

I believe that, with the obvious exception of genuine

handicap or injury, the vast majority of us are failing even to scratch the surface of our potential. I believe that any child, given the optimum help and encouragement, can do what I have done. And I believe that, three generations from now, the intellect of which I am master, and that you perceive to be so unusual, could actually be the norm. All we have to do is ensure that our children are exposed to the optimum diet, the optimum exercise, the optimum stimulation, the optimum educational aids, the optimum attention, the optimum teaching, and combine this with isolating them from bad influences and frivolous distractions, tell them that we expect them to succeed and chastise them – not physically, but by depriving them of company and attention – when they fail us, and they will all emerge significantly more accomplished than their contemporaries or, indeed, the generation that precedes them. I don't just believe this, as a convert to Catholicism swallows wholesale the concept of transubstantiation, I know it to be true. I am, after all, empirical evidence that it is so.

I believe that any child, from any background, however dissolute, however unpromising, can not only benefit from the upbringing I myself received, but actually flourish. I do not believe as others do that I am some sort of anomaly, a sport in the pack. I am the product of hard work, dedication and the will to succeed. And I intend, over the next twenty years, to prove this to be the case . . .

Chapter Twenty-Five

The Bitter Truth

'Did you know about this?' My fingers are aching from gripping the headset so tightly. The pain joins the ache in my eyes, my sinuses, the back of my neck, my brain, my back and my stomach muscles to form a generalised ache that just goes to emphasise the savagery of my emotions.

Carolyn doesn't say anything apart from 'Um, er—'

I scream down the telephone. 'DID YOU KNOW ABOUT THIS?'

She continues to stumble over her words: Carolyn, the only person in my entire childhood whose vocabulary occasionally failed her.

'You did, didn't you?'

'Oh, Anna,' she says lamely.

'You fucking knew, didn't you?' My voice rises again. I don't seem to have any control over it at all; I've been going from rag doll to howling banshee over and over again all night, Harriet and Mel and Dom trying to feed me tranquillisers and tea and vodka, following me round the tower surreptitiously pocketing breakables and things I might hurt myself with. Now they're sitting in a row on stools at the kitchen counter, drinking strong coffee and watching me with grey-edged eyes.

Even Henry, usually the kindest of friends when one of

us is upset, usually the first one to come and put his paws round your neck and press his face against yours, has realised that there's not a lot he can do given the circs, and has retired to the safety of the cushion on Harriet's painting chair and curled up in a tight ball, one eye watching balefully over his chicken thighs to check that I'm not coming in his direction.

'YOU KNEW, DIDN'T YOU, YOU BITCH! YOU KNEW AND YOU NEVER TOLD ME!'

I can hear Carolyn scrabbling around for her cigarettes. At nearly seventy, she has still never managed to give up, and cites the fact that she was never allowed to smoke at work as her justification for carrying on now. 'It's not as simple as that, Anna. You must know it's not that straightforward. It wasn't my—'

I interrupt. 'I trusted you,' I say, and another huge sob comes out as I say it. My intercostal muscles are aching from the stretching I've been subjecting my chest to. 'You were the only person I trusted, and now look.'

The click of a lighter. I can imagine her now, still in her dressing gown as it's only seven o'clock in the morning – I would have called her earlier but the others physically stopped me – face grey with no eyebrows as she's had no time for make-up, hand trembling as she fumbles the cigarette from the packet and lights up. 'Oh, Anna,' she says, 'I'm so sorry.'

'Oh, yes. I bet you are. I bet you thought you'd never have to face me, didn't you? I bet you're sorry I found out and now I can see you for the lying fucking bitch you are.'

'Please—' she says. 'Please don't think so harshly of me. I tried, really I did. I tried to tell them that it was wrong, but what was I supposed to do? I was only a secretary. They could have got rid of me at any time. At least this way I got to stay and do what I could to help you.'

'Oh, help *me*, is that what you call it? Help *them*, more like. Help them steal my name, help them steal my identity and my personality. Help them steal my fucking *soul*.'

'I was *frightened*, all right?' she cries back. 'I'm not clever like all of you. I didn't know what to do! You don't understand. I knew what they were doing was illegal and I didn't know what to do! It wasn't like now when you can just go out and buy a child, it was illegal and I'd known Grace since she was only a kiddie herself, and she would have ended up in prison if anyone had found out. And once I'd let it happen, I would have ended up in prison myself. I didn't know what to do!'

I'm so tired. 'Tell me about my mother,' I say.

'Anna, it's seven o'clock in the morning. I've only just woken up. Can't we talk about this later?'

'No. No. I don't want you thinking up a cover story. You've already had twenty-seven years to think up a story. Tell me now. Who was she?'

'She didn't want you, if that's what you want to know. You weren't kidnapped. She handed you over in exchange for money and registered you in your mother's name.'

'My mother's?' I ask sharply. There's no way I'm going to let that woman be called my mother now. The very suggestion makes me sick to my stomach.

'Well, Grace's. Your grandfather paid for her to fly out to Argentina and live there until you were born, then Grace put you on her passport and brought you home. And everyone thought she was some kind of feminist heroine having a child without a husband to support it. That was what the climate was like at the time; Germaine Greer, burning bras, a woman needs a man like—'

I cut through this monologue; the last thing I need right now is a lecture on social history. 'So who was she?'

'Just a girl,' says Carolyn. 'A tart. Catholic, so she couldn't have an abortion, though her religious scruples didn't seem to stop her selling herself in cars down by the canal. She was eighteen and had been working the streets of Doncaster since she was fifteen. I only met her once, just before they flew off to Argentina. Tiny, like you, and stick thin; little arms poking out of a tank top, bare legs, platforms, acne, lank hair. She drank. It's a miracle you didn't have foetal alcohol syndrome. And when Grace came along it was obviously an answer to a prayer. Didn't have to dump you on the authorities, able to drink herself through the recovery period with some cash in her pocket.'

'How did you find her?'

'Your grandfather.'

'Not my grandfather.' I'm going hot, and cold, and hot again by turns.

'Mr Waters.' After twenty-five years in my grandfather's employ, Carolyn had never progressed to first-name terms with him, even in the democratic seventies.

'What?'

'He went looking. Found her working a back street, her belly out to here, approached her. She didn't take much persuading. I don't think she'd ever even heard of him and your mother. Sorry, Grace. They were just punters, as far as she was concerned. Punters with ready cash.'

'Approached her'. An image of my grandfather, with his big beard and his solemn, patronising expression, leaning out of the window of his Hillman Imp and striking up a conversation with this street child flashes across my vision. The sick old fuck. Wonder if he tried the goods before he paid for them.

'And my father?'

Carolyn pauses. 'Anna, she was a prostitute.'

'And what would they have done if I'd been – black, or something, or there had been something wrong with me?'

She doesn't answer. Stupid question, really. If a supplier sends you shoddy goods, you send them straight back.

After a while, she says again, 'I'm sorry, Anna. I did what I could. I tried to make things better for you, but it wasn't easy.'

To some extent, this is true. Carolyn was the one who used to slip me pieces of chocolate, loosened the floorboard in my bedroom so I could have at least some small place to hide things from prying eyes, would occasionally smuggle reading matter outside my grandfather's prescribed curriculum in for me to hide there. I remember Carolyn for the warmth she brought with her: the smell of talcum powder, the smear of lipstick, the odd soft, fluffy hug in the bosom of her bright pink mohair sweater. Not a lot, but beggars don't have a lot of choices.

'Well, thanks for that,' I respond eventually.

'I am sorry.'

'I know you are.'

'Will you forgive me?'

What do you do? I shake my head.

I don't know what she takes a silent response to mean. 'Anna, I think I should come and see you. I can get on a train this morning, be there at lunchtime.'

I can feel another rag-doll phase coming on. In a few minutes I will be lying full-length on the sofa, crying silently again. God, let me be angry. If I'm not angry, that means I've accepted it.

'No,' I say, though my voice sounds a long way away. 'No, I don't think that's a good idea.'

'Anna, *please*.'

'No.'

Her voice, of all things, is wheedling. She sounds like a child begging forgiveness, asking for sweets.

'It's not up to me to forgive you,' I say. 'You'll have to work out how to do that for yourself.'

'Anna, won't you—'

'Goodbye,' I say, and replace the receiver.

Chapter Twenty-Six

Haven

Screaming round the byways of East Anglia towards Belhaven, one hand on the wheel, Harriet shouts, 'Okay, Mrs Humphreys, thanks. You're a star. We'll see you in an hour or so,' into her phone, hangs up the phone and drops it into the drinks holder behind the gear stick. Says, 'Oh, Christ. I hadn't thought of that.'

I wriggle in my seat, sniff and say, 'What?'

'I should have realised this would happen. They always turn up when something happens. Any chance to blag a few nights' freebie.'

'What?'

She shakes her head, lights her twentieth red Marlboro since we left London and says, 'Mrs H says that the Inbreeds have descended.'

We've reached the D roads that lead from the C roads that lead from the B roads ten miles from Belhaven, and Harriet is driving the whole thing on gears. I'm not sure if she's ever actually been shown where the brake is on this car. Or if she has, she thinks it's something you use only in case of small children on the road. Approaching the half-mile of hairpin bends after the Soldier's Downfall, she momentarily takes her foot off the gas, changes down into third, then hits the accelerator again to get a grip on the road. I close my eyes, hold my breath, and, when there is no sound of rending metal and I don't find myself showered with shattered glass, open them again and say, 'Oh, bugger.'

'Yes. Sorry. I'm really sorry, Annie. And there was me thinking we would get a few days' peace and quiet. Are you going to be okay? We could always go somewhere else and book into a hotel or something.'

'No, old dear. Don't worry about it. I'm sure we can dodge them most of the time.'

'I should have thought,' she says. 'I don't know if Gerald asked them, or they're just there, but Mrs H says we should be okay if we stay in the Kennels. You know they never stray more than fifty yards from the drinks cupboard. She says she had a feeling I might be down soon and she's made up the beds already.'

We scream round Old Nick's Kneecap at sixty miles an hour and Harriet says 'Sorry' again, though I'm not sure this time whether she's referring to her driving or the fact that her cousins have come to stay.

'Can't be helped,' I reply, a phrase that I think probably covers both eventualities. 'Who's come down?'

'Cair and Vif and Roof,' she says, which after years of knowing her I have learned refers to the Honourable Caroline Moresby, the Honourable Veronica Sewell and Lord Rufus Byng. A lot of the upper classes, I have discovered, go by these Teletubby diminutives, as they're so much easier to pronounce with hare lips and cleft palates. Harriet herself seems to be referred to as something like 'Hairier' among her kin.

'Ah,' I say. I've met Cair and Vif and Roof several times over the years, because somehow whenever we've made a dash for the relative peace and quiet of Belhaven, at least one of them has been in residence.

'I really am sorry,' Harriet apologises again.

'Stop it, Harriet.'

'Well, this is hardly going to be the break I promised you. I wanted you to have a chance to think things out, and now we're going to be relly-dodging all week.'

I actually manage to smile at this. 'It's still going to be better than London at the moment,' I reply. 'Honestly. Thank you.'

Harriet – and I sort of wish she wouldn't, because I feel unsafe enough as it is – smiles and takes a hand off the wheel to pat my knee. 'You're family,' she says. 'More family than my real family.'

'Well,' I say gloomily, 'looks like you're my *only* family.'

'Chin up, monkey,' she says, 'one day you'll look back at all this and laugh.'

Yeah, right. The screaming laugh of one in Bedlam, probably.

One-handed, she swerves round another corner, and Belhaven comes into view. It's hard for it not to, really. Like all the great houses, Belhaven's architecture owes as much to the desire to dominate the landscape and let everyone know just who the local boss-family is as any need to provide anything by way of fortification. It was built, as Carolyn would say, more for show than blow. Coming in on the Ipswich road, you begin to catch glimpses of the chimneys as far away as Much Hadham, popping out from behind the grand parkland trees that – there are those who would ascribe this to another Godiva-driven miracle – emerged unscathed from the Dutch elm epidemic. Her brief period of residence, after all, coincided with their survival, and lots of things can be construed as miracles if you're looking for one.

Harriet starts to hum. The *William Tell* overture, though the theme from *The Lone Ranger* is probably a bit closer to the truth. Girding her loins for the joy of Moresbys en masse. I pick the Marlboros up from the dashboard and light one. I've decided, as a figure touched by tragedy, to take up chain-smoking; Camel Lights in the blue box sit in my pocket as I huddle in the passenger seat and stare through the window with scratchy eyes. I'm dressed from head to toe in black: black workman's boots up on the seat, black socks, black trousers, black vest and a black silk Mao jacket. My face hurts. I've been crying for two days solidly and my skin feels dermabraded. People will mistake me for a friend of Elizabeth Taylor.

Henry, after two hours of vocal protest, has finally fallen asleep in his wire box on the back seat and twitches as he chases dream mice round a dream factory. 'Better go up the back drive,' mutters Harriet, and accelerates past the front gates and the signs for the coach park. The phantom decorators have been back, tying ribbons and bunches of flowers to the bars of the gates. I notice that the old Minnie Mouse dolls have made a reappearance. I've never got the Minnie Mouse thing. I mean, you can understand it when it's a child that's died, but why on earth would anyone think that a piece of Disney tat was a suitable memorial for a full-grown woman?

We follow the wall for another couple of miles, then swing in to the left and follow a Roman-straight one-track road through the woods. It's empty, as always: the back drive is hardly used, even by the people on the estate; it leads down to the Kennels and the stables and the kitchen door, and everyone – guests, staff, tourists, VAT inspectors – in this democratic age, likes to think that they are approaching a great house as a cherished equal. If it weren't for family, the back drive would never get used at all. You could drive down here in a psychedelic bus with loudspeakers playing *Sergeant Pepper*, and nobody but a few squirrels would notice.

Harriet suddenly swings the car over into a passing place and croaks on the handbrake. Henry wakes briefly, stands up, stretches his back, tail forming a perfect question mark, yawns and lies down again. 'Got your towel?' asks Harriet, hauling him from his nest and dropping him on the verge, where he sits, blinking, dividing his time between sniffing the air and looking indignant.

'Somewhere in the boot.'

'Get it, then.'

Like many of the most effective pieces of nature, the Belhaven woods aren't natural at all. They were transplanted here in the late eighteenth century, planted to shield the house from any risk that it might be infringed upon by the rest of the world. Over the years, they have adapted the landscape to themselves, great mounds of springy golden loam beneath swooping silver trunks, roots wrapping round the ice house and the grotto so that when the walls finally crumbled, the caves remained. Belhaven Great House groans with the guilt of generations, but their woods are a dappled kindness of muffled birdsong and ancient secrets.

Harriet would know them blindfold. Children of great houses are often ignorant of the workings of the formal gardens, careless of frescoes and statuary and the delicate stitching of commemorative tapestry. But show them an outhouse, and they'll show you where the servants used to carve their names, show them an attic and they'll show you a priest's hole, show them a wood and they'll show you the grave of a favourite foxhound.

Harriet leads the two of us – Henry starts out on my shoulder, but soon plops down and stalks along with us, tail in the air, ears wobbling – confidently through the under-growth, skirting hollows where chanterelles grow and rot unpicked on fallen logs, ducking beneath branches, hopping over scattered stones. I know where we're heading, but have never approached it from this direction before. Harriet marches forward confidently, as though she were following a path. Perhaps she is, but it's one that only she can see.

The weather has finally turned to full summer: I've been surprised on our drive, as those of us long-pent in cities often are, to see that the wheat fields are already turning, green giving way to gold and earth turned hard and red beneath the sun. We stroll in silence under trees heavy with the rush of new growth, skirt patches of bracken that play host to midge raves. I take off my jacket and sling it over my shoulder, grateful for the kiss of warm air upon my chilled skin.

Then I see the buttocks of a statue of Diana, her hunting bow slung gracefully over her shoulder, and I know where we are. A broad walk runs across our path, its middle divided by an old stone watercourse down which cool spring water trickles over cleansing moss. We make a right, head slightly downhill and come to the bathing pool. The haven.

It's not large; certainly not a swimming pool. Circular, maybe three metres across all told, buried in the heart of the wood, surrounded by a lawn of moss and creeping thyme that crushes beneath the feet and fills the air with somnolent perfume, walls of rhododendron screening it from the rest of the world. I don't think anyone has used it apart from us since the big pool was built in the old orangery back in the forties. In the spring the gardeners come down and drain it back, clear it of the previous autumn's leaves, scrub down the grey stones that line it and reopen the watercourse that feeds it. And then they leave it to the murmur of blackbirds and the rustle of peaceful growth.

Henry, after a bit of sniffing and a couple of prowls, finds a stone bench in a shaft of sunlight and settles down to pretend to be a statue. Conserving energy for tonight's violence, when he will deposit three adolescent rabbits and a thrush on the Kennels doorstep. We shed our clothes in the stone-built changing-hut sunk in the bank that hides the spot from the park, and, leaving them neatly piled on the floor, run starkers across the lawn and shallow-jump into the water. It is only five feet deep, but, shaded by trees, the water is cold enough to wrest a scream from my lungs as I surface. My nipples go bullet-like, like pink icing rosettes on a wedding cake. I flail, gasp and wait until my body adjusts. By the time it's done so, Harriet is already gently backstroking from side to side, face to the sky, composed and relaxed. My heart stops hammering. I drop onto my back and frog lazily back and forth. 'Aah,' I say eventually.

Harriet, floating, raises her head. 'Better?'

'Mmm.'

She executes a lazy crawl over to one of the seats let into the wall, spreads her arms along the top, smiles.

'I always feel better when I swim here,' I say from the middle, bobbing.

'I know,' she replies. Squints up at the sun. 'Everyone feels better when they swim here. It's a known fact. I wish Gerald would come here occasionally: then he might not walk around like he's got a stick up his arse the whole time.'

'Takes a lot to wash a stick out of your arse,' I say.

'Yes, but you have to start somewhere.'

Then we don't say anything for a bit. Henry does his long, thin sausage-cat thing, lets out a single yow and potters off into the bushes to bully the local insect life. Once he's gone, a blackbird tentatively starts up a song. Harriet runs water down the length of her arms, watching the hairs rise and fall with the temperature changes. I just float, and feel free, tension lifting for the first time in weeks from my shoulders and arms, stretching calf-muscles that have been encased in lead.

'You know,' says Harriet, 'they all hated her here. That's the grand irony of all this fuss and niceness now, that they couldn't find a nice word to say about her then.'

Godiva used to come down here as well, play at water-nymphs; that's how Harriet developed the habit. I think she mostly only brought Harriet down here when boredom, or the cold shoulders of the family, drove her to find solace and entertainment in her daughter, but the place has that magical property of happy memory for Harriet nonetheless. While everyone else was mixing gin and tonics and waiting for the cubbing season to begin, Godiva and Harriet would be splashing blondely about in the pool, the odd ones out.

'Even Daddy went sour once she'd left. I mean, I can't blame him, what with the stuff she said and everything, but I get really angry with these people who pretend they were her friend now. I mean, it was as if my relationship to her didn't exist. I guess that's how it works with the Moresby blood: the incomers simply don't matter. It was just extra-ordinary. She'd get up after lunch and say, "I'm going for a walk. Then you can all talk about me," and the minute she left the room they'd start in.'

Harriet slips suddenly into the accent of her forebears: an accent so exaggerated that no cockney comedian would attempt it. ' "I sumplih daren't knare, Gerald," they'd say, "wuh yer wur thinking abar." ' Gerald was Harriet's father's name; the Moresbys have shown little by way of imagination in the last couple of hundred years. 'Or, "Air *pleease*. Wut un *arth* does the thank she *lurks* like tuday?" '

Harriet grins. 'I think the best one was Vif, when I was about twelve and she was about eighteen. Mummy had been down to visit and I was hiding on a window seat in the white drawing room, reading behind a curtain where they couldn't find me because I didn't want to say goodbye to her and I knew that the minute she went someone would come and try to make me go and do some exercise, so I don't think she knew I was there. But she burst in with Aird – ' Aird is Edward Sewell, a second cousin whom Vif married when she was twenty-five – 'and they were laughing fit to bust. And you won't believe what they were going on about.'

'What?' I've floated over to the wall and am lying with my chin on my hands.

Harriet starts to laugh. Half bitter, half entertained. 'Aird goes, "Blurry 'all, earld gull. Did you *see* the size of thet dimund?" and Vif goes, "Air, I knair. End my *deah*, thet bairgas ecksunt." '

I laugh. 'How the hell did you manage not to end up like them?' It's always a wonder to me.

'Because, thank God,' says Harriet, 'half of me doesn't belong to them. Since she died, they've been busy covering up where she came from, pretending she was one of them, but she brought a bit of healthy blood into the family and that's what I've got. I think I'm the first half-Moresby since the Industrial Revolution.'

We're quiet again for a bit. I pluck some strands of moss and build a little pile by my hand. There's a certain irony in the fact that the blood that saved Harriet from her hare-lipped fate should have come from someone with such obvious flaws of her own. But you know, maybe Harriet *did* get her ability to reinvent herself from her mother: after all, if anyone showed pluck and imagination on that score, it was Godiva.

'What I'm saying, though,' begins Harriet again, 'is that it doesn't matter where you came from.'

'I know,' I reply. I'm not stupid. Obviously she brought me here to give me a talking-to.

''Cause that's what Godiva did. They may not have liked what she was, but at least she was a figment of her own imagination.'

I nod.

'It doesn't matter, you know,' says Harriet. 'I know you've had a shock, but you'd already stopped being what you'd been meant to be years ago. It's still the same.'

I feel tears pricking at the back of my eyes again. 'I know, Har,' I say.

'She's only telling you now because she wants to hurt you. She thought she could control you, and she can't stand it. But you don't have to do what she wants you to do now, any more than you did before. You don't have to be anything anyone tells you to be. You're doing fine as you are, you know.'

I quickly dip my head beneath the water, as the tears are starting to spill again. When I resurface, I say, 'I know. Thanks.'

'Thanks, arse,' says Sweary Mary. 'Fuck 'em, that's what I say.' She pushes off and splashes to the middle of the pool. 'I don't live here,' she says, then shouts it out. 'I don't fucking LIVE HERE and I never will!' Kicks water into my face so that the only thing I can do in response is start laughing again and kick back.

A strident, confident voice interrupts our shrieks and pushes us both beneath the water, where we crouch and look up. Three figures tower over us, dressed identically in Driza-bones, flowerpot hats and walking sticks. ''Scyurze me,' says the voice, 'you do knur that thus us priver prupty, daren't yuh?'

'Oh,' says Harriet, swimming to the edge. 'Hello, Cair. How are you?'

Chapter Twenty-Seven

1959: A Night Up West

'What did you say your name was again?'

'Geraldine West.'

'Geraldine, eh? And how old did you say you were?'

Geraldine, now an ex-Pigg, recites the magic formula that Kiki has given her. 'I'm twenty-one, Mr Flowers.'

Rodney Flowers considers his latest applicant with narrowed eyes, says 'Are you sure about that, Geraldine? You look younger. What's your date of birth?'

She's been practising this one all night. 'Fourth of April, 1938, Mr Flowers.'

Rodney nods, pleased with the response. 'Very good, my dear. Convincing. Now, you know, don't you, that you have to be twenty-one to work here, or in any establishment like this?'

'Oh, yes, Mr Flowers, I certainly do. I've been wanting to break into interpretive dancing for years now, so it's been terrible having to wait.'

'Well, your audition piece certainly showed a high degree of ambition,' he replies. He smiles, the smile of a well-oiled gecko, swirls the brandy round his bucket-sized snifter before inhaling deeply of the bouquet. It is ten in the morning and he feels that the day is about to go well. The tiny figure standing before him wrapped in a towel is just the sort of girl his customers – and he himself – have a particular taste for: blonde, stacked in the chest department, round of buttock and very, very young – seventeen, eighteen at the most. And she's hungry.

'So, Geraldine,' he says, 'tell me a little about yourself. What about your family? What do they think of your chosen career?'

'I'm an orphan, Mr Flowers. I've been an orphan since I was six-years old.' Geraldine affects a little pout, looks up at him speculatively through her thick eyelashes. Very pretty, thinks Rodney Flowers, very talented.

'I'm sorry to hear that, my dear. How did it happen?'

'My mother was killed in the Blitz when I was two-years old. A buzz-bomb. They found me unharmed in my cot beside her body.'

'All too common a story,' says Rodney Flowers, 'I'm sad to say.'

'Father was an officer in the army. He died in a prison camp in the Far East a year before VJ day.'

'Mmm. Mmm. And who raised you?'

'Neither of my parents had any family,' she announces confidently. 'I was raised in a government orphanage until I was old enough to look after myself.'

A likely story, he thinks. No government orphanage I've ever heard of pays for the kind of elocution lessons this one's had. Her voice still bears a slight trace of a Northern accent, but no doubt that's something that will iron itself out in time. 'And all this time,' he asks, 'you've wanted to be a dancer?'

'Oh yes,' she announces. 'All I've ever wanted to do was come to London and take to the West End stage.'

He puts his glass down, smiles again. 'And what better place to start? Why, you'll be right in the heart of the West

End working here. You do understand, though, don't you, that the job requires more than simply dancing? We have some very friendly gentlemen through these doors, many of them distinguished in their own right, and they are looking for more than just a performance on stage. They will be wanting you to socialise with them as well. If you know what I mean.'

Not a hesitation. 'Yes, Mr Flowers. I know what you mean. And I think you'll find that I can be very – sociable.'

He throws an arm over the back of his chair, relaxes, all formalities taken care of. 'Well, I'd say that you might well fit in here. We like a nice sociable girl in this club. It's what we're famous for. There's just one thing . . .'

She leans forward in interest, and a curve of bosom reveals itself elegantly before him. A practised little minx, he thinks. She's spent years in front of the bedroom mirror getting that one right.

'The name, Geraldine. It's hardly the name of a West End star, is it?'

Geraldine looks reluctant, then certain. 'No, I suppose not. I don't mind changing it. I'll do anything to get this job. What do you think I should call myself?'

'Well,' he considers his latest acquisition. Very nice. Very nice indeed. 'We generally like to give our girls names that are as close as possible to their original ones as we can. Saves confusion.'

'Absolutely, Mr Flowers.'

'Let's see – ' he looks away from her, as if to pluck inspiration from thin air. His eye runs down the rows of bottles behind the bar, lights on the gin section. He has thirty brands of gin, from the obscure to the tawdry. And in the middle, a flask of Geneva Spirit.

'That's it,' he says. 'Geneva. That's nice. Has a ring to it.

198

Classy. Geneva, like Jennifer, only not. How does that suit you?'

Geneva squeals with pleasure. 'Why, it's wonderful, Mr Flowers! I love it! Geneva West! Couldn't be better!'

'Well, Geneva it is,' he smiles again. Picks up the snifter once more, breathes deeply through the nose and sits back.

'So, Geneva,' he says, 'what would you do to get this job?'

He sees her make little fists with her fingers, sees her eye his belly, his old man's chicken legs, breathe in the aroma of dinner jacket worn night after night in a cloud of cigar smoke. Then he sees her breathe in and plaster a beautiful, angelic, willing smile across her face as she replies, 'Why I'd do anything, Mr Flowers. Anything at all.'

'Anything?'

'Yes, Mr Flowers,' she says firmly. 'Anything.'

The lazy lizard smirk reappears, and his tongue flicks ever so lightly across his lips. 'Call me Rodney,' he says.

Chapter Twenty-Eight

Theory of Relativity: Alternative Version

Life at Belhaven has a surreal quality as it is. And yet we always make the mistake of getting wasted before we enter the fray, which makes things totally wild and woolly. There was no chance, once the Inbreeds uncovered our presence, that Gerald wouldn't bring a couple of retrievers down to bully Henry, and take the opportunity to issue a three-line whip on dinner. Sadly, he did it after Harriet produced a Tupperware box of hash brownies that Shahin cooked up for us as a bon voyage present. So by the time we actually make it to the two-hour pre-dinner drinks, neither of us is really able to communicate at all, which is not such a bad thing, as neither are our hosts.

As we're staying at the Kennels, we enter Belhaven Great House through the kitchen door, so it's not until we're actually going in to dinner that Harriet notices that the chinoiserie cachepots in the hall seem to have sprouted a pair of Swiss cheese plants. Even I notice them, and I'm practically impervious, having grown up in surroundings whose appearance was dictated by practicality, to these obscenities of style that put others' teeth on edge. This doesn't look like a Geraldism to me: it's rather more the style of Sofe, his wife. Sofe, after all, once tried to carpet the long gallery.

We're all following each other in a large group, and everyone apart from me is bellowing with hilarity at a story a man called Neil is telling about an encounter with a group of anti-foxhunting demonstrators in Newbury, so I'm the only one to notice the slight hiss as Harriet spots the offending plant-life. She develops a sudden and exaggerated limp, hops along a couple of paces and then drops to her knee beside the first cachepot. 'Sorry,' she says to Roof, who scarcely notices, 'stone in shoe. Have to get rid.' The more time Harriet spends around her relations, the fewer words she uses. It starts with the pronouns and works its way down through adverbs and adjectives until pretty much all that comes from her mouth is a jumble of nouns peppered with minimal verbs and the odd conjunction. 'Gin, tonic, fag,' she'll say, 'and bed.' 'Walk, lake; take dog?'

I kick her ankle as I pass, which has no effect at all, glance over my shoulder as we go into the dining room and see that her hand is deep in her bag. Poor old Swiss cheese plant. We will never see your like again.

It's a relatively small dinner party for the size of the table; twelve of us strung down the sides with Gerald at the top and Sofe hanging off the end like a good hostess. There's me, Harriet, the Inbreeds and Aird, the Master of Foxhounds and his wife and a pair of men who go round in a Range Rover with Gerald, shooting things. My ears are adjusting gradually, tuning in to a world without consonants, so it only takes me a couple of seconds to translate and reply when one of the shooting buddies, the one who's not Neil, turns to me as we take slices of bread and butter for our smoked trout and says, 'Wurra view cu'fra thea'?'

'London,' I say, 'I share a house with Harriet.'

He looks at me. 'Lyki' there?'

I think for a second, weigh it up and say, 'Yes, I do, actually. It's—'

But he's barked out his own judgment – 'Burry awfore place' – and turned his back to engage the MFH's wife in conversation. I squeeze a mingy slice of lemon over my trout and settle back to another Belhaven dinner. Shooting buddy is booming, 'Marvlus day. Fifteen brace a head, nobody hit a beater, had to plough the lot under or we would've knocked the bottom out of the game market up that way.'

'Fantastic,' says Mrs MFH. 'Not too much trouble with the Krauts, then?'

'Five thousand pound a head I think I'll put up with a bit of trouble,' says Shootist, and they both collapse in laughter.

Other Shooter, next to Harriet, is shouting up the table. 'Good trout, Gerald. Come from the estate?'

Gerald laughs. 'Marks and Sparks,' he replies. 'No point in using fish from here when we can package it up with the crest and sell it at double the going rate. You won't believe what people will pay for a bit of packaging.'

'Associative glamour,' interjects Harriet, but her words fall on deaf ears.

'Very good,' Shooting friend says. 'You've got a good business brain there, Gerald.'

'Oh,' Gerald says modestly, 'not really my idea. Got it from the Duchy of Cornwall. They've been turning a profit from bran sweepings for years.'

'Bright chap, Wales,' says Shooting pal reflectively, and I manage, just, to suppress a snort of laughter.

'So, Gerald,' says Harriet, who knows that the answer is a souvenir Godiva plate with scenes of her life and interment, 'what are the best-selling lines in the shop at the moment?'

'Haven't the foggiest,' he replies blithely. 'Leave that to the accountant people. So when did you get down? Why didn't you tell us you were coming?'

'Oh, I was going to,' she lies, 'but we came down in a hurry and thought we might get in a couple of days' sleep before we bothered everyone.'

'Nonsense,' says Sofe. 'It wouldn't have been a bother. I mean, you've balanced the table for us tonight.'

I'm not quite sure what she means by balanced. The scales seem still to be firmly dipped to me. Harriet and I look at each other and, because we're both thinking the same thing, giggle like stupid teenagers who've invented a secret language to annoy the grown-ups. I polish my plate with my bread, take a sip of wine, take a sip of water, glance at my watch. Probably only another couple of hours to go.

The man next to me turns reluctantly from the MFH's wife and has another go at conversation. 'D'you shoot?' he booms.

Oh, yeah, I think. I'm dressed from head to toe in black, I have a small tattoo of an ankh on my left breast, a pierced nose and live in London. Good question. 'No,' I reply.

'Oh,' he says, turns away once more.

A plate of something that looks vaguely like overcooked beef lands in front of me, then a pot of jam. I take some jam, pass it on, help myself to a couple of roast potatoes, take a third because I realise that I'm going to need something to do with my hands, then a fourth because I've developed a serious case of the munchies. Think about fiddling with my cutlery, realise that there must be some green stuff on the way and clench my hands together in my lap.

'Jolly nice-looking venison, Gerald,' says Harriet's shooting partner. 'This come off the estate?' God, they're obsessed. It's like listening to allotment bores comparing marrow yields.

'Oh, yes,' says Gerald, 'Can't sell deer for tuppence. Great

British Public won't touch the stuff. Venison and rabbit. Got this one denuding a young chestnut in the park. Bang, single shot to the head, had to get it inside before the gates were opened or there'd've been hell to pay. Eat nothing but bloody deer in season. Deer for breakfast, deer for lunch, deer for dinner, deer pie, deer pâté, deer pasties, deer fricassée, deer curry, deer Wellington, deer with prunes, deer in cider, deer à la mode . . .'

Once Gerald gets started on a theme, there's little stopping him. Aird helps himself to frozen peas from a Sevrès serving dish and, as I take a couple of tablespoonfuls myself, starts to cross-question me.

'So what are you up to these days, then?'

Aird doesn't read much. To be honest, I'm not entirely convinced that he can read at all.

'I work in a restaurant, Aird.'

'. . . deer provençale, roast deer, braised deer, deer olives, smoked deer, deer salad, deer sandwiches . . .' drones Gerald.

'Restaurant, eh?' Aird almost perks up. 'So you must know Bob Portsmouth, then.'

Um. 'Sorry,' I say. 'I don't think I do.'

'But you must,' insists Aird. 'Went to school with me. Nice chap, bit dim, good at rugger. Owns a restaurant. In London.'

I shake my head. 'Sorry. I've not come across him.'

Aird looks deeply suspicious. 'But you must have come across him. You did say you worked in a restaurant, did you?'

I nod.

'In London?'

'In London.'

'But so does he. You've got to know him.'

'. . . deer quiche, deer risotto, deer in red wine, deer in Guinness, deer chops, deer steak, deer chasseur, deer burgers, deer à la king, deer . . . Oh, God, what are those things, Sofe, you know, long thin things made out of venison offcuts . . .'

As Aird turns to Sofe and says, plaintively, 'I don't understand. Harriet's friend says she works in a restaurant in London, but she doesn't know Bob Portsmouth . . .', I notice that the woman who has been serving the peas, and is currently leaning over Harriet's shoulder, is Margaret Burge. So noblesse oblige has won out over droit de seigneur, after all. Either that, or there's no one else in the village who knows how to carry a serving dish without dropping it.

Harriet looks up, smiles. 'Hello, Margaret,' she says, 'how are you?'

'Thank you, Lady Harriet,' mutters Margaret, and shuffles back to the door as fast as her stubby little legs will carry her. Margaret has put on a couple of stone since I last met her, and the low hairline and duck-hipped waddle you see a lot in the villages around Belhaven are becoming more pronounced in her as middle age approaches. Honestly, the more I see of rural communities unaffected by immigration, the more firmly I believe that miscegenation will save the world.

Aird turns back to me. 'But everybody knows Bob Portsmouth,' he announces.

'Sorry, Aird, but I honestly don't.' I look up to see Harriet's eye, and we both catch a cackle before it breaks for the hills.

'Well,' he concludes, 'I don't believe you really work in a restaurant, then.' And with that, he turns back to Sofe and I turn to my food.

Gerald is still going on. 'No, he says, don't tell me . . . something loud . . . come with herbs in most of the time . . . herbs and breadcrumbs . . .'

'So,' Cair shouts over to Harriet, 'have you sold any paintings?'

Harriet looks up. 'Not lately, Cair, no.'

'Oh.' Cair chews a mouthful of venison, chomps and slurps it down with a swig of claret. Then she says, 'How old are you now, Hairier?'

'I'll be twenty-nine next March,' replies Harriet.

'Twenty-nine? Aren't you getting a bit long in the tooth for this sort of thing?'

Harriet rolls her eyes. 'What on earth do you mean?'

'Well,' Cair continues, 'everyone has to grow up at some point, Hairier.'

'And what,' Harriet enquires, 'do you mean by growing up?'

'Well, I don't know,' Cair replies, then adds, proudly, 'I'm not clever like you. But I must say, you're a bit old to be playing at Bloomsbury Group.'

'What are you on about?' asks Harriet.

'Well, you know,' Cair nods and giggles. 'Like this afternoon.' She raises her voice and projects it in the direction of Gerald. All dinner parties at Belhaven seem to be conducted at megaphone levels. 'You'll never guess where we found them this afternoon, Jair!' she shouts, though it sounds more like 'yerlnare gaswur wefarndum sarfnoon'.

'That's it!' cries Gerald 'Venison bangers! Where?'

Aird and shooting man have now put their elbows on the table and leaned their heads on their hands so that their entire shoulders are presented to me, and my plate is thrown into shadow as they block out the paltry light from the two candelabra that have been lit for the evening.

'In that old pond in the woods,' says Cair. 'Stark bollock naked. Tits to the wind. Bouncing around like a couple of jelly babies.'

There's a small silence, then the MFH says, 'Really?' in that voice that would have gone along with a good deal of moustache twiddling a couple of generations ago. Then Mrs MFH says, 'Really?' in a voice that still goes along with folded arms today.

'Really, Hairier,' says Sofe, in a voice that she learned at nanny's knee forty years ago, 'you must try to be a bit more discreet. The whole park's open to the public, you know. You'll end up all over the papers again.'

Harriet says, 'No one's ever gone into the woods in my memory. They always stick to the gardens and the lake.'

Gerald takes a great slurp of claret. 'Don't see that she could do any more damage, anyway. Might as well go into glamour modelling and have done with it.'

Suddenly, everybody loses interest in their conversations, looks over at Gerald, then at my friend. Harriet stares down at her empty plate and says nothing. Many families revert to their old power structures the minute they get together, and the fact that the Moresbys have thirty bedrooms doesn't make them any different.

'Do you know,' Gerald continues, 'that not one Moresby had been in the press for anything other than being born or dying, or the occasional speech in the House, for nearly two hundred years, until her mother came along?'

This is an old, old speech. And it's always conducted as though Harriet were not even present in the room. Harriet makes no effort to respond though the whole table has turned to take notice.

Roof speaks up. 'Well,' he says, 'like breeds like, I suppose.'

Harriet shifts in her seat, throws him a gimlet look, bites her lip.

'She's still a Moresby, though.' Vif is obviously under the impression that saying this will make us all feel better.

Gerald waits a couple of beats for maximum effect, then says something I've never heard him say before. I mean, I know he hated Godiva for busting up his parents' marriage and then busting up his father's reputation, but I've never heard him take this tack. 'Ah, but do you really think she is?'

A perceptible intake of breath. Then Cair, who despite having the hide of a rhino, still sounds a bit shocked, says, 'What on earth do you mean, Gerald?'

'Well,' says Gerald, 'if she were a Moresby, she would behave like a Moresby, wouldn't she?'

Harriet lays down her cutlery, pushes her plate very slightly away from her body.

'And how does a Moresby behave, Gerald?'

Gerald nods at an armorial shield on the wall to the right of the fireplace. 'You know how a Moresby behaves. It's not just a motto. It's a description. It's how we've always behaved. "Constancy, Discretion, Valour". It's not just a matter of training, and God knows she's had enough of that; it's innate. It's so deep in the make-up of a Moresby that they could never betray those values. Whoever we've married, the children have always held those qualities most dear, acted with dignity, acted with pride, acted correctly. And now we have this cuckoo in the nest who has none of those qualities. What conclusion do you expect me to come to?'

Another perceptible breath.

Then Harriet says, quietly, 'But maybe, Gerald, I don't want to be all Moresby. Maybe I want to be the mongrel I am.'

Cair actually lets out a cackle of laughter – part nervous, part genuinely entertained – at this outlandish concept. 'Don't be silly! Everybody in the *world* wants to be a Moresby! Of course you're a Moresby!'

'Yes. I'm a Moresby. As far as I know, I'm half Moresby. And half Pigg. And I'm my own stupid self. I am the sum of my thoughts and experiences, and if I'm different from the rest of you, it's because I've had a different life.'

'Oh, dear. She's been reading self-help books again,' scoffs Sofe. 'You don't really believe that nonsense, do you?'

'Of course I bloody do!' cries Harriet.

Sofe does a little sneer. 'Grow up, Harriet. If you want the privileges and position of being a Moresby, you have to start behaving like one. How can anyone believe you really are a Moresby when you behave like a guttersnipe?'

'But *you're* not one,' I say. 'You only became one by marriage.'

She turns her sneer on me. 'I think it's probably time you grew up as well,' she says. 'You didn't get your brains from nowhere, did you? No. People marry the right people, and that's how everything is passed down. Moresbys marry people from families with similar qualities, a similar understanding of what's appropriate and what's not. It's in the blood. Gerald's father had a brainstorm and married Harriet's mother, and see how it's turned out? I don't think you need any more proof than that.'

'So what you're saying,' says Harriet, 'is that I'll never fit in.'

'No, Hairier.' Sofe turns a face of kindly reason on her half-sister-in-law. 'I'm not saying that at all. But you have a natural disadvantage, and you have to pay attention and fight it. Gerald didn't mean what he said, he's just upset. We all know you're one of us. But it's up to you to do what you can to let your good side come through and keep an eye on your unhealthy impulses. We're only saying it for your own good, for heaven's sake. You don't want to live like this for ever, do you?'

Harriet drains her glass. 'To be honest, I hadn't thought about it,' she says.

'Well, do think,' Sofe says kindly. 'You've got such a lot to live up to, but I'm sure you could do it if you tried.'

Chapter Twenty-Nine

Aaaargh!

I pull the kitchen door to, and Harriet immediately lets out a yell.

'Aaaargh!' she shouts. 'Aaaargh!'

And I join in as we run past the stableyard and down the wooded track to the Kennels. 'Aaaargh!' I shriek. 'Urgh, ugh, *aaaargh*!'

We pound through the warm night air, letting out the bellows of laughter that have been aching to get out all night, throwing our arms out and back to relieve the cramps in our chests and diaphragms. 'Aaargh!'

Harriet kicks open the door to the cottage and we tumble inside, propping each other up and bashing each other in our hilarity. A furious Henry is sitting just inside the door, glaring out his what-sort-of-time-do-you-call-this? message. Poor old chap's been shut in while we were out; we wanted to make sure the retrievers were put to bed before we let him roam.

'Aaargh!' says Harriet again. 'Do you know, I forget every time. It's like childbirth. I am simply unable to comprehend that anything can be as awful as a night with my relations until I'm in the middle of another one and it's too late to do anything about it.'

'Your relations,' I say, 'give a whole new meaning to the phrase "blood is thicker than water".'

'My relations,' she replies, 'are like the plagues of Egypt. Spotty, bloody, obsessed with the first-born, constantly killing cattle, benighted, swarming over food and drink like there's no tomorrow . . .'

'Your relations,' I say, because we've been playing this game for years and each make up analogies between times to make it look like they've just fallen from our witty lips, 'are like steam trains. Slow, inefficient, chuntering across the countryside and only really attractive to bores.'

'A night with my relations,' declares Harriet, 'is like an entire night of modern opera without the interval. And you can't even boo at the end.'

'A night with your relations,' I rejoin, 'is like eating sago wrapped in shortcrust pastry.'

'Drink?'

'What have we got?'

Harriet reaches into the magic bag and brings out an entire decanter of port that she has contrived to carry all the way home without the stopper coming out. I'm lavish with my praise. 'Top dolly. I name you Dido, queen of thieves.'

'You want a drink, then?'

'Got, got, *got* to have a pee.'

Harriet shrugs and goes into the kitchen to set up some glasses. Henry follows me into the bathroom, sits down to watch me as I hike down my knickers and sit.

'Prowl,' he says, politely but firmly, once he's sure I'm settled.

'Now?' I ask.

He blinks, gives me that are-you-totally-stupid? look and says back, 'Now.'

'I'm on the loo, Henry. One minute.'

Another blink. 'Now. Out *noowww.*'

Oh, bloody hell. I get off the loo, throw open the window. 'Go on, then. Bugger off.'

He takes himself up onto the sill, pushes his chin forward and sups the damp night air for signs of life. Thinks for a while, sniffs again, then, with a cursory 'Mwanks' over his shoulder, drops softly down onto the concrete.

There are few things more satisfying than a good horse-piss when you've been holding it back for a couple of hours. Something about the big house leaves me totally inhibited when it comes to bodily functions; I'm always happier when I can go to the loo elsewhere. With a sigh of utter bliss, I hunker down on the chunky wooden seat and let thunderously rip. Aaaaah. Victorian plumbing: adorable. So luxurious, so energetic, so gloriously echoey.

The Kennels are furnished with what used to be the nursery furniture when Harriet was growing up. When I emerge, she is lying full-out on a two-seater sofa, head up on one arm, legs dangling over the other. On a plate on her stomach are the remainder of Shahin's chocolate treats. 'We have pudding,' she announces. Pudding up at the house was some manky old stilton and a slice of chalky brie, then before the port arrived to cheer it up, we were sent off to the white drawing room to drink Nescafé poured from a silver jug in tiny eggshell porcelain cups and discuss the latest medical news on GMTV with Sofe and Mrs MFH. Harriet must have sneaked back to the dining room after the men came through and graced us with their presence an hour later, flushed with port and important talk.

'And you'll never guess who just called me at this hour,' Harriet continues. 'Only Leeza Hayman.'

'What? It's after midnight, for God's sake!'

Harriet huffs. 'She said some bollocks about not wanting to disturb me in the middle of my shift.'

'What did she want?'

'Oh, I don't know,' she says dismissively. 'Something about a march for Mummy that the Fawcett Society seems to be organising in a couple of weeks and wanting a quote. I told her to piss off and ring me at a decent hour.'

I throw myself onto my stomach, grab a tumbler and a brownie, light a cigarette.

'God, I'm sorry,' Harriet says for the umpteenth time, already leaving La Hayman behind her to return to the Moresbys.

'Shut up, Harriet. At least your brother keeps an excellent cellar.'

'Well, yes, but most of it's left over from Daddy. God, this really wasn't what I meant when I said coming down here would make you feel better.'

I take a bite of cake, roll onto my back and say, 'But the funny thing is, I do.'

She sits up, splutters, 'What the hell are you talking about? Have you gone stark staring mad?'

'No, come on, Harriet. One night with that lot and you can't help but feel better.'

'Well, yes, on the banging your head against a brick wall principle,' she concedes.

'Yeah, and . . .'

'Oh, excuse me,' she says. 'Are you implying that you feel superior to my noble and elevated family?'

I don't bother to answer, just smile at her.

Harriet chews a mouthful of brownie, washes it down with a slug of thirty-year-old port.

'Well, I suppose,' she says, 'at least they're not Frankensteins like your lot.'

This is still a bit tender. 'Yes, but the point is that my lot aren't my lot, are they? My lot are a tart and some pissed-up brickie whose name she never knew. Your lot actually *are* your lot.'

'I'm a Pigg, remember,' she states.

'Yer. On both sides by the looks of things.'

'I really do hate Sofe,' says Harriet. 'She's the most insufferable prig, isn't she?'

'Piggs, prigs, they're all the same to me,' I say, and because Shahin's present is already beginning to top up the levels we'd attained before dinner, we both snigger roundly.

Then we fall silent for a bit as we mull over the evening's events. My brain is already a tad fuzzy, as though someone's lined the synapses with cotton wadding. Oh, dear, don't think about cotton wadding. Thinking of anything absorbent always makes me feel queasy when I'm stoned. Cotton wool. Oh, bugger. I sit up, pinch my arm. Harriet, reclining again, has a hand flung above her head and stares at the ceiling like Pre-Raphaelite consumptive.

'Of course,' she says eventually, 'I can't expect them to understand me.'

'And why's that?'

'Well, I'm an artist,' she says grandly.

'Piss artist more like,' I reply. She ignores me.

'You see, none of them has anything they actually want to *be*. It never occurs to them that you could actually be anything else than what they are already. So it confuses them. They think something's gone wrong with me.'

'Well, they're not far wrong there,' I reply, because sometimes insulting your friends is the best way of sympathising.

She sinks back into thought for a bit, those wool-covered cogs going clunk-clunk-clunk, then says, 'There's nothing wrong with having an ambition, though, is there?'

''Course not.'

'So why,' she asks, 'don't you have one?'

Oh, blimey. I hadn't really thought about it. It's only recently that I've learned to live for the day. I think, hard, then reply, 'Do you know what?'

'What?'

'I think I'm living it right now.'

'What do you mean?'

'I think maybe I had ambition rammed down my throat so relentlessly when I was a kid that it's been burned right out of me. Does that sound stupid?' She shakes her head. 'Uh-uh.'

'But you know, I'm happy right now. Well, obviously not right now, but generally I am.'

'But, like, for ever?' she asks. 'I mean, I know it's fun knocking around and picking up men and staying up all night and stuff, but . . .'

'No, obviously not for ever. But you know, I think I'm doing pretty well considering. 'Cause, you know, in a lot of ways I feel like I'm about fifteen right now. I'm miles behind everyone else and I need to catch up.'

'You?' She turns her head to look at me. 'You're as old as the hills.'

'Well, yeah, in some ways. But everyone else I know had an adolescence, and all I had was an education. There's all this stuff I want to do, and it's all the stuff I'm doing right now. I never *got* the bit where you run around and learn to drink and snog boys and sneak out to all-night parties. It was all I ever wanted to do when I was a teenager, and I never got the chance.'

Harriet nods. 'Fair enough. And when you've finished?'

Do you know, I've never really thought about this. Like I say, learning to live for the day was a big achievement. So

I think now. I think about the picture of adulthood they sold me when I was a child: a life of relentless toil, of competition, of trusting no one for fear of the knife in the back and the stolen idea, and I realise that ambition scares the bejasus out of me, that this aimless life is a natural reaction to the threat of success. And I think: yes, but maybe this aimless life is actually the life I want, maybe it's what I'm good at. Maybe the training never took because I am, quite simply, not an ambitious person. And then I think: maybe that's why so many people are unhappy at the moment despite our material well-being, why there's this dreadful malaise afflicting the Western world: that there are millions of people walking around with this huge burden of guilt because in their heart of hearts they don't really want to *be* anything. And we're not allowed to have no goals these days; to have nothing one's aiming for is a bigger sin than cheating a business partner. We're no longer allowed to be contented with the old virtues – live well, do no harm, love your children. It's not so long since 'to live well' meant to be kind, to have an eye to the welfare of others, to observe your religion; now it means to equip yourself with all the luxuries. To have no ambition in the modern world is tantamount to admitting you don't deserve to exist. And maybe that's what my vocation is: to lead the vanguard of those who say 'Stop. Enough. Be content'. And having thought all this, I reply, 'Dunno. Maybe I'll think about it.'

Harriet starts snoring.

Chapter Thirty

LEEZA HAYMAN
The thoughts of a woman, the voice of the people

As you all know, I'm a single mum, and that's why I speak out for single mums everywhere. God knows, it's hard, working your fingers to the bone to provide for your little one, let alone have a social life, and sometimes you feel like you're banging your head against a brick wall, but there is one thing that makes it all worthwhile. It's that moment when you pop in to kiss him goodnight and a little voice says sleepily, 'I love you, Mummy'. When you hear that, all the sacrifices, all the struggle, all the tears mean nothing. There is nothing in this world more precious than the love between mother and child.

And there are few things more offensive than an ungrateful child. And some children really take the McVitie's HobNob, as my mum used to say. Sorry to go back to this unpleasant subject only a fortnight since the last time, but what can you do? Some people just don't know when they were born lucky.

As you know, the Godiva Fawcett Trust is organising a mem-orial march through London in three weeks' time to mark the great lady's birthday and demand that something is done about giving her a position she so richly deserves. The Vatican, by the way, is digging its feet in and claiming that only Catholics can be saints.

Typical, I say: what does a bunch of dried-up old farts who've never even been with a woman know about the real world?

Never mind: we can change their minds if they know that there are enough of us out there who care. If you want to show you care before the event, buy one of the pink-and-gold striped ribbons available at tills in major supermarkets now, and wear it with pride. I've been doing my bit, drumming up cel-ebrity support, and the *Sparkle* is fronting the money for the pathol-ogist's investigation into why Godiva's body remains untouched by the ravages of time. I care. Do you?

You would have thought every-one did, wouldn't you? Well, it seems not everyone does. Who?

None other than our old friend the Ungrateful Daughter, of course. La Moresby, it seems, is too busy flitting about her top people's parties and 'working' in her knocking shop to bother to get involved in any way.

I phoned her the other day to give her a chance. Silly me. Far from gratitude, I got the usual tirade of abuse. I'm not going to give this foul-mouthed slattern the honour of column inches, but here are a few choice phrases, to give you an idea: not qualified for sainthood; mischief-making drunken old hag; latching on to causes for your own self-aggrandisement; b****** off.

Very nice. Very grateful. Maybe we should feel sorry for her. She certainly has problems. Maybe it's difficult living in the shadow of someone as incandescent as her mother and she's never managed to grow at all. Sure looks that way. But I've got some advice for you, Harriet. If you can't say anything nice, try saying nothing at all, okay? You may be jealous of your mother, but if you can't learn any other lessons from her life, at least try to inherit some of her dignity. Your mother never slagged anyone else off, however hard she was pushed. Maybe you could try a bit of that yourself?

© Daily Sparkle 2000

Chapter Thirty-One

The Silent Scream

Five days at Belhaven puts us right, gets us back on track. We sleep, we take health-giving strolls, we eat wholesome, if flavourless, food and spend time licking wounds and talking. By the time we rattle back to London, we're feeling like we can take on the world. It takes five days at Belhaven to start the healing process, and a single night at the Ladies' College is enough to put us right back where we started. Well, it's not so much the Ladies' College itself, but the fact that Simon Clamp turns up.

Maybe he's one of the 20 per cent of the public who feel themselves to be above the tabloids, but he seems, among his stag-night buddies, to be blissfully ignorant of the fact that we are there, Harriet or me. Not that he would give me the time of day anyway. He looks through me tonight with exactly the same uninterested contempt as he did the first time I saw him, when I was seventeen years old; the uninterested contempt of an arrogant man encountering a servant, the uninterested contempt of 'in' meeting 'out'.

It takes me a couple of minutes after I've spotted him to work out who he is, and in the end it's the fact that he pays me no attention at all that makes me realise. I offer him the pudding menu, and he dismisses me with a cursory wave of the hand without looking in my direction. And it's at that moment that I remember, with a rush of those old worm-like inadequacies, exactly who he is, because this is just how he always behaved when I was in the vicinity. Jesus. Ten years and he's gone from twenty-two to forty-three years old. The romantic fringe, the lean rider's muscles, the lightly tanned outdoor skin, the blue-blue eyes, all sucked and sub-sumed into the corpulence of City success. Jesus. Simon Clamp.

And just as it's all coming to me and I'm thinking: oh, Christ, here comes trouble, I see him suddenly sit up like a bloodhound that's caught the scent and start to study Harriet intently. I try vainly to catch her eye, but she's busy taking beer orders and fending off happy hands, and never looks at me. And then, as she gets round to his side of the table and asks him, without looking at his face herself, what she can do for him, he reaches out and touches her arm, says, 'You could answer a question for me. You're not Harriet Moresby, by any chance?'

Simon Clamp. Such a stupid name for someone so important. Simon Clamp, the very mention of whom can take me back to when things were so not-all-right that I thought I would never survive. Simon Clamp, handsome, privileged, snob, scumbag. Simon Clamp who knew that people were whatever he decided they were, and was deter-mined that, if he had anything to do with it, they would never be anything else. Simon Clamp, who has lost his hair and gained three stone, and is eyeing Harriet with a combination of glee and horror. I can tell that he can't decide which to feel – his face is a picture as malicious gossip and love of aristocracy fight a pitched battle in his heart. Harriet doesn't even throw a glance in my direction, just smiles and lets a look of pleasant recognition dawn upon her face.

Simon Clamp. I remember him in a nightclub below ground in Oxford, purple velvet pianos and neon-strip dance floor, giant posters of peanut-packet women in half-buttoned waistcoats on the pillars; untouched seventies grunge that had gone the full revolution to retro chic. And I was there for my first ever big night out, in borrowed clothes, painfully aware of my gaucheness, that I knew no one and wouldn't know what to say to them if I did, terrified by the amount of flesh that Harriet had made me reveal. And as we sat on a velvet-covered banquette and I nursed my rum and Coke, Simon Clamp leaned forward in the crap-DJ lull between tracks and, without looking at me, but so clearly intending me to hear it, shouted into Harriet's ear, 'I see you've brought your charity case, then.' Simon Clamp, who smirked at Harriet as the music started and took himself off onto the dance floor as my face flamed and I struggled to look like I hadn't heard, didn't care. And inside, I found myself, once again, screaming. Do you know what it's like to scream on the inside? To feel the roar begin in your stomach, rip its way through your heart, your lungs, your ribcage and never allow your mouth to open lest someone should hear? I haven't screamed out loud since I was five-years old, but I've known all about the silent scream. There have been times when it was all I could hear.

'Why, Simon Clamp,' says Harriet. 'You haven't changed a bit.'

'Nor have you,' he replies, not seeming to notice the veiled insult. 'What on earth are you doing here?'

'Working,' says Harriet. 'And what are you doing here?'

'Stag night. You work here?'

'Yes.'

'How long have you worked here?'

'Three months or so. We both have,' she replies evenly, gesturing towards me with her order pad.

His eyes flick in my direction, pass over me, move away. He doesn't recognise me. Not surprising, really, because even if he remembered me, all I would be was another little gonk who hung around in the background waiting for the sting of his acid tongue. The friends have all stopped gurgling and are watching this scene unfold. I busy myself with clearing ashtrays.

'So what are you up to these days?' Harriet asks after a pause that's infinitesimally longer than is polite.

'Property.' Simon Clamp sits back, starts fiddling with a cigar that he's produced from his breast pocket, rolling it up and down between his fingers and sniffing at the middle. He's probably said 'Rolled on a maiden's thigh' every time he's smoked one in the past five years. 'Qualified as a surveyor five years ago.'

'Ah,' says Harriet, 'an estate agent. How nice. There's money in that.'

'So where are you living?' he pushes, seemingly oblivious to the mild distaste with which she is eyeing him.

'London,' she says breezily. 'Can I get you something for pudding, Simon? Only I've got eight other tables to attend to. Crème brûlée? Tapioca? Jam roly-poly? A good slapping?'

'I'll have a light for this, if you don't mind.'

I hand her a matchbook from the front pocket of my gymslip. Harriet flicks out a match and bends over Simon to light his cigar. He sucks, he chews, he dribbles, and finally he exhales.

'I bet,' she smiles benignly, 'you could do with a cup of coffee to go with that. Maybe a sticky or two?'

'Well,' he beams, 'don't mind if I do. Armagnac, if you don't mind.'

Interesting. He's already getting comfortable with the toff-as-servant role. He'll be calling her 'dear' in another fifteen minutes.

'Coming right up.' She spins on her heel and sashays towards the kitchen. I tuck my matchbook back in my pocket and follow in her wake.

Ten years ago. He probably still wonders what hit him. I stared around me like a mole that suddenly found that it had surfaced in an alley full of tom cats, gazing in terror through my pebble glasses as all the people who had won the charm lottery reaped the benefits of their wealth. I found myself clutching at the hem of my dress and twisting it round and round my fingers as the scream welled and ebbed. *Why? Why did you think these people would accept you? Why did you think you could come out among them and be anything other than a figure for their witty contempt. Look at them. Dancing and draping themselves decorously round each other's shoulders, and laughing. What on earth made you think they wouldn't be laughing at you?*

I talked to myself a lot in those days.

Simon Clamp took to the floor with Madeleine Bethany, one of those unspeakably beautiful girls-reading-English who lived on our floor in college and was a hopelessly dreary junkie by the time we left, sniffing and acting superior in an attempt to cover up the fact that her brain had been replaced by mashed potato. They executed some ridiculously showy-offy Easter holidays dancing-class move among the bobbers and weavers, slid forward a few steps, and then I saw him whisper into her ear. And as the howl in my head drowned out even the sound of KC and the Sunshine Band, I saw her glance over in my direction, and say something, smiling, back into his ear. And then they laughed.

Harriet seemed to have her head stuck in her handbag,

rummaging about with the same look of blank concentration with which she greeted the earlier comment. Even at eighteen, Harriet always carried a bag so huge and so full of tat she looked like she was packed and ready to flee an advancing army at a minute's notice. She sat up, leaned in to me and said, quietly but distinctly, 'There's more than one way to skin a cat,' unfurled her legs and danced away, leaving me alone. Cut a swathe through the dance floor, hands in hair, hips giving a bizarre suggestion of not actually being attached to the tops of her legs, while men and boys fell back gasping like airborne trout. For someone who's so contemptuous of her looks, Harriet sure knows how to use them.

Through the fog, I watched as she danced towards the Clamp party, smiled at Madeleine and patted Simon firmly but fondly on the back, moved on. She circled the floor and returned to my side. 'So,' she shouted over the din, 'you want to leave now, or you want to stay and watch?'

'Go,' I muttered. 'I want to go, please.'

Harriet shrugged. 'As you want.'

I was already on my feet, scrabbling for my coat. So I missed the first strike. And the second. But by the time I turned round, even I couldn't miss the commotion. Harriet was standing there, arms lightly folded, smiling like an indulgent mother watching her little ones enjoy a spot of cat-kicking, watching the dance floor, where Simon Clamp whirled choppily round in a mysteriously clear space that had opened up about him. And one by one, each time he whirled and turned his back to them, people threw their drinks over him. He had already taken a couple of pints, a glass of white wine and a pina colada full in the nape; his ears dripped with cocktail goo, and his hair, plastered to his skull, lent him the eerily demented air of an Australian politician.

Splat. A half-pint of Coca-Cola flew through the air and caught him on the left temple. As he turned to see who had inflicted this humiliation on him, another measure of lager flew from behind and washed the back of the dinner jacket he'd worn on from some fools' dinner or other. Madeleine Bethany, caught in the crossfire, had retreated from harm's way and was dabbing at her dress.

Then Harriet started to laugh. Grabbed me by the arm and pointed, blatantly, at Simon as he trickled onto the flashing neon lights.

And then I, too, began to laugh. Bubbling up from somewhere inside, the bully's hilarity overtook the scream, brought it roaring to the surface. I staggered, I choked, I coughed, and finally, a sort of cross between a howl and a guffaw crashed through the defences and the tears began to spill. Jaw pulled open, I stood and allowed them to roll as I held my belly and shook. You might not call this laughter, but it was the first time that I could remember that I'd done *anything* in public.

Simon Clamp, eyes popping as even Madeleine joined the cackles, ducked once more to avoid a flying screwdriver. He was as sticky as a stick preserved in honey. Clutching Harriet's arm, I sobbed with laughter, wept with laughter, wailed, bawled, keened and whimpered with it. And as she led me towards the door, Simon Clamp, as the DJ realised that something was going down below him and killed the music, stamped a foot and, in a voice full of rage, fear and tears, cried, 'Why? Why are you doing this to me?'

We slipped out into the night as the bouncers moved in to break things up. I don't think they minded so much about what was happening to Simon – he was an arrogant shit who was well known for never looking barmaids in the eye – as much as the cost of cleaning up 150 flying beverages. In the night, clacking down the alleyway arm in arm, I continued to laugh until I had another entirely new experience and was sick in public, in a waste bin, in a shopping centre, in the middle of the night after a big night out. Harriet mopped me up with a roll of bog paper she produced from her handbag, helped me totter along in my borrowed heels while I said, 'I don't understand. What happened?'

'Aah, come on,' replied Harriet. 'There's nothing someone like Simon Clamp can dole out than can't be sorted with a bit of Sellotape and a sign saying "Soak Me." '

Our lovely Shahin. Always comes up with a solution when something sneaky is needed. Harriet stays out in the kitchen while I help Roy fetch brandies and malts and Benedictines from the bar, and when I finally come through, the two of them are hunched over the coffee tray, on which Shahin has put three cups of filter coffee, two espressos and a cappuccino. Harriet is, as ever, digging in her bag.

'Keep an eye out,' he says. 'If you see Roy coming, let me know.'

I go over to the door and stand by the round window, half looking out, half looking in.

'Ah!' Harriet's face lights up and she brandishes the bottle of eyedrops. 'Found them!'

'What are you doing?'

'I want him out of here,' she states baldly. 'I don't want him here.'

'You're not going to get violent again, are you?'

Harriet shakes her head. 'Trust me. I promised last time. We're just going to get rid of him. He won't even know it was us.'

She unscrews the lid of the eyedrops, hovers over the far right-hand coffee cup.

'How many?'

'Four or five should be enough.' Shahin rests his ladle on his shoulder and glances over at me.

'This is your idea?'

'But of course.' The ladle flies through the air as he gesticulates, and droplets of mulligatawny end up on top of the extractor fan. 'We used to use to get rid of polisman when he come to our house. Everybody know that, don't they? Eyedrops are giving people instant sheets.'

'Instant sheets?' It takes me a moment to translate. Then, 'Oh. How instant?'

'Five minutes, ten minutes. Much faster than salmonella, much faster than botulism, much faster than senna tablet. Only one person, no one else affected. They think it something they eat earlier. Have a test, nothing show up. Easy.'

'Christ,' I say. 'Roy will kill us.'

'Well, don't tell him,' says Harriet.

'I'm not going to be able to stop you, am I?'

The two of them grin evilly and shake their heads.

And then I think: I've never really had my own revenge. Maybe it's time I did. So I step forward, give the coffee a stir. 'Mind if I have the honour?'

Harriet grins, pats me on the shoulder. 'Be my guest, old bean. Be my guest.'

Chapter Thirty-Two

Customs and Excise

I hold the door open and keep my disciplinarian's pout fixed as the last of the party of twelve in the name of Prescott shuffles gingerly through the door and into the night. Simon Clamp is long gone, buttocks clenched, but his friends have sympathetically made a night of it. 'Thank you,' they say as they pass. 'Thank you. Thank you.' 'You've all been very naughty boys,' I reply, 'and I expect to see you back in my study very soon.'

'Yes, miss,' they say, and at least one rubs his arse and looks like he's a returner. They've spent over a thousand pounds and tipped heavily. I want them back and so will Roy. But right now I want them to sod off. I count to ten as they wobble off down the street, then shoot the bolt on the front door, turn round and lean against it. There's one blissful moment in restaurant life, a moment of meditative calm, of rushing relief and idyllic happiness, and it's the moment when the last customer leaves and you're all alone at last. Of course, it's only a brief moment, and then you have to clear their table, balance the till, clean out the coffee machine.

Shahin is sitting at the bar. 'Holy Cow,' he says. 'I was beginning to think they are never going to live.'

I'm not entirely sure which verb he's actually aiming for. This particular party has taken so enthusiastically to the idea of corporal punishment that I've wondered myself. My caning arm aches.

Harriet has her hands on her hips again. Roy has gone down Columbia Road and replaced the late lamented window display.

'If any of those plants die,' I say, 'I'm telling.'

'You promised me,' says Harriet.

'I didn't. I promised I'd try to persuade him not to, but I didn't promise I'd succeed. And anyway, he's got a point. We need something in the window. You can't just have an uninterrupted view from the street.'

'But I—'

'No,' I say firmly. 'Harriet, if you do, I swear . . .'

'Can't he just – why can't we have things that *flower*? It's not natural. It's horrible. Plants are meant to *do* things. They're meant to produce flowers and fruit and berries and shit. They're not meant to just sit there being . . .'

She pulls a face, whacks at a large, glossy spade-shaped leaf with the cane and utters the word.

'. . . *variegated.*'

Shahin and I exchange looks. 'How's the kitchen?' I ask. 'Did you change the fan filter?'

He nods.

'Right, well, you might as well go,' I say. 'Thanks for staying.' It's always more difficult getting rid of stragglers when Roy's gone; that looming masculine presence at the bar is pretty essential.

'Welcome,' says Shahin, drains his glass of Coke. I've never known anyone get through so many sweet fizzy drinks as Shahin. Must be an Islamic thing, I guess. I empty the tips pot and hand him his share. He counts it, looks pleased.

'I'm going for a drink,' he says, happily fingering his fifty quid. 'You coming?'

Harriet shakes her head. 'Can't. Sorry. I've got to sort out the cellar.' The Health and Safety people are coming tomorrow and sorting out the cellar is her penance for taking time off without notice. Me, I've got to input the last month's incomings and outgoings on the spreadsheet for Roy to take to the accountant the day after tomorrow. He may have his benign moments, Roy, but you always end up paying later.

'Do it tomorrow,' he orders. 'I want to try out that new place that Laurence is managing. The Amish Bar.'

'What's that, then?'

'Apparently all the staff have had to grow big beards,' says Shahin, 'even the ladies.' And curls up laughing.

'I'm not sure why you find that so funny,' says Harriet, 'considering the moustaches on the birds where you come from.'

This makes him laugh some more. Shahin is nice to have around; it doesn't take much to raise a giggle from him. 'So you come,' he says.

Harriet demurs again. 'Darling, I'd love to, but they're due at eleven tomorrow, and I think I might be going down with something. I can't risk not being able to get up at seven to do it.'

Shahin shrugs. 'Up all night, then.'

'Probably.'

'Hokay.' He jumps down from his stool. 'I will go anyway. You change your mind, you know where to find me.'

He shambles out through the kitchen. The alleyway door bangs to behind him. Harriet sits down at the recently vacated table, puts her head in her hands.

'Are you okay?'

'Yeah, fine,' she says. 'Well, I'll be fine. I just feel a bit groggy, that's all.'

I go over to look at her, and she turns a face to me that

has a positive tinge of green about it. 'Christ,' I tell her, 'you look awful. When did this come on?'

'It's sort of been building all night,' she admits.

'Why didn't you say anything?' I feel her forehead, and it's warm and slightly clammy. 'I think you've got a bit of a temperature. Why didn't you tell me?'

'I didn't want to let anyone down,' she says. 'Sorry. I didn't realise I was going to end up feeling like this.'

I sit down opposite her, take her hand. In contrast with her forehead, it is slightly cold and clammy. I don't think she's going to die, but she must feel awful.

'You're really not well, sweets. You must go home.'

'I can't,' she insists. 'I've got to do the cellar.'

Oh, dear. I know I'm going to regret this. 'Don't be silly, honey, you're ill. I'll sort it.'

There. I regret it already.

'No, Anna,' she protests feebly, 'I can't just dump it all on you.' And then she shivers. A strand of hair has worked loose from her schoolgirl ponytail and clings limply to her forehead.

'Just accept this, Harriet,' I reply firmly. 'You've got to go home. You look like shit and you obviously feel like shit and I don't want you getting any iller than you can help. Come on, love.'

She looks up with large, wounded eyes, and her lower lip wobbles slightly. 'I'm sorry,' she says, and because she's ill, she says it slightly tearfully. I give one of those half-laugh-half-sobs as I look at her; the sight of someone else in trouble always fills me up. 'I really don't feel well,' she finishes.

I squeeze her hand, brush the strand away from her face. 'I know, darling. So go home.'

A tear drops out of one of her eyes and she wipes it away with the back of her hand. 'Stupid. Sorry. Bugger. Pathetic.'

'Come on. Go home. Stop worrying about it and get into bed. I'll see you in the morning.' I help her to her feet, put her into her coat. It's like dressing a small child. I get the tips pot and press the contents into her hand. 'And take a taxi,' I tell her. 'I don't want you walking, do you understand?'

She sniffs, apologises again. Then with heavy feet she trails out through the kitchen and the alley door bangs behind her.

I switch the Gaggia back on and wait for the steam to build up. I reckon a quadruple espresso should do it. At least until four in the morning. While I wait, I cash up. Not a bad night. We've taken nearly two grand despite the fact that huge tables usually mean that everyone else leaves early. Maybe I should think about opening a restaurant of my own when my trust comes through; if you're successful, it's practically a licence to print money. I stuff the cash in my money belt and take the credit-card slips downstairs to add to the shoeboxful already there.

It doesn't get any better, the cellar. Something scutters away into a corner when I switch on the light; I don't know what and I don't want to know. Eyeing the cobweb by the fusebox, I feel my way down the stairs and click on the anglepoise on the desk. Boot up the computer. It grunts. I sit down. I can't even kick off my shoes. If the punters could see the damp in here, they would never order another drink again. The quiet hum of computer and freezer scarcely disguises the fact that this room is unnaturally silent, oppressive, full of shadows. Everything in here seems to throw a shadow; the freezer, the bottle racks, the piles of spare crockery, the basket from the dead deep frier, the crossed lacrosse sticks over the box files. Joy of joys.

The computer beeps to let me know that it's finished

booting up and I open the shoebox. Rest against the chair-back and start to leaf through the receipts within. Roy's been stowing the incomings and outgoings in the same box again, damn it. I sigh, take a slug of coffee and settle down to separate them.

Boring, boring, boring. There must be a better way of raising income than this thing that combines excruciating tedium and gnawing terror in equal quantities. The combined hours wasted nationally on sorting pieces of paper into in and out, taxi and bus, vegetable and mineral, electricity and telephone would probably fund the entire NHS on their own. I hate it. I hate Customs and Excise and their right to come into people's premises whenever they feel like it and subject their lives to humourless scrutiny and wordless accusation. I hate that gnawing dread that starts up a month before the returns are due in. But most of all, I hate the boredom. If I could sue the government for the amount of boredom they've caused me in my life so far, I'd be a millionaire.

By the time I've got to box two, my eyelids are drooping. It's two in the morning already, and there are five screens' worth of dreary figures glowing ghostly white before me. The weight of the house above me seems to be pressing down on my back in the thick air, and my concentration is shot to shit. Picking up a handful of already sorted receipts, I realise that I've been assigning them randomly, simply staring dumbly at them and then dropping them on whatever pile my hand had drifted towards. I yawn, rub my neck, sip cold coffee and feel the tears of boredom begin to slide.

I've got to do this. Come on, Anna. Do this and then you can go home.

Perhaps just a little nap.

Come on. Pull yourself together. Arcoroc glasses, six dozen . . .

Just a small sleep. Will concentrate better when . . .

I pinch myself. Come on. You stay up much later than this without trouble when it's fun. Come on. 28 June: Table 6: dinner, 4 pers, 117.75 . . .

Just a bit. If you laid your head down on the desk and closed your eyes . . .

I can't help it. Bundling up my jacket for a pillow, I rest my cheek upon it for a few moments and everything goes black.

At first, I don't know what's woken me. I've been so heavily asleep that I haven't even been aware that I was, and finding myself in the cellar comes as an unpleasant surprise. Even more unpleasant is the discovery that I've been drooling, and my cheek and the shoulder of the jacket are smeared with stale-smelling sog. I smack my lips, raise my head and groan. Damn it. What time is it?

The computer says that I've been asleep fifteen minutes. I don't feel even slightly better for it; feel heavy and grimy and deeply depressed. Funny. I usually sleep for forty-five minutes if I take a nap. Wonder what woke—

Footsteps. That's what woke me. There's someone in the kitchen. Shahin forgotten something and come back half-cut to get it, maybe, or Roy come down to check on me. Ah, well: might as well make another coffee while I talk to them. I pick up my mug and get to my feet, and as I get to the bottom of the stairs, I'm about to call out. And then I hear the footsteps again, and stop.

That's not the footstep of someone pissed. That's a furtive footstep. There's someone up there, but they don't think they should be.

Oh, yeah, I'm awake now. Freezing cold and perspiring

at the same time. Oh, shit. There's someone up there. I didn't lock the back door and now there's someone in the kitchen, and they're making their way towards the restaurant.

Slowly. It's, like, footstep, pause, footstep, pause, two steps, longer pause. Whoever they are, they're in no hurry. They're being careful. And me in the cellar in nothing but a gymslip.

Oh, God. What do I do?

The shadows close in suddenly and my temperature drops another couple of degrees. I know what I want to do. I want to run away. But there's nowhere much to run from a hole in the ground whose only exit lies in the path of the intruder.

Maybe he'll go away. Please, God, make him go away.

A stealthy new approach towards the kitchen door.

Fuck. He's going to come through in a second and see the light shining out under this door. I have to do something.

What? What? Oh, for God's sake don't make me have to go up there.

To my astonishment, my feet seem to have made the decision for me while my mind was panicking. I am creeping up the cellar steps and I want to scream. *Please, God. If you exist. I'm sorry I said you didn't exist. Please.*

Two steps from the top, I stretch out as far as I can reach and take the old-fashioned button switch between thumb and forefinger. Slowly, slowly, millimetre by millimetre, I pull it downwards. Don't let it click, God. Just let it cut the connection and set me free.

The bare lightbulb behind me fizzes, dies.

It's still light, for God's sake, you stupid tart. The light's on on the desk.

I've started talking to myself again. Decision-making in order, and the internal dialogue is pumping away.

Can't I just hide somewhere?

Don't be stupid. He'll see you.

Why did this happen to me?

Nothing's happened.

Yet.

Yet. But it's going to.

What did I do? Why me? What did I do to deserve this?

Shut up. Do something.

There's a five-year-old child bawling and wailing and shouting inside me. I can hear it, and I can hear the blood surge in my veins.

Shut up.

Stupid. I actually think he'll be able to hear me breathe. Kick my shoes off at the bottom of the steps. Tiptoe across the cellar floor, snap off the light.

The kitchen door creaks open. Whoever it is is standing in the doorway. Probably deciding which way to go first. Looking around. To his left is the bar, and the cash till and the alcohol. To his right is the cellar door. God, let him turn left.

Frozen, I realise that I am still not entirely in darkness.

Fuck. Computer's still on. God.

Maybe it's not enough light. Maybe it's okay. How much can you see by the light of a computer screen?

Stupid. Stupid stupid. If he comes in and sees that the computer's on, of course he'll know you're here. Stupid. How could you be so careless? You think *he's* being careless?

Maybe he won't know.

Just turn it off.

He'll hear.

Turn it off.

I can hardly bear to breathe as I creep round the desk and feel along the underside of the monitor. He's still standing in the doorway; hasn't moved. Listening. My fingers find the switch. Thank you, God. I depress the raised end.

Beep.

I'm down in the kneehole of the desk before I've thought; knees and ankles and elbows and head crammed in like noodles, mouth hanging open in the gasp I don't dare let out.

He's heard. He opens the door.

I stop. Completely stop breathing. I think my heart actually stops. He's standing at the top of the steps, and he does nothing.

I don't know what they mean when they give you all that guff about adrenaline kicking in, or your mind being overtaken by calm in crises. Every hair on my body, every pore of my skin, every nerve ending within, is pure fear. Freezing, sharp-edged, paralysing fear. The only part of me that is not screaming at this moment is my mouth. Oh, God, make him go away. Make him go away.

The light comes on.

Silence.

Heart.

Silence.

Heart.

Silence.

A word forms in my mind: God knows where it came from. It's the word brave men use when facing death on the battlefield. It's a word that takes me totally by surprise.

Mummy.

I have to breathe. Take my hand from my mouth and, with infinite stealth, allow air to stream into my shuddering lungs. Let it out again. In again.

Silence.

Breathe.

Silence.

Breathe.

He speaks.

'That's all right,' he says. 'You're not going anywhere.'

Steps backward. Turns off the light. Closes the door.

He's playing a trick. He's still inside. Waiting. I can hear his heartbeat. Smell him. Upstairs, footsteps cross the restaurant floor. It's my heart. He must be able to hear it.

They cross back, pause once more outside the cellar door. Then a sound I really don't like.

He laughs.

Kitchen door creaking. Make him go away, God. Please.

He stays. I hear the scrape of Shahin's stool at the central island. He's sat down. At least I can breathe. Briefly, this improvement in my circumstances is enough. I haul air into my body, uncurl my legs to make more space for my chest. That's fine, stupid, but you're still trapped.

I know.

Get out.

I can't.

He's waiting.

I can't.

You must.

How?

The mobile. You stupid bitch, the mobile.

My bag is on the floor beside me, round the back of the desk out of his eye view. The mobile.

Save me.

It's off. I stuff it under my tunic and switch it on, muffling the beep. The welcome message takes half a lifetime to load; all the time, I can hear him shift about on the stool. What's he doing?

Menu.

No bars.

Shit. Basement. Widest coverage in the UK, my arse.

What's the use of a network that lets you talk from a beach in Cornwall when you can't talk from a basement in London?

I cast around. There is nothing here, no way out, nothing. We had the coal hole blocked up when we brought the computer down here in case of burglars. Good joke.

He's waiting.

You've got to go to the top of the stairs.

No.

You've got to do it.

I start to cry, stifled wimpers which I cover with my sleeve. *Please don't make me. I'm so afraid. Please.*

You have to.

Please.

You've got to GO.

And I know I'm right. But I'm snivelling like a cornered bully and the five-year-old's screams have reached full volume.

GO NOW.

I go. Crawl out from under the desk and, because my legs won't hold me, slither over the slimy floor to the foot of the steps.

He shifts on his stool and I make ready to bolt back to my hiding place. But then he settles down.

Please, God, please, please.

Don't let the steps creak. I go up slowly on my knees, weight all thrown over onto the wall side. Check the bars on the phone as we rise. One. Nothing. Two. Nothing. Three. Nothing. Four. Nothing. Five. Nothing. Six. Nothing. Seven. Nothing. Eight. The display flickers; for a split second a bar appears, then nothing.

There are only two steps between me and the door. My legs are shaking.

Go on. Go up.

I can't.

GO UP.

I go. Nearly drop the phone because of the sweat on my hands.

He's humming in the next room 'My Heart Belongs to Daddy'. And there's a strange scraping noise, like metal on metal. What's he doing?

A bar. I punch in 999 with hurried fingers, as though failing to act will make it go away.

It rings, it seems, for ever, then a woman's voice.

'Emergency. Which service?'

'Police.'

'Sorry, caller. Can you speak up?'

It sounds to me like I'm shouting already. 'Police,' I repeat.

'Putting you through.'

The line crackles, starts to ring again.

'Hello, police. What's your emergency?'

Suddenly, I can't say anything. Draw a couple of sobbing breaths, then, 'Please help me.'

'What's the nature of your emergency?'

'I – there's someone here.'

'Speak up if you can, caller.'

'I can't,' I whisper. 'He's just outside the door.'

Suddenly, background noise drops away. 'Where are you?' she says.

'Chelsea Ladies' College,' I say.

'What's the address?'

I give her the address, but my voice is shaking so much it comes out as a gurgle.

'I couldn't hear that, caller. You'll have to repeat it. Tell me the postcode.'

I whisper, very slowly, very clearly. In the kitchen, the scraping continues. I don't think he's heard me.

'Is that a school? Are there minors there with you?'

I almost laugh. 'No. A restaurant. I'm in the cellar.'

'And you have an intruder?'

'Yes.'

'Stay on the line, caller,' she says. 'There's a car on its way.'

Stay on the line? What kind of fucking idiot are you? I've hung up and started back down the stairs before you can say constabulary.

The stool in the kitchen scrapes back. He's standing up.

Everything racing again; internal organs scrambling to be first off the ship. I'm going to scream. I will scream. No time to get to the desk. I throw myself off the steps and scrabble in among a pile of cardboard boxes underneath. The thunder and rustle of my landing effectively disguises everything else. I scramble in as close to the wall as I can, don't even look for spiders, shrink down, make myself tiny. Maybe he won't see me. Maybe I'm invisible.

Silence. No sound from upstairs, no creak of door hinges.

Where's he gone? Is he in here already? Standing on the stairs, listening? Waiting for me to move and betray my position?

My nose is pressed against a Del Monte logo; cling peaches. We sell a lot of tinned peaches and cream because the punters like to throw them at each other. Back when life was simple. I chew the back of my hand, wait like a prey animal crouched in bracken as a buzzard sweeps overhead.

Silence.

No way. Don't even think it. He's in here, and he's waiting.

Silence.

The display on the mobile says it's been five minutes. Surely no one can go five minutes without making a noise.

You have.

I'm frightened.

He can too.

I'm getting cramp in my hip.

Don't even think about it.

Aargh.

Don't. Don't fucking move!

Aargh.

Footsteps upstairs. Oh, God. Careful footsteps, making their way across the kitchen pausing by the island. Shuffling. Moving on.

Pushing open the kitchen door. Pausing on the threshold. I shut my eyes.

'Hello?' A different voice, a London accent, trained in authority. 'Police?'

I explode from my hiding place, cardboard boxes around me, jump up and down and try to shake the pain from my upper leg. 'HAAAAH!' I shout. Then, 'I'm down here!' Then I collapse on the floor and start to kick, hard, at the prop on the stairs. The door opens and a couple of men in hats stand looking down at me in concern.

'Are you all right down there?' asks the man in front, who looks a good ten years older than his near-adolescent companion.

'Haaaargh!' I reply, almost laughing through the agony, the relief is so great. 'Cramp!'

They come down the stairs two by two, and the elder grabs my ankle, pulls. I let out a howl of pain, and everything stops.

'Christ,' I mutter from the floor.

'Blimey,' says young copper. 'Thought you were hurt for a minute.'

I take a moment to compose myself, sit up, wiping my eyes. 'No. I'm okay. Just scared witless.'

'We had a report of an intruder,' says older copper.

'Yes. That was me.'

'You're okay?'

'Yes. Thank you.'

'No sign of anyone upstairs now,' he says. 'And no sign of a break-in. How did they get in?'

I don't know how many hours they spend on the subject at training college, but I've never met a policeman yet who didn't manage to make you feel like a total fool. 'Stupid.' I say what I know they'll be thinking anyway. 'The other staff left and I forgot to lock the door behind them. Sorry.'

Young copper offers me a hand up, which I take. Stand there, brushing bits of ancient distemper off my clothes.

'That's not very sensible,' says older copper. Christ. He can't be more than a couple of years older than me, but it feels like getting a lecture from a headmaster.

'Doh,' I reply. It's amazing how quickly you can get your sarcasm back after a fright. 'I think if I'd remembered I'd've done something about it.'

Older copper gives me a big smile. Nice teeth, nice eyes. Short, sandy hair under the checkered hat; probably quite good fun down the pub.

'No harm done,' he says. 'Though I think you'd better come up and have a look at something.'

I've been thinking the same thing myself. I've had enough of this cellar to last me a good deal longer than the very short lifetime I recently thought I was going to have. I follow the two of them up into the restaurant. They've turned on the top lights. Tables four, five and six, shoved together for the big party, look sad and grimy, half-drunk brandies lolling among seedy ashtrays. 'We had a late table,' I explain. 'We were going to clear it up tomorrow.'

The two of them nod wisely. I'm still shaking. Pop behind the bar. 'I need a drink. Can I get you anything?'

'Thanks, no,' says younger copper.

'I thought that not drinking on duty thing was a myth?'

'No,' says older copper. 'You can drink under special circumstances.'

'Oh, yes?' I pour a couple of fingers of brandy into a snifter, sling in some ice. 'And what are those?'

'Well, obviously you can't if you're a common–or–garden uniform,' says older copper, 'but it's absolutely essential under certain circumstances if you're a pathologist.'

'Or a forensic psychiatrist,' says younger copper.

'Or if you work under cover,' says older one, 'specially if you handle guns. But you've got to have one particular qualification.'

'What's that?'

'Full membership of Equity,' says younger copper.

Ah. Comedians. Just what I need.

'So have they taken anything?'

'I don't know, love,' says older copper. God, I hate it when people call me love. 'You'll have to tell us, I'm afraid.'

Nothing has changed in the restaurant. It looks no more and no less crappy than usual. I shake my head.

'You do believe there was someone here, don't you?'

They both nod. 'Oh, yes. We believe you.'

Older copper nods back towards the kitchen. 'You haven't sacked anyone lately or anything, have you? Had any business rows? Fallen out with anyone?'

'Nope. Why?'

'Well . . .' He pauses. 'I think someone's not very popular around here.'

Oh, Christ. 'What?'

'You'd better come and look.'

He leads the way into the kitchen. Shahin, thank God, has made a good job of clearing up before he cleared out, and everything gleams under the neon strip-lights. So it takes, like, seven-tenths of a second for me to see what's out of place.

The two big knives have been taken from the butcher's block and lie, their tips worn away, on the worktop on the central island, by the stool. And scratched into the stainless steel, remarkably deeply by a determined hand, is a single word.

TRAITOR.

Chapter Thirty-Three

A Question of Race

My nerves get the better of me, and I don't want to go and hang about on the street waiting for a cab. So we sit in the front of the restaurant, back door firmly bolted, and have another brandy while we wait for a minicab. Roy's gone home, cursing me because there's no way the insurance will pay out for the worktop when I left the door unlocked and the alarm switched off, and Shahin has finally been persuaded to go home because I think that he'll probably get banged up himself if he makes one more promise to hunt down and kill my assailant.

'I'm so sorry about this,' says Harriet. 'It never occurred to me that any of them were nutty enough to do something like this.'

'Not your fault. If we should blame anyone, we should blame Leeza Hayman. If she wasn't stirring up all this grief none of this would've happened.'

'I don't know,' says Harriet. 'It's not like Leeza Hayman holds the copyright on stirring up the mob.'

'What did you actually say to her when she called down at Belhaven? Did you really say the things she said you did?'

'Well, sort of,' says Harriet. 'You know what it's like. Cut out a couple of sentences in the middle, and you can make someone say anything you want to.'

'So what did you say?'

'Look, I didn't really think about it. I picked up the phone while you were in the bog, and it was the Witch of Hayman on the other end going on about this beatification business and organising some sort of march or something, so I said that I didn't think there was any way that any church in the world would accept that a polygamous former stripper was qualified for sainthood, however much good she'd done, and that anyway, if I wanted to get involved in some sort of campaign, it wouldn't be one run by a lying, mischief-making drunken old hag like her and would she please get off the line. So then she said something like "So what you're saying is that you don't want to have anything to do with cherishing your mother's memory", and I said no, I don't want to have anything to do with her pitiful attempts at latching on to causes for her own self-aggrandisement and would she please bugger off and leave me alone as I was really busy. And then I hung up.'

'Oh, Harriet.'

'Don't oh Harriet me. You'd've done the same thing.'

'Um, I'm not the one who seems to be permanently in the firing line. How many emails have you had now?'

She raises her eyes to the ceiling, counts. 'Something around the hundred mark, I guess. But you know, email's pretty harmless. It's not like they've got our address or anything.'

'Yes, but it's still pretty unpleasant.'

She shrugs. 'Well, obviously. But it's hardly like I'm not used to being public enemy number one. Everyone hates me. Nothing new there.'

'I don't hate you, Haz.'

'You don't count. You're not allowed to hate me. You

owe me. We're inextricably bound together by bonds of duty.' She smiles grimly.

'Come on,' I say. 'I actually think you're brilliant.' Poor old Harriet. Things never seem to rain in her life when they could pour.

'Don't turn fruity on me. I've got enough fruitcakes to deal with without you going the same way. You should be mad as hell at me for getting you into a situation like that, not being all forgiving. I mean, what if this is only the beginning? What if we're going to spend our entire lives being pursued by crazies out for my blood? What? Are you going to stick around saying how brilliant I am then?'

I think for a bit, have a drink, then nod. 'Yeah.'

'Yeah what?'

'Haz, I don't have a choice in the matter.'

'Of course you do.'

'I don't. Aside from the fact that you're my best friend and I love you and I don't want to see you in trouble, there's the small matter of race.'

'Oh, fuck,' says Harriet. 'What are you on about now?'

'You know,' I say. 'I can't walk away from you and you can't walk away from me. I'm an Arab and you're Chinese.'

Harriet drains her drink. 'Good God,' she says. 'I'd forgotten about that.'

'I hadn't.'

Chapter Thirty-Four

1967: Knowledge is power

Leonard Wildenstein is having a high time of it. With Mrs W safely tucked away, recovering from her latest bout of corrective surgery behind pink stucco walls in Los Angeles, he is making the most of his freedom. He smiles at his reflection in the mirrored lift walls, chuckles with enjoyment and steps silently onto the thick carpet. It's been a long day, but Leonard Wildenstein is used to long days, and long nights. The difference, he always says when asked the secret formula, between men who succeed and men who don't, is stamina. He has had little sleep over the past four nights, and fully intends to get little more between now and Thursday. He is, after all, in Swinging London, most happening city on the planet, and what you do in Swinging London is swing. Every which way. Up, down and sideways. And when you've finished, you swing some more.

Looking in the mirror, Leonard Wildenstein enjoys what he sees. He enjoys it because he knows how the world really works, and that there is virtually nothing that a mirror can reflect that can't be overcome by a couple of million in the bank and a line of credit with the Winston corporation. It entertains him that a man who is very nearly as wide as he is tall, a man whose face and neck are permanently coated with a fine layer of sweat and whose remaining strands of hair are plastered to his scalp like seaweed should have the pulling power of Narcissus.

But it's been a long day. Sometimes even Leonard Wildenstein's stamina begins to flag after twelve straight hours watching them parade past, say their five lines' worth and fix him with a speculative pout. He feels old tonight: twelve hours in a theatre chair after the six hours' exercise he treated himself to last night is a lot for a fifty-nine-year-old body to deal with. He fancies a long bath and a short cocktail, and maybe a little lie-down in his Ritzy-titsy bed with its clean new sheets, maybe a little room service.

A knock.

'Who is it?' shouts Leonard Wildenstein.

'Concierge, sir,' comes the answer.

'Don't bother tonight,' he replies. 'I don't need turning down.'

'No, sir, I have an urgent package for you.'

He raises his eyebrows; he wasn't expecting anything until the morning when another batch of CVs is due from the casting girl.

He glides over the thick cream carpet, opens up.

'A package?'

'Yes, sir.' The concierge is wearing a tail-coat which hangs a bit tight over the shoulders; must be hotel issue. Certainly not made to measure.

'Who brought it?'

'A young lady, sir. She's waiting in reception. She wanted to come up but as she didn't have an appointment . . .'

'What does she look like?'

'Small – petite, I should say,' begins the concierge with the assurance of one who notes everything about everyone who passes through his doors, 'very, very blonde. Young. Not more than twenty-four I'd say. Holds herself beautifully, speaks well, well turned out. Pink suit, well-cut, good figure, though it's probably not my place to say so. Ladylike. That's the main impression.'

Ah. Another one trying to get round the audition procedure. All dressed up to suit the part. 'What did she say her name was?'

'Godiva, sir. Godiva Fawcett.'

'Well, tell her to apply via her agent like everyone else. I'm a busy man.'

'Er—' The concierge stays in the doorway, looking uncertain. 'She claims she knows you, Mr Wildenstein, sir.'

'Never heard of her.'

'Well, if you'd be so kind.' He offers a padded envelope. 'She said if you look at this, you would remember who she is.'

Wildenstein sighs. Takes the envelope, tears it open with the paper knife thoughtfully provided on the baize-covered desk. Half-pulls the contents out, glances briefly at it and, face betraying none of the emotion he feels, says, 'Send her up. Give me five minutes.'

The concierge bows, stands for a moment looking hopeful. Wildenstein sighs again, digs in his trouser pocket and palms the man five shillings. Feels a twinge of resentment: it's bad enough that the guy should bring a situation like this without expecting a tip into the bargain.

In the five minutes left to him, he reassumes his jacket, combs his hair, quickly places a low, hard chair in front of the desk before assuming the power position in the padded leather throne behind it. Spreads out some papers, lights a cigar and waits.

Another knock.

'Come,' cries Leonard Wildenstein, and begins to stare intensely at his papers, chewing all the while on the stogie. He's learned a trick or two in his years in the business;

Leonard Wildenstein has never needed a self-help book to show him how to wrong-foot a rival.

Quiet steps across the carpet; the squeak of expensive leather shoes, then silence. 'Gud eev'ning, Mr Vildenshtine,' says a quiet voice of cut-glass precision, then nothing more.

He is strongly tempted to look up; this is not the sloppy cockney of last night. This chick has studied the greats: this is the voice of Audrey Hepburn in *My Fair Lady*, of Joan Greenwood in *Kind Hearts and Coronets*, the rose-garden nostalgia of *Mrs Miniver*. With an effort of will, he keeps his eyes clamped on the page, replies, 'Wilden*steen*. Take a seat, why don't you?'

'Thenk yuh. I pruffar to stend,' says Godiva. She's learned a trick or two of her own. She continues to stand, quietly, waiting for him to make the first move; he can see the pink pointed toes of her stilettos held just so in first position.

Eventually, the waiting becomes too much. He crumbles, looks up, gets the surprise of his life. Last night's cut-price Marilyn has transformed into a glassy Tippi Hedren: Nordic hair swept back into an elegant, understated beehive, the fuchsia lips now smeared with something palely pink and barely there. Classy, he thinks. The dame's got class. And she can act, too, or so the evidence suggests.

'So what's with the Godiva thing?' he says.

She shrugs, replies, 'That's my real name. For obvious reasons, I don't use it in the club.'

'Quite a name,' he says.

She nods. 'I like it.'

'Chose it yourself, huh?'

She simply smiles, waits for the next move in the game.

'So what do you want, young lady?'

'Oh.' She smiles once more, a quiet little smile where one

side of her mouth only curls up and those emerald cats' eyes do nothing at all. 'I'm here for my audition.'

'And what audition would that be?' The cigar comes out of the mouth and is pinched between thumb and forefinger. Then he lays it quickly, slightly sheepishly, in the ashtray as a picture of her fingers doing something quite similar flashes across his memory.

'I want to play the part,' she says, 'of Melanie DuChamp.'

He's been expecting this. 'Honey,' he says, 'I've got every actress in London chasing that part.'

'Ah,' replies Godiva, and the cats' eyes twinkle merrily, 'but I have special talents, as you know.'

Leonard Wildenstein picks up the envelope delivered by the concierge. Takes his lighter from beside the ashtray and sets fire to one corner. The photographic paper inside catches, blooms, burns blue and orange. He continues to hold it until the flame licks his fingers, then, smiling, drops it beside his cigar butt.

'Oh, what a shame,' says Godiva, and from her elegant little clutch bag comes another envelope. 'I was afraid you might have an accident,' she says, 'so I brought you some more to replace those ones. And don't worry. I have plenty more in a safe place if you should need them.'

She looks around the suite: the fresh flowers, the stark white of the billowing nets across the windows, the rich upholstery of the reproduction Louis Quinze sofa set. 'I don't know,' she says. 'If I had a room like this, I'd want to show it off rather than spending an evening in a bachelorette flat in Soho. It's so clean. You never know what you might catch on unfamiliar turf.'

'You couldn't even remember my name last night,' he protests.

'Well, no,' says Godiva, and from the bag – it's amazing

what a woman can fit into a leather pocket the size of a paperback – comes a reel of audio tape. 'That's not strictly true. It was more that I wanted to hear you say it yourself for me. It's always so nice when a gentleman introduces himself. Makes you feel more – I don't know – secure. And a girl needs security in this tough old world, wouldn't you say?'

Chapter Thirty-Five

Make Your Feelings Known

Leeza's march takes place on a deliciously sunny Saturday two weeks later. I go down to act as Harriet's eyes and ears, drink in the sights and sounds to give back to her later. As usual they've closed Westminster tube station, so I schlep all the way up the embankment on foot and arrive five minutes before the march is due to move off. And as I emerge from round the back of the abbey into Parliament Square, the first thing I see is the drag queens. Magnificent drag queens, dozens of them, each one at least a head taller than the tallest of the rest of the crowd, platform shoes playing havoc with the grass on the square. And every single one a Godiva. They've come as every stage of her career; period Godiva, bikini Godiva, Western Godiva, Duchess Godiva in tiara and sash, Charity Godiva, cute and demure in ankle-cropped khaki trousers and an open-necked shirt, even a couple in white drapey dresses, wings and haloes, only their smooth white beehives and pussycat sunglasses suggesting that they have jumped the gun and become Sainted Godivas. Harriet would love this.

The drag queens are deeply excited by the presence of the TV crews, and are striking poses and waving their hands elegantly when asked, chattering like starlings to anyone who'll listen. 'Ooh, I loved her,' they say, 'even more than

Joan Crawford. Even more than Princess Grace.' 'Darling, she was faaabulous.' And as usual, the TV crews are reciprocating, ignoring the hundreds of normal people gathered in the square, tutting with impatience as a small child in dungarees runs, shouting with joy, into shot, saying, 'Excuse me, we're trying to film here,' in pointed tones to anyone who dares to give tongue in their vicinity. But I can understand why. TV always favours the freak above the average, and media people find it hard to register enthusiasms as anything other than the province of the mildly cracked. There must be a thousand representatives of the 'real' world gathered on this lawn today; once the march reaches our screens tonight, it will seem as though the crowd consisted of forty-odd drag queens and Leeza Hayman.

I step over to take a couple of pictures. I know Harriet will be so happy to see that the Divettes are still in action, as Godiva would have loved it in her lifetime. Imagine: there can be no greater compliment than to have the world's queens want to be you. A couple of Duchess Godivas spot me and start to cackle and point, putting one hand on their hips and the other behind their heads, thrusting their hips towards the camera and pouting.

As I press the shutter, a voice beside me says, 'Well, I call it disgusting,' and I know that I have fallen in among the hard line of the Fawcett Trust. I hadn't even noticed I'd done it. That's the trouble with Fawcetteers; they look so bog average that it's hard to spot you're among them before it's too late.

'Don't you think it's disgusting?' says the voice again. Then, to me, 'You shouldn't encourage them.'

Oh, bugger: it's the Solemnity of the Occasion group, the scariest and most hard line of the lot. These were the people who tried to tear down the gates of Belhaven to express their disapproval of the family's ostracism of their idol, the ones who tune out all facts, however well established, that they find inconvenient. It will be from among this group that the hatemails are coming, the You should be ashamed to be alive, the You've let down her memory, the Your life's not just your own, you know, it belongs to all of us, the I know where you live, the You don't deserve to be alive when she's dead, the Don't you know how lucky you are? the Why did God take away an angel and leave us you? messages.

Actually, I should have spotted them, considering the reason that this crowd has gathered. They are the Byrite women, those women who have a plastic bag permanently welded to their wrist, who tart their crappy hair up with jaunty little plastic bows, who wear brave lipstick on their downturned mouths, who feel that life has dealt them out a hard card and are determined to make the point by refusing to waste money, ever. Their lives have been blighted by the fact that real men never produce the passion of the romance novel. They wear their victimhood like a sash of honour and honestly believe that, had Godiva met them, she would have been their best friend, would have understood their woe, brought them solace in their grief. Imitating Godiva, they talk about spreading love and understanding, about accepting people for what they are, and, when confronted with a Godiva drag queen, react like Klan members outside a synagogue.

I lower the camera and smile sweetly. 'I think they look lovely.' And then I add something that perhaps is unkind under the circumstances. 'And anyway, Godiva was really proud that she had such a massive gay following.'

The air fills with the rustle of plastic bags as eight pairs of arms fold across chests. Eight chins retract like pigeons' crops. Then, 'You don't know what you're talking about,' says the main spokesperson, and her black plastic bobbles jiggle in dispute. As my eyes drift over her, I realise that I don't look out of place at all, because she, too, is dressed all in black. And so are her companions. The gaggle of Godivas looks like a gang of rogue birds of paradise invading a convention of gannets. No wonder they stand out.

Suddenly I'm glad that Harriet has avoided coming down here. People have brought bunches of flowers, and are laying them, still in their cellophane, at the foot of Winston Churchill's podium in the abscence of an image of the woman herself. They mill about, talking in hushed tones like guests at a funeral, spotting faces in the crowd and enfolding each other in sympathetic hugs. I guess that many of them turned up for the real thing fifteen years ago and are taking the opportunity to renew old acquaintances; the square is thick with the fug of nostalgia and a muted, but palpable sense of party.

The woman near me raises her voice so the drag queens can hear her, says, 'It's disgraceful. They should show more respect.'

A black Godiva, egg-sized diamonds setting off her rhine-stone-covered slip dress, looks over with a brilliantly rehearsed look of contempt that I've seen on Harriet's face a million times, raises her own voice and says, 'Don't worry, darlings. She's not been out of the house in fifteen years.'

Oh, good, I think, a ruck. But then a microphone clunks on and everyone turns to hear what's going to come from the platform over by the traffic lights.

'Hello, people,' says a voice, and I am immediately consumed by hatred. I don't believe this. How the hell did she manage to get herself into pride of place? I edge closer to confirm that it really is her, and find myself standing near the Divettes. I am so embarrassed that I'm wearing black; they must think I'm one of them.

A bikini Godiva, balls strapped down so that only the Gymbody six-pack betrays her gender, cranes over her elegant shoulder and says, 'Oh, God, girls, it's the harlot Hayman.'

'What's she doing here?' cries a Duchess Godiva. 'We don't want her!'

They start to boo and catcall, feet clattering like hooves on kerbstones. 'Off! Off! Off!' 'Shut your catflap!' 'Moo! Moo!' but the ego of Hayman fails to notice and she ploughs forward.

'Thank you all so much for coming today,' she says, and the thousand-odd mourners before her preen with gratification. 'I know,' she continues, 'that Godiva would have been so proud to see you all here in her honour.'

This, at least, is partly true; Godiva liked anyone turning out in her honour. Then again, she would, perhaps, have liked the cream of showbiz to turn out in designer mantillas, rather than all these frowning matrons and two representatives of morning television. Even Christopher Biggins has failed to show.

'I have no need to tell you,' continues Leeza, 'how important what you're doing today is. We all know, deep in our hearts, that Godiva Fawcett was the greatest woman of our lifetime and that she deserves respect from the powers that be. I know it's important to me, but it's important to all of us.'

'Yees!' cry a few voices from the crowd. The Divettes let off a collective squeal and wiggle their hips. Then they resume their chanting. 'Ditch the bitch!' they cry. 'ME! ME! ME! ME! ME!'

'Now I want,' continues Leeza Hayman, 'everyone here

to hold hands and we'll have a moment's silence in memory of our lady.'

Bloody hell. She's taken over from the Virgin Mary now.

I look around in alarm, terrified that I might be caught on camera handholding with people who've been sending threats to Harriet, but to my surprise, black Godiva totters over to me, grabs one of my hands and firmly puts the other into the hand of a Western Godiva. Then they all drop their heads, close their eyes and compose themselves: thirty-odd beehives bent to the centre, thirty-odd pairs of lips pursing and unpursing. And as the minute progresses, and gradually strangled sobs begin to break out from the rest of the crowd, I notice that these naughty faces are solemn, some of them working hard to keep back their own tears.

Good God. She really did mean something, after all. I sneak a look further out into the crowd and see that everyone – respectable grannies, men in T-shirts, mums shooting looks to rioting children, Byrite women, the odd City gent in yellow spotted tie, secretaries, artists, girls who have obviously come running down from their morning shift behind the counter at Boots – seems to be filled with a solemnity, a genuine sadness. Was there more to Godiva than the sum of her parts? Was she more than a platitude, a placebo and a magnificent death? What would she have thought about this gathering in her honour?

Knowing Godiva, she probably would have been pissed off at the low turnout.

The microphone clunks again, and Leeza says, 'Thank you.' My companions shift and start to tidy each other's mascara, sort out banners and placards from the stack by their feet.

'Right,' says Leeza. 'We're going to move off now. I'm sure you all know the route, but we'll be walking up Whitehall, through Trafalgar Square, down Pall Mall, along Piccadilly and finishing in Hyde Park where there will be speeches and a funfair. And, people, let's make sure that we show how a peaceful demonstration's done. Let's make this fun, and friendly, and get as many people joining us as we can along the way. Let's do it for Godiva!'

A cheer rises from the crowd, and despite myself I feel a shiver of emotion, but you can get a shiver of emotion from practically any large group of people applauding the same thing. If there's one thing they discovered at Nuremberg, it's that.

We shuffle off, milling about as the wheelchairs move to the front, then the mums with kindergarten-age children all dressed in their party gear, then the grannies and the grandads. After that, everyone falls in with their pals from the Godalming Godiva Memorial Society and the Bradford Mothers' Exchange. And among them, me, trying to stay both with and apart, keep myself separate from the gannets – separate from everyone, to be honest. I'm only meant to be here as an observer, to report to Harriet the things she won't see on the news – the Divettes, leggy and sparkling, a huge pink banner proclaiming them to be the Gay Godivas. Oh, I wish Haz could see them. She'd want to kiss every one of them.

I drop over to walk on the pavement, weaving my way round the scatter of tourists outside Downing Street who turn to watch the parade go by. More flowers are laid at the Cenotaph, people wave in the sunshine, beckon the pavement lurkers to come and join them. A lovely sunshiney day out, and some of the people on it really believe that they are doing something big, something important. It passes in waves through the crowd. We're going to change the world. We're going to make the world a better place. This is how we make our feelings known, how we make the people that don't care sit up and take notice.

Slowly I realise that there's been someone walking along beside me, keeping pace with me, for a while. I glance over. A tallish man, faintly familiar, fair hair trimmed to just below ear level at the back, a starburst of heavily-cropped curls at the forehead, open shirt, loose jacket, faint suntan as though he spends a good deal of time outdoors. 'Anna?' he says, and I think: okay, good, he's familiar because we've met, and then because I don't feel that I have to be nervous of him, I notice that he's extremely good-looking: lean, muscular, long legs, big hands; a calm expression, one of those I'm-in-control looks that make you feel instantly safe.

I can't for the life of me remember who he is. Someone I chatted up once? Someone I slept with? No. I'd remember. He's the sort of guy you would remember. He'd be the kind of guy you'd allow to stay for breakfast, even let lounge around your house reading the Sunday papers. He smiles at me with lovely strong teeth; a slight gap in the middle ones. We all know what that means.

'Hello,' I say. 'Sorry, I've—'

'Mike,' he replies. 'We met the other night.'

Nope. Rings absolutely no bells. Mike. Mike from where? A friend of Mel's perhaps? Lindsey's? Definitely not someone I know well, but equally definitely someone I've been glad to see when I've seen him.

'Hi,' I say with that false smile of social recognition. 'How are you?' Wonder whether to kiss him, then think: no, I don't think I know him that well. He's out of context, that's why I can't place him.

'Fine,' he says. 'You?'

'Yeah, good. Thanks.'

'Got over the break-in?'

Okay, so he knows about that. He must know someone who knows us quite well, then.

'Just about.'

'Have you sorted out your security?'

'Too bloody right. I don't think you could break *out* of the place now.'

He nods. 'Good. You can't be too careful. And your flatmate? What's she done?'

'Um,' I say, 'well, we're sort of hoping it was a bit of an isolated incident.'

'Hmm,' he says.

We walk along together for a bit, then I try another tack. 'What are you doing here, anyway? You're not a Godiva fan, are you?'

'Me?' He stops for a moment, laughs, then moves on again. 'I'm working.'

Working. Right. A journalist. Damn.

Then he laughs again. 'You haven't got the faintest idea who I am, have you?'

I blush, shake my head. He sticks his hand out. 'Mike Gillespie,' he says. 'PC Mike Gillespie. I fished you out of your cellar the other night.'

Older copper. Of course.

'Oh, God,' I say. 'How are you? I didn't recognise you—'

'With my clothes on,' he finishes for me. 'I must say, you look quite different out of school uniform.'

'I should hope so.'

'More, well, grown up. It took me a while to find you.'

I'm suspicious again. 'Find me?'

'Don't worry. I just figured you'd be here somewhere. Thought I'd keep an eye out for you.'

'Thanks.' I'm flattered.

'Lady Harriet not with you?'

263

'No. I'm reporting back to the homestead.'

He nods. 'Probably wise. I don't think everyone here is well disposed to her.

'Please, by the way,' I say, 'don't call her Lady Harriet. It makes her really uncomfortable.'

'Not uncomfortable enough to remove the Lady from her bank cards.'

'Of course not. You get much better lines of credit if you've got a handle to your name.'

We merge into Trafalgar Square, and instead of wheeling immediately left, the crowd seems to be being guided up to the open area beneath Nelson's column by a line of uniformed policemen strung from the bottom of Admiralty Arch all the way along to the far side of Pall Mall. 'What's going on?' I ask.

'Oh, mmm. You're all going to have to wait here for a bit. There are two more marches going on today. Farmers for Hunting and Pensioners for a Fair Deal, and everyone wants to go past Downing Street. The Farmers are being taken down the Mall to Horseguards and the pensioners are being diverted up to Piccadilly Circus. That way you don't clash.'

'Bloody hell. So no one can drive anywhere in central London at all today.'

Mike shrugs. 'It's called democracy. And it's probably better than having gridlock on three consecutive Saturdays.'

'Hang on. I thought it was Afghans for Equality next weekend.'

He gives me a penetrating look. Those eyes really are very blue; dark blue like the Mediterranean. 'You really are a funny one, aren't you?'

I plonk myself down on the wall of the fountain between

two groups of drag queens who are moaning and applying sticking plasters to their heels.

'So what kind of trouble are you expecting today?' I ask. 'Surely all these housewives are a pretty law-abiding lot, wouldn't you say?'

'Crowds always contain an element of risk. We'd all be sacked if we just left a thousand people to wander the streets of London without supervision.'

Suddenly, trouble starts anyway. Duchess Godiva, three down from me, suddenly leaps to her feet and bears down on a sturdy matron, spitting and screaming. 'Say that again to my face!' she shouts, voice suddenly full basso and loud as a foghorn. 'Come on! Say that to my face!'

Matron squares up to her. 'I said,' she shouts back, 'that people like you should be kept off the streets. It's people like you that give homosexuals a bad name!'

Duchess puts a hand on a hip and snarls, 'Well, it's people like you that give women a bad name. Look at you. I'm surprised you even bothered to take your curlers out before you came down here.'

And matron responds, 'Well, at least I'm not spreading disease like some people I could mention.'

Eight more Godivas, who have been listening intently and nudging each other, let out a concerted gasp of offence, leap to their feet and head for the fray. Sturdy matron finds herself surrounded by more muscles and spangles than at a Hulk Hogan fight. 'Who are you calling a disease spreader?' a voice rises up. 'Perhaps you ought to try spreading your legs a bit more often and you wouldn't be so angry!'

Sixteen sturdy matrons are running to the aid of their friend. 'Leave her alone! You get off her!'

Black Godiva rounds on a grey-haired woman who is prodding him with her handbag. 'Oh, go and buy a dildo,

265

you silly old cow!' he shouts. She shrieks, pulls her arm back and gives him one full in the face. For a moment he staggers and I think he's going to break his ankle, but natural balance kicks in and he plunges forward, rips off her hair bobble, waves it in the air triumphantly.

Someone knocks his wig off.

Someone else grabs someone's handbag and lobs it into the fountain.

The remaining Divettes leap to their feet and start applauding. 'Cat fight! Cat fight! Go for it, girls!'

All hell breaks loose. Mike gets to his feet and moves cautiously forward while the uniformed branch start running towards the melee of dropping hair, straining Lycra, ripping polyester, popping bobbles. I don't know whether to laugh or laugh. So I laugh. Stand up to get a better view and move out into clearer ground because I come up to the belly buttons of some of the Godivas and can't see for sparkling hotpants.

I'm only dimly aware of the fact that a small crowd is gathering around me as I stand. A beehive flies ten feet into the air, catches a gust of wind and spirals sideways. False fingernails clatter to the ground, elastic pops. A black figure attempts to crawl out between someone's legs, but a large hand reaches out and hauls her back, leaving only a pair of hexagonal, tan-rimmed spectacles on the pavement.

And then suddenly there's an arm round my stomach and a hand over my mouth, and I'm pulled backwards and off my feet. I try wildly to look behind me to see who's doing this, but they're holding my head too firmly and all I can do is roll my eyes. I flail out with my arms, and more hands grab my wrists, pin them back so that all I can do is thrash hopelessly with my legs.

To begin with, I'm annoyed but not frightened; think that

someone I know has snuck up on me and is playing a stupid practical joke. And I think: well, fuck it, if you're going to do something like this, I'll join in. So I bite down, hard, on the hand, which whips away with an angry 'Ow!' And then it comes back, harder this time, clamps over the whole lower half of my face, covering my nose so I struggle to breathe. 'Come on. Get on with it,' says a man's voice, one I don't recognise, one with a strong London accent and an element of calm that I really dislike. No one's laughing behind me. They're just pulling me away from the crowd, over towards the kerb, and there's nothing I can do.

'The little fuck bit me.'

'Well, don't cry about it.'

The arm round my stomach loosens, throws me further up, grips again. I kick out, as hard as I can, catch someone a blow on the leg. He swears. Then a hand grabs a handful of my hair, jerks my head agonisingly back, and a voice hisses, 'Stop that. Any more of that, and I'll really fucking hurt you.'

The voice says, '*He's really going to fucking hurt you anyway.*'

We're far away enough from the fight that I can hear their heavy, struggling breathing and the scrape of boots on pavement. We must be near the road now; surely someone can see me? I heave in his arms, manage to get my face free for a second and scream. 'Help me! Someone!'

And then the hand clamps back down and fingernails dig into my cheeks. How many are there? Two? Three?

They swing round and I see a white van, back doors open, parked on the kerb. Oh, God, they're going to stick me in there. I'm being kidnapped by White Van Man. I know that if they get those doors shut on me, it's all over. The dark interior gapes at me; a couple of spanners, a roll of carpet tape. Oh, God, I'm in trouble. I brace my feet against the sill, push against it.

The man holding my stomach swears again. 'Someone get round there,' he snarls. 'Break her knees if you have to.'

And then he goes, 'Oof,' and drops me. I land on my bottom, catch the back of my skull on the tow bar sticking out from the back of the van, teeth jangling, crumple up, dazed, and lie with my face on the road among the burger wrappers, half-leg Doc Martens missing my nose by inches. Raise my head in time to see Mike with the heel of his hand in the face of a looming skinhead, pushing him backwards, while a man in uniform catches another a full-on whack round the ear with a nightstick. Then I drop my cheek back onto the tarmac and go to sleep.

Chapter Thirty-Six

The Start of Something Big

'And it never occurred to either of you to tell anyone about this?'

I feel about yea high.

'No.'

Mike looks up from the screen, says, 'So there's been all this stuff coming in, and you thought it didn't mean anything.'

My head is splitting despite the ibuprofen and the tea. 'No,' I say wearily. 'I'm sorry, but it didn't.'

'Why on earth not?'

I lean my elbows on the desk and my head in my hands. 'Because they usually go away after a while.'

Now he's really giving me the look. If he hadn't just hauled me out of a bunch of Millwall's finest, I might be a bit hacked off at being treated like a stupid teenager.

'They usually go away after a while,' he repeats slowly. 'Now, just talk me through all this. Your friend makes a habit of getting these?'

'Um.' I can't think of any way of ameliorating the answer, so I finish, lamely, 'Yes.'

Then I say, 'Not all the time. Just when there's been something in the news. Anniversaries and that.'

'And,' he says again, 'it never occurred to you to tell anyone?'

I slap a hand hopelessly down on the desk. 'Mike, her mother used to get this sort of thing all the time. Well, obviously not emails, but she'd get letters in block capitals practically every day, and no one ever actually followed through. And my mother gets the odd one too.'

'Your mother.'

'You don't want to know.'

'Who?'

'Grace Waters. But we don't talk.'

Mike does a little grimace. 'I'm not surprised. You don't seem like you'd be exactly compatible.'

'Thank you.'

He turns back to the screen. 'So you think that "I know where you live" is a normal sort of anonymous email to get, do you?'

I attempt a shake of the head, stop when tears of pain spring to my eyes. 'No, of course I don't. But this sort of stuff is always meant to scare you, and if you let yourself be scared, they've won, haven't they?'

'And "I wish you were dead instead of her"?'

'Well, they probably do. That doesn't mean that they're going to do anything about it.'

'Good God, woman.'

He runs the cursor down Harriet's inbox, glancing at the subject space as he does so. Subject: You should be ashamed. Subject: Why don't you kill yourself? Subject: Disgusted. Subject: Better look behind you. Subject: You're no Lady. Subject: If I had a daughter like you, I'd have drowned her at birth. Subject: She didn't deserve this.

Mike shakes his head in disbelief. 'You know, when I met you, I honestly got the impression that you were pretty bright. And Harriet, too. And now I see this lot, and I begin to wonder. I mean, didn't it occur to you at all that there might be a link between the break-in and this lot?'

Maybe a glass of water. I go over to the sink and, while I wash up one of Harriet's paint-stained mugs, say, 'Well, of course it did. But you can't be paranoid. The kind of people who write that sort of thing hardly ever actually do anything. They get it all out of their system by writing it down, don't they?'

He growls. Not the sort of noise you expect to hear from Her Majesty's Constabulary. 'Have you ever heard of stalkers, stupid?'

At which point I burst into tears. It's bad enough being dragged off and concussed without someone calling you stupid.

He's on his feet in an instant and over by me with an arm round my shoulders. 'Sorry. Look, don't cry. That was very harsh.' He squeezes me a bit harder in that clumsy man-sympathy sort of way. I can't tell if it's fatherly or something else. Whatever, it's nice. An entirely inappropriate occasion, but I allow myself a small burst of feeling horny. Well, it's been weeks since the ocker took off for Barcelona and it's going to be a week at least till he comes back. A girl could shrivel up and die in that sort of time.

He gropes around on the counter, finds some kitchen roll, tears a bit off and holds it to my nose. 'Come on. Blow,' he says, and suddenly I feel all little and pathetic, and I want looking after. So I cry for a bit, and then I spin it out for a bit longer because it's nice being comforted for a change.

'Anna, it'll be all right,' he says. 'Now I know what's going on, it's only a matter of time before we pick up whoever it is and things get back to normal.'

'But I don't understand why they tried to grab me,' I wail. I've got enough on my plate as it is.

271

Mike pats me and says something that sounds suspiciously like 'There, there,' then continues, 'it's just bad luck. If they are a stalker, they're obviously not a very good one. Look. Why don't I make you a cup of tea?'

A man who makes cups of tea. A man who saves you from skinheads and makes you cups of tea. I could get used to this. Well, maybe not the skinhead bit, but it's nice to know he can do that if needs must. 'Okay,' I snuffle. Go over and curl up on the sofa. Yawn.

'When's Harriet due back?' he asks as he fills up the kettle. Looks at the pile of mugs on the draining board, pulls a face and eventually selects the one he thinks is the cleanest.

'I don't know.' I yawn again. 'I think I should get some sleep, you know. I feel really crappy.'

Mike puts a teabag in the mug, finds the milk, spoons some sugar in. 'I don't take sugar,' I protest.

'You need sugar,' he replies firmly, 'you've had a shock.'

'Is that something your granny used to say?'

Blue eyes look up and smile at me. 'Yes. How did you guess?'

'Never mind.'

He makes the tea, brings it to me, sits down in the armchair. 'How are you feeling?'

'Like I've just had a big bang on the head.'

He nods. 'You'll probably feel like that for a couple of days.'

'Listen,' I say, 'I really think I should get some shut-eye.'

'Okay.' He makes no move to leave. I realise that he's planning to stay.

'Look, there's really no need for you to hang around.'

'Bollocks,' he says. 'I'm not leaving someone with concussion on her own.'

'I'll be fine.'

'And if you're not, it'll be all my fault. I'll hang around until your flatmate gets back. It's the least I can do.'

I take a single sip of tea, realise that I'm not going to make it through to the end of the mug. Hold it out to him. 'I'm not going to finish this. Do you want it?'

'That mug's filthy,' he says.

'You really are a policeman, aren't you?'

'Don't get lippy, son.'

'I'm not your son.'

'Listen,' he says, 'you'd better go to sleep. And if you don't do it in an orderly fashion, I'll have no recourse but to arrest you.'

He picks up the blankey that hides the big burn hole in the back of the sofa where Harriet spilled lighter fuel and then dropped a cigarette a couple of years ago. Sees what's underneath, rolls his eyes and says, 'I think you two need some help around here.'

I put my head down on a cushion, say, 'A woman's touch?'

'Not on the balance of current evidence,' he replies. 'Do you want the cat?'

'No thanks. He'll only try to sit on my head.'

And then he shakes the blankey out over me and, to my amazement, tucks it in. No one's ever tucked me in in my life. I pull it up around my chin, eyelids already dropping. Just before I slide from the world, I manage to remember my manners. 'Mike?' I mumble into the darkness behind my eyelids.

A creak as he sits back down in the armchair. 'What?'

'Thanks.'

A single word follows me down into the underworld. ''S'kay.'

Chapter Thirty-Seven

Meteor Maid

Search:

Godiva Fawcett

Sources:

All

From:

1969–72

Publication:

What's on at the movies

Byline:

Ken Griswald

Date:

18 05 69

Headline:

New Talent: Godiva Fawcett

Only just nineteen years old, and Godiva Fawcett has
already packed enough into her life to make a movie of
her own. By now, we're all familiar with the tale of how she
landed the lead in Stephen Swift's take on Martin Stack's
bestseller of a couple of years back, *The Power Machine*
[out this week: see review, p.17], as the result of a chance
meeting in a coffee shop in London, England. As producer
Leonard Wildenstein tells it, 'I had been over there a week
conducting auditions and nothing seemed to have gone
right. I had a very clear picture of how Melanie should
look and act, but although I had seen dozens of very fine

actresses, none had the exact qualities I was looking for. Melanie has a special combination of innocence and sophistication, and it was proving to be very hard to find a real-life woman who could combine those qualities in the right proportions. Melanie is a true English rose, and I had dreamed that England was where I would find her.'

And then he dropped by the Starlight Coffee Bar, and, in true Hollywood style, the Starlight produced a star. 'She brought me my coffee,' continues Wildenstein, 'and the moment I clapped eyes on her I knew I had found my Melanie. I offered her the part on the spot. She was so ladylike and dignified, and yet had such warmth, such a *glow*, to her, that I knew it would work. I had wanted someone completely unknown in the States, but I never imagined I'd find someone who was completely unknown in her own country as well!'

Others who have worked with her on the movie are equally enthused. Fawcett says that working alongside co-star Charles Hollis was 'The single most thrilling experience of my life. I've worshipped him from afar all my life, practically, and I never dreamed for a minute that I would actually meet him!' Veteran director Stephen Swift is, she says, 'without doubt the wisest man I've ever met', and the director is quick to return the compliment. 'I have to say, I wasn't sure, when Leonard produced this kid, if we were doing the right thing. She had no acting experience, after all, and seemed pretty green to me. But we spent a couple of days shut up in a hotel going over the part, and by the end of that, I was convinced. The girl has talent, I can tell you that!'

But what is she like, this lass from the old country? So far, there have been few opportunities to find out: Wildenstein and Swift have kept her firmly under wraps, and, though lucky residents of Malibu have been able to see a bit more of her during the filming of Kurt Hamilton's *Beach Bunny Massacre*, due out later this year, we the public have had few chances to judge for ourselves. She's certainly made an impression among Hollywood's glitterati. Hamilton fondly speaks of her as 'my little lollipop'. Veteran actor Jeff O'Malley, soon to star opposite her in Harman and Cohen's modern western, *Bruck*, calls her 'Talented, extremely talented. I was unsure at first about what I could get from someone so young, but let me tell you – she's already taught me a thing or two!'

Wildenstein, one of her greatest fans, says that she is 'an old head on young shoulders. Godiva may look peaches-and-cream, but underneath is a steely will to succeed, an ambition and a willingness to have a go at pretty much anything that I am sure will carry her through. I truly believe that this girl is capable of anything'. Lara Siskovich, co-star in *Beach Bunny Massacre*, says, only half-jokingly, 'I truly hate Godiva. She loves the camera and the camera loves her. When she's on the screen, the rest of us simply don't stand a chance.'

Meantime, she's been making quite a splash on the party scene. Young and inexperienced she may be, but this girl's innate charm has turned quite a few heads. Out here for under a year, she has already been linked with such members of Hollywood's aristocracy as Marlon Cambridge, Joe Visconti, George Nightingale and Richard Loudon. Sophisticates in the know, it seems, are queuing up for a bit of quality time with our Miss Fawcett. An inside source says, 'It's amazing. The girl has such power it's frightening. It seems that all she has to do is smile and grown men fall to their knees.'

I caught up with Godiva at the modest three-bed hacienda-style house she has been renting in Beverly Hills for the past six months while she decides 'where I want to make my home'. The house is a combination of easy California charm and a very British kind of elegance; between shoots, she says, she has been shopping, filling her house with antiques and knick-knacks, creating a home-from-home to replace the one she lost at such an early age. 'I need to have beautiful things about me, Ken,' she says in that quaint and impeccable British accent that has won her so many admirers. 'It's not just that I'm an artist and need the tranquillity of art about me, it's because, although I've adopted America as my home and love everything about it, I'm English to the core. The English have a very strong aesthetic sense, as you can tell from the interiors of our homes, and my mother, particularly, had a wonderful eye for interiors, which I've inherited.'

Over the very English ritual of afternoon tea, served by the pool in a delightfully shady hibiscus bower, she continues, 'This has just been the most amazing time for me. I'm still pinching myself. People have been so very, very kind. I still can't believe how much they seem to have taken me to their hearts.' She gazes at me with those famous emerald eyes, and I can understand, myself, how this child-woman, with her maturity way beyond her tender years, can have cast such a magical spell over so many of Tinseltown's harder hearts. She offers me an English muffin – 'a little luxury from home' – and says, 'The thing is, there are so many more opportunities for a girl like me out here, and I just love the people, but at heart I am still the plain little English girl I always was. Sometimes I just long for those cool, damp mornings, the mist on the fields, the great oak trees, the smallness of everything. There are times when I long for a good old-fashioned winter evening toasting crumpets over an open fire. It's the simple things I miss.'

So if she had the chance to go back, would she take it? 'I don't know, I really don't. I'm so happy here, and with the work I'm doing, I can't see that it would make sense at the moment. Anyway,' she says, and fixes me once again with those eyes, 'tell me about yourself.'

This is typical, it seems, of Godiva. 'She's amazing,' says my party source, 'so little of the sort of ego you find in your average movie star. Always wants to know everything about everybody she meets, never wants to talk about herself. No wonder popularity has skyrocketed!'

With difficulty, I get her back onto the subject in hand. Her new-found wealth must come as a bit of a shock to her, I say. 'Well, yes and no. I was absolutely desperate when I met Leonard [Wildenstein], doing anything I could to get by. But though everything went after my parents' tragic death, I grew up in a good family, and I still remember what it was like to have lovely things about me.' Her eyes mist over as she remembers her happy childhood. 'They were lovely, my parents. They taught me all my values. I still miss them, think about them every day. They weren't grand folk, they were simple, good people and I like to think that I take after them. Material things are lovely, of course, but they could never replace real things, like love, and goodness, and a happy family.'

How is she getting on on the set of *Beach Bunny Massacre*? 'Wonderful. Hilarious. I was nervous at first about showing so much flesh, but everyone makes it so easy I can't allow modesty to get the better of me.' It's quite a departure from the part of Melanie DuChamp, I say. 'Ooh, I know.' She giggles. 'Melanie's such a natural lady, so dignified and accomplished even though she's only young; it's been a real challenge getting into the mind of someone like Sandee Carlton after that. She's a typical Californian girl: all fun and frolics, maybe a bit superficial, but good at heart.

And it's been great getting to act all scared! Very difficult when you know that what's on the other side of the camera is Kurt and his whoopee cushions!'

So there you have it. Godiva Fawcett: lady, child, star of the future. She may have come from nowhere, but I predict that she won't be going back there. We'll be seeing a lot more of this actress before she's done.

Search:
Godiva Fawcett
Sources:
All
From:
1969–72

Publication:
> Variety

Byline:
> Beebee Sachs

Date:
> 11 31 69

Headline:
> Review: Beach Bunny Massacre (AA). Dir. Kurt Hamilton.

Good old Kurt Hamilton, King of Schlock. He's never made a good movie yet, but they never fail to entertain, not least with the timing of their release. After the arthouse success of *Ski Chalet Killers* in the summer, the eternal joker brings us *Beach Bunny Massacre*, a stabfest set in and around the cultural wasteland of Malibu. It's all the usual stuff: cheap film stock, inadequate lighting, unknown actors mugging to camera, largely female cast whose primary talents seem to consist of a combination of *embonpoint* and the ability to stuff both fists in their mouths at once.

As usual, plot consists of a thinly disguised excuse to get a girl, make her wet, make her clothes fall off, make her run. This reviewer tends to find this level of sophistication a bit heavy going after the first ten minutes, and after thirty, I would scarcely have been awake but for one little thing: Godiva Fawcett, the little English lovely who raised all the hoo-ha earlier in the year when she turned in a not-half-bad showing in *The Power Machine*. Aptly named after a lady who lost all her clothes in medieval England, this girl spent practically every frame in a bikini in various stages of decrepitude. From the moment of her first appearance, to her last little vignette with a big rubber ball after the action was over, I was glued upright in my seat. I don't think I've ever seen anything like it. The girl was awful. The girl stank like eight-day-old fish. Her attempt at an American accent was so laughable it was contagious. Her reactions were so wooden, so scripted, so utterly risible you wondered if she was taking a rise from

279

the director. Fawcett? Force-it, more like. Natalie Wood looks lifelike by comparison.

In other words, perfect casting. This absurd tale of bikini wax and screaming bimbos has all the hallmarks of another Hamilton cult classic. See it in a fleapit, see it with a quart of tequila, see it if you dare. Word has it that Fawcett has already landed another part in Stephen Swift's upcoming wartime drama *Calais, Mon Amour*. I can hardly wait for them to storm the beaches.

Search:

Godiva Fawcett

Sources:

All

From:

1969–72

Publication:

The Moviegoer

Byline:

None

Date:

02 15 70

Headline:

'Surprise' Oscar nominee rates chances

Godiva Fawcett, the outsider who has come from the back to be a surprise nominee for this year's Best Supporting Actress Oscar, has been speaking to the *Moviegoer* about her chances of winning. 'I'm just stunned to have been nominated,' says the British twenty–year-old, whose more recent role in *Beach Bunny Massacre* received universal brickbats on opening a couple of months ago. 'I haven't got a hope of winning, not with the sort of talent I'm up against. I'm only thrilled that I'll get the chance to go to the ceremony at all.'

You said it, Godiva.

Search:

Godiva Fawcett

Sources:

All

From:

1969–72

Publication:

Information Weekly

Byline:

Staff Reporter

Date:

06 28 70

Headline:

Not so much amour on location

Rumours reach us that all is not peachy on the location shoot of *Calais, Mon Amour*, where Miriam Baylor is kicking up rough about favouritism. Youthful blonde co-star and recent Best Supporting Actress loser, Godiva Fawcett, it seems, is copping all those little on-set luxuries so beloved of the thespian community, and Miriam is spitting mad. 'I wouldn't mind,' she was overheard saying to a dining companion in a local French eatery the other night, 'but we all know her deal was finalised in the restrooms at Ciro's.'

What can she mean?

Search:

Godiva Fawcett

Sources:

All

From:

1969–72

Publication:

Fish-Eye Lens: the alternative movie magazine

Byline:

Orange John

Date:
02 13 71
Headline:
Go-diva!

What is it about a British accent that makes otherwise able men lose their heads altogether? We've just seen an early print of Stephen Swift's *Calais, Mon Amour*, and the thing that beats this correspondent is this: how come Godiva Fawcett? The girl's pretty, but there are thirty thousand girls as pretty in the Beverly Hills area alone. She can act, a little bit, as long as no one asks her to stretch herself beyond the two faces – haughty duchess putting down retainer and soppy duchess bringing soup to farm cottages – she's at home with. What she has to offer beyond that beats the hell out of me. One thing's for sure: after a brief vogue in the early months of last year, we can fairly much say that the girl has turned to box-office poison. *Calais* is reputed to have run over budget to the tune of $2m, mostly because of extra film costs run up by the need to reshoot vital scenes, and previews suggest that the film is likely to get a week in mainstream auditoriums at most. I for one won't be sorry if this chick disappears from our screens altogether; that De Havilland simper is beginning to make me want to reach for my Six Shooter.

Search:
Godiva Fawcett
Sources:
All
From:
1969–72
Publication:
Daily Express
Byline:
Hickey Column
Date:
10 06 71

Headline:

The pull of Hollywood gets weaker for Godiva

Godiva Fawcett, who left these shores three years ago for the lure of Hollywood and stardom, is to return to Blighty after a spell of 'resting' in her Beverly Hills home. 'In the end,' says the plucky twenty-year-old star of *The Power Game*, *Beach Bunny Massacre* and the ill-fated *Calais, Mon Amour*, 'I just miss England too much. The Californian lifestyle is fabulous, but it's such a shallow, bitchy world and in the end I found it hard to live with. People make so many promises, and in the end I felt terribly let down. I was constantly in work, but increasingly the roles I was offered were undemanding, and I want to do more with my life than just spend it in front of the lens. I have always been interested in charity work, and intend to get more involved once I'm back on more caring shores.'

Godiva is also to star in a pilot for a new ITV sitcom, *Daddy's Girl*, and has high hopes for its success. 'The part I'm playing is right up my street,' she claims. 'She's a real old-fashioned English rose, just like me. I can't wait to get started.' She is also hoping that her love life will enter a more settled phase when she returns. 'I dated a lot in America,' she says, 'but there was never anyone special.' And is there someone special now? 'Yes.' She smiles. 'There's someone special: an Englishman who I met while he was over here looking for new investment opportunities.' And does this Englishman have a name? 'It's early days yet,' she says with typical discretion, 'and he's the sort of person who hates publicity. We'll just have to see what happens.'

Chapter Thirty-Eight

Cleopatra, Queen of Denial

When I wake, it's dark outside and Harriet, in a cheerful voice, is saying, 'So she kept griping and moaning all night: this wasn't good enough, that wasn't seasoned enough, she didn't want radicchio in her salad, only rocket, and why hadn't they asked her, going on about how Linds – she's the other waitress who was sharing the shift with me. She's still a mate, actually. You'd like her – should've been filling her wine glass before it got down to halfway empty, there's no hand cream in the Ladies and what on earth was she paying all this for if they weren't even going to put hand cream in the Ladies, that sort of crap. A really horrible woman. She'd probably have nicked the hand cream if there had been any. One of those people who thinks that because they've scored a bit of money they've become magically exempt from the basic book of manners. And Linds knew that after all that running around, she was going to turn out to be a really mean tipper. You always know the mean tippers from the way they don't even look at you in case they strike up some relationship and get a twinge of guilt.'

Ah, the teapot, I think, close my eyes again and drift for a bit while she finishes. Register that Harriet definitely sounds a bit different from usual: sort of like she might be batting her eyelashes while she talks. If I didn't know better, I would almost suspect that she was flirting.

'So once she's pigged herself on four courses and three refills of the breadbasket, she wants fresh ginger tea because she says that the food has given her indigestion, and Linds is thinking: yeah, perhaps if you'd eaten less of it . . . So anyway, Linds tell the kitchen, and someone has to stop making food right in the middle of the busy period in order to go and blag some sodding ginger from the Chinese restaurant down the road and chop it up. And then obviously they have to leave it to infuse for a bit because ginger doesn't take just like that, so it's ten minutes before Linds can get it to the table.'

Harriet's companion murmurs, shifts in his seat.

'So when she arrives, this old bat goes, "Where have you been? I've been waiting for hours. Do you keep all your customers waiting like this? I call it terrible service. Don't expect a tip from me. Give me my tea," and Linds apologises and points out that ginger takes a while to infuse, and she goes, "Takes a while to have a cigarette out back when you should be working, more like," and Linds gives her her tea and goes off to take some deep breaths. And the next thing she knows, this woman's clicking her fingers at her – God, you've no idea how annoying it is to have someone click their fingers at you like you're a sea lion or something – and going, "You've let this tea sit around for so long it's stone cold. I wanted hot tea. Go and get me some hot tea."

'What a bitch,' says the bloke. 'I think she'd've got her tea in the face if it had been me.'

'Too right,' says Harriet. 'But Linds did something else which worked much better. She took the pot back into the kitchen, where they had a ceramic hob for keeping sauces warm and that. And she turned it up full and put the pot

285

on the hob for, like, five minutes with her hand sitting on the lid so it got immune to the heat, and waited until it was really, really boiling. And then she carries it through with her bare hand and sets it down on the table in the front of the woman, and says, "There. I hope that's hot enough now, madam," and walks away. So when the old hag goes to pour it out, there's a shriek and the whole restaurant practically bursts into applause.'

'Bloody hell,' says the man. 'Remind me not to tangle with your friends. What happened?'

Mike. It's Mike the copper. Mike the fanciable copper with the blue eyes and the way of stepping in to rescue you when you least expect it. Of course. I'm not asleep because I've drunk too much; I have a headache because there's a great big lump blistering up under my scalp. I open my eyes.

Harriet is cross-legged on the floor, a glass of something colourless, cold and delicious-looking nursed in her fingers. Mike is still in the armchair, spread out now like someone who's been here for months, feet under the coffee table, hands hanging down the sides. A can of beer sits open on the table. He hasn't taken a glass.

'Nothing. That's what's so brilliant about it. Lindsey picks up the pot and stands there holding it, going, "Is there a problem, madam?", and puts on the "Well, you told me to heat it up. Didn't you tell me to heat it up?" act. And because she's holding it, no one can exactly . . . Oh, hi, soldier, you're awake.'

Mike tears his eyes from Harriet's face and gives me a smile. 'How are you feeling?'

It takes a couple of seconds for anything to come out. 'Has Henry been anywhere near my mouth? Only it feels like it.'

They both laugh. 'He's out doing his Henry thing,' says

Harriet, which means that there will probably be a disem-bowelled something on the doormat in the morning. He likes to bring us presents, but he can rarely be bothered to carry anything up the stairs. 'How's the head?'

I groan. 'Agony.'

'Well, you were lucky Mike was there,' she says glibly. 'You might not have a head at all.'

I sit up. 'Harriet! This is actually serious, you know!'

'Oh, I know.' She takes a sip of her drink. 'But if you can't have a laugh when someone tries to kidnap you, I don't know when you can.'

Harriet always reacts to bad stuff with wisecracks. It's a posh thing, I think. 'Anyway,' she continues, 'it could have been a random thing.'

What's more, the wisecracks really get on my tits when they get out of hand, and it seems like she hasn't taken in just how scary this latest episode has been. 'Listen, Cleopatra, get real. There's obviously someone on our case and we need to think what we're going to do.'

'Cleopatra?' asks Mike.

'Queen of Denial,' Harriet tosses at him, and glues her crown firmly to her head. 'What evidence have you got that there's anything personal about what's happened lately?'

'Urr. Doh. What evidence have I got that it's not, stupid?'

'Okay. So someone broke into the restaurant. People break into restaurants all the time.'

'They usually empty the till and nick the drink,' Mike points out mildly. 'It's not that common to carve "Traitor" into the kitchen surfaces.'

'What would you know about it?' says Harriet. Which I take to be more evidence of denial.

'Someone broke into the restaurant two weeks after all the tabloids went big on it,' I say crossly. 'Pretty big coincidence.'

'And don't forget the emails,' adds Mike.

'No, I continue, don't forget the emails.'

'Oh, please.' Harriet waves this away. 'I get emails like that all the bloody time. If I started crying and running to the Plod every time I got one my complexion would be completely ruined. Anyway–' she gets up, rattles Mike's empty beer tin, trying to change the subject – 'Another?'

He shakes his head. 'Thanks. I've got to be going. I was only waiting around to make sure that Sleeping Beauty didn't slip into a coma or anything.'

He picks up his jacket, swings it round to put it on without getting up, and something made of black plastic falls from his pocket, clatters on the floor. 'Oops,' he says. 'It's always doing that.'

'Mobiles,' says Harriet, 'are the bane of the twenty-first century.' She comes over to pick it up. 'If they're not going off in church they're falling out of your pocket and costing a million quid in upgrades.'

She's about to hand it to him when she looks down and frowns. 'What on earth is this?' she says, holding it up on display like a spokesmodel presenting to camera on QVC. Instead of a keypad, it has two dials and a digital numerical display.

'Oh, that? That's my radio.'

'Radio?'

'Mmm.' He puts his hand out for it.

'Like in alpha alpha tango foxtrot?'

He nods.

'Sierra bravo cartwheel tampon goblin two-four?'

'Sort of thing.'

'What are you, a policeman or something?'

'Well, yeah,' he says.

'You didn't tell me.'

'Oh, sorry,' he says, 'I thought you knew.'

'Why on earth would I know?'

'Well, we have met before. And you acted like you recognised me. So I assumed you—'

'Well, I did recognise you. But . . .' She frowns off into the distance. 'So why did I . . .? Christ. You're not the Plod that came to the restaurant?'

Mike nods. 'The self-same Plod.'

'Good grief.'

'Love you too,' he says. Then manages a laugh despite the fact that I think I'd be more than a tad browned off in his position. 'Anyway,' he says, 'this Plod has an early shift tomorrow, so I'm going to proceed towards my motor vehicle, if you don't mind.' He digs in his jacket pocket, jangles some keys in his hand. 'You going to be all right, midget?'

Midget. Huh. I attempt to stand up, slump back onto my cushions. I guess if he can take being called a Plod without demur, I can deal with slurs on my height. 'I'll be fine,' I reply. 'And Mike?'

'Mmm?'

'Thank you. Thank you for everything.'

He puts on a policeman's voice. 'That's all right, madam. All in the line of duty.' Then he says, in a normal voice, 'But you two have got to think about the stuff that's been happening. I don't think anyone but your friend here would think that the two incidents were unconnected. With the emails and that.'

Harriet glares silently. He makes for the door.

'I'll come back in a couple of days and we can discuss your possible best course of action under the circumstances.'

Oh, goody, I think. It's nice when a man's sense of duty brings him winging back. I don't know how Harriet didn't actually pick up that this man was a copper. He has all the verbal inflections, dipping in and out of a formal, structured way of speaking, as though he were in court trying to sound official.

He reaches the door, Harriet still standing there glaring, and turns to face the room. 'Oh, and girls,' he says, 'when I come back, I don't want to find anything like this lying around where I can fall over it.' He holds something up between index finger and thumb. It is a piece of rolled cardboard, secured within a Rizla, one end ragged from contact with many lips, the other slightly charred. 'I know policemen are supposed to be stupid,' he says, 'but you should maybe think about emptying your ashtrays from time to time.'

Oops. I go bright red. Harriet suddenly smiles.

'I'll escort you to your vehicular transport,' she says.

Chapter Thirty-Nine

The Cute Policeman

She returns, Henry draped over her shoulder looking smug as she says all those girl-things like 'Who's the most bee-you-tiful boy in the world, then? Who's the coolest cat in London? Who's the coolest cat in the world? Have you had adventures, my fine gentleman? What did you get up to? Didjoo killsome bugs? Didjoo catch an urfworm?'

Henry yawns pinkly, eyes turning inside-out, great vampire teeth dried by stinky cat-breath, and stretches a long golden front leg down her back as he shifts his body weight to get more comfortable. 'Wooaaah,' says Harriet, running a hand over his head, down his back, rubbing the base of his tail to make him squirm. 'Who's my baby?'

If there were a man in the room, he would no doubt be making cracks about biological time-clocks at this juncture. It takes a very rare man to understand that the thing between women and their cats is nothing to do with babies. Yes, we like to baby them, to pick them up and turn them over and cradle them, to talk nonsense and coo at them while they fix us with placid stares of patronising contentment, but it's not a baby thing. It's an admiration thing. Henry is the dude I respect most in the world.

Cats are everything we aspire to be. Look at them: they're long and slinky and elegant, with no awkward lumps that get in the way when they're running. They never get bed-hair, and if they do, all they have to do is run a paw over it and it's perfect. The perfect slashes of eyeliner beneath their lashes never streak when they get overexcited. They have cheekbones to die for. They never let themselves be pushed around. They sleep eighteen hours a day and no one ever tells them that there can be such a thing as sleeping too much, you know. When they curl up and try to look cute, they actually look cute instead of looking mad and blobby. Their primary talent is finding quiet places on major thoroughfares where people will take the time to stop and pay homage, and instead of being called egotistical, everyone admires them for it. They can stay up all night and still look great the next day. But most of all, we love them because they accept love as it is not how they think it should be: never lie awake obsessing about imagined slights, never complain that someone's not there for them, never sit up stuffing their faces with chocolate and playing *Wonderwall* over and over on the record player.

She sits down on the sofa beside me, says, 'Go on, give us a kiss,' and Henry lazily raises his head for a moment, presses the tip of his nose against the tip of hers and resumes fur-tippet position, eyes closed in sybaritic repose. 'Thank you,' says Harriet, 'that was a lovely kiss.' And then she says to me, 'I know he's cute and all that, but what's with the copper?'

I knew this was coming. Harriet has a strange aversion to policemen. I think it comes from the time she was stopped for riding her bike through a pedestrian precinct at three in the morning and got banged up for the night for asking if the Plod in question didn't have a burglary to go to.

'He's a very nice policeman and he was worried. What

was I supposed to do? Say thank you for saving my life, now bugger off?'

'Well, I don't know,' she says. 'Couldn't you have written a cheque out to the injured coppers' fund or something?'

'I suppose so. But you're not supposed to leave people with concussion on their own, and he didn't seem to mind. Anyway, what's the big deal?'

This stumps her, so she just strokes the back of Henry's neck and glares at me. Eventually, she says, sulkily, like someone who knows that they're just about to be told they're talking bollocks, 'He'll have seen the mess.'

There's not much I do in response to this but laugh.

'No,' she says, 'no. Everyone knows that policemen are terribly respectable. He'll have taken one look at this place and put us on the at-risk register or something.'

I laugh again, though it busts my head to do so. 'Darling, I think we have to be children for him to do something like that.'

'Don't laugh,' she says. 'We'll probably have the drug squad round tomorrow because you're so bloody careless.'

I shake my head, which hurts as well. 'Not me, darling.'

'Well, it certainly wasn't me.'

I shrug. I'm not too bothered, to be honest. If Mike were going to do something, he'd have done it, or he'd have gone away and said nothing and come back later with half a dozen large dogs and some blokes with guns. He certainly wouldn't have just waved the roach around and wagged his finger. 'I think it's okay, Haz.'

'And what about this kidnapping business?'

'Ah, yes,' I say.

'When are we getting the visit? Giving the statements? Having our hard drive taken away for monitoring? Getting the phone tap put in?'

I feel pretty pissed off about this. No, actually: a lot more than pretty pissed off. I've been stalked, manhandled, concussed and frightened shitless, my entire family history has been turned on its head and I'm still dealing with the fact that I have effectively become an orphan, and all Harriet can do is worry about her precious privacy. 'Oh, don't worry about me, Harriet,' I find myself snapping, 'I protected your precious anonymity. I sat there telling them that I didn't have the faintest idea what had happened while I was having this huge lump on my skull X-rayed. No one knows it's because of you. After all, people get dragged into vans by bunches of skinheads every day in London. They've just made an incident report and forgotten about it already.'

'Well, apart from that bloke. He's going to be on our case for ever now.'

I feel very, very tired. 'Well, maybe he ought to be, but I don't think he will.'

'Huh,' says Harriet, and I come as close to hitting her as I ever have in the course of our long and chequered history.

'Huh?' I ask in reply. 'What's "huh" about?'

She doesn't say anything.

'Don't huh me and then bloody go into your shell. I'm sorry he found the roach, but he also saved my life, probably, while I was doing you a favour this afternoon.'

'Oh, good one. Ever so sorry to have asked you to do me a favour. It won't happen again.'

I sigh wearily. It's amazing how you can love someone to distraction and still find them more infuriating than anyone in the world. Suddenly, I don't want to carry on this conversation; I can tell it's going to turn into an argument.

'Can I go to bed now,' I say, 'if you're not going to take this seriously?'

'I am taking this seriously.'

'You're not, Harriet. We're going to have to think about what we're going to do. I don't want to spend the rest of my life looking over my shoulder.'

'How's the head?'

'Throbbing. And I feel sick.'

'I'm really sorry,' she says. 'Do you want Henry?'

I sigh. You can try with Harriet, but you can turn blue in the face before she'll concede a point. 'Yes, please.'

'Want a painkiller?'

'I took some just before I went to sleep.'

Harriet hands me Henry, who immediately struggles out of my arms and sits on the floor looking murderous.

'Right.' I push myself up on the arm of the sofa like an old lady, stand there rubbing the small of my back like someone pregnant. 'I'm going to sleep. Can you check if I'm still breathing in the morning, please?'

'I'll come and throw a glass of water in your face,' she says in her usual loving manner.

I wobble towards the door. Then she goes, 'Oh, here's something that'll cheer you up. Niggle called.'

'Who?'

'Niggle.'

'Who?'

'Your Antipodean playmate.'

'Ah.' I feel instantly more cheerful.

'He says he's going to be back in London for the weekend. Said he couldn't wait to play dress-ups.'

I can't stop a smirk. 'Ah.'

'Which,' she continues, 'I suppose is some Wagga-Wagga euphemism I'm not familiar with.'

The smirk creeps a bit further over my face. 'He comes from Perth.'

'Oh, good . . .' she says.

''Night,' I say.

'. . . because I wouldn't like to think you were involved in something kinky with your uniform.'

''Night.'

''Night,' she says.

As I reach the door, she says, 'Oh, and Anna?'

'Mmm?'

'He was a very cute policeman.'

I give her a grin, head down the stairs.

Her voice follows me. 'As policemen go,' it says.

Chapter Forty

1992: Virginity

And the first person, as always, that I want to tell is Harriet. At eight in the morning I cycle like the wind back through the early Saturday streets, take a punt on riding down the pedestrianised Cornmarket and get away with it – everything seems to be on my side at the moment – dump my bike in the bike rack inside the side gate without even bothering to lock it and pound up the stairs to her room. Bang on the door and, scarcely waiting for the sleepy invitation to enter, fling myself through it and onto her bed.

'Omigod!' I cry. 'Omiguurd!'

A green eye stares at me from a gap between tapestry cover and pillow. Harriet and I both have a habit of sleeping with the bedclothes pulled up to cover every part of our bodies, like retreating into a warm, fuggy cave. I bounce up and down on the bed: nineteen years old and behaving like a six-year-old. Feeling like a six-year-old. I've felt increasingly like a six-year-old over the past two years, only having never felt like a six-year-old when I actually *was* six, it's taken me almost as long to realise that that was what I was feeling.

Finally the cover is pulled down to reveal the squashy bedface of my saviour. 'You're a student,' she opines. 'You aren't supposed to get up for at least another three hours. Have I taught you nothing?'

I bounce some more, fling myself down so that I am crammed, full-length, between her and the wall. Nuzzle furrily into her shoulder. 'But I haven't gone to bed yet!' I cry. 'Well, I have, but . . .'

A flurry of bedclothes, and Harriet, tossing me aside like a fallen leaf, sits bolt upright, pink Victorian bosom barely covered by a clutch of sheet and blanket. She stares down at me, takes in the black velvet minidress, the bobbling earrings, the ruffled hair, the make-up down to there, the livid red of the lovebite on my neck . . . Her eyes pass on for a moment, then flick, sharply, back to the neck. An expression of wonderment dawns on her face. 'Anna,' she says, 'you aren't wearing any tights.'

And I can't stop myself grinning because I've been grinning from ear to ear for the past eight hours.

'Omigod.' She echoes my earlier announcement. 'Omiguurd! You haven't! You have! Omiguurd!'

Harriet pounces upon me, clamps my head between surprisingly powerful palms and plants three ceremonial kisses, French style, on my cheeks. 'Omiguurd!' she cries, leaps from her pit and tiptoes naked between the piles of clothes on the floor to the mini-fridge under the table under the window. I remember my first sight of this fridge as one of the first moments in my life when I was really impressed. I mean – imagine, a student having the foresight to instal an object of such sybaritic luxury in their grotshack rather than spending everything on booze in their first week and grumbling about stolen milk thereafter. I, of course, didn't come from a background that encompassed frivolities like fridges in bedrooms; any extra left lying around after the purchase of high-potency vitamins tended to be spent on extra RAM for our computers.

'Oh, darling, darling, congratulations!' says Harriet from

behind the door. 'Welcome to the land of the fallen. Ah.' There's a rustle and a clank, and from the depths she produces a bottle of Perrier Jouet, brandishes it like an Olympic torch. 'How does it feel? How was it? Was it agony? Was it bliss?'

I roll onto my back as she busies herself washing out a couple of toothmugs with the aid of a squirt of shampoo. Stretch and wriggle and say, 'Why didn't you tell me?'

'Tell you what, my little sinner?'

'I knew it was meant to be fun, but no one ever told me – oh, I don't know—' I am handicapped by my vocabulary. I am totally equipped to describe the shape of something, its every nuance of colour, its density, its absorption of light, but how do you describe the total, utter, squashy, sweet and sweaty blissiness of good sex? How do you say it? How do you describe that moment when you bite for the first time into a perfect watermelon? That crack of a shell ripe to bursting, the caressing stickiness of honeyed juice running over your wrists, the texture, that sigh of stunned pleasure as you sink your face into the firm but generous flesh? Because despite all the indications to the contrary, I have taken to sex like a cat to sunlight and I know that nothing, now, will turn me back.

She comes back to the bed, pulls the covers back over her lap and tells me, as she pops the cork, 'No one in the history of the world has been able to describe it in the same way that anyone else experiences it, oh adorable one. Was it wonderful? Was it luscious? Was it nectarines?'

I take my valedictory champagne. 'It was a dinner of nectarines and oysters and foie gras in a jacuzzi filled with cream,' I tell her.

'Was it diving into a tropical lagoon?'

I nod. 'From a cliff. Naked.'

She clinks her mug against mine. 'Oh, darling, I'm so pleased. You've finally popped your cherry.'

I sip. Oh, Grace, if you could only see me now. Everything you raised me to avoid, all the fripperies of the world, the joys that make other lives brimful, one by one I have fallen to their lure. Alcohol, drugs, staying up all night for no other reason than the hell of it, the cosseting friendship of women, vanity, the deep, deep pleasure of the unnecessary, lying abed watching the shadows creep across the ceiling, the heat and ecstasy of arms around my body. Oh, yes, I am a sinner, but if God didn't want us to enjoy our lives, every aspect of them – not only the development of intellect, but everything, the whole shebang, the physical and the emotional, then why did he give us bodies in the first place? I have fallen from Grace, but today my soul is full. 'I didn't know,' I repeat.

'You do now,' she says, yawns. 'I'm proud of you, my chick. Were you scared?'

Not so scared that a bottle of wine and three martinis couldn't sort out. 'No,' I say. 'Were you?'

Harriet yawns again. 'I scarcely remember.'

'How old were you?'

'Goodness.' Harriet does that looking up and over thing, says, 'Fourteen, I think.'

'No!'

'You forget,' she informs me, 'I was at a convent school. He's cute, Robert Saxby.'

'Ooh,' I reply, 'he's laaarvly.'

'I did wonder,' she says, 'if last night might be the night. It was the way he was gazing into your eyes, and instead of reacting like a startled lemur you were gazing right back.'

I'm high on luurve. Laugh, drink my nourishing breakfast

drink. 'Men are lovely,' I declare. 'Sex is lovely. Why don't you do sex any more, Harriet?'

'Oh, darling, you don't want to know,' she replies, 'this is your morning.'

'Yes I do! I do! I mean, I didn't know what it was like before, and now I don't understand why you aren't doing it all the time! I mean, you have men buzzing around you like bees round a honey pot, and all you do is wave them away!'

'Swat them like flies on shit, more like,' says Harriet. 'Darling, it's good for you, but it's not for me.'

'But how can it be good for me and not for you? I don't understand.'

'Because we're different people,' she says, with an air of finality. I push it.

'And?'

'I don't trust men much,' says Harriet, tries once again to sound as though the statement has brought the conversation to an end, but I won't let it go. 'Why? Why not? You just said that they were good for me. Why can't they be for you too?'

Harriet drains her mug, pours us both generous top-ups. Then she says, 'I said, Anna. We're different people. You've got to stop believing that I know everything, that everything I know is good and everything you know is bad. I'm trying, myself, you know. I'm trying to unlearn things just like you are, and men is the most important.'

'How do you mean?' I can't imagine that anyone could want to unlearn the things I learned last night. That stuff about mouths and hands and the way human bodies were designed to fit together so perfectly, so slippy and hard and soft all at the same time. I know I've discovered a pastime that will stand me in good stead for ever: how could anyone turn something so delicious down once they've tasted it?

301

Harriet says, 'You and me, we were taught opposite things when we were young, and both of them were wrong. Grace wanted you to think of men as totally unnecessary, and that's so wrong. I mean, obviously not if you're a lezzie, but a life lived without ever knowing what it's like to be totally consumed by lust, totally mad for someone, totally into playing, is only half a life.

'But you see, Godiva – no, not just Godiva, all the men around me as well – taught me something just as bad, and that's that men are the only thing. That they're how you get what you want, that the way they see your body is your best route to success. I did so much of that when I was at school. Being the most invited, the most chatted-up, the most wanted, and it wasn't until I was seventeen that I woke up one day and realised that they didn't want me at all. They wanted what I represented. They wanted my body, they wanted my connections, they wanted the fact that everyone else wanted me, but the one thing they weren't thinking about was what was inside here.'

Harriet jabs resentfully at her head with a long, elegant finger.

'And I thought,' she continues, 'yeah, I could carry on with this. I could be like my mother, or Sofe, or Gerald's mother even, and use them for what they could give me in return, or I could stop and try to be the first woman in my family in God knows how many generations who tried to do something for herself. So I stopped.'

'But surely,' I cry, 'you could do both?'

She shakes her head. 'I don't think so,' she says, and there's a twinge of sadness in her voice. 'I think the training's gone too deep. I don't think I can do men until I've done my own life.'

'But if— You'd turn him down if he came along? The perfect man?'

'What's a perfect man? I don't know where you'd find him. I want someone who wants me for myself. Someone who will look at me and say, yes, I see the faults, I see the scary bits and the messy bits and I don't give a damn about the family and the hair and the eyes and the fact that she looks like her mother, I'll just take her on and let her be, but no one will ever, ever do that. They know who I am from the moment they see me, and that's what they want. I don't believe I'll ever find someone who will see anything else. So it's better if I steer clear altogether.'

I am heartbroken for her. So I tell her. 'That's the saddest thing I've ever heard. You can't mean that. But what about sex? What about love?'

She smiles. A wry, sad little smile. 'Sex isn't all it's cracked up to be,' she says.

No. It's far, far more. 'I never want to go without sex again as long as I live,' I tell her. And I mean it too.

'I'm so glad,' she replies.

'But you. How can you—'

'Good God,' says Harriet, 'I'm not planning to actually regrow my virginity.'

'So, what?'

'I think I'm going to hold out for love,' says Harriet. 'I'm going to hold out for something that matters. I just don't want to give myself away for approval, or power, or popularity or vanity any more.'

'But that's not what I'm planning to do either,' I stutter lamely. 'Surely . . .'

'You,' she says, 'have a whole lot of catching up to do. It's not the same. You've got to have the hell-raising, wild living, crazy time you never got. But it's not a loss to me. Doing that will be part of your achievement. And not doing it will be part of mine. It's okay, lovely. It's life.'

I think about last night, about the shudder of absolute astonishment and delight when I discovered how it feels when he enters, when he sighs with pleasure and begins to move inside you, and I can't suppress a shiver of recollection. Oh, God, let this be just the beginning. Let me feel this excitement, this languor, this strength, again and again and again.

Harriet, over her mug of champagne, sees what I am thinking and begins to laugh. 'Oh, boy,' she says. 'You're really hooked, aren't you?'

'Oh, darling, it's the best. The best.'

'So are you seeing him again?'

Blimey. In all the excitement, I forgot about these pieties of good behaviour. 'I don't know,' I say, 'I didn't ask. He was asleep when I left, anyway.'

'Would you like to?'

'Do you think he was good at it?'

Harriet considers, delivers her verdict. 'Yes. I think he probably was.'

'And how many are, do you think?'

'Some. Quite a few, probably.'

'How do you tell?'

'Experimentation.'

And I think: oh whoopee, I know all about experiments. I've been doing them all my life, gathering empirical evidence and jotting it down for future reference. 'Then I shall just have to experiment some more,' I declare, 'until I get it right.'

Chapter Forty-One

A Head Case

I've had three bangs on the head in my short life: once falling off a table when my heels gave out from under me, once standing up carelessly in the loo built in the coal cellar under the all-you-can-eat Chinese banquet by South Ken station and once being rescued from skinheads, and apart from the blinding headache and the three-day nausea, the really familiar side effect is wild and stimulating dreams. After the Chinese loo, I spent some time in the Underworld, only the main problem was less the uncrossability of the Styx than the fact that it had turned into an open sewer and I didn't want to try swimming it in a satin ball dress. After the table incident, I spent hours looking for a sky-blue minidress in a huge town-square market where the clothes were beautifully cut and wonderfully finished in soft, light, drapey cloth that came only in camel, charcoal and cream.

Tonight's dream is a doozy, though. When I put my head on the pillow, I have a couple of those vertical-fall slumps into sleep where I wake clutching the edge of the bed and puffing with alarm, then everything goes black and, when I see light again, I'm standing in a courtroom, and my mother is the judge. And the jury and the witnesses and the counsel for the prosecution, and the stenographer and the usher and shuffling, tutting public. And I seem to be attempting to conduct my own defence; the table behind which I'm sitting is bare of papers and the chair next to me is empty. And I don't know what the charges are, but I know that this is deadly serious.

My mother, grim beneath her wig, glares at me through wire-rimmed specs. Twelve mothers stare damningly at me as my mother strides up and down and enumerates my faults. '. . . was seen wearing shiny knee-boots in a public place . . . Has an established history of sexual dalliances with under-qualified men . . . known associates are dilettantes and frequenters of places of rowdy public entertainment . . . can no longer recite the periodic table without prompting . . . rarely gets up before eleven in the morning . . . eats kebabs despite early training . . . dyes hair . . . shows no remorse . . .'

I want to stand up, say, 'Hey, hang on, none of these things are actually illegal, you know, what am I doing here?' and it's then that I discover that not only am I glued to the chair, my tongue seems to be glued to the roof of my mouth and the only noises I can make are muffled urks. I can only lift my hand with the greatest of efforts.

My mother turns and points accusingly in my direction, and says, with great force, 'Ladies of the jury. I put it to you that the accused deserves none of our sympathy. It was given the best of everything, provided with all the accoutrements necessary for a constructive life and DELIBERATELY chose to eschew these advantages for a life of which none of us here can approve. I put it to you that it is GUILTY.'

The jury bursts into spontaneous applause and I realise that I'm condemned before I've even been heard. But I make a superhuman effort and rip my thighs from the chair, lumber to my feet, peel my tongue from the roof of my mouth and shout, 'No! I am not an IT! I am a human being!'

The court erupts. At first, I think they're laughing, but

then I realise that they're making ape noises. Forty Grace Waterses jumping onto their chair seats, hooting and scratching at their armpits, picking at each other's scalps, thumping their fists in the air and going, 'Oooh! Oooh! OAAAH! OAAAH!' And I realise that they're imitating me, that nothing that comes out of my mouth makes any sense to them, that I'm a lower form of animal, one they would gladly use for experimentation, whose screams they would ignore for the greater glory.

In my dream, I start to cry, which only brings on another wave of hoots and hollers. And then they start to laugh, to point at me and laugh, and as quickly as the laughter dies it is replaced by boos and catcalls. 'Get rid of it!' they shout. 'Guilty!' 'Send it down!' I fall to my knees and grab the hem of my mother's gown, but she whisks it from my hand, retreats as though I am contagious.

Judge-mother bangs her gavel, and her face is twisted into an expression of hatred. Indifferent justice this ain't. 'Order! Order!' she shouts. Then, 'Order is all! Without order there is no science! Can I take your order! I order you to desist! I order you to obey! You will obey! Those who disobey will be condemned!'

'Condemned!' repeat the crowd. 'Condemned!' repeats the jury. I hang my head, try to mumble but no sound comes. 'Condemned!' says prosecutor-mother, and I wriggle with misery, cringe with shame, and all the time try to shout, 'No! It's not fair!' while nothing comes from my mouth.

Judge-mother bangs once more with the gavel and the court falls quiet. 'Anna Waters,' she says, 'you have been found guilty on all counts, namely failure to do your duty, failure to thrive, disruption of the order, lack of gratitude. You are condemned. You are cast out.'

She casts a gimlet glare round the waiting courtroom, then

shouts for all to enjoy. 'We will have no more! We will excise it! Take it away!'

An arm clamps round my stomach, another over my mouth. Hands pin my arms to my sides. Oh, God, not again, I think, as I find myself hauled backwards, ribcage caving in beneath rough hands. I drag my feet on the floor, struggle, try to cry out for help, but nothing gets past the hand clamped over my mouth, my nose. I throw pleading looks from side to side as we proceed up the aisle, and all I see is row upon row of Graces, arms folded, gazing at me with the silent contempt of a pest exterminator gazing at a cockroach.

The doors swing open at the back of the court and I see the pavement in Trafalgar Square. Parked beside it, doors ajar, is the white van. Three skinheads lean against the sides, smiling a smile of triumph. And inside the van, crouched down like a spider, is my mother, dressed in floral prints and running her finger over the sharpened edge of an axe.

Chapter Forty-Two

Dispatched, Matched, Hatched

Search:
> Duke of Belhaven

Sources:
> All

From:
> 1971–5

Publication:
> Daily Monograph

Byline:
> Diary

Date:
> 06 28 71

Headline:
> none

What's going on at Belhaven Great House, stately seat of the Duke of Belhaven? Rumour has it that, since the fifty-two-year-old Duke's return from a lengthy trip to Los Angeles, the corridors have been ringing to the sound of prolonged shouting. The aristocratic pair, it seems, have forgotten the ancient maxim, not in front of the servants, and below-stairs gossip suggests that all is not well on the upper floors. The reason? Certain 'friendships' struck up by the Duke on his 'working' vacation seem to have displeased the Duchess, and she is making her displeasure known. Suffice it to say that the Cadogan Gardens mansion flat is currently considerably more in use than it has been in recent years. The couple have a son, Gerald, who celebrated his thirteenth birthday at Eton last week.

Search:

Godiva Fawcett

Sources:

All

From:

1969–75

Publication:

News of the Nation

Byline:

Diary

Date:

08 19 71

Headline:

Godiva in Toffs' love-triangle

The love-rat Duke of Belhaven finally got his divorce application from the Duchess yesterday – citing his adultery with none other than twenty-one-year-old actress Godiva Fawcett. And it doesn't seem like she's going to have to work too hard to prove her case – insiders on the recent Bangladesh Famine telethon, where the *Beach Bunny Massacre* star did a stint as a guest presenter, reckon that she's got more than a couple of biscuits in the oven. 'Every time the camera was off her, she'd make a beeline for the toilet,' says a cameraman on the show, 'and come back looking so green the make-up people had trouble covering it up.' Let's just hope the House of Lords can rush the divorce through in time for the new arrival.

Search:

Duke of Belhaven

Sources:

All

From:

1969–72

Publication:
Times
Byline:
Court and Social
Date:
03 31 72
Headline:
Marriages: His Grace the Duke of Belhaven and Miss
Godiva Fawcett

The marriage took place, quietly at Belhaven Great House,
on 29 March 1972, of His Grace the Duke of Belhaven to
Miss Godiva Fawcett. The honeymoon will be spent at home.

Search:
Duke of Belhaven
Sources:
All
From:
1969–72
Publication:
Times
Byline:
Court and Social
Date:
04 04 72
Headline:
Births: Moresby

On 31st March, at St Mary's Hospital, Paddington, Lady
Harriet, daughter to Gerald Moresby, Duke of Belhaven
and Godiva (née Fawcett) Duchess of Belhaven, a sister
for Gerald. Mother and child are doing well.

Search:
Godiva Fawcett
Sources:
All

From:

1969–72

Publication:

Chat Magazine

Byline:

Georgina Ponsonby

Date:

16 06 73

Headline:

Taking on a new role

Godiva, Duchess of Belhaven, throws open the doors of
Belhaven Great House herself. 'Welcome, Georgina!' she
cries. 'Please! Come in!'

I am surprised to be greeted by the Duchess in person;
I had expected a housekeeper or a butler, or a personal
assistant at the very least. I tell her so as I follow her
through the grand entrance hall, and she laughs merrily.
'Oh, no, Georgina. I never bother with formalities like that.
You've got to remember, until recently I was a simple
working girl, shopping in the local grocery and making my
own little bachelorette suppers in the evenings.'

Typical modesty from a twenty-three-year-old best
known to the world as Godiva Fawcett, the actress who
gave up stardom, critical acclaim and the Hollywood social
whirl for love and motherhood last year when she married
Gerald, Duke of Belhaven following his divorce from his
wife of twenty years, the former Candida Revere, and
gave him a daughter, Harriet, now a year old.

Harriet plays around our feet as we talk in the white
drawing room. She is the image of her mother, with the
same white-blonde locks, retroussé nose and rosebud lips
– not to mention those famous emerald cat's eyes – and
mother and daughter display an enviable degree of
devotion. 'Of course she has nannies,' says the Duchess,
'but I like to spend as much time with her as I can. Who
wouldn't? Just look at her. She's a peach, isn't she?'

She certainly is. Has motherhood changed Godiva at

all? 'Why, of course!' she beams. 'It's my greatest role yet! I had no idea it was possible to love anyone so much. I love Gerald, desperately, madly, but nothing will ever compare to my feelings for my daughter.'

It would be hypocritical at this juncture not to pursue the subject of her love for the Duke. Their meeting, and the Duke's subsequent divorce, was, after all, subject of the greatest society scandal of the last two years. Godiva's usually sunny face clouds over as I ask her. 'Oh, Georgina,' she says, 'I wish it could have happened some other way. Neither of us meant it to happen, we fought it for as long as we could, but we couldn't help ourselves. We just fell in love, it's as simple as that. But don't think we weren't guilty about it. We were. Both of us, completely. I can't tell you the nights we both lay awake, crying in each other's arms. And especially about how awful I felt about the effect that all this would have on Gerald's son, Harriet's half-brother.'

But things are settled now, aren't they? Godiva attempts a brave smile. 'Of course. It will take time, but I'm confident that young Gerald *(Gerald, Viscount Ditchworth, heir to the Belhaven estates)* and I will eventually become great friends. But there are forces trying to poison him against us, and there's very little I can do but put up with it and try to keep smiling.'

What sort of forces? 'I don't want to talk about it too much,' she says. 'There's been too much mud-slinging in the past eighteen months as it is, but I do think it was vindictive of Candida to name me in the divorce petition. I know that she holds me personally to blame, but the marriage had been over in all but name for years. It was only a matter of time before he went looking for love if he couldn't get it at home. A man needs – I don't know – to be cherished, to be appreciated, to be admired. But now young Gerald has something concrete to cling to when he sees me, and I think it will be hard for him ever to give me a fair hearing.'

So how does she feel towards her husband's first wife

now, I ask, but her natural discretion blocks the question. 'No, Georgina, I said I didn't want to talk about it, and you can't draw me out. I'm sure Candida is a thoroughly decent person. It's just a shame that she doesn't seem to be able to get over her bitterness.'

Does she miss the glamour of her old life? Godiva laughs that tinkling, infectious laugh that came from the screen and caught audiences up in its magic. 'Not at all! No, really! Of course I enjoyed every minute that I was an actress, but in the end it's a shallow life, and Hollywood is a shallow place. I have always had more to me than just being a pretty face prancing across a screen, and the time has come for me to show the world that this is true.'

And how is she planning to go about showing this side of herself to the world? 'Well, obviously, my first duty is to my husband and daughter, and to his son, who badly needs some love and attention,' she says. 'But after that, I am planning to throw myself into my charitable works. As you know, I have long been interested in helping those less fortunate than myself, all the little people who need a spokesperson, someone who will stand up for them when they can't stand up for themselves. I have always felt that this was my destiny, and now I find myself in a unique position to help. After all, who better to speak for these people than someone who is already a household name, someone whom audiences recognise immediately? I'm saddled with my fame, after all, so I might as well put it to good use.'

And how is she going to go about this? 'Well, I'm open to offers!' she jokes. 'I've been working quietly in the background for various organisations, but now I think it's time to come out into the open, to stick my head above the parapet, as it were. So now I'm looking to do more, similar work, really get out there in the field, get my hands dirty. I plan to become a spokesperson for the front-line organisations, show the world that things can be done. It really is very, very important to me. I don't think people realise how much it matters to me that I be seen to be concerned. I know lots of cynics will probably pooh-pooh what I'm doing, but I know that I can make an important contribution.'

Godiva sighs, looks out again over the lands of Belhaven. 'You know, Georgina,' she finishes, 'this really is the most important thing to me. One day, the world will look back and know that I cared.'

The Duchess of Belhaven would like to make it known that all fees for this interview have been donated to charity.

Search:
Godiva Fawcett
Sources:
All
From:
1969–72
Publication:
Daily Express
Byline:
William Hickey
Date:
23 10 73
Headline:
Good God-iva

A little bird tells me that, after over a year of public breastbeating, Godiva Fawcett, better known these days as the Duchess of Belhaven of the *troisième part*, has finally managed to land herself a role as public spokesperson for a high-profile charity. And a good thing too, thinks Hickey: after such an adventurous early life, it would be a shame to see the lovely Godiva sink into a future of fete-opening, hunt-following and choosing the proper knife and fork. No news as yet as to who the lucky organisation is, but doubtless the beneficiaries of her largesse will not be suffering from anything too disfiguring to make a nice photocall. Expect much baby-dandling, orphan-cuddling and sincerity. Don't expect anything to do with scars, pus or contagion.

Chapter Forty-Three

Liggers' Paradise

I actually forget all about the dream until we're passing through Trafalgar Square on the bus on Thursday night. The bang on the head was heavy enough that I didn't wake up, despite my desperation to do so, and by the morning all I had left was a cross-looking Henry and a vague sense that something had happened in the night. But as we pass the spot where my kidnap happened, it all comes flooding back. 'Good grief,' I say.

Harriet, painting her lips a vivid scarlet with the help of a trimmed-down paintbrush, lowers her compact and says, like your teachers used to tell you not to, 'What?'

I tell her. As I speak, she raises the compact once again, smacks her lips a couple of times, clamps down on a Kleenex and pouts. Then she says, 'Good grief indeed.' Then she says, 'Blimey O'Reilly. So you're still obsessing about your old girl, then?'

The cheek. 'I think it was more metaphorical than literal,' I protest. 'Dreams usually are, you know.'

Harriet shakes her head. 'No. That's dreams about big old houses you've never been in, or flying or stuff. When you dream about your mother, you're dreaming about your mother.'

'Balderdash. If you're going to say that, you might just as well say that I was dreaming about your bloody stalkers.'

Harriet humphs. She's still deep, deep in denial. 'I don't have a stalker,' she says, to illustrate my point.

I sigh. Harriet has only received another dozen or so creepy emails from her non-stalkers since the march ('Saw you didn't even have the grace to honour your mother's memory on Saturday. Shame. I was looking forward to seeing you there. I had a present for you'), but the blinkers are still firmly on. I've tried screaming, and shouting, and pointing to the lump on my head, and talking reasonably, and even threatening her, but all she does is set her mouth and say, 'Well, obviously I'm going to be careful.' So, silly me, I'm scared to go anywhere without her, insist on following her everywhere, as if someone my size would be any use against a nutter with a hotline to London's skinhead community. Then again, it seems to have worked: nothing seems to have happened in the past five days, and now I can take a night off because we're going to be surrounded by Everyone Who's Anyone, Darling in the London restaurant community and no one, but no one, who shouldn't be there will get past Lydia's bouncers.

They have to have bouncers. Of course they've got boun-cers. All new bars these days are built with aquarium windows so that the handbag thieves have plenty of room to scope the yuppies before they pop in and set themselves up for the night. So when there's a launch, everyone within a mile's radius knows about it within seconds of the paper coming down from the windows. Bars have been known to go bankrupt on the backs of their launch parties. Obviously, underfinanced bars run by nitwits, but it's still a fact.

Of course, the owners of the Ski Bar probably think they've got bouncers because it lends them a certain exclusive cachet, like chrome swipe cards and a no-suits policy, but fortunately for them, they've hired Lydia to do their launch, and what Lydia doesn't know about bouncers, their uses and abuses, probably isn't worth knowing.

Lydia is Dom's new boss. Lydia specialises in top of the market launches and plucked Dom from the obscurity of front-of-house at Barley Cane to start at the bottom in her PR company. He's been there four weeks now, still in the middle of the honeymoon period, and we've already discovered the perks of having a mate in restaurant PR: that we will never, ever have to pay for a drink on Thursday night again. Because Thursday night is launch night, and all the PRs go to each other's launches when they're not doing launches of their own, and nobodies like us get to tag along.

Despite the fact that she eats out three or four times a week, Lydia is pencil-thin to fit into the designer gear she blags from her fashion PR friends in return for setting them up with the wherewithal to dine their clients without paying. Lydia has bags of energy and is always bestest, bestest friends with her staff in between the eighteen-month tantrums when she sacks them all, which usually precedes a five-week holiday somewhere in the Arizona desert. But she's the best in the business, everybody knows that, and Dom says he reckons he'll have learned everything he needs to know by the time she sacks him, and then he'll be able to set up on his own. 'It's a licence to print money, love,' he says. 'And I don't want to be living on catering wages when I'm forty.'

As we stand in the queue, Harriet says, 'So you're still thinking about that horrible old bat, then?'

I nod. Grace is rarely off my mind, though God knows I'd like to expunge every memory if I could. She hasn't, of course, been in touch. I didn't expect her to be. And I'm damned if I'm getting in touch with her.

'Poor old you.' Harriet makes an effort to sound sympathetic. 'All that and a headache too. How are you feeling?'

'Okay,' I reply. I've pretty much recovered. For four days, I nursed a headache and a sense of approaching doom, and though, obviously, I didn't have to work on Sunday and Monday because we were closed, things were pretty tough on the following two shifts. Even Harriet decided to lay off for a while, and behaved immaculately, taking up the slack when I had to pop off and sit down on a chair in the alleyway for a few minutes and close my eyes, though a strange virus seems to have struck Roy's new botanical collection, and their leaves are beginning to mottle and curl. But she's added a new twist to her act, trussing up her victims with liquorice bootlaces, an idea she introduced just as Roy was starting to ask questions, and he was so thrilled that he forgot all about his line of thought.

Dom's working the table in the foyer, scanning lists of names and ticking them off. He looks harrassed. 'Look,' he is saying to a man in a ski jacket that looks like it's been inflated with a bicycle pump, 'you're the third Adam Collyer who's come in tonight. You can't *all* be Adam Collyer.' Dom isn't just being firm because it's his job. He has certain standards and this man, who seems to have had his hair cut in the highlighted beach-bum curtains of 1991 despite being thirty-five if he's a day and is blessed with a set of teeth that some roebuck somewhere must be sorely missing, doesn't live up to them. 'Well, it's hardly my fault that someone else is pretending to be me, is it?' he is saying. 'Which ones were they? I'll go and find them.' Yer, right. Like no one on a door has ever heard that one before. 'There have been over three hundred people through the door already tonight,' Dom replies. 'I wasn't keeping an eye on what the Adam Collyers looked like.'

'Rich and Stinky are going to be *siriusly* pissed off about this,' says Adam the Third. Dom treats him to a welcoming smile. Rich and Stinky are the owners of this new glamour spot, a pair of former City traders who jumped over the wall to set up a company promoting off-piste snowboarding holidays for other Sloane Rangers. The business has done well, branching out into a healthy trade in branded skiwear, lipsalve and so forth, and now they're launching the Ski Bar to make some cash in the four months a year when the snow's gone from the Alps and the rest of us are treated to the sound of braying in the streets of London. They've even managed to get cigarette sponsorship from St Moritz, boom-boom.

'Ah!' says Dom, 'you're a friend of Rich and Stinky's! Why didn't you say?'

'Didn't think I had to,' says Adam the Third.

'Well, we can get this sorted out in no time,' says Dom, turns slightly to his left and says, 'Rich! Stinky! I've got Adam Collyer here!'

Rich looks up from where he and Stinky have a small blonde woman pinned at bay against a coat rack made from old chair-lift parts. Her suntan would make a Spanish shoe-maker wince with pride. 'Air Yair?' he says. 'Wear?' and I realise that he and Stinky must be distantly – or of course, not so distantly – related to Harriet. I stand back in amazement as they speak. Not a word emerges unscathed. You don't *learn* to speak like that; you're born to it. Liz Hurley could practise in front of the dressing-room mirror for the rest of her life and still never learn.

'Here.' Dom points at Adam the Third.

'Well, he'snur A'am Coyer,' says Stinky. 'Who the blaryal ar year?'

Adam the Third, unabashed, sticks out a hand. 'Ha-o

Stinky. Rory Cottrell. Wazza school waya bra'er. Met at that fraferl Jane creacher's chalet at Zermatt.'

'Air furguards sake,' says Stinky, catching him a violent slap on the upper arm. 'Why didn't yer sayser? Wappened to the Jane creacher, anyway?'

'Married some Franch skiern strata. Nafterer furra moneya course. Slarve.'

'Well, dafta be larve. Couldn't be furra sex appeal, could it?'

'Too righ. Sirius paper bag job, that one.'

'Yah, *sirius*.'

They roar and treat each other's upper arms to another bout of violence. Dom sighs, turns back and puts a third tick beside the fated Adam Collyer's name. 'Hello, darlings,' he says, kisses us both. 'Avoid the gluhwein like the plague. Ranjiit's behind the bar.'

Then he turns to the pair of scarecrows jiggling in line behind us and says, 'Hi, there. Can I have your names, please?'

Lydia is in the middle of the main room, talking to Terry Marshall. Terry is the bar correspondent for the *Evening Argus*, and wrote a book last year called *How to Get Drunk for Free*. Terry hasn't paid for a drink since 1987, and the whites of his eyes have been yellow since 1992. It doesn't take much to get Terry going these days, and he has already started singing. 'Have you heard this one, then?' he yells into Lydia's ear as she gamely smiles her welcoming smile. '*Lid*dia oh *Lid*dia say *have* you seen *Lid*dia, Liddia the *tatt*oed *lay*dy . . .'

'I have, Terry,' says Lydia, who has heard it from these very lips every time she's done a launch since she entered the business in 1993. 'Very good.'

'Music hall,' barks Terry, 'you can't beat a bit of music hall. Ah. Now. Who have we here?'

Lydia's eyes light up. 'Anna! Harriet! Welcome! Have you got a drink? Have you met Terry Marshall?' and before we're even able to say, 'Yes, Lydia, we were only spanking him a month ago,' she has slipped off into the crowd. This is what's technically known in the trade as the Teflon Shuffle, that ability to pass on anyone, however sticky, without ever seeming to have been there. Lydia's ability with the Teflon Shuffle is renowned throughout the industry. PR companies actually send their trainees to her launches to observe how it's done.

'Hi, Terry,' says Harriet. 'How are you?'

'Well, well,' bellows Terry, wiping the corners of his eyes with a wad of crumpled bog paper he's brought out from his pocket. 'Bloody awful launch, though. Never seen so many ugly people in one room in my life.'

Mr Marshall has a point, though. The press may offer little to write home about, but their leather-patched tweed jackets look positively tempting beside Rich and Stinky's field of acquaintance, who have turned out en masse to lig every last drop they can. Because what is just about acceptable in the low-lit wooden schnapps bars of Kandersteg is just *so* not attractive in the less kindly illumination of the urban wilds. Because, you see, though skiboarders like to think of themselves as the surfers of the mountains, it's not like that at all. They're more like the trolls of suburbia.

Where surfers are long and lean from a diet of shellfish and amphetamine, these people are square and squat from a diet of dope munchies. Where surfers have smooth, blemishless skin from constant exposure to sunlight and salt water, these people have rashes on their necks from constant exposure to man-made fabrics. Where surfers chug the occasional beer from the neck of the bottle, these people chug anything they can get, and their chapped lips are perpetually blackened by the berry stain of gluhwein. Surfers come from the coast, where the air is clean and long legs are a great aid in breasting sand dunes. Skiboarders come from the central counties, where short, thick little legs are a great aid in dipping sheep. You can't take a boy from a farm in Gloucestershire and turn him into an Adonis: it just won't happen.

Harriet executes a perfect Teflon Shuffle on Terry Marshall. She appeals to his sympathy. 'We've been here twenty minutes, Terry,' she lies, 'and we still haven't managed to get a drink. I'm going to die if I don't go to the bar. Can we get you something while we're there?'

'Poor old you,' says Terry. 'No, you're all right.'

We slip away and Terry disappears among the cackle of trolls. I brush against a pop-eyed brunette who has obviously stolen her teeth from a chain-smoking buck of the same family that Adam the Third got his from. She goggles, says, 'Mind out.' Then, she tries to take a puff of her Silk Cut extra-long with lips that have difficulty stretching closed, trails smoke up through her seagrass hair. 'You okay, Biccie?' says a bloke with a bobble hat. Oh, please. 'Yeah,' says Biccie. 'Though obviously some people can't see where they're going.' Puts a glass of red wine to her face, pushing lips forward in a trough to meet it, and a trail of spare goes down her chin to join the rest on her collar.

'Biccie,' I say, 'it's meant to go in your mouth,' and I move on while she's still goggling and trying to think of a response.

Ranjiit, tidy little goatee and hard-trimmed hair, hasn't worked a launch for a while, and is looking harassed. Presses up on the bar to give us kisses and drops back down again. 'They're animals,' he says. 'It's a feeding frenzy.' Waitresses attempt to come out of the kitchen doors with trays of canapés, get four, maybe five steps into the crowd and have to turn back because their trays have been sucked as clean as bleached dinosaur bones on a Montana hillside. He stops for a minute, picks up a cloth and a glass to look like he's doing something. 'How are you both? Haven't seen you since you left the Bean Bag Bar. You've been in the papers a lot.'

'Please don't start,' says Harriet.

'No, it's cool,' says Ranjiit. 'I was really proud. Did you really swear at Leeza Hayman?'

'Sort of,' says Harriet. 'I called her a bibulous old fishwife, if that counts as swearing.'

'Respect,' says Ranjiit, and gives her a high five. 'D'you two want a drink?'

We nod. We need a drink.

'What do you want? White wine?'

'Great.'

Ranjiit selects a nice bottle of Aussie Semillion, pops the cork and hands it over with two glasses.

Biccie shoves an elbow under mine, heaves me off the bar. 'I'll have one of those as well,' she says.

Ranjiit shakes his head, smiling nicely like a well-trained little boy. 'I'm sorry,' he says. 'I'm not allowed to hand out bottles.'

Biccie goggles. 'But you gave *her* a bottle.'

'Ah,' says Ranjiit. 'She's special.'

'Well, I'll have five glasses of wine, then,' says Biccie decidedly.

'Sorry.' Ranjiit shakes his head again, but nicely. 'I'm not allowed to do more than three glasses at a time.'

'Why on earth not?'

'Well,' he says slowly, 'because people often take advantage at things like this and get half a dozen glasses for themselves at a time. Which means that the drink runs out in the first half hour, and then there's nothing left for the people who come later.'

'You're patronising me!' she says accusingly.

Ranjiit smiles a lovely smile, blinks a couple of times. 'How clever of you to notice,' he replies. 'Three glasses of white, was it?'

We finally track Linds and Mel down to a corner by the window, where they perch on a stack of piled-up tables and share an ashtray made from an empty St Moritz packet. They are deep in conversation with Max Kershaw and Bob Pruitt.

'. . . Sort of person you'd have to gob in their food,' I hear Linds say to Max as we approach.

'An Amis or a Winslet?' asks Max.

'Oh, a DiCaprio at the very least,' she says. 'It would definitely have to come from the back of the throat.'

'Good girl,' says Max. 'He can't cook to save his life, anyway. Did you see the other night? Bloody bacon and tomatoes in the same pan, as though that was some sort of revelation.'

Max and Bob are both food writers. Max works for a glossy freesheet distributed in expensive hotels in the central zone, has a signet ring on his little pinkie and believes vehemently in capital punishment. Bob wears bow ties, and is obscenely, magnificently fat. I'm not talking unfashionably fat, here: Bob is a walking bell jar, a titan of fatness. Bob has to squeeze to get through doors, and that's when he's already turned sideways. I once sat in a booth in Livebait backing on to the one Bob was sitting in, and when he laughed, he catapulted me face-first into the person opposite me's bouillabaisse. Bob writes recipes for a Sunday paper that begin with declarations like 'There is no chip that compares with one fried in home-made beef dripping.' I love Bob.

He is also amazingly strong for someone for whom the very effort of standing up produces the sort of panting you usually only see in a Grand National winner. He picks me up in huge arms and squashes me into the folds of his tummy. 'My dear,' he declares, 'it's always so nice to see the rude girls. Have you insulted anyone yet this evening?'

'It would be hard not to,' Harriet splutters after receiving the same affectionate treatment. Bob is a lovely guy, but it's hard to breathe when your face has been buried in three tons of lard. 'Anna found someone called Biccie.'

'Biccie?' says Max. '*Biccie?* What sort of a name is that?'

'Biccies?' Bob looks around him wildly, hopefully. 'Are there? I'm fainting from hunger.'

'No, no,' says Max. 'It's a *name*. What do you think it's short for?'

'Biscuit, obviously,' says Harriet.

Mel gives me a big cuddle round my well-squashed shoulders. 'How's the head?'

'Better.' I push my hair back to show her the bruise.

'I say,' says Max, 'been tangling with that chef of yours again?'

'Oh no, far more dramatic,' says Harriet, 'she got kid-napped. Had to be saved by a very cute policeman.'

'How cute?' asks Linds.

'Very cute,' we chorus together, and I look at her in mild surprise.

'Kidnapped?' asks Bob, to whom the idea of someone picking you up and carrying you away seems an entirely alien concept.

'Don't worry,' says Harriet. 'She got a police escort home.'

'Hang on,' says Mel, 'last I heard you had that nice Australian boy in tow.'

'Well, yes, but he's in Barcelona until Sunday. And then he's off back down under.'

'Still keeping them lined up like chocolates, then,' teases Mel.

'Chocolates?' Says Bob. 'Where?'

'It's a crime against humanity,' Max fulminates.

'What?' asks Linds.

'You can't call a woman *Biccie*. It's like calling your dog Cressida.'

This goes over everyone's head. Especially Bob's. 'I wish you wouldn't keep mentioning biccies,' he says. 'I might have to slip through the crowd and see if I can't get a bit closer to the kitchen.'

We all turn to watch Bob slip through the crowd. It's one of those unmissable phenomena, like the parting of the Red Sea. He lumbers away from us, going, amiably, 'Excuse me, excuse me,' and ploughing forward without waiting for a response. People topple like ninepins before a bowling ball. A swathe of clear floor opens up behind him.

'I'm going to see if I can't get into his slipstream,' says Mel, 'see if Ranjiit can do us another bottle.' And she slips through the crowd in his wake.

'Which one's Biccie, anyway?' asks Max.

I point across the floor. 'The brunette with the brown velvet skin.'

'Well, *that* narrows it down a bit.' He laughs. And then he does something very odd. He cups his hands about his mouth and shouts a single word:

'Caroline!'

For a moment, the room falls quiet. It's as though a mobile phone has gone off in a bar full of bankers. Everyone looks around to see who's calling them, then, like a herd of startled sheep, they begin to talk again, odd bleats joining up to become cacophony once more.

'That's brilliant.' Lindsey giggles. 'Can I try?'

'Be my guest.' He gestures expansively towards the room.

Linds cups her mouth, yells, 'Chaaaarlie!' out over the throng. The hoots and brays die away once more, heads crane like compys in *Jurassic Park*. 'What a lovely game,' she says. 'Lovely.'

'The trick,' he explains, 'is to not do it too often. Every ten minutes or so is about right, or they begin to learn, like Pavlov's dogs.'

'A little-known fact about Pavlov's dogs,' Harriet butts in, 'is that, about twenty times after they'd rung the bell and salivated, they realised that there wasn't going to be any more food and started attacking their trainers.'

Everyone falls silent to contemplate this for a moment. Then the Jurassic crowd parts once more and Bob Pruitt bears down upon us with a tray of canapés held high above his head. 'No biccies, I'm afraid,' he announces. 'But I managed to get these.'

We all fall upon them as though we haven't eaten in weeks. 'You saviour,' cries Harriet, 'you little star!'

Bob beams round a handful of bruschetta.

Mel pops out from behind him. She has a bottle of red in one hand and a bottle of white in the other. 'I'm getting quite good at this for a librarian,' she says. 'Ranjiit's a sweetie, isn't he?'

'Where do I recognise him from?' asks Max.

'He used to work at the Bean Bag Bar with us,' I tell him. 'And before that he was the barman at Polka!'

'Polka! Of course!' cries Max. 'He used to make a blinding schnapps martini! With little sausages on the side!'

'They were Kabanos, I think,' Bob corrects him.

'No, no they were definitely sausages,' says Mel. 'By the way, I just played a blinder.'

'Oh, yeah, what was that?' asks Linds.

'Some toad with bloody wraparound sunspecs on was leaning over me telling her stories about his bloody skiing holiday. Adam something-or-other. Never been so bored. You know me. I wouldn't know a schuss from a scheiss. And he's leaning further and further forward to look down my dress and it's getting more and more obvious. So I said, "Oooh, look, there are my food-critic friends over there. I must go and talk to them." And he said, "Ooh, must you go so soon? I was just getting to know you. I'm going to an orgy in Fulham later. Want to come?" '

Harriet opens her mouth and mimes putting her finger down her throat.

'If it were up to me,' says Max, 'I'd horsewhip the lot of 'em. If ever there was a justification for bringing back hanging . . .'

'So,' finishes Mel, 'I said, "Ooh, but I wouldn't want to monopolise you. There must be other breasts you want to talk to." '

Max sighs. 'Ghastly, these things. Ghastly. Don't know why I bother coming. Hate every minute of them.'

'Me, too,' says Harriet in her most blasé voice, though I know for a fact that she's spent the entire day getting excited about getting to go for a night out without having to serve anyone. She had three baths. Count 'em. Three.

'I swear, this is it,' says Max. 'Complete waste of time.'

'Dreadful,' agrees Harriet. 'Absolutely pointless.'

'Sick of bloody canapés,' he says.

'I know,' she says, ducking under Bob's arm to help herself to a miniature duck pancake with hoisin sauce dripping from the ends. 'Never want to see another one.' She pops it in her mouth, chews, closes her eyes slowly in ecstasy.

Max pauses, lights a Dunhill in a small bone cigarette holder. 'Going to the launch of that new gastropub on the river next week? The Cox's Head. Down by Putney, good views of the boat race.'

'Probably,' says Harriet. 'Haven't decided yet.'

'Good,' agrees Max. 'Me, too.'

Chapter Forty-Four

Revolving Doors

Grace has won a Brit Award. No, really. We're watching the highlights in stunned silence when the buzzer goes at half past five on Sunday, and, while I'm still going, 'Good god. What if she'd turned up and collected it?' I think: blimey, he's keen. He's not due till six thirty. I've not even had a chance to have a shave yet. I'm still drinking sugary tea, and Harriet, who has promised to go out, is still elbow-deep in the glue and cat litter from which she is constructing a *faux*-gravel path in a 3-D representation of Highgate Cemetery after, as far as I can see, a nuclear holocaust. Blasted trees of coathanger wire and unthinned oil paint hang over leery gravestones and scattered chicken bones. We've been arguing desultorily about whether she is ever going to clear up the popcorn on the stairs, which must be riddled with beetles by now.

We're both so gobsmacked by the sight of the bald little man in a suit who has been sent by her record label to collect Grace's Brit that neither of us hurries to answer the door. He only comes up to the shoulder of the fashion-model-in-platforms who announced the We're Not Complete Philistines, You Know Award, and she is standing behind him as he mutters acknowledgement of the entire orchestra that were hired to back up my mother's xylophone-playing. It's lucky that she's black, really, as otherwise, what with her décolletage and push-up bra and the fact that he is dipping his head towards the microphone in the manner of people unused to public speaking, one would think that she'd suddenly sprouted three tits.

Halfway through his speech, a gigantic photograph of Grace, looking particularly grim, is projected onto the backscreen, and the assembled crowd of musos drop their don't-care act to emit a unified gasp of fear. I know how they feel. The last time I saw my mother, I had my hands clamped over my mouth to stop myself from screaming.

The buzzer goes again as an Indie artist in a dress that looks like a pine cone comes forward to announce the Hammiest Overacting in a Promotional Video Award. Still reeling, I wander over and press the speak button on the intercom, go, 'Hello?'

'Hi, it's Mike Gillespie,' comes an unexpected voice.

Harriet looks up, raises an eyebrow. 'Oh, hi.' I press the buzzer. 'Come up.'

Harriet goes over to the sink and begins to swarfega her hands. 'Well. What does he want?'

'I don't know.'

'Hmm,' says Harriet. Then she says, 'You're not going to sleep with him, are you?'

This gives me pause. 'Gosh. I hadn't thought about it,' I half-lie. 'D'you think I should?'

She rolls her eyes. 'I wasn't giving out orders, Anna. Keep control. Just because someone asks you a question doesn't mean that the answer is yes.'

'D'you think that's why he's here?'

'Well, I don't think he's planning to walk in here and rip your gear off, no. Anyway, for heaven's sake, you've got

Niggle turning up in an hour. What's wrong with him, all of a sudden?'

'He's going back down under after the weekend.'

'I think,' says Harriet, 'he'll be going down under before then.'

'Eugh,' I say. 'Lurid and unnecessary detail.'

Harriet squirts a couple of pints of cream onto her hands, rubs it up to the elbows, puts her rings back on.

'So, what? Our PC Gillespie is to be the next victim?'

'Christ, you make me sound like a black widow spider,' I say.

'Well . . .' she says doubtfully.

'What?' I'm used to Harriet calling me a slag, but this is slightly unusual.

'He's a nice guy, that's all,' she says. 'I'm not sure if he's the quick-fling type.'

At which I laugh. 'Harriet, every man in the *world* is a quick-fling type if you give him the opportunity.'

'Cynic,' she says.

'Takes one to know one,' I reply.

The buzzer at the bottom of the stairs sounds and I clunk him in.

'Seriously, though,' I say, 'even *you* thought he was cute.'

Harriet nods. 'Yes. He is. And nice.'

'So what do you think?'

'It's not up to me. Why don't we see what he wants?'

I suppose that this could be a good plan. 'Look,' I say, 'whatever, I don't want to give the impression that there's a revolving door to my bedroom. He's pretty respectable . . .'

The door begins to creak open. Harriet nods hurriedly at me and we both turn to give him a welcoming smile as, panting slightly, he staggers the last couple of steps over the lintel.

'I thought I was reasonably fit,' he announces.

'Good stairs, those,' says Harriet. 'Designed to wear burglars out before they get here.'

'You must have had fun moving in.'

'There's a winch on the balcony. They carried everything *down*stairs.'

Harriet looks at her watch. 'Well, the sun's passed back under the yardarm. Would you like a beer, or does your duty to the public preclude the ingestion of an alcoholic beverage?'

'I'm not on duty,' he replies, and a small line that appears beside his left eye is the only indication that he's taken in the jibe. 'I'd love a beer, if you've got one.'

Slightly to my surprise, I find that there are half a dozen tins of Stella in the fridge. Neither of us really bothers with beer, on the grounds that it fills you up too much to really work, so it's not often you find it in the house unless I remember to swipe a couple of cans from the restaurant. Harriet must have been thieving. I pop the top on one, cast around for something to pour it into. The sink is piled with glue pots.

'Don't worry,' says Mike hastily, 'I'll have it from the tin.'

Relieved, I hand it over.

'So to what do we owe the pleasure of this rare visitation from Her Majesty's Constabulary?' Harriet continues with her mick-removal, flopping down on the sofa in her paint-stained jeans. I'll give her this: she's certainly making an effort to be friendly. She usually grunts and carries on painting when a bloke comes into the room.

Mike sits in the armchair. He already looks comfortable in that chair, as though he's been sitting in it for years. He looks good in his mufti, even if it does veer towards the well-pressed collarless grandad shirt and Hush Puppies style.

But there's something quite appealing about a man who's so obviously in need of a bit of help. I'm hardly the first woman to think so.

'I just thought I'd check up on you,' he replies, once he's settled. 'See how Midge's head is and find out if you've done anything at all.'

'My name's not Midge,' I say, because you have to stamp on these things early or they get ingrained and the next thing you know you have a nickname. It took me five years to shed Fanny, and I'm not going to start again now, 'and thanks, it's much better.'

'Still got a lump?'

I think: ah, a chance to get a bit of the old physical rapport going, say, 'Huge one. Size of an ostrich egg. Want a feel?' and present my scalp to him.

He feels around above my ear, eventually locates the remains of the lump and says, 'More of a bad mosquito bite, I'd say. Hurt at all, does it?' and takes his hand back to rest on his beer can.

Bums. Mike Gillespie's hand felt extremely right, stroking around my earlobes. I would have preferred if he'd kept it there a bit longer. 'Not much any more. It's better now.'

'She made the most of it while it lasted,' says Harriet. 'I was bringing her meals in bed for two days.'

Mike takes a slug of beer and says, 'And have either of you thought about who's been doing this, yet?'

We exchange glances. Rather embarrassed ones. Harriet says, 'Well, nothing else has happened since . . .' and dries up.

I light a cigarette.

Mike sighs. 'Well, I'd not entirely expect something else to have happened in a week, but that doesn't mean that you shouldn't be at least thinking about it.'

Harriet puts on her stubborn look.

'Come on,' says Mike. 'Can't we at least talk about it?'

'So which days off do you get, then?' Harriet effects about the most blatant change of subject I've ever seen. And he cooperates.

'Hard to predict,' he says. 'I usually get Sundays off, but we all work on a rota that gets mapped out ahead of time. I get a reasonable amount of notice, unless someone's ill or injured or something.'

'Blimey,' I say. 'Must play havoc with your social life.'

'You get used to it,' he says non-committally. He's got a touch of the Clint Eastwoods about him, a sort of yes-ma'am laid-backness that makes my skin contract. Pleasantly, you understand. 'I don't suppose it's any worse than working in a restaurant.'

'Ah, but *our* friends can come and hang out at our place of work. I don't suppose yours can do that.'

'Not much,' he agrees. 'Though I seem to get people from the Chamber of Commerce in the back of my Panda at least once a fortnight.'

'What for?'

'Meant to be a community spirit-building thing but everyone knows it's just to give them a thrill. They love it when we put the siren on, especially if we go through traffic lights.'

'Can I ask you a question?' says Harriet. Mike nods over his beer can. 'Do you ever put your siren on when you don't strictly need to?'

'How do you mean?'

'Well, you know, when you're bored, or when it's time for your tea break, or when you've, like, bought a curry or something and don't want it to get cold?'

The humour line comes back by his eye. Then he smiles,

a lazy, naughty, calculating smile. 'That would be an abuse of my judicial powers,' he replies. And despite the fact that I'm going to get plenty of naughties tonight, a little voice inside me goes: *you can abuse your judicial powers with me any time, sonny.* And then I notice that Harriet is holding his gaze, and I think: blimey. If I didn't know her better, I would think they were exchanging meaningful glances.

'Well, doh,' says Harriet. 'Why do you think I'm asking?'

He laughs. 'I don't feel myself at liberty to divulge that information under the current circumstances,' he says. The cheeky minx, I think, she's flirting with him. Harriet never flirts. She saw so much of her mother flirting to get her own way that she rejected the practice as unsound in her early teens.

'Anyway,' continues Mike, 'you're changing the subject. Have you had any further ideas about who might be sending these emails?'

'Probably dozens of people,' says Harriet. 'It's hardly a challenge to work out what my address is.'

'Have you thought about changing your address to something more anonymous?'

'Bollocks to that,' says Harriet. 'I'm already ex-directory and anonymous on the council-tax list. I've got to have *some* way that people can get in touch with me. What would happen if some gallery owner wanted to buy something and they couldn't find out where I was?'

Yer, right. That's happened *so* often.

'Well, look, there's nothing I can do to force you to ask for help,' he says, 'but at least will you take my phone number and my badge number in case you need it?'

Now, there's a novel way of getting a chick to take your number. 'Thanks,' I say, 'that's really sweet of you.'

'No problem. It's just that I feel sort of responsible now I've got involved. You know how it is.'

'Oh, yes,' says Harriet. 'We know.'

It's five past six. I'm definitely going to have to get this guy out of here in the next ten minutes. I still can't work out what's going on, whether he's interested or not, but law four of promiscuity states that facing a potential lover with the evidence of the one before is the most effective way of failing to get anywhere after asking someone to marry you and have your babies. Unless he's the sort of man who's kinky for other men's women, in which case you should steer well clear, as rule five states that if you get any inkling that you're about to become a trophy shag you should cut and run.

I give Harriet a look.

She gazes vaguely back, showing not a sign that she's taken in my meaning. The bitch is going to torture me.

'Would you like another beer, Constable Gillespie?' she offers.

'Yes,' he says, 'thanks. That would be nice.'

Damn you, you cow. You're doing this on purpose.

Harriet slowly unglues herself from her seat, meanders over to the fridge. Opens it and stares for several seconds at the five cans of Stella inside. Closes the door, stands up and says, 'Damn. I thought there was more. I'm very sorry, but we seem to have run out.'

Good girl. My mate.

'Never mind.' He settles back.

'There's only one thing for it,' she says. 'I'll have to take you out and buy you one.'

'Good God,' he says. 'There's no need for that.'

'No,' says Harriet, 'I insist. It would be a travesty if you were to come round here on your night off and go away on a single beer. I won't hear of it.'

'It's fine,' he says. 'I'm perfectly all right. Really.'

'Well, look, you can do me a favour, then.' She comes back towards him, bends forward so that a small flash of cleavage peeks out from under her work shirt. Harriet learned this one from Godiva. Done right, the flash so small that the victim barely takes in that he's seen it, it works brilliantly, like subliminal advertising. Mike Gillespie is like a large dog on a small chain.

'It's my night off too, and I could really do with getting out of this place for a bit,' she says. 'I've been indoors all week and the last thing I want to do is stay cooped up in here all evening. Why don't you come down to the river with me and let me buy you a beer?'

'I wouldn't want to intrude,' he says slowly, eyes revolving in his head. Women don't need twirling watches to hypnotise a man; all they need is their top two buttons undone and a sky-blue bra.

'You wouldn't be intruding,' she says. 'You'd be doing me a favour. Anna's got to wait in for a phone call from Taiwan, so I'm stuck if you won't come with me.' She puts her hands between her knees, presses her elbows together. Mike is on his feet like a shot. 'Okay,' he says. 'Just for a while.'

'For as long as you want.' Harriet bats the cat-likes in his face and begins to walk towards the door. 'If you'd care to proceed in an orderly fashion, I'll show you the way.' The invisible chain lets out a little bit, goes taut, tweaks, begins to pull. Mike never even thinks of pulling against it.

'Thanks, Mike,' I call out as they head to the top of the stairs. 'You've saved my life again.'

'You're welcome,' says Mike from a great distance.

'See you soon, yeah?' I command, in the hope that he will take me up on it.

'Sure,' he says.

'No, really, I mean it. You're welcome here,' I insist.

'Thanks,' he says, but it's obvious that the trance is way, way too deep for him to give much mind to anything else.

'Have a good time.'

'Thanks,' they both reply.

I wait as their footsteps recede down the stone stairs, listen for the clunk of the door at the bottom. Then I leap to my feet and run for the bathroom.

Chapter Forty-Five

Wash and Brush Up

Bugger, bugger, bugger. I have precisely fifteen minutes till take-off. Hair, skin, fingernails dirty, no make-up, cat-litter armpits, gorgonzola cleavage. And nothing to wear. Nothing in chest of drawers but an old Bart Simpson T-shirt and some leggings. Leggings? When did I ever wear leggings?

No time to think. Nice Mike the sexy copper: hope he comes back, but in thirteen minutes there will be a brown beach-boy from Barcelona on my doorstep and get your priorities right, girl. Toss through the pile of clothes on the floor like a tornado, resurface with the perfect thing: short, black Lycra, clingy around the boobs, cut gypsy-style off the shoulder, flared skirt just above the knee. Best five pounds I ever spent in Brixton market, and it doesn't even have any stains on it. Well, not that can't be covered up with a casually tossed-on turquoise silk bolero. Which is creased from lying over the back of the chair for a month. I put it on a coat hanger, run to the bathroom with it over my arm.

Pull the shower curtain, let the cubicle fill with steam and hang the jacket from the rail to iron itself out. Brush my teeth, look in the mirror and blench. It's worse than I thought. I never got round to washing my face after we fell in through the door from work, and there's mascara smudged under my eyes. No wonder PC Mike didn't want to stroke my hair for too long. Grab the apricot facial scrub, rub my skin red-raw and take a few blackheads with it.

Ten minutes. At least if I'm washing my hair, I don't have to waste time scrubbing my fingernails. Hang the jacket outside the shower, jump under the steaming water, scream, jump out, turn up the cold, jump back in again. Lather, rinse, repeat, scrub like the wind at the old cheesy bits. Absolute terror as blunt razor scrapes over pits, shins; no time for anything else. Please God, no blood-letting tonight. God is on my side; a tiny nick below the knee decides just to bubble up a little and leave it at that. Hopefully he won't notice.

Harriet and PC Mike must be almost at the water by now. I only hope they find something open.

Seven minutes. Thank God for short hair. I stand in front of the mirror rubbing vigorously with the towel while I check that I've brushed my teeth thoroughly enough. No green bits. Chipped varnish on toenails; nothing I can do about that now. Hair half-dry, shove on some mousse to make it stand up as though it's meant to look like that.

Five minutes. Glop on face. Second thoughts, glop everywhere. Especially on breasts, shoulders, stomach, bum. Lovely and smooth. Sometimes, girl, you can pull it off.

Stumble on stairs as I pull my dress over my head, catch my knee an almighty clunk, scream out a string of words that would make Captain Haddock proud. Waste twenty seconds rocking like a madwoman, teeth gritted. Deodorant. Damn. Pull dress down and slop it on, snap dress back into place. Shoes in bedroom. What shoes? Which ones? Ah, sod it: let's go for the natural look. I run, barefoot, upstairs in search of my handbag.

Two minutes. Two minutes till my lovely boy is due. I'm starting to get excited. The pounding of my heart is no longer only because I'm late; in ten minutes, if I'm lucky, the dress will be on the floor and no one will care about stains any more. No time for foundation. I slick two lines of black kohl pencil inside my lower lashes, two coats of mascara, a quick finger lick and I smooth down my eyebrows. Suck in cheeks, pout into hand mirror. No cheekbones. Damnation, why didn't you just give me cheekbones and have done with it?

I find a dark red lipstick, draw rapid stripes of colour onto my face, rub it in. Too strong. More haste less speed: they always told me that. Grab a manky old tube of face cream from the nether regions of my bag, rub some over the lippy, smear it all backwards towards the hairline. Yes. Yes, yes, yes.

The doorbell goes. I run over, clunk the open button, finish off my lips. Two lovely morello cherries slashed across a pale, wide-eyed face. Lovely. How can he resist? Right. Time for a deep breath and a fag.

No there isn't. The jacket's still in the bathroom, Goddamn it. I hit the front door button and belt down the stairs. Drop the jacket over my shoulders, take a last glimpse in the mirror and slow my breathing right down. Hi, love. Here already? What, this old thing? Just something I threw on.

I step out onto the landing as he comes in through the front door, go down to meet him.

He looks delicious. Delicious and tired and brown and warm, just like I remember. We meet five steps from the bottom, fold into each other's arms. His mouth is soft like toffee. I stroke his upper arm muscle and rest my head against his shoulder. 'Hi, love,' I say. 'How are you?'

He pushes me back, looks down at me, a little smear of fresh lipstick at the corner of his mouth.

'Christ,' he tells me. 'You look good enough to eat.'

And I give him my foxy smile and say, 'Whatever you want, master . . .'

Chapter Forty-Six

1977: Our Lady of the Earthquake

Our Lady of the Earthquake is standing on the dust-laden, crumbled tarmac of another indistinguishable foreign street, hands in the back pockets of her cropped-ankle jeans so that her breasts thrust forward in her immaculately pressed, checked lumberjack shirt. We are looking at her in profile, for she is gazing, lost in thought, at the devastation around her. The cameraman briefly changes his focus so that, instead of each perfect hair in Godiva's elegant but suitably unadorned chignon, we see instead a row of Soviet-grey concrete blocks of flats which have tipped sideways as their foundations gave way and are leaning one against the other like hay bales.

From their windows, or from where the windows were before the fronts of the buildings toppled into the street, hang the pathetic remains of family life: curtains, bedsheets, clothes, are draped like ghastly bunting put out to welcome triumphant death. Scuttling among the ruins, tiny people cup their ears to listen for sounds beneath the concrete, a skinny, tan-coloured dog scrabbles at rubble, an old woman veiled in black holds the sides of her head and rocks silently back and forth as though the pain inside will cause her to explode.

Godiva heaves a sigh, turns back to the camera, which

swings sharply into focus in time to register that the emerald eyes are brimming with tears. She takes a hand from her pocket, gestures helplessly, as though even she realises that donating her beauty to the Third World will not in itself be enough. 'This is the aftermath of an earthquake,' she tells us. 'Doesn't look so bad, does it? No screams, no blood, no gunshots.'

She pauses, looks back down the street. Continues. 'But that's because, apart from a very few, the people of Kalechi-stan have given up their dead now. Five days after these buildings – less than a week ago home to hundreds of families, thousands of people – were destroyed by the terrible earthquake that devastated this town, they have relinquished the digging, put mourning aside, for the very business of survival threatens to overwhelm them.'

Godiva holds out her hands, sweeps them criss-crossed, says, 'Cut. Cut.'

The cameraman switches off, the sound man rests the pole to which the boom is attached on the crumbled soil. Everyone mops their brow with their sleeve, for earthquakes do little to lower the temperature in the mountainous regions of Central Asia. 'Is there a problem?' asks the press officer from the Kalechi Earthquake Fund.

'Of course there's a fucking problem,' snaps Godiva. 'I haven't had a thing to eat since we left the hotel and my concentration's all shot to hell. Didn't anyone bring any sandwiches, even?'

Everyone looks about them as though with enough concerted will, a sandwich will materialise in an earthquake zone at noon in the middle of Ramadan.

'I'm afraid not,' says the press officer.

'Oh, right,' says Godiva. 'And if we had the press along, rather than just me having to do this whole thing by myself, would you have remembered to bring something to keep us from starving to death?'

'I'm sorry,' says the press officer.

Godiva tilts her chin so that her head turns away. 'Right,' she says. 'Well, I suppose we'll have to get on with it.'

She sighs, says, 'But this is so unprofessional.'

The cameraman lifts his equipment back up to his shoulder.

'Well, excuse *me*,' says Godiva, fists on bony hipbones. 'D'you *mind* if I have a little make-up first?'

'Sorry,' they all mumble.

The make-up artist rushes forward, dabs another layer of powder on the perfect complexion, brushes the essential touch of pink onto the perfect cheekbones. Holds up a mirror for the Duchess's scrutiny. Godiva tilts her head from side to side, wets her lips and pouts a little.

'This actually matters, you know,' she lectures her crew. 'I'm not just doing this for vanity. They've done loads of research that proves that people are more likely to listen to people who look good. It's a fact. The better I look, the more exposure we get, and the more exposure we get, the more money we raise. It's important to me, this, even if it's not to you.'

The make-up artist applies a quick layer of Frosted Teacake to the perfect lips and everyone is satisfied. 'Children ready?' asks Godiva.

'Yes,' replies the press officer.

'Good,' she says. 'And can you get Abdullah to keep his finger out of his nose for five minutes?'

She resumes her former position. 'Right, let's take it from the last pause, shall we? Count me in, someone.'

In the absence of a clapper holder, the press officer goes, 'Three . . . two . . . one,' and Godiva once again pauses to look back down the street and continues. 'But that's because, apart from a very few, the people of Kalechistan have given up their dead now. Five days after these buildings – less than a week ago home to hundreds of families, thousands of people – were destroyed by the terrible earthquake that devastated this town, they have relinquished the digging, put mourning aside, for the very business of survival threatens to overwhelm them.'

She pauses to change gear, and somehow, her eyes seem to begin to glow. 'Their families dead, their belongings destroyed, their very means of eking a living shut off from them, these people face starvation, disease and hypothermia. Those fortunate enough to escape from these blocks when death came thundering through in the small hours of the morning now face a struggle equally as terrible to continue to stay alive. The International Community seems to have forgotten about these people. The country's too small, not politically powerful enough, the people haven't emigrated and formed communities with political pull in richer nations, they're not the right religion. You must help. Britain has donated the princely sum of $10,000 in aid, which will buy maybe twenty makeshift tents to house the homeless. America's contribution has amounted to some $20,000, or 0.007 of a cent per capita of that country's population, or 0.25 of a cent per capita here. We must do something – you and I must do something. This cannot be allowed to continue.'

Again she pauses, and this time brings her hand up to rub, like a small child, the area just below her left eye. You can think what you like about her, but Godiva was a professional. 'There are signs of hope here,' she continues, 'but hope can only flower where it is watered by kindness.'

Godiva waits another beat for the statement to sink in;

the power of cliché should never be underestimated. Then she turns, crouches down and puts her arm round the shoulders of a small girl in a baggy, blue cotton dress who stands between two slightly larger boys. Their eyes are huge and round, and gaze without expression at the camera as though all that they have seen has driven the thoughts from their heads. She is beautiful, though, this child: round and smooth of cheek, smooth strong hair rough-cut in the gamine style, lips like plums. 'Maryam, Abdullah and Jamal lost their parents and grandparents in one terrible minute on Wednesday night.' Godiva looks once again at the camera, then turns to Maryam and runs a Frosted Teacake fingernail down her cheek. Maryam continues to stare ahead, lower lip jutting, while Godiva bends forward, showing the viewer just that tiny hint of cleavage, presses her mouth to the child's forehead and lowers her eyelashes in empathy. 'They have no family, they have no home, they have no future. But fortunately, they have friends.'

Pulling Jamal – or maybe it's Abdullah – into the benediction of her arms, she gestures with a jerk of her perfect little chin at a building behind her which has somehow come out of the earthquake almost intact. 'The IERF has established an orphanage in this safe house. Here, children like these can find safe harbour, have some chance of rebuilding their shattered lives. Here, over one hundred lost children have found shelter. For the time being, they are safe. But Jamal and Abdullah and Maryam face an uncertain future. What is to become of them?'

A beat, two, three. Again, Godiva's eyes fill with unshed tears. 'I think of my own daughter,' she bravely croaks, 'and wonder, how would she cope? What would she do? She's so innocent, so young, so sheltered; what would I feel if it were her? And I'm asking you today to wonder the same thing.

Ask yourself: if these were my children, would I want them starving in the streets, or surrounded by love? Given a handful of rice and a cup of water and sent on their way?'

Godiva takes time to gaze lovingly at Maryam's expressionless face. Turns back to her audience. 'You can make a difference. I can make a difference. We can all make a difference. What I'm asking you to do today is take the first steps to make that difference. I know *I* don't want to live in a world where people ignore those poorer, smaller and weaker than themselves. If you're like me, and want to live in a better world than that, send your cheques to the International Earthquake Relief Fund at the address below, call the numbers below to make your pledges, or make donations to our collectors, who will be out on your local High Street this weekend. Don't do it because I tell you to. Do it because you care. Do it for Maryam and Jamal and Abdullah. Won't you? Please?'

Her expression, half smiling, half tearful, is directed straight to camera for a full five seconds until the press officer says, 'Cut,' and everyone lays down their equipment. She lets go of the children, pulls a handkerchief from her jeans pocket and wipes her hand. 'Someone needs a bath,' she says. 'How was that?'

'Marvellous,' says the press officer. 'Fabulous, wonderful. You are so kind to do this, and you've done such a fantastic job. I can't tell you how grateful we all are. You were brilliant.'

Godiva straightens up, brushing dust from the knees of her jeans, stretches her body in the sunlight, eliciting a hiss from the old lady in black ten yards away.

'Was I?' she asks. 'Was I really? Do you think they'll like it? Will they like *me*, do you think?'

Chapter Forty-Seven

Things Hot Up

Nigel packs up his rucksack and leaves while I'm still asleep. When I wake up and realise he's gone, I feel sort of sad, but sort of glad as well, because I hate saying goodbye, especially when I've got fond of someone. It's day-off Monday, so I stay dozing and enjoying little flashback memories of beach-boy running his hands over my stomach, over my hips, over my thighs, and cuddling Henry, who submits with the good grace of someone who's glad to have his bed back, until the direct sunlight passes off my window, which means that it's gone seven o'clock in the evening and, even if I haven't noticed it yet, I ought to be hungry.

On the landing just outside my door is a note scrawled on the ripped-off back page of a paperback novel. I flip it over and see that it's come from a battered copy of *The Beach*. I'm not sure whether to be entertained or insulted. But at least he's not the sort of anal character who can't break the spine on a paperback in case someone might spot he's actually been reading it. In clear, teacherly script it reads:

Hi, kiddo,

Call me an old romantic, but I like the fact that my last sight of you was a mop of black hair and an arm sticking up from under the bedcovers. We wouldn't have known what to say to each other, so I thought it was best just to go without a load of drama. But I also want to say thanks for the best time, and I won't forget you. It would be hard to. You've changed my view of the English for ever! You're a great chick, and I wish you well with everything that goes on in your life.

And listen: ignore this bit if it makes you uncomfortable. But if you need a friend, or just need somewhere to go for a bit, you've got a crash-pad in WA if you need it. No strings. I'd just like to feel that you knew you could if you wanted to. Or maybe come out and see what fun you could have when it's not so blimming cold 24–7! We could go down to Margaret River and eat crayfish. Hang with the hippies. They've got trees down there you wouldn't believe.

Think about it. My number's at the bottom of the card if you want it.

Take care, Anna. I won't forget you.

Love always,

Nige

Sweet. Sweet guy. A lovely interlude and an invite to the sun. Not bad for one night's work at the GeogSoc. Maybe I'll take him up on his offer. It's not often you find someone who's that – well – *compatible*, if you see what I mean.

I tuck the card away in the letter rack on my desk, carry Henry upstairs to shoot the breeze with Harriet.

To my surprise, there's someone already up there. Mike is back, sitting in his chair with a mug of coffee clutched in his hand. Blimey. I know I told him to come round any time, but I didn't expect him to take me up on it *that* quickly. They're chatting in easy tones, go 'Hi' without pausing when I come in. Harriet says, 'Sleep okay?' and I say, 'Yeah. Like a sloth.' Then, to Mike, 'I didn't hear you arrive.' He sort of shrugs. You often don't hear the doorbell from my room; I guess I must have been more asleep some of the time than I thought. 'You look rough,' I continue.

'Mmm,' says Harriet. 'We ended up making a bit of a night of it.'

'Four bottles of red wine,' says Mike, 'I think my head's going to burst.'

I rattle the ibuprofen, which are still sitting on the coffee table alongside the CD cover. 'Took some,' he says.

'I asked Mike if he'd like to stay for something to eat,' says Harriet. 'I hope that's okay.'

I'm more than happy. PC Gillespie may be looking rough, but rough can suit a man. Today he's wearing a black T-shirt that moulds over a nice torso which reveals itself to be built more for speed than lifting, and a pair of upper arms that make my knees go weak. They bulge like well-fed pythons, and the shirt, cut for the leanness of the body, is stretched beyond patience. He gives me a sheepish grin, looks a bit like a handsome Stan Laurel. Bless.

'He can stay,' I say.

'Great,' says Harriet. 'Then he can set up the barbie.'

An hour later, we've realised that, competent though he may be in many departments, Mike Gillespie is absolutely pony at getting a fire going. Nothing works. I mean, I know the charcoal's a bit damp from sitting out on the balcony, but, as I point out, a real man can make a fire from two sticks and a magnifying glass.

'All right,' says Mike. His face is purple from puffing on the tiny single flame he managed to produce for two minutes before it sobbed its last and died. 'As you're so clever, perhaps you'd like to try.'

I hunt through Harriet's art supplies, find the white spirit and a lump of cotton wool.

'No,' says Mike. 'You cannot be serious.'

'Why not?'

'Because people die in barbecue fires every week, that's why.'

'I think it's out.'

'It's definitely out,' says Harriet.

'They're about as famous last words as "Somebody lend me their lighter I can't see where the smell of gas is coming from".'

'He's quite sensible, our pet copper,' I say to Harriet.

'Very sensible,' she replies.

'Tell you what I'll do,' I say. 'I'll make cotton-wool balls and put some on and throw them on the barbie.'

'Please don't,' Mike begs. He's looking seriously worried now.

'So what are we meant to do? Starve?' I tease. Men are so sweet when they're trying to look all brave in front of chicks.

'You don't have a grill?'

I laugh hollowly.

Harriet says, 'I tried to heat up a pizza and fell asleep.'

I explain, 'She got drunk and tried to heat up a pizza and passed out leaving the plastic salt pot on top of the stove. By the time I came home, there was melted plastic salt pot all over the grill and smoke everywhere.'

I put some white spirit on a wad of cotton wool. Stand just inside the doorway ready to throw it. 'Please don't,' begs Mike.

'Duck, cissy,' I reply, and throw it.

Nothing happens.

'See?'

I douse another wad, throw it again. It lands four or five inches from the first, settles on the coals.

'I know what I'm doing—' I start to say, turning towards him.

Whump!

A ball of flame shoots up from the barbie, making me jump. The wind is blowing towards the french windows, and carries a thick cloud of acrid black smoke into the room.

I swear. A lot. Slam the windows shut. 'What else was there on those coals?'

'I don't know,' says Harriet. 'There's loads of stuff out in that shed.'

We throw open the window on the other side, and the smoke gradually begins to clear. On the balcony, the conflagration dies back to a mild roar, settles to a healthy burn.

'Please don't do something like that again.' Mike dabs exaggeratedly at his forehead. 'I don't know if my heart can take it.'

'Aah, you big wuss.' I elbow him in the ribs. Deliberately stay there for a second against his body. Yes, this may be a little forward of me, but Nige has gone now, and you know what they say happens to she who hesitates. 'You're going to have to develop a stronger constitution if you're going to hang around with us, you know. If you're really good, we'll teach you how to make napalm out of diesel and soap.'

'Stinks, though, doesn't it?' says Harriet. 'Petrolly.'

'That's just left over in your nose. It'll have burnt off by the time we put the food on.'

We make piripiri chicken from the freezer, potato and melon salad with chives from the windowbox, and a big tomato salad. We camp out on the balcony to eat, sitting in a row on chairs against the wall, feet up on the railing, food in our laps, watch the light die from the sky, the trains clatter past, and wipe the juices off our plates with half an old baguette Harriet has found in the freezer and revived on the dying embers. It's nice. Sort of family without the grief. When it gets too cold, we go inside to kick back around the coffee table.

I make coffee, and we all light cigarettes.

'I didn't know you smoked,' I say to Mike.

'I don't really,' he replies. 'I just like to have the odd one so nobody can call me a non-smoker.'

Harriet, lying full-length on the sofa, slaps her tummy. 'Boy, that was good,' she says. 'It's nice to eat proper food for a change.'

We mumble in agreement, fall silent.

'Tell you what,' Mike says after a while, 'I can still smell that smoke.'

'Me, too,' says Harriet. 'We must remember not to do that again.'

We're quiet again for a bit, then Harriet says, 'Tell you what, I can *really* smell smoke.'

'So can I,' I say. 'Is the barbie out?'

'Yes. I think so.' She goes out onto the balcony to check, comes back nodding. Walks over to the staircase door, saying, 'What's that noise?'

Mike is suddenly upright in his chair. 'What noise?'

'Weird. Can't you hear it?'

I can, now she's pointed it out. It seems to be coming up the stairs. A sort of explosive crackle like—

'Popcorn,' I say. 'It's popcorn.'

Harriet makes to open the door, and Mike leaps from his seat, covers the distance in half a second flat and hurls her to the ground. 'Don't open that!' he shouts. 'Get away from the door!'

'Ow,' shouts Harriet, more discombobulated than hurt. 'What?'

'Don't you get it? There's a fire down there!'

'What?'

'Shh!'

We all look at each other, suddenly solemn in the machine-gun staccato of Harriet's corn kernels exploding on the stairs.

'Christ!' says Harriet.

'Where's the phone? I'll call the fire brigade,' says Mike, who has suddenly assumed that air of authority I remember from the restaurant. Despite my fear, I think: he's a good person to have around in a crisis. Impressive.

Mike locates the phone under the *A–Z*. Listens for a dialling tone. 'Dead,' he says. 'Someone's cut it.'

Harriet and I exchange guilty glances. 'Well, actually we forgot to pay it.'

'Oh, bloody *hell*,' he says. 'Can't you two do *anything*?'

I give him my mobile. '*Okay*,' he says. Dials. 'Oh, hi, Lorraine,' he says. Good God. He knows the people on the emergency switchboard. 'It's Mike Gillespie, Chelsea. Fine, thanks. You? Good. The kids? Good. Yes, well, I was wondering if you could patch me through to the Pimlico fire people. No. We've just got a bit of a fire here.'

Harriet and I retreat onto the balcony. I don't believe this. This is just totally un-bloody-believable.

'He's gossiping,' says Harriet, who also seems to be thinking about our companion rather than the situation. 'He's bloody *gossiping*.'

'Keep your hair on.' To my amazement, I'm quite calm. And the fact that Harriet is pacing like a caged tigress merely serves to make me calmer. Maybe I've just had too many crises now; maybe I've got inured.

'Keep my *hair* on? It'll all be burnt *off* by the time he finishes asking about Lorraine's sister-in-law's father's lumbago.' Harriet seems to be panicking enough for both of us. I put a hand on her arm and she freezes like a rabbit when a hawk passes overhead.

'Don't exaggerate. He's only being polite.'

Mike sticks his head round the door, phone glued to his ear. 'What's the combination for the front gates?'

We tell him. He goes back in.

'Well, there are times and times for politeness,' she says, 'and in the middle of a bloody great fire isn't one of them.'

Mike appears, giving me back the phone. 'They're on their way,' he says.

'Oh, good,' says Harriet. 'I *do* feel better.'

'I've wet that blanket on the sofa and put it over the door,' he says. 'We should be reasonably safe up here. Everybody okay?'

He walks round the balcony, looking down at our small empire: the yellowing rowan, the brackish waters of the lock, the piles of rusting metal that used to be bits of Thames barges.

'Only problem is,' he comes back, 'do you have any idea how strong that bridge is?'

Harriet shakes her head.

''Cause they're going to have to get the ladder over it, and that's a heavy bastard.'

'The ladder?' she asks.

'Yes. Retractable crane thing with a platform on the top. For lifting us off this balcony.'

'What do we need that for?'

'How else were you planning to get down?'

'Well,' I say, 'I guess we thought we might use the fire ladder.'

Mike explodes. Very quietly and that, but an explosion nonetheless. 'Why didn't you *say* you had a fire ladder?'

'Well, I'm sorry you think we can't organise a cockfight in a gay bar,' says Harriet. She seems to be rallying. 'But we'd hardly be allowed to live at the top of a very high tower with only one staircase without one, would we?'

'Well, where *is* it?'

Harriet gestures at the shed.

The ladder is a slender, lightweight thing made of aluminium, but it takes a certain amount of bulk to get down six floors and it takes the three of us to manouevre it out of the shed and over to a clear patch away from the front door. Mike, slightly chastened, proves to be a good team-worker now that he's not taking control in his copperish way. It's him that suggests we try rolling it rather than carrying it, and it's him that bruises the palms of his hands banging the holding pins through the holes in the hooks, works out how to attach the weights to the bottom so that, when we flip it over, the ladder drops down straight and true to the earth below. Then he says, 'Okay. Who's first?'

'I'll go,' I offer. It's not courage that makes me volunteer, but the fact that I've got no knickers on. Well, you don't always put on knickers when you've been anticipating a quiet Sunday night lounging around the house. I want my hemline firmly on the ground by the time anyone else shows up.

He helps me up onto the railing and when I look down to rest my foot on the first rung, I realise just how high up we are. Funny. I never noticed it before. 'Oh, God,' I say, look back, panic-struck, into his eyes.

He looks back. Long and steady. It's just me and him, alone in space. *Don't flake on me now,* say his eyes. *We've done well so far. Keep going. You can do it. I'll fall,* I reply without speaking. *I'm afraid I'll fall. I'll be swinging out in the air and the ground is so far away.*

Mike says, quietly, firmly, 'Get both feet on the first rung. Take a grip and just stay there until you're sure.'

I can't.

'Don't look down. Keep your eyes on mine.'

I find the rung with my foot. Slot it in.

'Good. Now the other one.'

I can't.

'Yes you can,' says Mike. 'Come on. You're safe.'

I unhook my other leg from its safe purchase, swing out into space. Lurch. Feel the contents of my stomach shift, grit my teeth and cling harder with the arm that's wrapped round the railing.

'That's good,' he says. 'That's the worst bit. Find the foothold. Go on.'

My foot finds purchase. Now I'm clinging like a Mabel Lucie Atwell baby, chin over the railing, eyes like saucers.

'One step at a time,' says Mike. 'Take it slowly and you'll be fine.'

I won't be fine. My hands will never hold me all the way down. I'll be by the bathroom window and they'll give up. Fear will make them lose their grip and I'll pitch out into space.

I gurgle and clutch tighter to the railing. 'You won't,' he says, and never takes his eyes from mine. 'You'll stay on the ladder and step by step you will go to the ground.'

No I won't. I know about falling. I do it in my dreams every night, only this time I don't have the wings that will save me.

'First step's the worst,' he says.

Then he barks, 'Anna, come *on*!'

This shocks me into action. I put a foot down, let a hand go, squeak again, grab the rung below and I'm moving.

Of course, he lied. The first step isn't the worst. The

worst is when you get below the balcony, when it's too late to swarm back upwards, where the ladder is braced against nothing but thin air, and you find yourself swinging back and forth with every step you take. That's the worst bit: when the wall in front of you approaches and recedes with jerky regularity and the ladder takes your spine through your stomach each time you put your weight onto a different foot.

A bead of sweat trickles from my forehead, avoids the eyebrow and lands directly in my left eye. Stings like Dettol and there's nothing I can do. Can't let go, can't reach my shirtsleeve with my face without sending the ladder into a wild St Vitus dance that clatters my feet against the wall. Come on, Anna, just go. I decide to close my eyes. Try to set up a rhythm: foot, foot, hand, hand, foot, foot, hand, hand, ignore the ache in my arms, ignore the sickly wobble, ignore everything but the process of moving down the face of the tower.

Suddenly, the ladder pitches wildly just as I shift my weight. Momentarily, I lose my grip, slip, dangle, gasp as I watch myself fall, find that, after all, the survival instinct has kicked in and I'm hanging with both arms wrapped round the vertical. Kick around and find the crossbar, get feet onto the rung, stop and allow a single sob to escape before I take three deep breaths and look up. Harriet is on the ladder above me and heading at what feels like breathtaking speed in my direction. Damn it: it's me that should be the little monkey, shinning up and down drainpipes without fear; instead Harriet, the lanky one, heads down the ladder with a confident athleticism that's liable to trample me.

I start down again. See my bedroom window drift past, the room inside misty with a pall of black and choking smoke.

It takes a moment to register. My room. I've covered two floors. One more floor and I probably won't die when I hit the ground. One more floor and I'm on quadriplegia. One more floor after that, maybe I'll break a leg or two. And one more floor after that, an ankle sprain from an awkward dismount. I look up again as the ladder does a renewed flail, see Mike's big feet appear at the top, Harriet still bearing down on me, close my eyes again, go down.

Foot, foot, hand, hand. Just keep going. You're almost there. And I swear, I will never make you hang over a height again. No parachuting, no hang-gliding, no microlights, no abseiling. Your feet stay on the ground from now on.

I put out my foot to find another rung, and find thin air. Grope again, nothing. Oh, God, what *now*? Don't look down. Don't be stupid, I have to look down. You can't be too far off now. I open my eyes, peer over my arm and, with a rush of relief, realise that there's no rung because, three feet below where I'm standing, is the tainted earth of my industrial garden. I'm there.

I jump. Collapse to my knees and very nearly do a Pope John-Paul with the ground. Look up to see where the others are and discover that they've stopped. In fact, Harriet seems to have started ascending. She's come up against Mike somewhere around the fifth floor. He's looking down, she's looking up and they seem to be arguing. He shakes his head. She nods vigorously, the bottom of the ladder where I'm standing whipping frantically from side to side. Again he gestures refusal and suddenly she starts up the ladder towards him again. Then he takes a hand off a rung, pushes a palm at her face. For a few seconds they are still, then Harriet begins to make her way earthward while, to my astonishment, Mike begins to ascend. What is going on? What the hell is going on?

He gets to the top, swings a leg up and over and bounds out of sight. Harriet is passing my room now, working her way methodically down: hand, hand, foot, foot, never a pause.

When she's at first-floor level, he reappears on the railing, and he seems to be wearing my black rucksack on his back. And when he swings back out, I see that the rucksack is moving. Not just moving: jumping about angrily on his back, wriggling, thumping outwards against the tightly fixed straps like John Hurt's chest in *Alien*, evidently throwing him off balance.

Henry. Oh my God, I forgot Henry.

Harriet jumps to earth beside me, looks up, rubbing chafed hands together. 'Has he got him?' she asks.

'Yes.' Thank God he's got strong arms. The bag is now jumping about like – like what? – like a cat in a sack, of course. They used to sell brilliant wind-up toys called cat in a sack on street corners in Covent Garden a couple of years ago: a sack with a big ginger tail sticking out, that rolled and wriggled just like Henry is doing now. As they pass the two-storey mark, a long yellow leg emerges from beneath the flap at the top of the bag, swats a couple of times with the claw at Mike's ear. Henry's furious head follows, and a yowl of pure rage pours down upon us.

'Oh, Christ,' says Harriet. 'He's going to jump.'

Henry breaks free from his confinement, and it's only when his hindquarters get loose that he seems to realise that he's not in a position to be fighting. He looks startled, scrabbles at the air in front of him a couple of times, and then a furry tummy and four straight-as-dowels legs are heading full-plummet for my upturned face.

I duck. He hits my back with a perceptible *doof*, knocks me sprawling to the ground, bounces, rolls, leaps to his feet.

If ever a cat was glad of nine lives, it's not Henry right now. He stands on tiptoe, tail like a pine cone, back arched in fear and fury, and shrieks the C-word at us through bared and howling gnashers.

'CAAAANT!' he howls. And then he shoots off as if his tail's on fire and disappears into the boat sheds.

Mike clambers down the last few steps, jumps to the ground and, hand clapped over a torn and bleeding ear, lets off a few expletives of his own. 'Never, *ever* again!' he yells, jabbing a finger at Harriet. 'Next time your cat wants saving, he can fucking *burn!*'

I have to say, he looks magnificent. If you ever want to see what a magnificent man looks like, try finding one who's swearing his head off after saving the life of your moggy.

'And if you ever, *ever* try to tell me that there's nobody after your hide,' he shouts, 'I'll come round and set fire to you myself!'

Chapter Forty-Eight

Safe House

There are police everywhere. Police in uniform, police with bomber jackets zipped up to the collar jingling change in their pockets, policewomen conducting by-the-book checks on our need for counselling, police swabbing our fingernails, police taking photographs, police writing laboriously in notebooks, police standing with their arms folded in reflective jackets in front of the gate to attract attention to the fact that there's been an incident behind it, police milling about going 'sierra tango bravo F-U Roger?' into radios, police just generally milling about. Burglars throughout the region must be cracking open the champagne.

It's a warm night, but someone following form has produced thermal blankets and insisted on wrapping us in them. Every time one of us tries to shed our covering, someone comes along and hitches it back up over our shoulders. The yard stinks of wet cinders and lock-water. The front door no longer exists apart from a few shards of soggy charcoal and some heat-twisted studs that have dropped, one by one, into the pile of ash on the ground. Behind it, the stairway gapes black and oily; there's been some puzzlement about the volume of smoke involved until word gets around about the popcorn, the tin of varnish and the bag of moulding resin that were sitting on the stairs. Then the post-facto wisdom of the fire service points out that flammable materials are generally best kept stored where they aren't going to catch fire. 'Sorry,' I say, 'I don't think we were expecting someone to pour a can of petrol through the letter box and chuck a burning rag in after it.'

I'm calm in all this milling about: calm but hacked off because no one will let me back up the stairs until the forensic people have finished their stuff, and until I've been upstairs I can't see what that thick black smoke has done to my belongings. At least my credit card was in the side pocket of the rucksack, magnetic strip facing away from Henry's offended claws.

But then something happens to break my calm. Harriet has been the centre of a huddle of men in bomber jackets for the past ten minutes, Mike Gillespie talking solemnly among them, frowning, listening, rejecting. Lost in thoughts of my antique chenille bedcover and the vulnerable brocade on the curtains, it's only when Mike breaks away and approaches me that I even notice, really.

And when he gets to me, he says, 'We're taking Harriet to a place of safety. Everyone thinks it's for the best.'

'Okay,' I reply, and make to follow him, but he says, 'I'm sorry. It's just Harriet.'

And all in a rush, I'm in a panic. It's like someone's thrown a bucket of freezing water over me. 'You can't be serious.'

He shrugs. 'I'm sorry. My superiors are under the impression that she's the one who's at risk, and they want to get her out of here as soon as possible.'

No. You're kidding. What am I supposed to do? What am I supposed to do without Harriet? Christ. 'And I can't come with her?' I ask feebly, because suddenly my voice has gone weak, like my knees.

'No. I'm sorry. It's just her.'

Harriet is arguing with one of the bomber jackets, shaking her head vigorously and pointing at me as he gestures to squad car parked on the other side of the lock. He tries to take her arm and she shakes it off with the irritation of someone brushing away a bothersome insect, and then she actually stamps her foot. Finally, she marches over in our direction, her attendant reluctantly following.

'Anna, I'm sorry,' she practically shouts when she gets within five paces. 'I don't know what to do.'

'Where are they taking you?'

'They say I'm not allowed to say.'

'You're kidding.'

She throws a poisonous look at bomber jacket, who looks glumly back.

'Why not?'

'I'm not allowed to tell *anyone*.'

'But this is *me*!'

'Can't she come too?' Harriet pleads to bomber jacket, but he simply shakes his head. '*Why* can't she come? What's she supposed to do?'

Bomber jacket addresses me. I don't like him. He has a big moustache and little beady eyes like a chipmunk. 'I'm afraid that Lady Harriet is our primary concern at the moment. We have to ensure her safety.'

'But why can't you tell me where you're taking her?'

I am assailed by an extraordinary combination of emotions: confusion, fear, anger, frustration, a wish to protect my friend. Harriet and I have never not known what the other one was up to for more than twenty-four hours in ten years. We look after each other. That's what we're there for.

'I'm sorry,' he replies. 'It would hardly be a place of safety if we told everybody where it was, would it?'

Patronising tosser. 'Why can't I come?'

'You can't.' Blunt, dismissive. He starts to pull Harriet away by the arm. And that's when I really panic. I start shouting. Screaming, almost. 'What are you *doing*? Where are you taking her? Harriet!'

And Harriet is dragging back against him, wide, frightened eyes fixed on my face. 'Anna!' she shouts. 'Oh, God, leave me *alone*! Anna!'

I turn to Mike, realise that he's not the one with the power, turn to the man in the bomber jacket, start to plead. It feels as though I'm pleading for my life. 'But you don't understand! What am I going to *do*? I've lost everything! Everything! I don't have anywhere to go! What am I going to *do*?'

'I suggest,' he replies, 'you check into a hotel for the time being. We'll let you know when we no longer need you.'

Oh my God. 'Do you think I'm part of this? Is that what this is about?'

He looks at me impassively, says nothing. Won't even commit himself, the bastard. Just leaves me with the mute accusation.

Now I'm shouting, 'You've got to be joking! What are you thinking?' and Harriet is shouting too, 'What are you *on*? You can't be serious! Haven't you paid any attention at *all*? She's had as much happen to her as me, for God's sake. She's been here all the time!'

What the hell am I meant to feel now? I've been burgled, beaten, burnt and now I'm guilty? This is too much. This is too bloody much. As he pulls Harriet down the path towards the lock, I can't stop the rage and the horror from hauling itself out. I clench my fists, close my eyes and let out a scream.

She breaks away from his hand, runs back up the path, throws herself on me. We cling together, thumping hearts, tears bursting hotly, and she cries, 'I don't think it! It's not me! It's not me! Anna, it's not me!'

Hands prise us apart and Mike Gillespie is holding me round the shoulders while bomber jacket and a uniformed policewoman pull Harriet by the wrists. 'It won't be for long,' she yells. 'I promise. I'll be back. I won't leave you!' and I'm sobbing without let, choking on my anger and my grief. Harriet is helped into the back seat of the car, people get in all around her and she's driven away, her white face staring at me through the back window.

'It'll be all right,' Mike says quietly. 'I promise I'll look after her.'

But now I don't care. I'm crying for myself now. 'Fuck you,' I sob at him. 'Just damn you to hell, you fucker. Screw you into the fucking ground. What about me? What am I going to do? I don't have *anything*.'

He lets me go, comes round to face me and takes my arms. Dips down to look into my face. 'You'll be okay. You'll be fine. Don't lose it now, Anna. You'll be okay. I'll take you to a hotel and get you sorted out, and you'll be *okay*.'

'I don't want you. I don't want you. You think I—'

'No,' he says firmly. 'No I don't. I've seen you and I know you and I believe that you don't have anything to do with this. They just have to play it safe, Anna. Calm down. It will be okay.'

'Don't tell me to calm down. You total, total bastard. You've done this on purpose, you bastard.'

And he just takes it, lets me cuss him out and scream invective. And when I start to slow, he puts a kind arm round my shoulders and I let him lead me through the gates to his car, which is still parked beneath the intercom, and buckle my seatbelt obediently when he tells me. An officer in a luminous jerkin looks at me curiously through the windscreen. Oh, look. There goes the suspect. I make a face and he waves us off.

Mike says, 'You'll be fine for tonight. What are you going to do after that?'

'I don't know,' I say. 'I can't go home, can I?'

He shakes his head. 'That's going to be out of action for a while. And to be honest, I'm not sure how safe you'd be there anyway. Is there anywhere else you can go? Maybe you should get out of London for a bit.'

'I'm wanted for questioning,' I say sulkily.

He makes a sort of pffft noise. 'Don't be dramatic. I'll sort that out. But I think it might do you good, if nothing else. Is there anywhere you can go?'

In my pocket, my phone beeps. I get it out, look miserably at it. There's a little envelope in the top left-hand corner. I pull up the text menu. Harriet mob it says. The message is short, left in a hurry.

I am ok pls b ok 2.

'So is there anywhere you could go?' Mike asks again.

I sigh, stare through the windscreen at the passing street lights. 'Yes,' I say. 'Yes, I think there's somewhere.'

Chapter Forty-Nine

SunnyView

I've been in Poole four days when Carolyn and I finally have The Talk. For four days she leaves me pretty well alone, finds a bowl for Henry, who I found sulking by the boarded-up front door when I went back to look for him and put in a cardboard box, and took him, complaining loudly, first into a taxi, then onto the tube and then onto a train at Waterloo, as Mike instructed me, so that no one could trail us by the car number-plate.

The British holiday season has already virtually finished its short flowering, so we get the front bedroom at Sunny-View, the B&B she semi-retired to when it became evident that only hubris had justified her wage packet from my family in the previous ten years.

SunnyView is on the edge of the shallow, muddy part of Poole Harbour, a thirties-built villa with swirly carpets, frilled curtains, and a lean-to sun lounge running the length of the sea-facing wall. Every available surface is covered with pink and white china knick-knacks, all of which seem to have a function that belies their decorative appearance: vases shaped like boots, clocks shaped like milkmaids, pen holders shaped like tulips, letter-openers shaped like fish, ring trees shaped like grasping hands, nail-brushes shaped like Scottie dogs. Whenever I've been here, I've always found it hard to believe that Carolyn could ever have shared a life with my spartan forebears. Where did she keep all this stuff in the old days? In a suitcase under her bed? In a lock-up garage surreptitiously visited in the wee small hours? Or is it a reaction to all those years of function and restraint, a late flowering like the reds and purples and lush velvets that characterise my bedroom?

We're in the sun lounge on a Thursday afternoon when she finally brings up the subject of my mother. I've told her about the stuff that's been happening to Harriet and me, and she's tutted sympathetically and shown no sign of nervousness. Henry, much recovered apart from a tendency to talk loudly and persistently at inopportune moments, has found a sunny spot on a pink and blue rag rug that probably came from a Women's Institute bring and buy, and is basking with all four feet up in the air and a ridiculous smile of self-satisfaction on his face. And Carolyn says, 'So have you spoken to your mother?'

'No,' I reply, rather hoping that this will be the last of it but knowing that it won't be. 'The last I saw of her was projected on a back wall at the Brit Awards. Looking as sour as limes, as usual.'

Carolyn, who seems to have taken up knitting in her dotage as well as alarming quantities of shocking-pink lipstick, clickety-clacks a couple of times, casts off or something that requires her to stick her tongue out of the corner of her mouth and frown, then says, 'Why not?'

'Why? Have *you*?' I ask suspiciously.

'Ooh, no, dear,' says Carolyn. 'Her assistant sends me a card at Christmas. That's about it with me and Grace these days.'

'Well, then,' I say triumphantly.

'Yes.' Another go with the tongue. 'But then again, she's not *my* mother.'

'I was rather under the impression,' I inform her huffily, 'that she wasn't mine, either.'

'Well, like it or not,' says Carolyn, 'she's all the mother you're ever going to get. You'll have to get used to it one day.'

'No I don't. She was a terrible mother. She was never motherly to me once.'

Carolyn throws me a small, sympathetic smile. 'She wasn't as bad as all that,' she says. 'You've got to remember, she did what she thought was best with the equipment she was given.'

Funny. A sentimental bit of me believed for a long time that most of what I in my deprived way thought of as mothering – the occasional cuddle, the smuggled treats, the comforting words – came from Carolyn. Maybe she was more of a godmother: the person who could spoil you and walk away, whose job was to show you that there were other lives outside that of your family. Grace, shut away in Shropshire, never saw anyone like that.

I give her a bit of a glare. And she has the temerity to laugh in my face. 'Besides,' she says, 'you've got most of your personality from her.'

'I have not!' I protest. 'That's so unfair!'

She gives me that look that southerners find so irritating in Yorkshire publicans: that sort of 'Tha knows th'art fooling thyself' look that plays around the mouth and makes you want to punch it.

'You,' she says, 'are far more like your mother than you know.'

'I am not! Look at me! I'm entirely self-invented!'

'Ah!' responds Carolyn. 'And where do you think you got

the strength of character to do that? You're like a terrier once you've got the bit between your teeth.'

Carolyn has always specialised in mixing metaphors in a way that somehow works nonetheless. It used to drive my grandfather potty.

'Most people with your upbringing would have found it very difficult to do what you've done,' she says. 'Of course, most people with your upbringing weren't also brought up to think that they could do whatever they wanted if they put their minds to it. I know your mother's disappointed by the results, but you've done exactly what she trained you to do, and you've done it brilliantly.'

'Oh, Carolyn, that's such – ' I'm about to say bullshit, but remember that, though she's always coped very well with the eccentricities of our situation, she's still of the older generation, and of the knitting, china-collecting older generation at that – 'poppycock,' I finish.

'And that's another thing,' she continues. 'You're just like your mother in that. Anything that doesn't suit you, you just deny it altogether. Flat contradiction. No manners, they would have called it in my family, but I suppose it has its uses.'

I think for a bit. Say! 'Well, whatever the truth in that may be, she's done some stuff that's pretty unforgivable.'

'I know, dear.' She lays down her knitting, folds her hands in her lap. 'But you're going to have to find a way of putting out the olive branch.'

'Carolyn, no!'

She nods.

'Why should *I* make the first move? It's not *me* that's in the wrong.'

'Well, as you see it.'

'As I *know* it.'

'And that's another way you're alike,' she says. 'So you'd rather never have anything to do with her again than go halfway?'

I'm firm on this point. I've had plenty of time to mull it over in the past few weeks.

'Yes.'

'You know you'll never see her again, don't you?'

I make a 'don't care' face.

She sighs. 'You're *so* alike.'

'Now what?'

'Both of you. Sometimes I could bang your heads together. If she wasn't six inches taller than me and twelve years younger . . . Listen to yourself. Can't you *hear* your mother when you talk, sometimes? You'd rather die than admit you might be wrong. You've always been like this. Someone does something, or something doesn't suit you, and you just slam the door and throw away the key. Sometimes I think you'd actually commit murder rather than be wrong-footed.'

I say nothing.

She continues. 'Of course, she was always exactly the same. But she's had no chance at all, really. At least you've seen some examples of how adults behave. You could always have a go at leading by example.'

'No,' I say. 'Look, she's the mother and I'm the daughter. I know I'm grown up, but in the case of mothers and daughters, she'll always be the adult and I'll always be the child. That's how it is.'

She sighs again. 'Anna. Just try for once to see things outside your own point of view. Think about your mother. You were the lucky one. You may have had a miserable time of it, but at least you got to mix outside the bubble. Think about what life's been like for your mother. Trapped with that *awful* man and no one else. Bred up for her life like a suckling pig . . .'

'No more than I was.'

'Much more,' says Carolyn.

'What exactly do you mean?'

'Oh, dear,' she says. 'You really don't know anything about your family, do you?'

I stare.

'Did it ever once occur to you to ask questions, Anna? Or were you so busy hiding everything you didn't have any room for anything else?'

'What are you on about, Carolyn?'

'If I tell you, you've got to promise that you're not going to blow up like you did last time. I really couldn't bear to have another scene like last time.'

'Yes, yes,' I bark impatiently. 'I promise. Now what are you on about?'

'Your mother,' says Carolyn, 'was an early experiment in this genetic thing they're all going on about.'

'What do you mean?'

'Well.' She thinks for a bit, then begins. 'I don't think it started that way, mind. I mean, obviously he'd always had the ambition to produce a genius. I don't think it would have occurred to your grandfather for a minute that any child of his could have been anything else. And I don't think he ever intended to share the limelight either. From what I've picked up about your grandmother, the whole thing was fairly much a temporary arrangement, anyway. It certainly wasn't a love match. He wanted a child and she wanted a good lump sum to emigrate with. She went to South Africa when they split up, you know. That's why she never put in any inconvenient reappearances. I don't suppose the Afrikaaner farmer she married would have been too chuffed to find out that his children weren't alone in the world, if you know what I mean.

'But then there was a spoke in the works.'

I suppress a smile, carry on listening.

'I don't know exactly what happened, but the baby didn't materialise. They thought it would be an eighteen-month, two-year process – bang, as it were and you're out – but nothing happened. I'm not sure if it was that Peter was firing blanks, but between you and me' – she puts a finger to her lips and looks around her as though we are surrounded by spies rather than sitting on wicker furniture in an empty conservatory on the south coast – 'I don't think he was a very *sexual* man, if you see what I mean. And as it turned out, there certainly wasn't anything wrong with *her* waterworks.'

By now, I'm riveted. This doesn't feel like my family history at all, more like one of those Channel Four documentaries where nonogenarians reminisce about bunk-ups behind the glue-works.

'Anyway. After two and a bit years, they realised that it just wasn't going to happen. So she said come on then, give me my money and I'll be off. And he said no, love, the deal's not completed. No kid, no cash. So she said you can't do that! and he said just try suing me in a court of law. I don't think a judge would take a very kindly view of an arrangement like ours. As a matter of fact, I think in those days a judge could have refused to give them a divorce altogether and they'd have been shackled together in perpetuity. So she said well, what do you want me to do about it? And he said well, if we can't get a baby this way, we'll have to go about it another. Obviously, they didn't have that artificial insperminination in those days. You used turkey basters for basting turkeys when I was young. And he didn't want just any old donor.

'So they cooked up this plan. There was a conference going on in London that summer – I can't remember which college, but it was something to do with science – and there were going to be all these Nobel prizewinners there. So he agreed to bung her an extra thousand, which was a lot of money in those days, believe me. You could have bought a whole street in Salford for that.'

She pauses. 'Still could, mind you. And she agreed to go along and hang around at all the social events and see what she could pick up, if you see what I mean. Conferences then were exactly the same as they are now. Knocking shops. Anyone who hasn't brought his secretary is looking to see what he can find among the delegates. Only difference was that there weren't so many female delegates to choose from in those days.'

'Good God,' I say.

Carolyn nods. 'Well might you say it. So anyway, Sylvia buys a new wardrobe of low-cut dresses and small hats and sets off to London to do some fishing. She targeted only Nobel prizewinners or men who'd got more than one doctorate.'

'How many?'

Carolyn shrugs. 'The conference lasted a week,' she replies. 'And bingo-bango, nine months later your mother pops out. Peter gets what he wanted, Sylvia gets a heavy handbag and everyone's happy.'

'So Grace is the first Nobel baby.'

'I suppose you could put it that way.'

'Good God.'

'So you see,' she says, 'you weren't the only experiment in your family.'

'Good God,' I say again, because it's taking me a while to

think of anything else to say. 'No wonder she's so obsessed with the heredity thing.'

'Exactly,' says Carolyn. 'You would be too if you'd been bought off the shelf like that. And don't think he didn't throw it in her face every time he didn't think he was getting value for money. Poor little thing. Never learned anything apart from disapproval and implacable hatred.'

I light a cigarette to give me time to think. Can't think of anything much to say, so stay silent.

'The stupid thing is,' says Carolyn, 'I look at your mum and, despite everything, I think she's done pretty well for herself. I mean, obviously not with you, but if you consider the start she had, you'd have expected much worse. It's just that Peter never thought about the fact that people need social skills as well as qualifications if they're going to get on in the world. Your mum's won prizes galore and everyone says they admire her, but no one's exactly going to be crying at her funeral, are they?'

I shake my head.

'It's all a question of presentation, isn't it? Your friend Harriet's mum, for instance, she was all presentation, but dying was marvellous for her public standing. You probably don't remember, but the public was getting pretty sick of her and her "poor me" this and her "admire me" that. I don't think we'd really even remember who she was today if she hadn't died like that. Your mum has had the misfortune to keep on living, and her reward is that she's got no friends and a daughter who can't even bring herself to hold out an olive branch.'

She's an effective persuader, Carolyn. I'm beginning to crumble. She's watching my face and sees that she's winning.

'So do you see now,' she starts again, 'why you need to try being a bit more forgiving?'

'Yes,' I reply slowly. 'Yes, I do. I understand. But it's not as straightforward as all that, is it?'

Once more, Carolyn lets out a sigh. 'Anna. I watched your mum go through her teens without any niceness at all. And I watched something similar happen to you. But believe me, you had more chance than she did. You're much better equipped than she was, even if it was tough. You really could try doing the adult thing. You're nearly thirty, after all.'

'Twenty-seven,' I correct her.

'Twenty-ni—' she starts, then colours slightly and shuts up.

'WHAT?'

'Silly me, I'm getting old. Memory like a sieve,' she stammers.

'DON'T EVEN TRY THAT! WHAT DID YOU SAY?'

'Oh, bugger,' says Carolyn. Funny how 'bugger' is a totally acceptable swearword to the older generation where practically every other is not. 'I've done it again, haven't I?'

'Are you telling me I'm twenty-nine? How the hell did *that* happen?'

'Forget it, Anna. It was a slip of the tongue.'

'Uh-uh. You don't make slips of the tongue. Tell me.'

'Just a silly—'

'TELL ME!'

'Oh, dear.' Carolyn picks up her knitting and starts, stitch by stitch, to unravel it.

'You were a small baby, you see . . .'

Chapter Fifty

LEEZA HAYMAN
She's young, she's fun and she takes no prisoners

If there's one thing that makes me sick to my stomach, it's the sight of a celebrity crying over spilt milk. So the sight of our own Lady of the Airwaves, Godiva Fawcett, aka the Duchess of Ditchwater, Bleeding Heart of Belhaven, weeping and beating her suspiciously perky breast this week had me on my knees by the nearest toilet. I mean, here we are, our boys are off in the Falklands, wives and mothers everywhere are waiting with hushed breath to hear whether their loved ones are going to come back alive, and this spoiled madam wants us to spare our sympathy for her misfortunes? Give me a break. There's no misfortune you haven't brought upon yourself, Godiva, so don't even think about trying it on.

In case you've been living on the planet Venus for the past week, Godiva Fawcett has been found out. And boy, has she been found out. Our sister paper, the *Sunday Sparkle*, did a bit of digging and discovered that practically everything this self-styled angel of mercy

has said about herself is untrue. And her response is a classic example of the way the famous try to pull the wool over our eyes, the way that, whenever the proverbial hits the fan, they will come out weeping and claiming that it was all someone else's fault. Well, boohoo, Godiva: you've been found out. And because you're so transparent, I'm able to deliver the Boohoo Guide to celebrity excuses:

Found Out: you're not a poor liddle Orphan Annie after all. Your aged parents are alive and ailing in a council old folks' home in Rotherham, where you grew up over a butcher's shop. And your name is plain old Geraldine Pigg.
Boohoo: You didn't want to tell anyone, but you had to cut off all contact and change your name because they were so cruel to you when you were growing up. It was only loyalty that kept you from ever revealing your injuries to the teachers, social workers, etc. who came into contact with you throughout your childhood and

never remarked anything untoward, but once you reached adulthood, you had no choice but to never, ever have anything to do with them again.

Found Out: You weren't a poor but honest waitress, but coworkers remember that you were an enthusiastic 'dancer' under the name of Geneva West in a Soho nightclub in the late fifties.

Boohoo: How could you have ever told anyone? You were so ashamed. You were only very young – fifteen when you started – and you were exploited by older, ruthless men who seduced you into the lifestyle before you were old enough to know better. And anyway, you were desperate.

Found Out: Papers left to be opened after the death of his wife show that your so-called mentor, the late Leonard Wildenstein, didn't discover you and promote you out of admiration for your talents at all. In fact, he hated you and only gave you parts because you were blackmailing him.

Boohoo: I can't believe he could say things like that about me. I loved that man with all my heart, even though he subjected me over the years to the vilest practices. I only went along with it in the name of love. I feel so *soiled*.

Found out: Your separation from your husband, the Duke of Ditchworth, wasn't amicable at all. He kicked you out, and won custody of the daughter you had together.

Boohoo: I've kept quiet about this for too long to protect the inno-

cent, but now I have to speak out to protect my own reputation. When I met Gerald Moresby, he seemed like the perfect gentleman, but once I married him I discovered a whole other, darker side to his character. He drank and often closeted himself away with his guns for days on end. Our marriage was a loveless sham from day one, and it was only from the great love I had for my daughter that I stayed as long as I did. And the custody hearing was a conspiracy: what chance does a poor, powerless commoner like me have against the combined might of the British aristocracy? They say that abused children often marry into similar situations, and that's as much as I am going to say. I want my daughter still to have a chance of loving her father, in spite of all the things he's done to me. Why does everyone have to concentrate on the negatives? Why can't people look at all the good things I've done? I've thrown myself into charity work since I discovered the emptiness of my married life, and I think I should be given credit for all the love and affection I have lavished on the suffering.

Yes, yes, I know she does a lot of work for charity, but don't let that blind you to the facts. This isn't the Slothful Seventies any more: it's the Help Yourself Eighties, and there's a lot of evidence that suggests that charity is a waste of time, just props up people who should be learning to stand on their own two feet. I know it's upsetting to watch Bangladeshi flood victims, but you've got to remember: if you choose to live in a flood zone, what do you expect? And why, just because Godiva-better-than-us-Fawcett says so, should we be giving money to people we've never met, and who are as unlikely to thank us as Galtieri is to organise a Polo friendly with the Royal Windsor, when we've got a lot on our plates at home.

We've got enough demands on our good nature what with whingeing miners and whining steelworkers without some over-privileged biddy in designer combats coming along and telling us to dig even deeper in our already overburdened pockets. Maybe once we've had a few tax cuts, Godiva, but lay off for now. And don't think that just because you've been seen playing kiss-chase with a few Africans that we're going to forget about your exploits closer to home.

© Daily Sparkle, 1982

Chapter Fifty-One

Studland

I'm not a wimp, but it's all quite a lot to take in in one go. Harriet and I keep in constant touch by text message, but it's not the same thing.

After The Talk, I sent her the following:

BIG NEWS. MOTHER BASTARD CHILD OF ANON NOBEL PROF, GRFTHR PIMP. I AM 29!! LIARS BASTARDS LOVE AXXX

and she sent, by return of receiver:

!**!?F**!! wot do u mean yr 29 yr older thn me & how come u sa anon didnt she no who shagging? Hxxx

to which I replied:

SHAGGED 5 IN 1 WK DIDNT GET THEIR NOS PETER PAID HER THEY PRET I WS 2 YRS YNGR 2 PRET I WS CLEVER XX

and she replied:

u r clever stupid but now I no why wrinkles. ruok? how is henry gvng u xxxxs I hope. miss him & uxxx

Which isn't quite the same thing as caning a bottle of rum and cussing out the world.

I'm still not allowed to know where she is. A representative of her Madge's Constab came down to take a statement from me and spent the whole time eyeing me balefully over his teacup. So word's got round, then. I think we're not meant to be talking, even: the couple of times we manage to get through on our mobiles, there's an odd constraint between us, as though someone's listening.

So I go for walks. I walk along the pine-lined avenues of suburban Poole, marvelling at the way rhododendrons can look dank even at the end of a hot, dry spell, fantasising about the terrible revenges I will wreak with my walking frame when I'm old.

I walk past fish and chip shops and shops selling little plastic buckets and tinfoil windmills. I pass grocers that stock pasties, crisps and fizzy drinks, past bait shops and newsagents and row upon row of insurance HQs. Beats me why all these insurance companies would want to site their headquarters in the very heartland of those most likely to claim, but there you go. I sit on seafront benches and watch middle-aged couples argue over windlasses and outboards, and I think: I wonder if I'll ever be like this, halfway to paying off my mortgage on the semi in Bournemouth and spending every weekend squabbling over mastery of ten square feet of boat.

I'm twenty-nine. Not such a big difference, is it? It bears no comparison with the eight years Godiva got away with knocking off her age, but I guess the effect an age difference has on you is directly related to whether you knew about it or not. And which direction it takes you in. If you've shaved a couple of years off here and there yourself, it's like you've clawed back a few more years' life; made your past more action-packed, your present more hopeful, your future more dynamic. Right now, I feel as though I've been robbed.

Because I have. All those years when I thought my early memories – learning to read, catching an aeroplane to the States, blushing as the owl eyes of my grandfather bored into me as I stumbled over my seven-times table – were from the phenomenal perspective of eighteen months old. Now I find they're a bog standard three-year-old's memories, with family weirdness tacked on top. And the worst thing is this: the barrier that stood between me and my classmates never really existed. I wasn't two years younger than them, condemned to the cold zone of Not Fitting by my age at an age when two years mattered a whole lot. All that wasted time, girls looking down on me as the freak, the little kid who had somehow infiltrated the hallowed sanctum of their maturity, and every bit of it was based on a lie. I wasn't two years younger: I was the scrawny midget I am today, ill-fed on beans and leaves to keep me small, puberty delayed by diet and stress, started off with a lineage where children have always been small, always been underweight, because poverty either makes you fat or makes you tiny.

And that's not all. Another piety I've held dear has been swept away, the one thing that kept my head held high all those years when conversation consisted of teachers going, 'Let's give someone else a chance for a change, shall we?' I was always at least able to blame the whole thing on my fabled superior intelligence. And now I don't even have that. I wasn't a phenomenon at all. I was the class swot.

And things have begun to change in my head about my mother. I don't see her any more as the omnipotent, the omniscient, the omnipresent Grace Waters. I know now that there's a chink in her armour, that she's as flawed as the rest of us. Because despite her famous rectitude, the straight back and the perfect grammar and the insistence on empiricism in everything, her scientific contempt for cheating and cutting corners and slipshod thinking, Grace Waters couldn't quite resist cooking the books when push came to shove. When it came down to the biggest experiment of her life, she couldn't stop herself from telling a couple of fibs to make certain that the results were as she wanted them.

It fills me with anger and sadness, but after a while I realise that there's another, strange emotion bouncing around shouting, 'Look at me! Look at me!' So I look, and I discover, to my astonishment, that it's a tiny nugget of glee. And once the glee finds the daylight, it grows and grows, and before I know it, it's towering over all the other feelings and making me jump for joy. Grace Waters, I've found you out. And now I know your dirty little secret, I will never be scared of you again.

Imagine. It mattered so much to you that you be right that you had to tell a whopping great lie to prove it.

And once I've thought my way this far, my attitude begins to soften. I start to see Grace in a new light, and I don't think it's a light she'd like me to see her in. I find myself thinking: poor thing. Poor lonely creature, trapped in a bubble, your whole life from the moment of your conception manipulated to fulfil the ambition of one inadequate man who couldn't even get it up enough to father you. I've spent my whole life pitying myself, and now I see that I was the lucky one. I was the one who escaped.

So I go back to SunnyView and, with Henry making a pest of himself because he's sensed the change in my mood, walking all over the paper and butting his nose against mine until I think I'm going to come out with bruises, I write her a letter. It's not a long one, but it takes almost four hours to complete.

Dear Mother,

I don't know if you were expecting to hear from me, but I've been thinking a lot over the last couple of months and feel that, whatever passed between us the last time we met, it's worse for us to be estranged like this than anything else. Things have been difficult for both of us, but I want you to know that, however disappointed you are in me, I am grateful for the things you have done for me. I know I'm not the daughter you wanted, but I am the daughter you've got, and if we took time to get to know each other, I think you might find that, although I've not taken the path you would have chosen, I am still an okay human being. I must be. Your values are values you have given me, and I wear them with pride. I am sorry that at the moment you can't see that any good has come from the time and the effort you put into my life, but I hope, one day, that you might be able to.

Please, the next time you're in Europe, can we meet up? Please? And start again, as adults. It would mean so much to me. Please think about it.

Oh, and congratulations on the Brit Award, by the way. I'm sure they thought it was far more of an honour than you did!

With love,

Anna

I know Carolyn knows what I'm doing up here, but I don't want to discuss it. So when I've finished, I slip out of the house to post my missive before I lose my nerve, or change my mind, or go back and edit in something spiteful. I buy a stamp from the shop at Sandbanks, and, once I've deposited the letter beyond reach, I take the chain ferry over to Stud-land and go for a walk on the beach.

I can't tell you what a weight has been lifted off my shoulders. I'm full of warmth and love and hope for the future, and my lungs are filled with salt spray from the running tide as it churns beneath the ferry. The railings are lined with painted boards advertising the joys of the Italian restaurant in Swanage and the *Best Fish and Chips in Purbeck*. A couple of teenagers with matching curly perms are stuck halfway down each other's throats, grinding crotches and taking occasional breaks to puff on Embassies that glow and splinter in the sea breeze. They're so ugly, and so horny, I even feel full of love for them.

We pull in on the far side and I walk down the gangplank as a couple of dozen cars vie to see who can do the fastest 0–60 handbrake start, and disappear towards the toll-booth a hundred yards further up the road. The teenagers saunter greasily towards the cafe. I walk up past the mysterious phone box buried waist-deep in a sand dune out where no one could possibly want to use it, and hang a left under the swing-barrier to Shell Beach.

It may be past the season for families, but the nudie people are still here. Some of them, judging by the deep mahogany of their skins, unbroken by lines of white where modesty usually prevails, have been here all summer, standing with their hands on their lower backs on the lower reaches of the dunes, pointing their bits to the prevailing wind.

They *are* strange, the nudie people. Where most people are content just to sit and read, or lie full-out and fall asleep in a whelter of glop and sunhats, nudie people always have to be standing, or walking, or doing tai ch'i or some other gymnastic pursuit that involves bending over or spreading your legs, or both, every few seconds. You don't stop on the nudie strip, or take too many detours from the flat seashore, for even if it weren't for the strangely un-naked people who perch behind the gorse bushes, one hand on the binoculars they have trained on the gymnasts below, everyone knows that the dunes further back are a famous place of assignation for gay men. Why anyone would want to have sex on a patch of loose sand scattered with the remains of sea-thistles beats me, but there you go. Perhaps they were attracted by the name.

While I walk, I think some more. Like I say, it's a lot to take in at once. I feel older, but I feel better too. All the lies have been excised now, and I can look at life full-on for the first time ever. I think: the bad stuff's done with now, you've got a good life. You love your job, you love your friends, you love your life. And you owe it all to Harriet Moresby. If she hadn't come along and picked you up and taught you the meaning of honour, and loyalty, and unquestioning love, you would never have learned to trust anyone; you would maybe still be in your cocoon, hiding from the world, afraid of your own shadow.

I think: Harriet was the first person to tell me the truth, pure and simple. Harriet is the only person who always *has* told me the truth. And that's the basis of our friendship. We come from families where nothing could be told, where everything was hidden away, changed, airbrushed, twisted to suit convenience, and we took truth, brushed it down, blew off the dust and went: *this is better.* Harriet Moresby saved my life. And I don't just mean the times she did it for real.

Then the phone rings, and I know, I just *know*, that it's her. I pick up, go, 'Harriet?' and her excited voice goes, 'Anna!'

'Harriet! Darling, how are you?'

'Anna.' Her voice is dancing, laughing, breathless, 'Anna,

it's over! We got him! We got him, the bastard, and it's all all right again.'

'Got him?'

'Yes! The man who's been doing all this. I caught him tampering with the car, and I was beating the crap out of him, and Mike—'

'It's okay?' I can't believe it.

'It's okay. You can go home. I can go home. Come home!'

'Mike was with you?'

'Yes! We're in the police station now! D'you want to talk to him?'

'I – yes—'

She's already handed the phone over. He comes on the line, and when his deep, serious voice goes, 'Anna?' I know, with a rush, that I am mad, crazy, wild about this man. It's not just a passing fancy this time, it's the real thing. Just like Harriet said, he's not a quick-fling guy, he's a stayer and, to my astonishment, I realise that I can be a stayer too. No more Happy Slapper, no more eyes across a crowded room, no more do you take milk in your coffee: I can be a stayer too. A month ago the thought would have filled me with horror, but now I know that I will pursue him to the ends of the earth. Because he saved us, he saved me, he's put our lives back where they were before and he's just so—

'Mike?'

'Hi.' I can hear a smile in his voice. 'How are you?'

'How do you think? Who is this man? What happened?'

'Sad fella,' he says. 'Angry little chap. The doofus actually has the same name as some of those emails. He didn't even give himself an alias before he sent them. Of course, he denies everything, but considering we caught him with the lid off the petrol tank and a box of matches, I think we've got our man.'

'You're brilliant. You're wonderful. Oh, Mike, I could kiss you *right now.*'

'Steady on, old bean,' says Harriet, who has taken the phone back while I was talking. 'Darling, when are you coming back? When are you bringing Henry back?'

'How's the tower?'

'Fucked,' she says. 'But we'll sort it out. Come back, Anna, I miss you. When are you coming back?'

'There's a train in a couple of hours,' I shriek. 'I'll be on it if it kills me.'

Chapter Fifty-Two

Have-a-go Heroes

We meet in the Synagogue, a bar under the arches near Waterloo. I run through the door, fling my arms round her and bounce with happiness. Then I fling my arms round Mike and kiss him firmly on the lips. 'Thank you! You're my hero!'

He looks a bit startled. 'You're welcome,' he says. He's looking just yummy in a black T-shirt bearing the logo of a restaurant in Nassau.

The waitress, in pinny and sensible shoes, comes over with a little silver tray with a doily on. 'Welcome,' she says. 'What can I get you?'

'Hi,' I say. 'What would you recommend?'

'For you,' she says, 'I'd recommend a cup of hot chocolate and an early night, but I suppose you'll be wanting a cocktail.'

'That would be good.'

'What would you like?'

'What's nice?'

'It's all nice,' she says. 'What, you think I wouldn't have nice in my house?'

'Well, what's the choice?'

She reels off a list. 'Dead Sea Breeze, Kiss of Bethlehem, Nazareth Fizz, Jaffa Sunrise, Eilat Iced Tea, Haifa Headbanger, Jerusalatini. Oh, and there's the Dome of the Rock if you want something without alcohol.'

'What's in a Dead Sea Breeze?'

'It's like a normal Sea Breeze,' she replies, 'but with a crust of salt round the rim of the glass.'

'Jaffa Sunrise?'

'Fresh orange juice, arak, grenadine.'

I don't even want to know what's in a Haifa Headbanger. 'I'll have the Jerusalatini.'

'Are you sure? It's very strong, you know.'

'Yes, thanks.'

'Well, it's your choice,' she says, and goes away.

I turn to the others, who sit triumphantly elbow to elbow, grinning at me. Harriet looks better than I've seen her in a long time. Mike really does look every bit as good as I remember him looking: frank blue eyes smile across the table and my heartstrings go ping. 'So tell me what happened?'

'Kapow! Zap!' says Harriet, with appropriate hand movements. 'Zing! Wham!'

'Slightly longer version?'

'Well,' she says, 'we were in the tower trying to sort things out. It's surprisingly okay, you know. The stairs were disgusting, but I promise I've got the worst of the melted stuff off the steps. And I'm afraid your room's awful. Everything's black. I think you're going to have to throw most of your stuff away.'

I take this on the chin. I had expected it, after all.

'I hope you don't mind,' she continues, 'but I thought I might as well bundle up most of the cloth stuff and just throw it away. There's no way any cleaner's going to be able to get the smoke damage out.'

Oh, dear, I think, my poor chenille.

She senses what I'm thinking. 'We'll bring some stuff up from Belhaven,' she says. 'The attics are heaving with crap.'

'Thanks.'

'So that's what we were doing. I'd filled up about twenty bin liners and Mike had taken them down to the bottom of the stairs, and the hall had got completely clogged, so we thought we'd better hump them along to the front gate.'

'It's incredibly sweet of you to do that,' I tell him.

'All part of the service,' he replies in that laid-back manner.

'If you can't rely on the boys in blue for a bit of rubbish clearance,' says Harriet, 'what on earth are we paying our taxes for?'

The waitress returns with my Jerusalatini, which turns out to be an ominous sky-blue in colour but contains two beautiful queen olives, and a small plate of falafel. Puts it on the table between us, says, commandingly, 'Eat!' and walks away. 'Did we order this?' I ask.

'You get a snack with every drink,' says Harriet. 'It's a gimmick.'

'Not very cost-effective.'

'You haven't seen the price of the drinks. Anyway, I was going down to the gate with, like, five bin liners, and I noticed some sort of movement out of the corner of my eye. Over by the car.'

'So of course' – Mike decides to make a contribution – 'she goes over there to look, doesn't she? Protective custody, and the first time she sees something suspicious what does she do? Goes off to investigate all by herself.'

Harriet continues. 'So I went over to look, and there's nothing there, but then I notice that the lid has been taken off the petrol tank. It's sitting there on the roof of the car.'

'Blimey,' I say. 'Weren't you scared?'

'Scared?' says Harriet. 'I was bloody livid.'

'She has a temper,' says Mike.

'I know.'

'Well, anyway, PC Bloody Plod is still dillying about over by the front door conducting some sort of discreet surveillance of his own backside, so I think: well, obviously it's up to me again. So I cast about for a bit, and then suddenly this bloke jumps out from the shadows by the boat shed and starts legging it towards the wall.'

'Poor sod,' says Mike. 'He didn't stand a chance.'

'Naturally, I thought it was my duty as a good citizen at least to make an attempt at apprehending the villain,' says Harriet. 'So I gave chase and conducted a citizen's arrest. Had him on the ground before you could say stalker. Bugger never knew what hit him.'

'I had to drag her off,' he says. 'You've never seen anything like it. Lucky she *wasn't* on the force or we'd have had a brutality case on our hands. I was only a hundred yards behind her, but by the time I got there, she had his face ground into the mud and was bouncing up and down on him shouting, "You tried to kill my cat, you bastard!" I nearly had to use the handcuffs on *her.*'

There's a small flash of something between them that I can't quite make out. The waitress comes back. Points at the uneaten falafel, sighs, says, 'And what's wrong with my falafel? You don't like the falafel?'

I'm immediately consumed by guilt, apologising. 'No, it's wonderful. It's just that none of us is particularly hungry . . .'

'Look at you!' she cries. 'You're skin and bone! You'll fade away to nothing if you don't eat. Think what all that alcohol is doing to your insides. You can't drink on an empty stomach.'

'Thank you,' says Mike, picks up a falafel, takes a bite. 'Delicious,' he announces.

' "Delicious", he says,' she mutters to an imaginary friend floating somewhere near the ceiling. Then, 'I suppose you'll be wanting more of those to ruin your health with?'

Mike declines. 'Thanks. I'm on early duty tomorrow. Can't afford a woolly head.' Harriet orders an Eilat Iced Tea and I take another Jerusalatini, which has proven to be very good even if my teeth won't be thanking me in the morning, and she settles back to her story.

'Of course, he's denying everything.'

'Of course,' says Mike, proving that in England you are still guilty until proven innocent.

'His name is Anthony Figgis,' says Harriet. 'He's a quantity surveyor from Dorking and his whole house is like a shrine to my mum.'

'Walls covered in pictures, scrapbooks full of press cuttings, memorabilia all over the place: *Beach Baby* T-shirts, posters, books, videos, old clothes . . .'

'He even,' she says, 'had ten of those dolls they made in the seventies. One for each of the costumes so he didn't have to change them.'

'But there must be dozens of people like that in the country,' I say.

'But none of *them* has been caught with my petrol cap off in the middle of the night,' Harriet points out.

'Or sent a couple of dozen nasty emails,' says Mike. 'He admits he sent *those*. Says he wanted to teach her some respect. Says he wouldn't harm a hair on her head.'

'He's lucky,' says Harriet, 'that I didn't have time to harm a hair on his.'

'Has he been charged?'

Mike nods. 'We've hit him with breaking and entering and malicious damage for the time being while we tie him in with the rest. Oh, and theft. He'd been into the car and half-inched a pair of earrings out of the ashtray. Excuse me.' He stands up, nods towards the Gents.

The minute he's gone, I lean forward and say, 'He's great, isn't he?'

'Mmm,' says Harriet. 'He's really great.'

'Has he been looking after you while I've been gone?'

'Yes,' she says. 'He's been brilliant. Really brilliant. I was so upset, and he's just been the best.'

'He was wonderful the night of the fire,' I say, 'after you went.' Suddenly, I feel shy about talking about him. Suddenly, after all these brazen years, I find it difficult to broach the subject of actual feeling with my best friend. Stupid. I can talk to her about anything, but I don't know how to use the L-word.

'He said you were in a state,' she says. 'I'm sorry, Anna. It really wasn't my doing.'

'I *know* that, Haz. But he was like the only person who believed me. I'll never forget him for that. He's the sort of guy you really want to have around.'

Harriet brightens. 'D'you think so?'

'Absolutely.'

'I'm so glad you said that,' she says. 'He will be too. He really likes you, you know.'

'Does he?'

She nods. 'He says you're a really spunky female, whatever that means.'

I'm pleased. 'Does he?'

'Yeah. He'll be really glad when I tell him you like him too.'

Deep embarrassment. 'Harriet! Don't!'

'Why not?'

'You can't do that. That would put him right off.'

'Sorry?' Harriet looks puzzled, then, suddenly,

discomfited. 'Oh,' she says. 'Oh, I didn't realise you meant like that . . .'

She trails off as he returns to the table, grinning, and sits back down. 'I must ask them,' he remarks, 'how they keep those plants in there looking so nice. I don't know what I've been doing wrong, but every plant in my house has dropped dead in the last couple of weeks.'

Chapter Fifty-Three

You Lied to Me

I can hardly wait for him to go, and I think he realises that, because, being a man of good grace, he gives it another five minutes, with me and Harriet staring across the table at each other and me speaking in monosyllables, and then he makes another reference to his early shift and takes his leave. Harriet hops up, walks him out to the street and I stay at the table, feeling like a prize pillock. No, not just like a prize pillock: like a prize pillock who's had the rug pulled out from under her feet and everyone's laughing. Like a prize pillock who's gone and fallen in love with someone who never even wanted her in a million years. Like a prize pillock who's just discovered that her best friend's been lying to her all along.

The waitress returns. 'One Jerusalatini, one Eilat Iced Tea.' Then she places a dish of hummus and a small basket of sliced cholla in front of me. 'I thought maybe as you hated the falafel, I'd give you this,' she announces. 'No one can hate hummus. It came from a shop, look.'

I thank her absently, and ask for the bill. I don't think we're going to be here a lot longer.

'Oh,' she says, 'must you go already? You've only just got here. I never see you, and now when you finally come, you're dashing off before you've even sat down. You've got better places to be than here, I suppose.'

I look at her. 'Does this work, this gimmick?'

She shrugs. 'Some of the time. We have to turn people away on Friday nights.'

'Friday nights?'

'You'd be surprised how many people leave town to get away from home and end up missing it once they're free.'

I give her my credit card, which is starting to look a tad frayed after all the use it's had lately, and smile even though I don't feel like smiling.

'I'll sort that out,' she says. 'Now, eat!'

Harriet returns, sits down and waits for me to say something. She has a way of wrong-footing you like that, Harriet. So eventually I say, 'Well. So I look a total dick, then.'

And she says, 'Don't be silly, Anna. You didn't know. You don't look anything.'

'And how long have I been making a dick of myself for?'

'You haven't,' she insists.

We stare each other out for a while, then she says, 'I'm sorry. I couldn't tell you because I haven't been alone with you since it happened.'

'God, Harriet, it's not as if it's some sort of solemn announcement.'

'Not for you, maybe,' says Harriet, and adds, slightly spitefully, or at least that's how I choose to interpret it, 'you've had more practice than I have.'

And then neither of us says a dicky bird for about five minutes.

She spends the first two minutes fiddling with her drink, stirring it with the straw, ducking the bits of fruit floating in the tan-coloured froth on the top, so they bob back to the surface with new bubbles attached. Then she folds her hands onto the table and gazes off round the room as the waitress brings the chit for me to sign and, looking disappointed, scoops up the hummus to recycle to another table. Then Harriet looks at my face again.

'I'm sorry I didn't tell you. But it's not as if it's some sort of long-standing secret.'

Paranoia makes me say, 'Must have been nice to have such a cosy place of safety to go to, then.'

'There's no conspiracy here, Annie.'

'Good to be able to get me out of the picture for a while, though.' I'm surprised at the level of bitterness that's crept into my voice. But you know, I've spent two weeks in exile, being treated like a criminal, and I *feel* bitter. So much for Gillespie and his assurances.

'For God's sake!' she explodes. 'What the hell do you think this is? Do you really think I could enlist the entire Metropolitan Police to get you out of the way so I could move in on some bloke you fancied? Get fucking real, Anna. You *know* it didn't happen like that.'

'Well, how did it happen, then?'

'Look, it just *happened*, okay?'

'Oh, right. Like your mother and father *just happened*.'

As soon as it's out of my mouth I regret it. But it's too late now. It's said.

Harriet's head jerks back, and she blinks a couple of times. 'Ow,' she says. 'That was harsh. You don't really think that, do you?'

No, of course I don't think that. Harriet, I don't think that. But I'm in pain right now and I'm standing back watching myself lash out.

And the pain says, 'Well, like mother like daughter, I guess. It's a bit of a family habit, isn't it?'

And she says, 'Well, I don't suppose anything would have happened at all if you hadn't used me as your beard while you shagged the last one in line.'

401

Ouch back.

'That's what happens when you behave like men are on some sort of conveyor belt for your pleasure. Every now and then one slips off, Anna, and you can't get too pissed off about it.'

God almighty. I'm not pissed off about *that*.

'You can't treat people like toys,' she continues. 'They have feelings.'

'Don't bloody lecture me,' I snap. 'If I ever heard an exercise in self-justification, that's it.'

Her haughty look comes out and she says, 'Well, I'm sorry if just this once I've failed to prop up your sexual confidence.'

Ouch again. You shouldn't have rows with people you know beyond a certain point. They know too well where to find your underbelly. This is way beyond tears. This is family betrayal. The two of us are hissing at each other like injured snakes, trying to cause as much damage before we die as we can.

'You lied to me,' I say.

'Anna, I never lied to you.'

'Oh, yeah, right. You were just economical with the truth.' She shrugs.

'I hate being lied to.'

'Oh, for God's sake,' she says. 'It's not such a big deal. I started a new relationship and didn't want to blab about it when I didn't know what was happening myself. Get over it, Anna. It's not the end of the world.'

'You don't get it at all, do you? It's not about the relationship, it's about the lie. You left me out in the cold for your own convenience and I'm pissed off.'

'Oh, grow up,' she snaps.

'Oho. The Fawcett charm. Or should I say the *Pigg* charm.'

She reels a little at this. 'Golly,' she says.

402

'Golly,' I say back.

Silence again. Everything is all twisted up inside my head. My guts are knotted and I feel like my heart is about to stop.

'Please let's stop this,' she says.

'I don't have anything more to say to you.'

'Don't be stupid.'

'I'm not fucking stupid,' I hiss, though I'd rather be shouting. 'Don't call me stupid.'

'Shut up, Anna.'

'Well, piss off, then. Just piss off. Go away. I don't want to talk to you. You're a fucking liar and I don't want to see you.'

She stops. 'You don't mean that.'

I turn away, dig my fingernails into my palms and fight back a scream. What am I doing? I can't be throwing the most important thing in my world away over a man. It's not possible. We're supposed to be inseparable. The Siamese twins. The Weird sisters. What am I doing?

'Anna, come on.'

'You can go now,' I say coldly and calmly once I've got my voice back.

'Anna, please, let's not do this. I'm sorry. I never meant to hurt you, and I'm sorry you're so upset. But let's talk about this. Come on—'

I interrupt. What is it with pride? I could turn round now, say something in return, heal the damage. There'd be scars, maybe, but people learn to live with scars every day. I could put my arms out and she would walk into them, I know that. And pride says 'I'll come and get my stuff when I've sorted out a van.'

'No, Anna, you don't have to do that. Come on. This is ridiculous.'

I say nothing, refuse to meet her eye.

'Anna, *please.*'

'Just go, Harriet.'

'Please can't we talk?'

'I don't want to talk to you. I don't want to have anything to do with you.'

'Look,' she says, and there's something interfering with the clarity of her speech, 'I love you. Nothing's changed.'

'But it has,' I say. 'Please just go.'

'Anna,' she says, 'look at me.'

I keep my back to her. If I turn round, she will see my face.

She stays there for what seems like an hour. I can sense her eyes on the back of my neck, feel her trying to find words.

Then I hear the rustle of her coat, hear her stand up. 'Come on,' she says. 'Don't do this. I can't bear this.'

But I say nothing. And eventually she puts a twenty-pound note on the table and walks away.

The restaurant is closed by the time I get back and let myself into the flat upstairs. When he hears the key in the lock, Henry leaps off the futon mattress, which is the only piece of furniture left after Roy moved out, and trots over, yawning and stretching, to rub his head against my ankles. Then he sees that something is wrong, sits up attentively, looking up at me, wide-eyed.

'How?' he asks tentatively.

'Not good, darling,' I reply.

He stands on his back legs, places his front paws on my thigh, gazes up into my eyes. 'Don't,' he says.

I haul him up into my arms, turn him over and squash him to my chest. He reaches up one gentle paw and pats it on my cheek.

'Don't cry,' he says. And I bury my face in his velvet coat and disobey.

Chapter Fifty-Four

LEEZA HAYMAN
When the World Weeps, She Weeps With Them

These are words that are hard for me to write, as the past few days have been hard to live through. It's been such a beautiful week, the sunshine mellow and gentle, dew on the morning grass. A week when everyone should be happy. A week for families and friends, for picnics and tennis and long lazy boat rides. Instead, we find ourselves in a veil of tears. For every morning, as we wake and see the sun streaming through the curtains, hear the excited shouts of children too young, bless them, to understand what has happened, we have thought: maybe it's just a dream. Maybe it's not true. Maybe it will all be back as it was before. And then the truth comes crashing down like waves upon the shore, as our heavy hearts cry once again, 'She is dead!'

I feel as though my heart has been ripped from my chest. For though I will admit that I was sometimes harsh in judgement of Godiva, let me also say this: people are often harshest in judgement of those they love the most. For I loved Godiva Fawcett, as everyone loved her. She was beautiful, she was kind, she cared in a way that few people can afford to care in this world. She offered to everyone, everywhere, her unconditional and shining love, and we loved her in return. And I cannot be the only one who has shed bitter tears when I think that perhaps, just perhaps, if I'd shown it better, she would still be with us today.

So let me say it now. Godiva, you were loved. You probably never knew how much. Let me say how much I admired you for your selfless courage in standing up for the causes you believed in. Let me tell you about the twinges of jealousy at your beauty, your goodness, your deep and palpable devotion to the child so cruelly ripped from your arms by an unfeeling judge. Let me tell you how I respected your dignity, admired the way you stood up and showed the way for women smaller of heart and weaker of will than yourself. You were loved, Godiva, and no number of tears will bring you back.

Nothing will be the same again. Never again will our lives be brightened by this shining star in our midst. Never again will our screens light up to the sight of that beauty, never again will our voices thrill to the sound of that voice. The children of the world have lost a champion, Godiva's daughter has lost a loving mother, and all of us have lost an inspiration, a role model, a yardstick by which to judge our own paltry efforts.

No doubt there will be cynics who will claim that the widespread sorrow over our terrible loss is mass hysteria, or crowd-pleasing, or any one of the insults that soulless intellectuals reserve for the simple emotions of real people. But today I say to them this: you are wrong. If you have been untouched by the loss of Godiva Fawcett, you will be for ever untouched by all of life's real meaning. If you remain untouched by the courage, the nobility of her death, you will never know nobility. And I say something else. Time will tell. When all you carping cynics are forgotten in your graves, the name Godiva Fawcett will live on.

It will live on in the hearts of all who knew her, and all who knew of her, and it will live on in the hearts of wide-eyed children who will learn of her greatness alongside the fairy tales they learn at their mother's knee. When all your feats have turned to dust, those of Godiva Fawcett will be the stuff of legend. For I am certain of one thing: we have, in our own time, witnessed the life of a saint. And one day, when the carping and the criticism is over, when the world can see with clear eyes and uncluttered judgement, it will be the deeds that live on.

Farewell, Godiva, and flights of angels sing thee to thy rest. A light passed from the world on Tuesday. We will never see its like again.

© Daily Sparkle, 1985

Chapter Fifty-Five

1994: Home at Last

We're still clinging to the fantasy that we're going to live healthily, have vegetables in the fridge and so forth, so I'm carrying four plastic bags full of salad and mineral water when I come home to find Harriet sitting on the floor streaming with tears, tiny Henry, still small enough to fit upside-down in the palm of your hand, clamped to her shoulder. She's on the floor because the vet's bills after we found him, poor blood-covered little mite, came to more than the cost of the glamorous Knowle sofa we'd been saving our tips for, and we're still trying to decide whether to save up again or just buy second-hand. So there they are, in the middle of a slightly singed Persian rug from Belhaven, Henry with his ragged ear and his broken nose and his half-closed eye, the burnt-off whiskers just beginning to sprout again, and Harriet crying like she's never going to stop.

I drop the bags, rush over and sit beside her. I've never seen Harriet cry but the once before, when she'd cut me down from the hook in my bedroom, and it's a sight that alarms me, makes me want to cry myself. Tentatively, I reach out to stroke her hair, which makes her both bawl even harder and duck her head to try to hide the fact that she's doing it. A great big tear plops off her cheek and lands squarely on Henry's head. He shakes it off, ears rattling, then stretches his neck, eyes closed, to rest his chin on her collarbone. Less than three months old, and he's already learned that cat thing of knowing the difference between crying and anger and taking the appropriate action.

'What's wrong? Darling, what's up?'

'There's nothing wrong, honestly, I'm fine,' she sobs.

'Well, why are you crying? You can't be crying if there's nothing wrong.'

'Well, I *am*,' she wails, and collapses against me. Henry, mildly confused, transfers himself onto my jumper, clambers up with needle claws to stand on my shoulder. He starts licking my ear, tiny rasping tongue giving me such a nice tickling that, under other circumstances, I would burst out laughing.

'So what's with the tears?' I put my arm round her and our little family circle is complete.

Harriet gulps. 'I was thinking,' she said, 'how wonderful it all was. I came home, and Henry came galloping to the top of the stairs to meet me, and I picked him up and gave him a cuddle, and then I was thinking about how brilliant everything was. We've finally got this place, and it's you, and me, and Henry, and I've never felt so – so – so *safe* before, and I never had any friends before, not really, just people one knew, not people who actually minded. And now I've got you, and Mel, and Dom, and Lindsey, and we've got this house where we can be anything we want to be, and I don't want it all to *end*.'

I shush her, lean my chin on her hair and stroke the back of her neck. 'Why do you think it's going to end, honey?'

'Because *everything* ends!' she wails. 'Everything!'

'But I'm not going anywhere, Harriet. You're my friend for life.'

And then she flops about a bit, and looks up and puts her hand on Henry's poor bashed-up little head.

'Look what they did to him,' she says. 'That's what. Look. He's only tiny and he never did anyone any harm, and look what they did! He's little and trusting, and they used him like a football and they shut him up in a box to die!'

My own eyes start to brim with this, and I begin to gulp along with her. 'But he's okay now,' I blubber, 'he's got us now. There will never be a cat in the world who's as loved as Henry Tudor.'

We both know we're not just crying over Henry, though I've shed many tears in surgeries up and down the city. You know, you suddenly find yourself responsible for something so small, so damaged, and your defences crumble one by one. The first time Henry came voluntarily out from behind the kitchen unit where he spent most of his time hiding and rubbed his scrappy little cheekbone along the length of my extended finger, I fell besottedly in love. I can't bear the thought that someone could hurt my baby.

But we're crying because, if you're damaged yourself, you can't bear to see someone else go through the same thing. That's the tie that binds the two of us together. Don't think we're so unaware that we don't know that.

'But what if . . .?' she says. Now that I'm crying, she's slowed down herself.

'Don't do what ifs, Harriet. We can't do what ifs.'

'Yes, but,' she says, 'this can't last. Something will come along that will destroy it all. We could get ill, or we could start to hate each other, or you'll go and settle down with some man—'

I interrupt. 'What the hell are you on about? I'm not going to leave you for some man, Harriet.' And then, because I'm more of a realist than that, I correct myself. 'Do you think I'd ever swan off with some man who didn't understand what you meant to me?' And as I'm asking it, I'm thinking about all the times Godiva did just that: called from New York to cancel an access visit because luurve took precedence. 'My daughter *wants* me to be happy,' she would crow to the press. 'She understands how hard it's been for me.' And Harriet, on the payphone from her boarding school, would echo her, 'That's fine, Mummy,' she would say dutifully, 'you *know* I want you to be happy'.

'You think that now,' she says, 'but men always get in the way. You love them. You're bound to want to be with one some day.'

And I say, 'Harriet, let's not think about that now. Let's just enjoy ourselves. We've finally found somewhere where no one can touch us, where no one can come in without our say-so, where we're totally safe. Just try to be happy. Don't spend your life waiting for it to end.'

Henry, finished with my ear, emits a little peeping miaow – he still talks baby-talk – and hops from my shoulder onto hers. She puts a hand up and wipes her tearstained face on his coat, something he doesn't seem to mind.

'Besides,' I add, with that sunny optimism borne of friend-ship, 'we'll probably end up a pair of mad old cat ladies quarrelling about your art supplies when we're seventy.'

She sniffs, gives me a watery smile. 'We'll never get a Stannah up the stairs,' she says.

Chapter Fifty-Six

Really Drowning

And I keep crying. There's nothing I can do to control it. All the tears I haven't shed come bursting to the surface and won't be stopped. I cry myself to sleep, I wake up and cry at the bathroom mirror as I'm brushing my teeth, I cry in front of the TV. She doesn't come in to work again, and two or three times a night I have to take off for five minutes or so to hide in the cellar and let the tears roll. I stop going out, and instead I cry as I prepare my solitary late-night suppers, I cry when anyone calls to see how I am, and I lose it every time Henry climbs up and pushes his worried, mournful face into mine.

I stop answering the phone because I don't want to run the risk that I might pick up and find it's her, then I cry some more because whenever the machine clicks on, it never is. It's as though she's vanished off the face of the earth. It's as though she's died: one minute she's there, filling up my life, irritating me and entertaining me and giving me worry and hope, and the next minute: nothing. Only, dying's not a betrayal. If someone dies, it's not stupid pride that takes them away from you. If someone dies, you can't blame yourself.

And nobody seems to be on my side. Shahin says, 'Anna, you are motherfuckin' stupid bastard. You are family. She is like family to you. How can you do this? Why you are so angry? It's only a man, after all.'

Oh, yes: they all know about *that*.

And I say, 'You don't understand, Shahin, it's not about a man, it's about the lies. Everyone has lied to me, my whole life. Until I met Harriet, there wasn't a single person who told me the truth, about anything. And now I find out that she's the same as the rest of them, and I can't trust her any more either.'

And Shahin clears his throat and makes a spitting noise, and says, 'Anna, you are crazy woman. I know all weemens are crazy, but this is really crazy. You think you're only person ever got lied to?'

'No, of course I don't. But this is different.'

Shahin makes a roar of Middle-Eastern frustration. 'Of *course* is not different! What makes you so special? I lie all the time. Everyone lies, all the time. Where I grew up, you had to lie, every day, every minute, because that was only way you stayed alive. Lying's not the worst thing you can do. Sometime it's the *only* thing you can do.'

And I say, 'It is to me, Shahin. How can I ever trust that someone loves me if they don't tell me the truth?'

'Many time,' says Shahin, 'people tell lies *because* they love someone. Are you really so blind you don't even know that?'

And then he says, 'You been lying to your mother for, what? Ten years? I hear you all the time, on the telephone. Yes, Mother, library, Mother, being good girl, Mother. Without shame.'

And I say, 'My point exactly.'

Mel comes over. She says, 'Anna, Harriet's in an awful state. Why won't you talk to her?'

I roll over on the sofa, wrap myself tighter in my blanket

412

because I seem to be cold all the time nowadays, even though it's only September, and I say, 'Mel, you don't understand. Harriet's got what she wants. She doesn't give a damn what it does to anyone else.'

Mel says, 'No, she rang me the other day and she could hardly speak, she was crying so much.'

I shout, 'Don't you think I'm crying? Do my tears matter so little to all of you? Why are you so concerned about Harriet's tears? What about mine?'

Mel leaves, and Lindsey comes round the next day and sits on the futon with her arms round me for an hour while I cry. And she says, 'Anna, Harriet never meant to hurt you. You must know that. It's the last thing she'd do on purpose,' but I can't listen to her. All I know is that everything is spoiled now, that nothing will ever be good in my life again.

You think I'm exaggerating? Live in my shoes. I've nothing left. Oh, for God's sake, this isn't *about* a man. It's about something important. It's about trust and respect and deceit, it's not about some poxy man.

Dom calls, all awkward, says, 'How you doing, mate?'

'I'm fine.'

'Really?'

'Yes.'

'Oh, good,' he says. 'So maybe you feel like coming out on Saturday after work? We were going to go to that new place on Greek Street where you get free drinks all night if you guess the weight of the bouncer.'

'No, thanks,' I say.

'You sure?' he says, all concerned.

'Positive.'

He's a bloke. He's relieved, though because he's a nice

bloke he tries not to show it. 'Okay, then,' he says. 'But if you change your mind . . .'

'I won't,' I reply. 'Thanks anyway, Dom.'

After he hangs up I hug a cushion for an hour before I fall asleep.

Roy says, 'For Christ's sake sort yourself out with that posh bint. This place is going to go down the tubes without her. Let alone the rent I'm not getting on the flat upstairs.'

I say, 'Thanks, Roy. I'm doing my best.'

He shakes his head, tuts. 'Well, it's not bloody good enough. You've got a face like a wet Tuesday and it's scaring off the punters.'

And I go down to the cellar and have a cry where he can't see me.

On the eighth day, she sends me a letter.

> Annie,
>   Please talk to me. Please don't walk away from me. I'm sorry. From the bottom of my heart I'm sorry. I haven't told him anything about this. He has no idea. He never did. I love you. Please talk to me. It's killing me, having you be so angry with me. I know you have reason, and all I can say is that I am truly, truly sorry. I'll finish it with him, if that's what you need; I just don't want to be estranged from you like this. I never meant to lie to you. I was going to tell you, I swear. Please, please talk to me, let me apologise to your face. We can't leave things like this.

I don't know what's got into me. Maybe I'm not my mother's daughter for nothing. I read it, and I miss her so much. It's like having had a limb amputated. I feel her presence all the time, turn to tell her something and remember that she's not there. And then the anger returns, and I screw the letter up, throw it into the bin. Then I get it out and read it again, and cry, and then, ritualistically, I put it in the ashtray and set fire to it, Henry crouching down in a corner, looking nervously at me like I'm going to set fire to him next.

So I think: maybe I'll go to Australia. Maybe I'll just bugger off to Australia and live on the beach and never come back, and that'll show them. So I dial Nigel at three o'clock in the morning and he picks it up at seven o'clock his time. 'It's me,' I say.

'Annie!' His voice is happy, relaxed, full of beach life. 'Annie, how are ya? I wasn't expecting to hear from you so soon!'

'I'm fine,' I lie.

'Really?' he asks. 'And how's the stalker?'

'Arrested.'

'Well, thank God for that. And how's Harriet?'

'All right, as far as I know,' I tell him, and burst into tears.

A worried, kindly voice on the other side of the world says, 'Annie, what's wrong? Why are you crying, Annie? What's going on?'

So between sobs I stammer out my story – well, the edited highlights, obviously, about the safe house and the loneliness and the fact that she'd been holed up with Mike all that time without telling me, not the bit about how I'd wanted him for myself, and Nigel listens like the sweetie he is, only saying the odd 'Aouh yeah?' and 'Go on' to encourage me. And when I'm done, he sighs and says, 'Poor old you. You've been having a rough time, I reckon.'

'Yes,' I sob, 'I have.'

'Guess you need a spot of the old TLC,' he says.

'Yes,' I reply, then, suddenly shy, I ask hesitantly, 'So is it all right if I – you know – if I come out and see you? Like you said?'

'Well, sure,' says Nigel, 'I can't think of anything nicer.' And then he pauses, adds, 'Once you've sorted everything out.'

'What?'

'Anna,' he says, his voice serious, 'I'd love to see you. You know I'd love to see you. I meant what I said. But I'm not going to help you run away from your problems. I'm sorry you feel let down, but you've got to sort this out. I've seen Harriet in action, and I believe what she said about not meaning to lie to you. You're going to have to talk to her. Get things out in the open. If you run away now, you'll end up being one of those people who runs away from *everything*.'

'I won't!' I cry.

'You will,' he says firmly. 'I'm sorry, but you will. Strikes me that you and Harriet are the only stable things in either of your lives. If you reject *that* when things get rough, you're pretty much saying that you're the kind of person who'll run away from anything. I'd love to see you. You know I'd love to see you. But I don't want to see you if all I am is a bolthole.'

Oh, God. Not one person is on my side. I say nothing.

'Come on,' says Nigel, 'talk to her. She's a good girl, you know that. And she's a good friend to you. You love her to death. Just sort it out, Anna.'

'I can't,' I mutter. 'She won't want to talk to me now.'

''Course she will,' he says. 'Come on. Just call her. For your own sake.'

Then he says, 'I've got to go now, Annie. I'm sorry, but

416

I was due over at Scarborough half an hour ago. I'll call you in a couple of days, yeah?'

'Okay,' I say.

'It'll be okay, Annie,' he says. 'Sort it out.'

And then there's nothing but me and a dead line. And I go back to the futon and crawl under the duvet and cry some more, because no one seems to be on my side, because I don't want to face life on my own any more, and because, deep in the very fabric of me, in the place that tears easily and never mends, I can't bear to be without my best friend.

Chapter Fifty-Seven

The Silicone Saviour

And of course, I don't do anything. Stupid pride keeps me crying in the miserable flat above the miserable restaurant, and my tips go down because Harriet and I, however much we annoy Roy, were a good team, and one of the others and I simply don't cut the mustard to the same extent. I give up going out. I just wander upstairs from work and sit on the futon with Henry eating leftover toad-in-the-hole and watching telly until I fall asleep. No one's heard anything from Harriet, or so they tell me. Mel says she's gone underground too. More likely living in her love bubble without a need for anyone else, I think uncharitably, steal several portions of bread-and-butter pudding from the restaurant and shove three helpings in my gob with cold custard before I throw it all back up again.

And then Godiva reaches out from beyond the grave once more. Three weeks after I last saw her daughter, I'm up early for someone who rarely goes to bed before three; *Rise and Shine* is still on when I turn on the black-and-white telly Mel's loaned me while I get my life straight. And the first face I recognise is Leeza Hayman's. There she is, bold as brass and twice as blonde, power suit and 15 deniers, legs crossed at the knee on the comfy sofa. I leap forward, turn up the volume to hear her say '. . . just as I'd always said all along. I've been saying for years that there was something fishy about the whole thing, so it hardly comes as a surprise to me.'

No, I think: nothing comes as a surprise to you. Surprise is a rare commodity among those who have the luxury of twenty-four hours in which to register their prescience.

'But Leeza,' protests Mandy, the forty-something co-host who seems to be chairing this segment, 'you've been one of the most vocal figures in support of her over the past few months.'

Leeza, evidently unrattled, replies, 'Yes, well, I always like to give people the benefit of the doubt, but in the end enough is enough.'

We cut to camera 2, and I see that, along with Leeza on the sofa, which is one of those corner jobbies that allow the maximum number to be seated within the narrowest camera angle, are what looks like a Church of England vicar, the Shadow Spokesperson for Contentious Issues and a woman in black who looks remarkably like she might belong to the Solemnity of the Occasion Brigade. No, Goddamn it: she *is* one of the Solemnity of the Occasion Brigade. She's the woman who told me off for taking a picture of the drag queens in Parliament Square. I sit down to watch.

Mandy turns to Solemnity. 'Mavis Rogers,' she says, 'you're a long-standing member of the Godiva Fawcett Trust. Would you say that there was some truth in what Leeza is saying?'

Solemnity colours, clears her throat and begins, 'Absolutely not,' she says. 'Whatever Ms Hayman's opinion may be, there are millions of people in this country who regard Godiva as a saint, and nothing the likes of the press can say is going to change our minds. She was a good, lovely lady, and any smear stories people like you' – she spits the last word at Leeza – 'may dredge up are nothing but that: smear stories from petty and jealous people bent on dirtying anything good to make themselves feel better. She will always be a saint in my eyes, and in thousands of other people's. I think they should carry on and deify her anyway—'

Leeza leans forward to get her face into shot, interrupts. 'That's just the sort of ignorance that's getting this country into trouble,' she snaps. 'It's not *deify*, for a start, it's *beatify*, and in case you didn't know, there are rules about this sort of thing. And aside from the fact that it's well recorded that she was hardly a model of virtue, the rules say that a body must remain uncorrupted, and I think it's been proven pretty conclusively that hers is not.'

'Yes it is!' cries Solemnity. 'I've seen it myself! She looks exactly as she did the day she died!'

'She died from a blow to the back of the head,' says Leeza. 'Hardly disfiguring. And as for the rest, it's all in the autopsy if you weren't too fat-headed to read it. Half her body was stuffed with silicone and the rest had been sucked so free of fat that there was nothing left to rot. It's hardly a miracle. It's called cosmetic surgery, dear.'

Shadow Spokesperson grabs at what he perceives to be a cue. He looks like a schnauzer and wears a well-ironed spotted handkerchief in his – horrors – blazer pocket. 'I think,' he says, 'that if ever there was one, this stands as a metaphor for the kind of government we've got at the moment. Godiva Fawcett's life was like the life of this parliament: government by spin, government by public image, all performance and no substance.'

Everyone turns to him with a look of puzzled boredom. Vicar, the man of peace, jumps in to save both the day and the flow of the discussion. 'As a man of the cloth,' he declares in fruity tones, 'I feel it my duty to see the good in everyone.

The saint and the sinner, as it were. And I think that Godiva was a very *real* person. Flawed, of course – and who among us can claim to be perfect – but good at bottom. And we must not forget the manner of her death. If ever there was a Damascene conversion, I would say that this was one—'

'Nonsense!' cries Leeza. 'It was the best career move she ever made!'

A tiny silence. Then Mandy, professional to the last, says, 'What do you mean by that, Leeza?' and Leeza continues.

'Godiva Fawcett was an actress, for heaven's sake. An actress and a publicity merchant. And her career had gone into freefall years before. She'd managed to prop it up with the bleeding-heart routine, but even that was wearing thin, and she knew it. I think it's fairly obvious that she decided to go out with a bang, that's all. Played out her greatest scene before the camera. And jolly effective it was too.'

Even Mandy finds this one hard to cope with. 'Well, that's certainly a strong opinion, Leeza,' she stutters.

Solemnity is unable to hold herself back. 'But there were the miracles!' she insists. 'Everyone knows about the miracles. She was always making ill people better. Why, my own daughter came out of a year-long depression just from seeing Godiva on the television talking about her own troubles . . .'

'Hardly a miracle,' says Leeza. Pulls the sort of face you see teenage girls making at dowdy rivals in discos.

'And I'm afraid we're going to have to leave it at that,' says Mandy hastily. 'Thank you so much for joining us, Mavis Rogers, Peregrine Hart-Dumplington, Leeza Hayman and Nicholas Redfern. Now some of you may remember' – she turns to face the autocue – 'that we reported a few weeks back on the case of the little Nottingham girl who was found to have a sycamore growing from her left ear. Well, news reaches us today of an even more amazing . . .'

I turn the volume down. So Godiva no longer qualifies for sainthood. After all that, she turns out to be little more than a tailor's dummy. And through various feelings of amusement and disappointment and relief, a single word is topmost in my thoughts.

Harriet.

Chapter Fifty-Eight

Reconciliation

And of course, the wolves are back outside the front gate, just as I knew they would be. Half a dozen of them gathered, hands in pockets, on the pavement, backs to me as I round the corner. Damn. I duck back out of sight before one of them turns, speed-dial our number, which is still stored under AAA in my mobile.

She's screening, of course. 'This is a machine,' says the machine. 'If you leave a message, it will not steal your soul. If you're lucky.'

It beeps. I speak. 'Hello, it's me.'

Pause. 'Harriet, it's me. Pick up the phone.'

She picks up. 'Annie?'

I'm quiet for a moment, then say, 'Hello.'

'I'm so glad you called,' she says. 'Are you okay?'

'I'm okay,' I say, feeling awkward.

I can hear her thinking, considering, then she says, again, 'How are you? How are things?'

'Fine,' I reply. And again, 'How are you?'

'Yeah,' says Harriet. 'Fine. Keeping busy. Have you heard the news about my mother?

'Yes. I'm sorry.'

'I'm not,' she says. 'Maybe the Solemnities will find

423

something else to get worked up about now. They've had to let Anthony Figgis go, by the way.'

'What?'

'Couldn't actually tie him in with any of the other stuff. Can't keep someone locked up on a single burglary charge alone.'

'I'm sorry.'

I can hear her shake her head. 'I don't suppose he'll be up to anything much else,' she says. 'I gather he's been scared witless by being pulled in as it is.'

Then I think: what am I doing, talking to her on the phone? 'Harriet,' I tell her, 'I came to see if you're okay.'

Her voice changes: fear, excitement, something else. 'You're outside?'

'Round the corner.'

'Oh, thank God,' she says, and the words come in a rush as though she's been holding her breath.

'Can I come up?'

'Yes! Yes, please!' It sounds like she is about to lose her voice.

'I'll tell you when I get to the gate,' I tell her. 'Then you'd better buzz me in. I don't want to hand the combination over to all those gits out there.'

'Fine.'

I drop the phone to my side, round the corner once again and walk with a determined stride towards the wolf pack. It takes a few seconds before they notice me, then they rush towards me like a wave towards a rock, break over my head in a hullabaloo of shouted questions, though, as there are only six of them, it would scarcely seem necessary. Half a dozen tape machines plunge towards my face, making me flinch. 'You'll take someone's eye out one day,' I tell a man in a polyester tie, and in return he shouts, 'Are you going to visit Lady Harriet? What does she think about the findings of the autopsy? Will she be appealing to the Vatican? Can I have a quote on her reaction? What's going to happen now?'

I smile sweetly and try to look calm, though inside I'm bricking it, scarcely able to keep walking. God, please let this go okay. I miss her. I can't help it: I miss her. We reach the gate and suddenly all fall quiet as they wait to see what I'm going to do next.

'Sorry, guys,' I say. Lift the phone to my ear and say, 'I'm here.'

A second later, the lock clunks and I slip inside, then lean all my weight against it to push it shut against the resistance without.

The yard hasn't changed much, aside from a few extra tyre marks from the police presence and a pile of bin liners against the wall. I don't know why I should have thought it would have. The car, petrol cap replaced, festers under the rowan, which is already covered in festive red berries.

And now I'm inside, I'm scared to go forward. I don't know what to say to her. Because I know nothing about reconciliation. I have experience in obeying, in punishment, in total and final estrangement, but I'm twenty-nine years old and in all that time I've never spoken bitter words and then asked for forgiveness.

I've slowed to a crawl. It takes me nearly five minutes of dawdling to get as far as the bridge. The weather has turned from blazing sun to one of those perfect early autumn days where the air is light and the light is clean, and you're suddenly aware that winter won't be far behind. What do I do? What do I say? Oh, God, let me go back to before, let me un-say the things I said, take back the thoughts, just be me and Harriet, cat-ladies for ever. My stomach is churning, my skin burns, there's a twitch in my cheek that won't be still.

And then I realise that I can't go through with it. I can't face her. I can't do this. Losing her the first time – throwing our friendship away the first time – was like a death. I'd rather die. I'd rather die myself, right now, than go through it again. I stop in my tracks, look at my shoes, make to turn back towards the gate.

And then the door bursts open at the foot of the tower and she's pounding down the path towards me, hair flying, face twisted with – what? – I don't know.

And then I do know. Because her arms are open and she's shouting and sobbing all at once, 'Darling, darling, I'm sorry! You came back and I'm sorry and thank you and oh God, Anna, you came back!'

Chapter Fifty-Nine

The Rules of Promiscuity

Thursday night. There are twenty-five church candles on the coffee table and it takes nearly five minutes to light them all. But it's worth it, because it gives me an opportunity to turn off the background lighting once the first one is lit, and then I know I look good with the warm yellow glow playing on my face and my backless dress falling lightly forward as I lean casually over them to reveal just the merest hint of breast. I use a long wax taper rather than a cigarette lighter to light them; it looks classy, and besides, I get an opportunity to pout delicately, looking all the while into his eyes over the flame, as I blow it out.

François sits back, arm along the back of the sofa, and watches in silence as I perform the ritual. Shoulder-length black hair, sleek and glossy like a raven's wing, angular, squared-off bones to his face like the rock Gods of Rapa Nui, arched, defined eyebrows, slightly slanted eyes that in the light are an intriguing shade of khaki and by candlelight are a vivid gold. They are slightly narrowed, speculative, as he watches me perform my task. He may be French by birth, but the blood is pure – well, part – Pacific.

I finish, sit back and smile. Am pleased to see him slightly adjust his posture on the seat. I lean forward again, pick up my brandy glass, lick a finger and run it round the rim to

427

make it sing. Which in the language of seduction is roughly tantamount to saying, 'Make *me* sing, big boy, why don't you?' François's eyes narrow a little more and a smile plays around the corners of his lips.

'So your flatmate,' he says in that smooth and fluid voice, 'she's not here tonight?'

I smile back over the rim of my glass, stop the singing and dip my finger in my Armagnac. Bring it to my slightly parted lips, place the tip between them, close and suck. Even the most basic learner doesn't need a lot of help in translating *that* gesture.

'No,' I reply slowly. 'She's staying at her boyfriend's.'

He nods with a hint of satisfaction. 'And the artist? That's her? Or you?'

'Her,' I tell him.

'Ah, of course,' he says. 'And you work in a restaurant.'

'Very good,' I tease. 'You're obviously a spy.'

He reaches out a hand, runs the backs of his fingers along the hairline on my neck. I shiver. 'You like?' he asks.

'Yes,' I reply, 'yes, I do. And next year I'm going to open one of my own.' You see, because I'm twenty-nine, I can make plans for what to do with Peter's money now. It's not just a pie floating far off in the clouds.

François sits forward. 'Aha. Your own restaurant. And what will it be like?'

'It will be lovely,' I announce, taking a lump of ice from my drink and rubbing it over my lips. 'It will be the perfect restaurant. Huge sofas and dark corners and candlelight, and food you eat with your fingers. Terracotta and azure and gold, and velvet curtains.'

'Beautiful,' he says, and this time I know he's not talking about the restaurant. He reaches out again, closes his hand over the hand in which I'm holding the ice cube and gently prises it from my fingers. 'Now close your eyes,' he orders. At last. I comply, fingers pressed together in my lap. Sensation: cold and kind, running down my upper arm, first on the outside, and then on the tender skin on the inside of my elbow.

'You like?' he asks again.

'Oh, yes,' I tell him, 'I like.'

The ice runs back up my arm, over my collarbone, works a line up my neck to the pulse point just below my ear. And then, after pausing a moment, it moves on, fingers replacing it with a gentle caress on my throat that brings an involuntary moan of pleasure from my lips. And with the ice, he runs on down the back of my neck, traces the line of my spine so that my whole body is suddenly tingling with anticipation. Oh, oh, ohhh.

'You like?' he whispers again, so close to my ear that I can feel his hot breath against the frozen skin. And all I can do in return is turn my mouth towards him, breathe in and swooningly press flesh to flesh.

The sixth rule of promiscuity: Get over it. Move on.

Chapter Sixty

The Secret Policeman's Ball

There are secrets that women never share, and Harriet and I have ours. Mike never knew – never will know, I think, at least until we are all so old and gnarled and used to each other that we can treat it as a family joke – the whole story behind Harriet and my estrangement. He knows, of course, that it was to do with him, but he believes that my anger was about being exiled while they developed their bliss.

Neither of us has felt it necessary to tell him more.

And bliss it is, I can see that. Not a bliss I want for myself just yet, but I can appreciate how sweet it is for them. They're crazy, mad, love-bubble people, riding the surf, plunging down the waterfall, diving through the water. They need nothing, right now: not food, not drink, not books or music: all they need to do for sustenance is look at each other and they're full again.

And besides, having a Plod around is proving to have its uses. It's been six weeks since the fire and nothing untowards has happened aside from Henry bringing in a dog-collar one night. And I don't mean the collar from a dog; I mean a dog-collar. Go figure. But Anthony Figgis has evidently had his fill, or the truth about Godiva has worked wonders, and we're almost back to normal.

Harriet, having vanquished the foe, seems finally free to

talk. 'The thing I don't get,' she says, 'is how a little guy like that could get himself so worked up in the first place. I mean, I can understand the sneaky things, but it's the other ones. The restaurant and the march. He just didn't seem that confrontational a type.'

Harriet is putting on make-up because she is going to the CID summer party with her beloved. This particular shindig is known as the Secret Policeman's Ball in the trade, because they try to keep quiet about the fact that it happens in case they come in for flak about taxpayers' money and lose even more Plod off the streets. I'll tell you what, there are some sacrifices I'd *never* make to be in the love-bubble. The bubblers even offered to take me along if I wanted, but somehow the prospect of a night listening to a load of blokes in bomber jackets share perpetrator stories over a pint of bitter is less enticing than a night in painting my toenails and watching old Take That videos. But Harriet is making an effort; she wants PC Mike to be proud, and proud he will be. She has on a fifties-style dress with a low neckline and full skirt in a red and gold brocade I'm sure I last saw dressing the Chinese drawing-room windows at Belhaven; she even has a matching fichu, starched and tied about the shoulders to frame her swan neck and Audrey Hepburn beehive. She looks beautiful.

'Well, yeah,' I say, 'but he obviously hired people for the march. Believe me, none of them were weaselly blokes with moustaches and anoraks. God, Figgis is much more like the kind of person Grace attracts than a man of action.'

The mention of Grace makes her change the subject, but this time it's not one of those clunking subject-changes that characterised the topic of her stalker a couple of months ago. 'I don't suppose that Grace has lived up to her name and got in touch with you after your letter?' she asks, though she must know the answer because she knows I would have told her.

'Uh-uh.' I shake my head. Look in the mirror and see a little pixie staring back at me beside the Titania that is my friend. 'I don't think she will either.'

Harriet draws lines in crimson around the outside of her lips. 'How do you feel about that?'

I pull a wry face. Because even though I know what Grace is like, I still have regrets that we can't get along.

Harriet stops painting, looks at me in the mirror. 'Strikes me,' she says, 'that maybe you ought to give up on Grace now.'

'God. I've got Carolyn on one side telling me I ought to persist and you on the other telling me to give up. It's not easy, you know.'

'No, look,' she says, 'you've tried the persisting bit. But in the end there has to come a cut-off point. Maybe it's now. If she's not been in touch, the chances are that she won't be.'

'Maybe . . .'

'Look,' she says again. 'The ball's in her court now. And she's made it clear what she thinks. She's had you over a barrel all your life and now she can't any more, she's taking her revenge.'

'Hardly revenge, Harriet.'

'Yes, it is. It's revenge. She knows what she's doing, and she's doing it to hurt you. Let it go, Anna. Let her get on with it. Grace Waters is obviously one of those people who never forgive anything. I think she'll carry her grudge with her until one or the other of you dies. There's no point torturing yourself about it any more. I've met her, remember. She's implacable. That's the only word I can think of for her.'

I sigh. 'Maybe you're right.'

'What would you do if she walked in right now?'

'I don't know. I think maybe I'd be glad.'

'Glad? *Glad?* You've only just got rid of the bitch.'

'Yes, but if she walked in now, it might mean that there was some chance . . .'

Harriet finishes off her lips, turns to me. 'It would be more likely that she'd come back for another go, Anna. You're better off without her.'

Mike looks like a copper. He's wearing a numbered baseball jacket over a checked shirt. God, they look odd together: the princess and the frog, the duchess and the bodyguard. Now that my own love-bubble has burst, I can't see what filled it in the first place. But Harriet can. She stands by him in the doorway, looks up at him with an expression of such soppy adoration that I think I might need to get her on a course of Prozac.

'You're sure you don't want to come?' he offers once more. 'We've still got a spare ticket.'

Like a hole in the head I want to come, I think. But I say, 'It's really sweet of you, darling, but I'm totally washed out.'

'You're sure you're going to be okay?' asks Harriet.

'Of course. I'm looking forward to a quiet night,' I lie. Actually, I'm beginning to think about maybe calling the lovely François and seeing what we could do with the set of handcuffs that Mike hasn't noticed I've swiped from his overnight bag and secreted in my bedroom. I wouldn't mind a rematch. François's body was made for climbing up cliffs and diving off them again. Lots of upper-body musculature.

'Well, if you're sure . . .' she says.

'Have fun,' I say. 'If your stalker calls, I'll be sure to say hello.'

They laugh. Come over and kiss me goodnight. And then they leave.

For a couple of minutes I just stand there, listening to the sound of their receding footsteps and adjusting to the silence. Henry's out rollicking somewhere; I have the house entirely to myself. I draw my feet up onto the sofa, wrap my arms round myself and have a little drum of the fingers. A whole night to myself. Funny. There was a time when that was all I had, and it drove me to attempt suicide. Now it's such a rare occurrence that I'm not sure if I want to bust up the tranquillity with activity. God, it's so quiet I can hear the drip–drip–drip from the leaky washer at the kitchen sink.

It's so quiet, I can hear my own thoughts.

And they're going: maybe Harriet's right. Maybe it's time just to let go of the past altogether now, move on as an effective orphan. Because, really, if I look at it, that's what I've been all along: the foster child, the changeling, tolerated only so long as I toed the line. All my life, I've had this fantasy that somehow my family would revolutionise itself, turn into a place of safety. Maybe it's time to let go of the fantasy and face reality. My mother is not like other mothers. So I don't need to persist in trying to be like other daughters.

Bad train of thought. Now I definitely don't feel like calling the lovely François. Thinking too hard about Grace Waters is like being doused with a bucket of cold water laced with bromide.

In my bag, I find a bottle of gorgeous green nail varnish I'd forgotten I had. That wonderful acidic, almost phosphorescent green that could never, ever occur in nature. I paint my left big toe, sit and look at it, smiling smugly. Yes. Lovely. Definitely not the sort of colour a hothouse genius would pick. I start to fill in the other toes, wiggling them against the bottle green of the sofa throw and feeling pleased with myself.

The phone rings somewhere over by Harriet's art stuff. She's gone and taken it off the charger and dropped it wherever she hung up again. Gingerly, I uncurl my legs, hobble on my heels over to the vague area where the sound is coming from. There's a certain amount of hurry necessary to the operation, because if the answerphone kicks in before I locate it, the chances are that it will stay hidden.

It continues to ring as I sift through the huge pile of assorted detritus on the table. Bills, more bills, Dom's press releases, loan offers, flyers from art shops, instruction leaflets on how to use glue ('Do not put in plastic bag and hold to face, as this could result in chemical alterations to the brain. Avoid smearing palms with adhesive and gripping hard objects, as this could result in unwelcome adhesion'), polystyrene packing chips, plastic wrappers, crisp packets, no phone. It rings again as I get on hands and knees and look under the table. Fluff, an empty wastebasket, no phone. Head for the chair and the answerphone kicks in. Damn.

The machine plays its message as I start to throw the pile of clothes on the chair seat onto the floor in a race against time. Harriet, in an unaccustomed bout of nerves, has spent an hour trying on outfits and chucking them away before settling on what she's wearing tonight.

Mel's voice. 'Hello, loves. It's me. Nothing important, just calling to say hi, really . . .'

Clunk. The phone slips from the pocket of a swing coat and hits the floor. I dive on it, hit the on button.

'So, er, yeah, hi,' Mel continues.

'Hi, honey,' I say.

'Oh, hi. Were you screening?'

'No. Harriet hid the phone.'

'Ah,' says Mel, not even slightly surprised. 'How you doing?'

'Yeah. I'm doing good. Having a lovely evening all alone with my toiletries.'

'Lovely,' she says. 'Love-bubble out for the night, are they?'

'Yes. They've gone to a Plod party.'

'Oh, blimey. Harriet's getting to all the glamour gigs these days. What's a Plod party like?'

'Plodding,' I reply. 'How are you?'

'Good. Well, fine. I just had to tell you about Dom.'

I go back to the sofa, settle down for a good chat. Mel is always ringing up with more evidence of Dom's masculine ineptitude. She collects examples like other people collect stamps.

'So what did he do this time?'

'I was in the bath, right?'

'Mmm?'

'And he came in looking all pious and going, "Mel, where does the dustpan and brush live?" So I said, "Darling, where it always lives." And he went, "Oh." Then he thinks for a bit and says, "And where's that?".'

I laugh. Mel and Dom have been living together for four years now, in a flat they bought together in Bethnal Green.

'So,' she continues, 'I said, "On the hook on the wall over the cat litter. Where I take it down and sweep up once a day," and he went, "Right. Well, I just thought I'd tell you, I'm sweeping up the floor around the fridge. It's got all bits of onion skin on it and it's disgusting." '

'What did you say?'

'What do you think I said?'

'Silly question. How is the little lamb?'

'Oh, he's fine,' she says. 'Gone out with the lads. Got me

out of the bath to find his blue T-shirt in the airing cupboard. Swore blind it wasn't there.'

'Oh, they are sweet.'

'Blind, more like,' says Mel.

'It's not really blindness. It's a sort of helplessness, isn't it?'

'No it isn't. It's deliberate. They know that if they allowed us to think they were competent at anything then they might have to do it themselves.'

I've got beeps. Irritating beeps that cut Mel's every seventh word off.

'I've got beeps,' I say.

'I know. Want to take them?'

'Think I'd better. They're obviously not going to go away.'

'Sure.'

I hit the star key, say, 'Hello?' in that 'You're interrupting me' voice, which is funny, because you'd hardly subscribe to call waiting if you *didn't* want to be interrupted, would you?

A cold, formal voice that I thought I'd never hear again says, 'Is Anna Waters there?'

Chapter Sixty-One

Grace of God

It's so unexpected, I take a couple of seconds to recognise who it is. 'Mother?'

'Yes,' she says.

Wow. 'Gosh, hi.' I allow an Americanism to slip out before I can stop myself. 'Sorry. Hello.'

'Are you still on the other line?'

'Yes. Hold on. I'll get rid of them.'

I click back to Mel. 'Darling, got to go. I'll call you tomorrow.'

'Okay,' she says.

'Bye.'

'Bye.'

I wait for her to hang up, and my mother is on the line again.

'Hello,' I repeat. 'How are you?' Stupid, stupid, stupid. Here I am, playing right back into her hands again, throwing my innocence down as a carpet for her to tread on.

'Are you alone?' she asks.

A slightly odd question, but I go along with it. 'Yes. Did you get my letter?'

'Oh, yes,' she says. 'I got your letter.'

A silence as I wait for her to say something more. 'Where are you?' I ask, eventually.

'London.'

Christ. And here was me thinking we could rebuild gradually by transatlantic phone call. 'Oh, right,' I say doubtfully. Then, 'Where?'

She names a hotel on Park Lane. Very discreet, very plush, very not my mother. And while she's telling me, I'm thinking: okay, this is an olive branch. She wouldn't be calling if she didn't want to see me. 'Would you like to meet up?'

'I was thinking,' she replies, and there's no warmth in her voice. Was there ever? 'Of coming to see you. I want to discuss your letter.'

I'm surprised. Grace has never wanted to come to the tower. It's too much of a symbol of her loss of power. 'Well, of course. Of course. Do you want to come now?'

'Not unless you're alone,' she says. Then, 'I don't want to be interrupted.'

Well, well. The great Grace Waters afraid of other people's judgements. 'It's fine,' I tell her, 'we won't be disturbed.'

'I'll be there in fifteen minutes,' she says and, in her customary manner, hangs up before we can get into the pleasantries of disconnection.

Fifteen minutes. Fifteen minutes. No time to make myself presentable, but she knows now. Trackie bottoms and a big jumper will have to do. But the flat's its usual mess and I don't want to give her ammunition. I don't even know where to start. Run around from pile of crap to pile of crap like a headless chicken for a minute, stop, take a deep breath and try to get methodical.

The method is this: no time to both wash up *and* clear the rest up. I have to clear now, sort it out later. I fling open the doors to the kitchen cupboards, push the contents backwards and stack as hard as I can to make room. Sweep my arm across Harriet's pile of papers and carry them, in two batches, to stuff into one cupboard. Kick scattered videos and CDs under the sofa, take a moment to straighten the throw so that it hangs to the floor and hides them. Bolt round the room collecting glasses, mugs, toast plates, pizza boxes from our night in with Mel and Lindsey two days ago, empty wine bottles, brimming ashtrays. Jump up and down on the pizza boxes to crumple them into quarters so they will fit in the kitchen bin. Follow them up with fag butts and wine bottles. Recycling is a luxury for those who have time. Reserve two mugs and two glasses on the draining board, pile the rest, like jackstraws, in the cupboard under the sink where the cleaning products live. Grab the Flash spray, gallop round the tops scraping off jam stains, crumbs, spilled salt, coffee marks, rinse the sponge and leave the spray out by the taps to make it look like it's used all the time. Run the hot water and speed-wash the mugs and glasses, polish them dry with the hem of my jumper – there's nothing like waitress training to teach you to get a glass dry in two seconds – and place them in the glass cupboard to make it look like they live there all the time. Scrub out the ashtrays and cast them casually about the room to look as though they are decorative, not functional. Why am I doing this? Why do I care what she thinks? No time to wonder. Just get on with it.

I'm running round the room scooping discarded clothes into the empty wastebasket from under Harriet's table when the buzzer goes. Throw the bin back into its proper place, take a moment to compose myself and answer.

'Grace Waters,' she says. Not 'me' or 'your mother', but the full monicker.

'Come on up.' I clunk open the gates, put the front door on the latch, check myself for smuts and start down the stairs to greet her.

Of course, the great Grace Waters doesn't get puffed. She's wearing a green wool loden and gloves, though it's not really cold enough to merit them, and for once she's not wearing her specs. 'Hello!' I say, go to kiss her, and she turns her face, as always, to present me with a cold cheek on which to place an obeisance rather than a mark of affection. But I'm different now. I'm thinking: she can't help it, poor creature. It's up to me to make the change.

So I say, 'You're the last person I was expecting.'

'I daresay,' she replies. Never one to waste words, Grace Waters.

'Come up.'

She follows me up. Enters the room and says, 'Well. It doesn't look as bad as I expected.'

'Sorry,' I say. 'We had a fire, so a lot of stuff's up here while we sort things out.'

'I know.'

Oh. So she's been keeping closer tabs than I assumed, then.

I say, 'I'm so glad to see you,' and she says nothing, just stands with her hands in her pockets drinking in the chaos around her. 'Sorry,' I repeat, and find it necessary to tell another whopper to cover my embarrassment. 'It's even worse than usual because I've got all my stuff scattered around.'

She still says nothing. I offer her coffee. 'You know I don't drink coffee,' she replies. Tea? Camomile? Water? She merely shakes her head, and I realise that things are not all right, that Grace and I aren't about to open a new chapter in our lives together. She's looking at me in that old, old way, like I've crawled out from the back of a cupboard.

So I think: grasp the bull by the horns. 'You wanted to talk to me?'

'Yes,' says Grace.

'Was it about my letter? Did you read it?'

'Yes,' she says again.

'Oh, good.'

A long, ominous silence. Then she begins, in a voice filled with poison, the voice of the wicked stepmother, the voice of the evil headmistress, the voice of a cornered serpent.

'Oh, good?' She mimics. 'Oh, good? What's so good about it?'

Taken aback, I start to answer. 'I thought maybe we – maybe we could talk. Maybe we could see the differences between us—'

She cuts in, steps forward so suddenly, like a prey creature pouncing, that I find myself recoiling in response. From her pocket, she produces the offending article, waves it, crushed between her fingers, in my face, her teeth bared in a snarl, eyes slits of malevolence.

'Oh, I think you've made your differences very well known,' she hisses. 'Oh, yes. We all know about *your* opinions.'

'Mother, I—'

'Disappointed in you? Disappointed?'

'I—'

'Grateful, are you? Do me a favour. What do I want with your version of gratitude? What would someone like me do with your gratitude? You wouldn't know gratitude if you were tied down and spoonfed it.'

I don't know what to say. I'd thought I was throwing oil on troubled waters, and it seems, instead, that I've thrown a lighted match into the tanker.

'Not the daughter I wanted? My God, what an understatement. You're no daughter. Anybody would be ashamed to have a whore, a pert, ungrateful little whore like you for a daughter. Your values my values? What values have you ever taken from me?'

Lost for words, I stare at her. Her eyes are blank, like sharks' eyes, her mouth a white line of tension and rage. Oh, God, it's not going to be all right. It's not going to be all right at all. It's going to be another night like the last one we spent together, only this time I don't have the option of standing up from the table and leaving. The phone rings. Grace's head snaps round like a lizard's, myopic eyes searching for the source of the sound. The answerphone comes on almost immediately; I didn't erase Mel's message after she called.

Harriet's voice. From a mobile, traffic noise in the background. 'Darling, I've just realised. Christ, Anna. I'm coming home right now. It's not Anthony Figgis. I can't believe I didn't see it before. I'm coming home, Anna. Wait for me. And for Christ's sake don't let anyone in.'

She hangs up. Grace, all sinew and tension, turns back from the room to look at me. An air of calm has descended upon her, an air I know of old. A small, white smile plays about her lips, and, as though a curtain's been pulled back to reveal a tableau vivant, I see with blinding clarity what all that reason, all that logic, all that prizewinning self-control has hidden from me all these years. My God, I think. You're quite, quite mad.

The smile widens slightly, teeth bared. She speaks, quietly, those clipped accents chilling me to the bone.

'It seems we haven't much time,' she says.

Chapter Sixty-Two

Love, Honour and Obey

'What do you mean?'

I know what she means. But you think, don't you: maybe if I can keep her talking, maybe if I can reason with her, maybe then I can turn this away.

'In the end, delegation is always a waste of time,' she says. 'In the end, I always have to do everything myself.'

What do I do now? What do I do now? She's standing between me and the door; the only way out of here is over the balcony.

'It's the same in the laboratory,' she continues, speaking to the air as though addressing an audience. 'You would have thought that someone with the privilege to work for me would at least make an effort to be conscientious, but no. In the end, it's always my responsibility. I have to set up the experiments, I have to oversee them, I have to double-check the facts and I have to dispose of the failures. One can't trust anyone else. One can pay them, one can think one's organised them, but when action needs to be taken, the only person one can rely on is oneself.'

'Mother, I—'

Her head snaps round and she is looking me full in the face. 'I thought I had made it clear,' she barks, 'that I am not your mother. I am not your mother. I am your creator.

To be a mother, one needs some affection. I never felt affection for *you*. You were an experiment. Nothing more.'

'I AM A HUMAN BEING!' I scream, slap my hand down on the counter, trying to bring her to her senses.

She shakes her head. 'And when an experiment is over,' she says, 'it is one's duty to tidy up. Remove the residues. Make certain that they are safely disposed of. Especially if an experiment has gone as badly awry as this one has. We don't want contaminants infecting the others, after all.'

She smiles again, and I realise that the coat and the gloves and the lack of glasses are a form of disguise. No one will know she was ever here.

Yes, but she's a creature of reason. Creatures of reason don't—

I don't even see the blow coming. She's across the room and upon me before I even have time to raise my hands to cover my face. Her bunched fist cracks down on my nose, and my mouth and my throat are instantly filled with blood. I gasp, choke, bend over double; the fight for breath consumes so much of my being that I don't see the second blow that explodes from above. Blood from my forehead, streaming into a ballooning eye. Two punches and I'm down.

I'm backed up against the kitchen cabinets, to get away from her. And all this time, her voice hasn't changed a bit. Even, emotionless tones, perfect pronunciation: if she answered the phone right now, the caller would never know that anything was unusual.

'I should never,' she enunciates, 'have allowed it to go on so long. I should have drowned you like a kitten. The first requirement for success is admitting when you have failed.'

She jerks forward as I strain backward to avoid her, so that her face is almost pressed against my own; I can feel her 'Ss' and 'Ts' as she spits them out, misting against my skin. Her hand shoots past me. Picks something up from the counter. Something hard and shiny.

Another blow, a heavy metallic blow behind the ear. An eruption in my head. I am instantly giddy, can see nothing but star-studded black, slip, as she steps back, to my knees, drop down onto my hands.

'But it's over now,' she declares. 'We'll put an end to it.'

She draws back a foot and kicks me at the junction of the ribs and stomach, knocking the wind out of me. I curl up like a hedgehog; spine out, stomach in, blood and tears and snot and coughing. And she kicks again, twice, at the small of my back so that I spring open instantly, howl with pain.

The foot comes round and takes me in the face, something crunching and loosening in my mouth, blood pouring between my lips. I'm screaming now, full-on shouting, trying to hold onto the ankle, throw her off her balance, stop her, but she shakes me free, kicks again.

Then she bends, sinks her hand into my hair and, pain ripping through my scalp, begins to drag me across the room towards the open window. The only way out, over the balcony. Oh, God. That long, long drop to concrete, bricks rushing past my face. Please don't. Please.

I realise that I'm actually saying the words. They spray from my mouth and she's deaf to them. Hands up above my head trying to claw her away, but she has talons of iron and I can't break free. Oh, God, I don't want to die, don't want to die, save me, please, God, I don't want to die.

And then a voice. Calm, firm, strong.

'Grace, stop it.'

I feel my mother's body shift, then she continues with her dragging.

The voice again.

'Grace. Stop.'

The grip loosens slightly, my mother standing over me like Herod Antipas, panting, bloodied. I twist, strain round, and Harriet is standing in the middle of the room, bizarrely festive in red and gold, white hair piled on a head held high, holding Grace's gaze with her own. And in this moment, she looks more like Godiva – beautiful, fierce, unstoppable – than I have ever seen her.

'Let her go, Grace.' Harriet's voice betrays no fear, no hesitation.

My mother's breath, heavy, a tightening of the hand that wrings a shriek from my lips.

'It's enough,' says Harriet. 'This is the end.'

'DON'T give me orders,' says my mother. She is out of breath. She pants and pulls once more at my hair.

'You will stop this, now,' says Harriet. Stock still, back straight, her eyes never flicker. 'You will stop this, and leave my house.'

Grace hisses, like an angry reptile. 'You don't know. You don't know. None of you know. I own her. She's not yours. She's mine.'

'She's nobody's. She belongs to nobody. Leave her, now. She is not yours to judge, she is not yours to pass sentence. Let go, and leave.'

Once again, Grace tightens her grip, and I gasp, but this time the grip is less certain, less determined.

'I did everything for her.' She speaks again, but this time there's something plaintive in her voice. 'I did everything, and she repays me nothing.'

'No debts,' says Harriet. 'No payment. You will leave now, and you will not come back.'

'I—' says my mother. And Harriet suddenly shouts into the salty silence, 'Grace, you let her go! You let her go now, or I swear I will never let you go as long as you live! I will

447

be at your back and on your shoulder and ready to find you whenever you forget. Let her go, Grace! You don't know what I can do to you!'

And Grace lets go. She sees the truth in Harriet's face, and she lets go.

Harriet takes a step to the side, clears a path for Grace, but never once do those eyes lift their gaze from her face.

Grace begins to walk. I slip to the ground and watch as she steps slowly towards the door, and Harriet turns to watch her go. There's blood from my face on her ankle. Grace keeps her head held high. As she leaves, her step becomes measured again, deliberate, the pace of the Nobel prize-winner leaving the podium.

She turns in the doorway, looks at Harriet. Harriet doesn't move, doesn't utter. And my mother speaks, and for the first time, I hear her lost, empty.

'I am not just,' she assures my friend, 'the sum of my genetic inheritance.'

Harriet stands with her back to me watching the doorway as the steps recede down the stairwell. Waits for the sound of the door, stays as it closes. I'm curled in a ball on the carpet. Pain everywhere, blood streaming from my mouth and my nose and pooling beneath my face. And I wrap my arms around myself and, mewling like a kitten, I rock, back and forth, back and forth.

And when she's certain that Grace has gone, Harriet turns and contemplates me. And then she steps forward, comes to my side, kneels down. With gentle hands, she helps me upright, with the strength of her body, she props me there. And she lifts a hand and strokes the only part of my cheek that isn't blackening, and looks into my eyes. And she says, 'It's all right. It's all right. I'm here.'

Chapter Sixty-Three

Noble Riesling

From: Waters, Anna
To: Moresby, Harriet
Subject: You *are* kidding?

I bloody hope you are. I know you've got luurve on the brain,
but do you really think I'm going to settle down with a geography
teacher? Even if he *does* have a body from God? Do you
know how many bodies from God there are in Fremantle alone?
Christ, remind me to wipe this from my sent box.

We're having a good time, is all. No, we're having a great
time. He's the kindest, sweetest thing, and he knows where we
stand and he's way cool about it. I shouldn't have been so
nervous about coming. I should have trusted him to be pleased
to see me, but I was almost sick at Changi Airport I was so
scared.

He almost didn't recognise me at the airport, though. Walked
straight past me, then stopped and said, 'Strewth, Annie, dig the
nose. I didn't know you had Cherokee blood.'

He brought me down to Margaret River after you rang to tell
me about Grace, to chill out and get my head round things
because I sort of lost the plot again for a couple of days. His
parents have a 'property' on Cape Mentelle where he reckons
no one will find us until I want to be found. Which may be a
while, I think. I don't know that there's much I can do, after all;
it's all out of my hands now. It's not like I'm going to be called
as a character witness.

Thank M for keeping stumm against his better judgement. And I'm sorry that it had to be your mother's mausoleum that got the brunt of things when she finally turned up. I'm sorry I was in too much of a state to tell you so at the time. But at least, thank God, there's no doubt in anyone's mind that someone who could turn up at a public monument with a batch of Semtex has to be pretty barking. And at least I'm in the clear now. I hope. I don't know what you feel about it. I know I'd feel weird if I were you, especially as it was obviously you she was trying to affect when she did it. Please tell me. Maybe it's a relief, in a way. At least the fan club won't have a focus for their obsession any more.

We got here three days ago and visited eight vineyards in the first 48 hours. Now sitting on the porch consuming the by-product and looking at the sea. Funnily enough, the view from a distance looks almost exactly like the parkland at Belhaven. Just think: all that money on landscapers, and all they could think of to do was replicate the look of a country they only thought fit for convicts. I almost screamed when I first saw this place: it's one of those things made of corrugated iron like you see in the movies, with a wood-floored verandah running all the way round to sit and swat flies on, and there was a kangaroo on the porch when we pulled up. N hoicked a rock at it and called it a bloody little menace, but now I really know I'm in Australia.

Listen: I love you more than I've ever said, old darling, old friend, and I can't wait to see you. Kiss my noble gentleman for me and tell him I love him too. I'll be back in a few weeks. N's job starts in the New Year, but he's going to come with me part of the way back so we can go and contribute to the destruction of the ecosystem of Lombok and say our goodbyes in style. And a jacuzzi, har har.

And yeah, I'm feeling a lot better, thanks. Ribs still get a bit antsy if I laugh too hard, which you'll be glad to know seems to be happening several times a day now. But, you know. It's going to take a while. A couple of times I've been talking quite normally and I suddenly find myself in tears. But he's brilliant about it. Just shuts up and waits until I've stopped and then cracks me open a drink.

Yesterday, he shoved a huge glass of Leeuwin Noble Riesling into my hand on the verandah, ruffled my hair, and said, 'I reckon you're all right, Kimosabe,' and you know what? I think I probably am.

Love for ever,
A
xx

Epilogue

The Martyr

Harriet has footage of the day her mother became a saint, because Godiva died as she had lived, in the middle of the circus, with a dozen cameras gathered as witness. She doesn't play it, but she keeps it in her box of secrets because it's the last she has of her. I don't suppose she has to play it to remember; the footage was aired so often and with such glee that Godiva's death is as familiar to anyone who was around at the time as is the first moonwalk, or Marilyn Monroe singing 'Happy Birthday Mr President' to theirs.

You may well remember it. Godiva, figurehead president of the International Earthquake Relief Fund, has been flown out, once again, to lend her voice to the appeal for the victims of the Balanistan disaster. The ten-minute film is intended for transmission just before the early evening news. Nobody setting up the flattering lights, the perfect angles, brushing at Godiva's cheeks with Rose Blush and smoothing her lips with Pearl Crush thinks that they are making a segment that will earn royalties that the Kennedy Foundation could only dream of.

It begins in much the same vein as countless appearances before: Our Lady of the Helpless in a disaster zone, dressed down in made-to-measure, the subtlest glint of gold at her ears, the lightest dab of silver below the eyes, the most modest splash of tan at the lips. To her side she clutches the sweetest orphan in town, and, hey, even if she's not an orphan, but has been picked for her looks from the local compound, people give more money to pretty orphans, it's the way of the world, and needs must when the devil drives. Godiva, in her handmade, kid-lined combat boots, strokes the orphaned head and, her eyes heavy with the weight of the sorrows she has witnessed, addresses the camera, scatters about her homilies on caring, sharing, generosity and love.

You can almost hear the crew yawning: it's a hot day, they've been up since dawn scouting locations and, though they know better than to blow their repeat fees by saying it, they've heard it all too many times before. For though people may have fallen for this stuff in the spangled seventies, it's now the hard-nosed eighties, and we're all too sophisticated to be taken in by this guff these days.

Compassion fatigue may be a real problem in the world of charity, but it's something of a necessity among those who have to find a grisly cadaver to emphasise their point. And even in the world of compassion, fashion is a driving force. And in the world of compassion, everyone knows that Godiva Fawcett is a force of the past: that the people want someone younger, less tarnished, more virginal, less – well, familiar. Godiva is sliding down the fashion scale; will probably lose her sinecure in the next year or so, go from Supercarer to B-list fete-opener.

Still. You don't get to be a cameraman without doing a professional job, even if it's the same as the job before. The focus pans in and out: from the golden strands of Godiva's sleek slicked helmet to the lone baby crying in a dust bath a little further up the road. Later, Godiva is to drop her speech halfway through a sentence and go to comfort the little creature; for now, she is under orders to merely look as though keeping herself away is the emotional equivalent of tooth-pulling.

So there we have it: disaster lite. A world where leprosy heals with empathy, where shattered lives can be put back together with a PR campaign, where a hug makes up for a lifetime's neglect and the problems of the Third World can be miraculously cured by a famous beauty from the first. Even at thirteen I was beginning to know that it didn't work like that. Even at thirteen, Harriet used to cover her face from shame when Godiva peddled her snake oil.

But today is to be different, for today, instead of the usual job of coming in as witnesses to someone else's catastrophe, these people find themselves participants in one of their own.

So to begin with, this priceless footage is as countless reels before it: the vultures descending to pick apart the bones of tragedy. Godiva is in grey today, a loose gauze *dupata* draped decoratively over her hair in deference to the religious scruples of those around them. And she looks deeply, lovingly into the camera, intones, 'For us, in our cosy homes, it is hard to imagine the scenes we see today. Hard to imagine what it must be like to live through them. And I know that it seems as though these disasters are ceaseless, that we can never do enough to help these people back onto their feet, that the hand of friendship can only . . .'

And then she trails off, and the look of a startled deer passes across her face. And the viewer becomes aware of a low rumble that builds as Godiva casts lamely about her, begins to totter, then stagger. And the camera begins to shake, drops down to film, juddering, the rubble on the side of the road. Then, jerking as though it's being thrown about by the hands of a careless giant, it comes back onto its operator's shoulder and we see buildings crack, piles of masonry that had seemed irrevocably fixed in mangled heaps begin to shift and tumble. And we hear screams of fear, warning shouts, yells of alarm as rock-pickers bolt for the safety of the open road. The roof of the orphanage cracks, caves, comes to rest on the floor below. And then, silence. Dead, trickling silence for one second, two, before the voices start again, the creak and groan of houses stressed beyond bearing as they try, and fail to find their shape.

And then there's Godiva. Visibly shaken, her mouth works and her hands begin to move. She looks at the camera, looks at the crew members who have staggered into shot as the earth heaved beneath them, stares at the sky. And then she sees what remains of the orphanage, and the voice that finally comes is shocked, and doubtful. 'Did they get out?'

No one responds.

She points at the orphanage, the beams that support the roof already screaming in protest.

'Did they get out?' she repeats. 'Did anybody see them get out?'

A flurry of questions, denials.

'*Are they still in there?*'

And then, with barely a glance to check that the camera is still running, Godiva Fawcett is bolting across the road in her designer grey, skirting piles of fallen stone, leaping the gaping crack that has opened in the ground.

'Shit,' says a voice off-camera. 'She's going in.'

'Are you getting this, Barry?' says another.

A word from the cameraman. 'Yeah.'

She reaches the doorway, pauses for a moment, peering into the gloom. And then she ducks, enters.

A shuffling, uneasy lull. 'What the fuck is she doing?' says a voice.

'I don't know. I think she went to get them out.'

'What the—'

'Jesus, that's all we need.'

'It can't be safe. What the hell does she think she's doing?'

'Always a one for the great set piece, our Godiva,' says another voice, cynicism breaking through alarm.

'What the hell are we going to do? I'm not going in there after her.'

People mill about, mutter, wander into shot, shading their eyes to con the crumbling façade. And all the time, the camera continues to focus on the point where Our Lady of the Earthquake disappeared.

'How long's she been in there?'

'I don't know. A minute? Two?'

'What the hell are we going to do?'

'Christ, don't ask—'

In the doorway, a knot of figures appears. Godiva, skirt ripped, face caked with dust, carrying a small form in her arms. From a distance it looks like she's got hold of a ventriloquist's dummy: overlarge head, heavy hands dangling at the ends of boneless arms. And around her, creeping silently, filthy, a handful of children cling to her skirts, cover their eyes from the assault of sunlight.

A collective sigh as the audience appreciate the drama before them. 'God, this is fantastic. Fantastic. We'll make every single channel with this. Christ, look at her. What a pro.'

Godiva gets halfway across the road before she drops her burden in the dust, feels for a pulse on his throat, presses her mouth over his lips and heaves air from her lungs into his. Does it again as Sandra, the make-up artist, comes into shot and kneels down beside them. 'Christ,' she declares. 'He's bleeding out. I need something to make a tourniquet.'

The little group of children begins to wail as experience sinks in. A cacophony of childish shrieks, shouts for help and the twisted groans of buildings, loosened by the tremor, giving up the ghost. And in the middle, Godiva, seemingly oblivious to the drama of her role, counts one–two–three–four–five as she pumps the chest of a dying child. She pulls the *dupata* from her head, pushes it at Sandra for a tourniquet, continues with her endeavours.

The scene falls silent as the sound man lays down his boom and steps into view, crosses the road towards them, takes over. Godiva staggers to her feet, looks helplessly down, then her jaw shoots up as something draws her attention to the dying building once more.

She turns back to the camera, begins to wave her arms at the invisible onlookers behind it, throwing a desperate hand out towards the orphanage. No one steps forward; the focus draws in to her face, pulls back out again to the dramatic scene behind her.

Then she is striding towards us, her face contorted with some emotion – rage, urgency, frustration; it's hard to tell when the words are lost – and she is shouting.

She grabs an arm, tries to drag an onlooker back the way she has come, but the arm shakes her off, pulls itself away.

She's standing now three feet from the camera, skin pale beneath the grime, eyes wide, white teeth flashing behind dirty lips. She stamps, she pleads, she holds a hand out dramatically at the crumbling building. And then she throws her hands up in a gesture of disgust.

And suddenly, her expression changes. The emotion drains away, is replaced by a transcendent, glowing calm. Age drops from her face, the cats' eyes narrow, blink, and throw the lingering look of old into our own. Slowly, she nods.

Turns, and runs once more towards the building. The camera remains steadfast to the last, focus perfect as she gains her distance. She passes the knot of first-aiders without a glance, pelts to yawning doorway.

On the threshold, Godiva Fawcett stops for one brief moment, turns, as though she knows that this will be her final exit, smiles one last, radiant, sparkling smile for her loving public. Raises a hand in farewell and steps inside.

And then, the aftershock.